BUILD
UNIVERSE

Nicole Petschek

Think Achievement
&
Make It Happen

© 2022 **Europe Books**| London
www.europebooks.co.uk | info@europebooks.co.uk

ISBN 9791220123242
First edition: August 2022

Printed for Italy by Rotomail Italia
Finito di stampare presso Rotomail Italia S.p.A. - Vignate (MI)

Think Achievement
&
Make It Happen

*I dedicate my first book with love and appreciation to my mother Margret Ellen Burke Petschek and to my father Ernst Nikodem Peter Petschek, whose love for each other transformed from emotions to matter.
I am the "Matter"*

To Hans Christian Beltermann, my soul partner, best friend, and life companion; the most challenging, inspiring and loving person with whom I have been able to use all the exercises and techniques in this book to prove they work on disbelievers and believers alike.

*To Roland von Bleichert aka "Rolo", a talented, connected young painter and illustrator with a spiritual sense of humour, who appeared in my life just as I needed an artist to illustrate:
THINK ACHIEVEMENT & WATCH IT HAPPEN*

*And finally, to all my teachers, mentors, family, friends, and clients who have left me with such a deep understanding of the mind and our infinite possibilities.
You have given me the situations to live those experiences from your teachings.
Thank you from the bottom of my heart.*

Start here…this is your beginning!

A memo from Nicole Petschek the author

This book consists of HOW TO'S and WHAT TO'S.

The correct way to read a self-improvement book is as if I am answering your questions. You will automatically recognise the advice that is relevant to you.

Use this book as your notebook. Underline what resonates with you as you go from page to page and put question marks after what is not clear to you. If you don't mark what rings true or important as well as a sudden inspiration at the time, or the key to unlock your obstacle, you will forget it a few pages later.

This is your notebook refer to it through life. In the future you will have noticed how far you have come. This will inspire you to always keep on learning. The more you know; the more you know how much you don't know!

Despite what others might have told you, or you believe now, you have what it takes to succeed.

I solemnly promise you that these 'How to and What to methods' will deliver you successfully to your goals if you take the action to make it happen.

CHAPTER ONE

LINKING YOUR MIND TO YOUR GOALS

The art & science
of
self-improvement & transformation

Quick Start Formulas 2 Success

Clear explanations of the scientifically proven use of spiritual energy to make success our default mode.
Proven methods, exercises & approaches for self-realization and empowerment
From grade school to eternity 'THINK ACHIEVEMENT & WATCH IT HAPPEN' is not so much about finding yourself but about 'CREATING' yourself.
Our time on earth is critical for living the life we want. Don't settle for a life that has less than what you want and deserve.

'THINK ACHIEVEMENT & WATCH IT HAPPEN' is a philosophy and method of modern day living while sharing what has produced positive and measurable results in the lives of my friends, my clients and myself.
Positive evolution of our lives happens also thanks to good advice. The genuine improved outcomes which manifested themselves excited me so much that I got fired up to help you transform your life into the reality you want it to be. As the saying goes: "If it is good for the goose, it is good for the gander".

I woke up one bright sunny morning thinking, "Nicole; there is more to life than what meets my eye. The vision of what is still possible for me to experience is still unknown to me. But I will create my new I.D."

If improvement, self-transformation, empowerment and your new 2.0 is a wakeup call to you as it was to me about 20 years ago; enjoy this book as it explains a universal truth. It is easy to understand but will take good will, an open mind and faith in your existing but untested hidden talents and superpowers.

Everyone has a different journey, and every book resonates in different parts with different people. Enjoy the parts that will take you to places you might never have even thought of discovering on your own.

'THINK ACHIEVEMENT & WATCH IT HAPPEN' shares exercises, explanations, and techniques from people who have already travelled their inner road to reach their better and upgraded outer destination.

Energy, the core of our being, impacts the matter of our bodies and transforms it at will. Invisible energy creates those visible realities.

Every thought whether conscious or not sculpts our core energy field. Thoughts are the tool for our personal improvement, transformation, and our personal freedom. Develop the habit of only thinking about what you want by noticing what you notice. Increase your self-awareness.

In the norm of your everyday reality whereby you have been conditioned to only believe what you see coupled to living in the age of instant gratification many lose out on the understanding of 'possibility', which is as vast as 'infinity'.

Most people know the word 'Responsibility' but have no idea what it really stands for.
Responsibility is the ability to respond. Thereby giving you total freedom in choice and outcome for yourself.
The words that you choose to follow 'I AM' will become you. Choose carefully who you want to be. "I AM' are the strongest most impactful words in all languages.

THINK ACHIEVEMENT & WATCH IT HAPPEN is borrowed, begged, stolen and mine. I have included the experiences of friends, family, and clients for 20 years… and have sifted through reams of advice, conferences, and workshops from giants in the industry, such as Bruce Lipton, Shlomo Shohan, Paul McKenna, Louise Hay, Joe Dispenza, John Asaraf, Jack Canfield, Christine Sheldon, Steve Covey, Nick Ortner, Oliver Madelrieux and many others who are also named as I proceed in the book.

Being a very down to earth person, living in a very materialistic society, and wanting to enjoy the benefits of that society; I used what had worked for other people, namely learning how to apply positivity to spiritual connections and allowing the energy applications to dance their dance and guide me through the baby steps which are allowing me to reach my goals while continuing to lead me onwards to more of my wishes, dreams and targets. I am trained in NLP and hold degrees in transformation as well as corporate coaching. My clients and myself are looking to achieve measurable results of improvement in the sectors we focus on.
'Think Achievement & Watch it Happen' guides you through the easy down to earth approach and step by step implementation of the exercises and the work that you

MUST DO. You must put the key in the ignition to start the engine.

An honest confession; when I was in my 40ies and took the decision to start my shift and create a new life for myself I became addicted to these nice warm and fuzzy books filled with feel –good content.
At the time the psychobabble chit chat at parties sounded like Fairy Tales with almost everyone having a great testimonial to talk about.
It was better than the normal boring talk of who went where for their last vacation or how sweet their domestic pet was. Nothing more nothing less, and certainly not something I was going to invest any time in.
Until one day I hit the proverbial wall and did not have any time to waste in applying slower methods to my recovery.
I broke my shoulder in the last minute of a polo match by galloping straight into a goal post during the semifinals of a medium goal polo tournament in Argentina, but it was well worth the break because I scored the goal by hitting the ball in at an awkward angle of about 20 meters giving us the win and qualifying our team for the finals in less than 2 weeks' time.
However, 30 minutes later with my left arm dangling like a limp raggedy Ann doll cloth arm, my doctor showed me the clear break on the x-ray and bracing himself for an onslaught of insults from me, he announced that even though the break was not serious, it was going to need 4 to 6 weeks so that my bones would mend and close. He instructed me that in the meantime, I was to always keep my left arm secured in a body-hugging sling and not use the left arm at all until he could safely remove the arm strap.

Since I did not qualify that often for finals, I was not ready to let this opportunity of playing in a 'final' slip through my fingers. I had to find the way to play in 12 days' time.

As per miracle, Louise Hay's book 'Heal Yourself 'came to my mind. I tracked it down somewhere in my heap of old books, thinking to myself that if she could have cured herself from a tumor as she wrote in the book, then I would give her spiritual and positive mentality approach a good try at closing my bone.

Not knowing anything about medicine or visualization I set my alarm clock for 60 minutes and for the next 10 days, every morning and late afternoon at the same time I shut my eyes and kept them shut until that alarm clock rang. During all that time I focused as intently as possible on imaging my broken bone to look like Rice Crispy cereal and marshmallows blending and meshing to mend the fracture.

I had no idea of biology, so I made the choice to give it a fairy tale feel and thought that Rice-Crispies and Marshmallows was a nicer image then bits of broken bones.

During the last 4 sessions I also added some imaginary grenadine juice to my wound which I chose as a symbol of my healing blood bringing the natural oxygen to wherever it was needed to close that break.

11 days later, I untied the sling from my body and standing full frontal in front of my mirror I gently instructed and willed my left arm to lift from the side of the body. Eureka, it moved, and I was able to lift my arm about 30 cm upwards and away from my hip.

Excitedly I drove as fast as my 1951 Chevrolet white Pick-Up truck could roll to my doctor who told to stop talking nonsense and go downstairs for an x-ray that would prove my bone was still broken.

30 minutes later I was back upstairs in his practice and witnessed his expression of utter surprise. He had to admit the bone was mended!

I had set the intention to play in the finals and it happened. I played in the final and could easily hold the reins and the whip in my left hand.

I had forgotten to set my intention to win though. But despite losing the finals I won a new lease of life. I discovered the creative powers of my imagination and the benefits of intention setting combined with conscious and disciplined focusing.

From that moment forward my life took on an ongoing permanently growing sense of excitement, learning, empowerment, and success.

Today I am overjoyed to share with you tried, tested and proven tools which have the undoubted and proven ability to make success our default mode of living.

Go back to your tender childhood and play 'make-believe'. Say 'I believe I AM ………………'

Fill in the dots with whatever you want to do and whoever you want to be.

I= INTENT

A=ACTION

M= MANIFESTATION

Change from the inside produces the results on the outside.

The brain's neural pathways are always on the move and transforming themselves.

Choose some of the exercises that you will find in this book and commit to doing them daily for at least 9 weeks. Set aside the necessary time daily for retraining your brain to discover higher meanings, and better actions that will guarantee you live your dreams and reach the goals you have set for yourself.

You are your own superpower. You are the mask that God is wearing. Allow the white light to shine and obtain clarity!

Your inner child is the Genie in the bottle… wanting and waiting to produce the magic in your life.

Ask and you shall receive.

Q.: Who do you ask? And who will give it to you?

A: Yourself! Know yourself, know your mind.

The mind operates at various levels of awareness, the Conscious, Preconscious, Unconscious and the Subconscious.

For the purposes of this book however I will refer mostly to the Subconscious mind since the Subconscious is ultimately what gets the job done.

Mind makes matter, and your mind is ENERGY.

Use your invisible energy for the vastness of measurable results it will deliver into your reality.

"The reasonable man adapts himself to the world: the unreasonable man persists in trying to adapt the world to himself. Therefore, all progress depends on the unreasonable man."

George Bernard Shaw, *Man and Superman*

Creation is the name of the game during your visit on earth

Key actions to unleashing your superpowers:

1. Transform your wishes into goals by making plans and strategies.
2. Consciously re-program your subconscious mind with intention.
3. Your subconscious mind is the driving and creating force in your reality.
4. Purposely re calibrate your brain for success.
5. Success loves speed. Do today what can be done tomorrow.
6. Install Self-Discipline and the rest becomes easy.
7. Mentally rehearse within the eye of your imagination the inner vision you have of yourself as if your goal has already been achieved, thus you are reconditioning your body to a new mind set.
8. Open your heart. Experience and live in the aura of peace, trust, and love.

Each human being is continuously manifesting their own reality by their known or unknown thoughts. Our thoughts linked to our emotions solidify into beliefs which are the sole creating ingredient of our life.
'THINK ACHIEVEMENT & WATCH IT HAPPEN 'will prove that when you swing and dance back and forth from knowledge to action; the universal laws of existence operate predictably. Create goals, meet them, gain confidence, and grow organically.

CHAPTER TWO

MIND'S MAGICAL MIRACLES

Q: What is a miracle?
A: An extraordinary and welcome event that is not explicable by natural or scientific laws and is therefore attributed to a divine agency.

Until something is explained and demonstrated it is called a wonder, an illusion, magic, or a miracle.
When clinical scientific studies demonstrate what happened, and the explanation allows the object or situation to be re-created at will by following a choice of certain procedures then magic transforms into a 'Technique'
The magic in our lives happens when we escape into our imagination. Wandering down familiar streams of our inner thoughts while traveling into the universe of our inner reality.

Gregg Braden wrote that an advanced genome analysis has revealed that the DNA that sets us apart from other primates is the result of an ancient, mysterious, and precise fusion of genes 200,000 years ago, suggesting that something beyond and/or outside of evolution made us possible.
Whatever that something was, it left us with extraordinary abilities of intuition, compassion, empathy, and self-healing that other animals and mammals do not possess.
We all do it, escaping into imaginary scenarios to live intense emotions. We smell scents, feel textures, hear sounds, and live the ups and downs of our emotions... all that without leaving our room.

But for the most part, those scenarios are doom and gloom. As you uncover your drama Queen or King patterns and inner dialogues, and you will find yourself having conversations with people in your mind.

Relax and rest assured you are not singled out by fate; everyone has their share of problems, and everyone sees themselves as unique and misunderstood. Humans believe their problems seem and feel the worse. They are on a private race as to who is the worst off.

Everyone to a bigger or lesser degree in life deals with challenges, fears, pains and more.

Acknowledge what is bad, but don't make it worse than what it is.

Sadly, not only do you hear yourself speaking to your inner voice, you also become the other person in the echo chamber of your mind and hear yourself speaking in their shoes giving yourself a negative suggestion or answer.

How much negativity can you self- inflict?

Your well-rehearsed negative elevator pitch story has kicked in so often that daily you find yourself projecting onto the screen of your mind a movie that you would never allow your children to see, nor be entertained unless you are a masochist. That is just a bad mental habit.

Are you slowly becoming aware how you keep on experiencing the same scenarios?

Each time you hope for a different outcome, an incident of one type or another out of your control happens; tipping over the orange cart and you end up once more at the same bottom line even if the characters in the story and the geographical location have changed.

Did you ever wonder why you can't jump off and out of the hamster wheel that you have been pedaling on throughout the course of your life?
The answer is simple. You are not aware that your subconscious thoughts are running your life.
Is there anything you can do about that?
Yes, RETRAIN YOUR BRAIN to notice what you notice! Get out of your left brains mechanism of jumping back and forth from the memories of the past to the projection of the same feeling into the future.
Everyone from every walk of life can do this.
Retraining a brain is just as achievable as improving your physical figure. Jump into your right-brain's imagination factory.
Retraining a brain to become success orientated is based on tried and tested principals. Principals deliver measurable results when you commit to them and spend time working on them consciously. Repetition creates the habit.

THINK ACHIEVEMENT & WATCH IT HAPPEN is about accepting and believing that you have the same magical ability as a magical wand. It explains the mechanisms of the mind and its control over your behavior.
By absorbing this knowledge and implementing it into your lifestyle you will master your mind and succeed in attaining your goals by getting the results you are aiming for.
Become your 2.0

MAGIC IS REAL

Q- How can you prove to yourself that you are a magic maker?
A-Be honest with yourself and allow the incidents of your life which you probably just discounted and wrote off to luck or destiny to become clear again.
Remember how many times something happened, and you thought… "I knew it, I should have listened to myself and not done it".
Remember the times you hesitated to do something in the first place… "Uhg... I knew I should have not done it in the first place, I knew it would not work"
Q- HOW did you know it would not work if you have never done it or tried it before?
A - The only way you KNEW it would not work beforehand is because you had lived and relived without even being conscious of your repetitive mind images that the disastrous outcome of your wish which lay in the depths of your subconscious mind would fail.
The brain has a default programing of failure instead of success.

To make matters worse if you are the type of person who tends to wallow in victimization, self-pity, or defeatism your energy levels are set to a negative frequency automatically.
Frequencies are invisible to the naked eye, but they are real, and they are the platform for what you call 'magic'. Inner energy frequencies can be measured with sophisticated high-tech machines.
More importantly they are immediately picked up by people and situations who will match your frequency.

Just remember that birds of a feather, flock together!
Without digging deep into molecular sciences, we know for sure that the atom is the building block for all matter. Whether that matter is platinum, steel, rocks, plants, fruits, animals, human beings and so on.
Inside the atoms are electrons. Some electrons are positive, and others are negative.
These electrons are twirling and swirling round and round attracting and blocking other energies from invading the electromagnetic field in and around our physical bodies.
The electrons dance, twirl, and swirl according to the melody created by our thoughts. Therefore, you might have heard the saying 'Thoughts are things.'
It is vital to self-discipline yourself into creating and shaping your point of view as to how you choose to see and believe in yourself and others.

If you want to prove to yourself how 'real' a thought is, and that thoughts are electromagnetic; take a 1 Euro coin and simply push it gently on to either the left or right side of your forehead above your eyebrow.
Then remove your finger and notice how that coin will stick to your forehead. Of course, do this sitting or standing up. If you are horizontal that does not count.
The explanation as to why that coin will stick to your forehead is that we are processing approximately 60,000 thoughts daily, of which at least 95 % are occurring in the subconscious levels of our billions of cell brains, which we will call the subconscious.
The conscious mind has no way of evaluating what those subconscious thoughts are.
According to Deepak Chopra the prefrontal cortex will run around 3000 thoughts per hour. And considering that

each thought has an energy frequency you now know why that Euro coin is sticking electro magnetically to your forehead. The average neuron contains a resting voltage of approximately 0.07 volts.
Thoughts become things. We are only energy.
That is why it is so important to develop awareness and to make the choice of creating enabling subconscious thoughts daily for the thoughts to become stronger and clearer.
At that point your thoughts have rolled themselves over into a critical mass of energy and will begin to manifest into your reality the object or situation of your desire.
A wish is not electro-magnetically strong enough.
You want to ramp up that wish to the energy frequency of a strong and persistent desire.
The higher the desire, the stronger the frequencies will emit.
To give you an idea of the actual force field of thoughts look at this:
17 seconds of focused thinking on one idea, or image has the energy frequency value of pedaling a bicycle for 200 hours non-stop.
34 seconds of focused thinking is equal to 200,000 hours And 68 seconds is equal to 2,000,000 million hours of pedaling along on a cycle or if you prefer to break it down, there are 8,760 hours in one year.

Simply getting into the habit of focusing your thoughts on the outcome of what you want for 68 seconds per day you are allowing the universe to deliver to you the results of what would take you many years in ego thinking work. The daily simple repeated exercise of imagining how 'you' want to be, will be the platform which will catapult you into being a CEO instead of the doorman of the company.

Beliefs are the proteins of your fundamental determining factor of happiness, success, health, financial abundance, and a fulfilled life.

Beliefs are building blocks. What you believe influences and creates the outcome of your life.

Ensure you take the preparation time to create beliefs that match your desired outcome.

If you are feeling confused and go through your daily motions in a daze, ask yourself if it could be because you have no idea what you are thinking and believing either consciously or unconsciously.

Question yourself if you have clear goals, or even any goals! If you are honest with yourself the answer will be a resounding 'no'.

The signature of your beliefs is the reality of your current life.

Maybe you are working in a nasty office, or have no sexual desire or satisfaction, perhaps your health is poor, or you are lonely with few or no friends, and not even a meaningful loving relationship in life.

The explanation is that you subconsciously built beliefs over time or after a trauma. You have become the product of your beliefs; even if you are not aware of them and even less so that you have created your current reality.

On the other hand, if you like your current reality; then keep on going because you are living a truly successful meaningful life, attracting to you the objects and situations of your beliefs and desires.

Positive thoughts emit positive frequencies thereby allowing objects or situations with a similar frequency to

attach themselves to you and develop into a manifestation.
Since you are emitting positive vibes, any matter or situation with a negative frequency will be repelled by your subconscious.

Emerging studies of positive psychology have concluded that to duplicate healthy emotions it is logical to study happy people who are healthy versus grumpy people who are ill and trying to get well again or better.
The same approach is now adapted in allopathic medical research. To look for a cure the research studies healthy people and not sick people.
For many years people have been searching in the wrong places to find the right answers.
This explains why today there are so many identified case studies of positive turnarounds, of which many of them are called placebo healings. There are more and more 'on demand 'healings' in all sorts of life segments. This has resulted in people admitting that as soon as they were made aware of the power of positivity, they applied all the tools they could until their results matched their vision.

Everyone can access their divine intelligence. We are all born with it. It is in us all We have just been looking on the outside for help in the form of a Knight in shining bright armor. That Knight is inside of us. The exercises in this book will help you to achieve to find your knight and ride the horse in your own shining bright armor.

When you are listening to a radio program of classical music on one frequency you cannot hear at the same time the pop music on another frequency on the same radio.

Be self-aware and make sure you are mentally listening to your enabling positive self-talk which is confirming to you that you have reached your goal.

Unexplained healings happen far too often and routinely to investigate and explain the details in this book. Those unexplained healings are called 'Placebo' healings.
Often the healed person said they had prayed or been prayed for. Without wanting to highjack religion, it is important to take a close look at Christian Science which was founded by Mary Eddy Baker in the mid-19th century in the Unites States of America. Mary Baker Eddy's foundational thoughts on Christian Science were the conception of God being a transgender all loving mother or father; made of pure divine love which in turn is the nuclear energy in each human. The Christian Science religion sees clearly that consciousness is the cause of ill and good health.
Energy is magic… and therefore magic is real.

In today's world thanks to high tech visual and analytical instruments which allow us to follow energy throughout a part in not all its course, as it transforms from one expression to another, we can scientifically explain magic.
We know that energy eventually turns to matter. Learned physicists have dismantled the mathematical calculations and formulations and explain how energy becomes matter.
Alchemy was a form of magic. Today Alchemy is mathematical knowledge of the formulations which will produce precious metals.
These methods are not a new discovery; but confrontation and proof that they had always existed and are only being rediscovered now.

YouTube shows many good videos of matter being created from sound or from vibrations of pictures and emotions. Everything is energy and so are you. You are pure energy. All matter is energy. We live and swirl in universal oceans of energy.
The energy which is yourself is your intuition.
Ask and program your own energy to manifest whatever you want to be, see, experience, give and have.
Allow your intuition to feed your mind and in turn feed your body the necessary powerful energy to manifest into matter what you want.

Q-Can you do it?
A-Yes
Q-Is it easy?
A-Yes
Q-Has It been done before?
A-You do it every moment of your life.

Everything you are, have, experience, see, and feel are only the symptoms of how you have been igniting your own thoughts and emotions in the past. Mostly unconsciously though.
Now is the moment to become AWARE and self-drive your energy.

Energy normally cannot be seen to the naked eye except to those who can see auras with or without the photographic method known as 'Kirlian photography'
In 1939 Semyon Kirlian realized that objects placed on a photographic plate and connected to a powerful source of high voltage energy could become visible to the naked eye.

The Kirlian photography method is used in research studies for alternative medicine.
Shakespeare said: 'A picture is worth a thousand words!"
The word 'Magic' exists to explain while keeping the secret of how thoughts are things, those things are energy.
So, your life is the result of your thoughts!
But remember you have 2 sets of thoughts.
One set are your conscious thoughts, and the other set is your unconscious and unaware thoughts pulsating in your subconscious mind which are produced at the rate of 60,000 per day.
Those thoughts are on automatic pilot. They are run and programed by your subconscious mind. The subconscious thoughts are the main blueprint which creates your reality.

That is how and why you will want to enjoy retaking control of your thought process via self-disciplining your conscious mind to invest in your 'Self Development Daily Private Time'
Claim your awareness, acknowledge your feelings, choose your thoughts, and watch your invisible energy become as familiar as your visible feet which get you from where you are to where you want to be.
Polish your inner lamp and allow your intuition to inspire you.

CHAPTER THREE

CONSCIOUS & SUBCONSCIOUS

This chapter is not about either or, it is about both.

THE SUBCONSCIOUS MIND

Use it to get from you are to where you want to be.
Mind transforms thought into matter. So, make sure your mind is programmed to deliver what you want. The two key aspects are to look closely at what it is that YOU want and not what you think 'other people 'want for you'. The 2nd key aspect is to be sure it is 'what you want' and not short-change yourself by 'what you think or know you can have, be or get'. Establish your 'want patterns' of thought based on: "If nothing were an obstacle money, time, age, health, and current or past realities what do I want to have, be, do, experience, etc.
Creation is the name of the game during our lifetime on earth. The subconscious mind accepts images and beliefs and transforms them into physical form.
"THINK ACHIEVEMENT & WATCH IT HAPPEN" will enable you to gain a simple overall view of what is happening in the correlation between the different entry points of a thought and the different options for the exit point of that thought becoming your beliefs before it becomes your perceived reality. It is easier to understand logically the imagery of the subconscious and the conscious, related to the body and to the outside elements of the body where reality plays out and thereby becomes easier for us to identify.

All physical substance is made of atoms and molecules. Inside the atom is an invisible yet measurable galaxy connecting energy hubs such as electrons, neutrons, protons and many more; they all have their divine intelligent connecting roles to carry out.

The Quantum field theory in physics has proven scientifically beyond a doubt that thoughts become things. To make more of your time better on planet earth take it for granted that as far-fetched as it may seem, everything in this book works and delivers the outcomes you want.

Of course if you are sceptical, that is also excellent because you can spend years reading up on the research and the ongoing research as to whether or not you really can create the life you want for yourself , and then you can spend more time to finding out if it really does work and by the time you are satisfied with the answers who knows how many years of possibility you will have lost on yourself!

The source of our subconscious mind is in our cerebellum situated at the junction of our skull and spine. It is also known as the Reptilian brain. When our umbilical cord is cut, the subconscious mind automatically kicks in with all the programs of physical survival it picked up during our 9 months baking time! The cerebellum is one of the seats of intuition. The other is the pineal gland. Medical science claims that the creation of our new neurons sprout partially in the cerebellum.

It is up to us to choose which habits we create, because those habits then create us. Habits automate most thoughts, feelings, and behaviors. Subsequently those habits get hardwired into the brain and unconscious triggers set up the default chemical output which causes you to stay stuck and go around and round in the hamster wheel. You have lost the control over your behavior and find it impossible to unwire and break those nasty habits even though you understand they harm you in the short and long run.

If your behavior is generated by your unknown and subconscious memories, beliefs and thoughts you will find it very difficult to take the necessary actions you need and want to take to reach your goals.

Be mindful and aware of the habits you don't want to have any more. Analyze yourself non-judgmentally to identify what triggers your reactions and feelings in the first instance. Be gentle in your self-analysis of yourself.

The subconscious pre-programming of our physical machinery kicked in around the 6th month when we were in our mother's womb. The skin and nervous system connect to the inner vibrations of our mother and our body falls into this divine mechanism which keeps us alive and ticking. We breathe, we see, we hear, we feel, and… and… and. The list is as endless as is the miracle of life.

The subconscious mind stores the cellular shelf and storage space for our wishes, wants, and beliefs in our life to be comfortably housed until they are replaced with new beliefs.

Welcome to Uncle Freud's favourite subject: 'The subconscious mind, home to all our beliefs". Your subconscious mind will determine the reality of your life. From relationships to finance via health.

Be willing and committed to going back to basics and reprogram your unknown belief system to accepting the instructions you give it. Of course, you will want to stack the odds in your favour so reprogram your mind with success principals. And the only way to reprogram a mind to

accepting a new principal or habit is to practice that principal every day for at least a minimum of 30 days.
As you progress through the chapters you will read about many different success habits.

The next step is to open your inner ears and listen to your intuition while developing your awareness. Note that I wrote 'Intuition' and not 'instinct'.
Instincts are based on what you have already experienced in the past, sometime that is bad, and sometimes it is good. But if you are in a stressful situation and in the past, you carried out a behaviour under stress, the likelihood of the outcome being good is slim. Nevertheless, as your instincts know that behaviour you will feel the instinct to re-enact that same behaviour only because it is familiar. That does not mean it was right or good!

On the other hand, 'Intuition' is an inexplicable message that is very often ignored because it feels illogical. In those cases, trust yourself and run with the message. That is intuition. Intuition is always beneficial for you even if it is illogical or inexplicable. Intuition is personal. The intuitive message is good for you, not necessarily for others.
Your reality will change subtly and gradually. Armed with your developing increased self-awareness realise how the events in your life are unfolding or happening as you have programmed your subconscious mind to believe they will.
The subconscious mind has no will of its own. It only obeys and executes the instructions of the conscious mind. It does not know the difference between a real or a vividly imagined event. The subconscious 'is' and the subconscious 'knows'.

Conclusions are based on emotions which are our perceptions and beliefs. The subconscious runs on auto pilot. It is the memory bank of emotions. The subconscious is constructed of frequencies dating back to our babyhood and pre-babyhood! But it is perfectly doable to take control and auto-regulate your own emotions, develop your self-awareness, and become aware of as much of yourself that you can. That does not mean that you are egocentric or self-involved. Quite the opposite it means you are positively productive.

The creativity work is to identify with as much clarity as you can conceive of to feel the emotions which you want to experience which you see in your mind's eye as already experiencing them.

An emotion just 'is' and does not question itself as to why it is or if it is good to be. The transmitter of the emotion is our neurochemistry.

Our body produces chemicals such as dopamine or others when our thoughts; either subconscious or conscious kick in letting loose the neuro adrenalin, thereby fuelling us up to act.

The subconscious default mode is 'BELIEF' which does not mean that if someone is sick, they should not use western or allopathic medicine. Of course, they should. If you break a bone... set it! If there is a cancer then cut it out, if surgery is needed to sew back a limb, then on to the sewing machine you go.

Our emotional and physical senses are only the minute tip of the iceberg. The real creating machinery lies beneath the surface, embedded in our unknown and subconscious belief system. Your unseen and ignored inner world, vibrating 24/7 in the trillions of your body's cells which are creating your visible and perceived world.

In Beijing China, there is a hospital called 'The Medicine-LESS hospital' where illnesses, many of them life threatening diseases such as cancers are cured within minutes by surgeons who don't cut but instead chant and see the patient as 'Whole and Healthy' before the physical body proves it is so.

Gregg Braden shows a live 3-minute film of a cancerous tumour disintegrating in real time as the surgeons are chanting sound vibrations in front of the patients as she lays down.
Even though the tumour is gone, and the patient has been cured the patient needs to adopt a new set of beliefs and live through those new beliefs emotionally every day until they become the patient's new inner belief reality.
That patent is creating a future memory in the present. Otherwise, if the body stays with the old memory the same physical symptom will reappear in your body. "Physician heal thyself" really comes into play here. This is when you must take responsibility for your health. Every physical symptom comes from an inner vibration which in turn stems from an emotion emanating from a belief. So, it is up to you to practice one or more modalities in this book daily to ensure that your energy field becomes and stays as peaceful, happy and positive regardless of your circumstances. Find one reason each day to feel gratitude and anchor it in. That is part of healing yourself.
For the results of any surgery to stick, the body must emit most positive energy vibrations to allow the healings to settle in. The kinder and 'more in the heart' a person is, the more of a healer they are. Love is healing! It's as simple as that. Create the right frame of mind to generate the

correct beliefs of love into your system. This is the act of co-creating your new reality.

Thanks to state-of-the-art medical imagery and brain scans; we are now able to see the energetic impact of a thought on the neurons and all the other related body parts. The frequencies of each thought develop into their own clear energy patterns.

Let's look at EMDR as one example. EMDR stands for Eye Movement Desensitization and Reprocessing. It is a comprehensive integrative psychotherapy approach, containing elements of many effective psychotherapies of which the structured protocol is designed to increase treatment effects such as psychodynamic cognitive behavioural, experiential and body centred therapies.

Every time you experience something, your neural pathways shift. If you experience the same thing often enough on a repeated basis, then the neural pathways solidify and that is the start of creating a physical reality. Very often this translates into the physical and mental health sector.

Our conscious mind is only responsible for 2 to 5% of our results. The rest is all down to the subconscious mind. USE… your conscious mind to issue clear instructions and beliefs in the form of 'It has already been done"

You can understand and accept that all you must do to reach your goal which has eluded you so far is to reprogram your 'old mental tapes 'today.

To find out what you have been unknowingly thinking and believing in the past, look at your current reality in the present.

Thanks to deep imaging technology we understand the workings of the brain and the subconscious mind better than ever before on a scientific level. It is all measurable.

That knowledge base now tells us how and why we want to reprogram our thoughts to obtain better results. Repetition is the name of the game Despite some mind coaches who say 90 days of repeated daily practice will do the trick, I like to advise at least 180 days but even better 365 days of daily reprograming exercises and whenever possible, at the same time each day.

Train your brain to imagine and feel what it is like that you want to experience and have. In the beginning, it is a bit tricky but by doing it daily after a while the neurons begin to open and then daily your imagination develops. I guarantee that you will become your own genie in the bottle, by manifesting all your wishes and goals by yourself. The repeated frequencies emitted from each emotion you imagine gain momentum and critical mass until such a time that they turn into a 'belief'. That belief will lodge itself in your subconscious emitting its frequencies automatically.

Q: What is a reality?
A: *Reality is that which is and when you* **consciously** *stop believing; it does not go away!*

By now you have understood that you can live the life you dreamed and hopefully still dream of today. So, make sure you spare a few minutes every day to first create that life in your imagination.

The subconscious mind is pure energy. It transforms its form but is always pulsating, transforming, and creating physical and measurable reality.

- The question is 'HOW' do we get our subconscious mind to transform.
- The answer is: 'Practice' whatever you are aiming to have in your life, you must learn and discover. And the way to do that is by practicing, which is nothing more than programming the highly trainable mind to the point where your spirit knows automatically what to do and does it automatically. You were not born knowing how to walk, talk and dance. You learnt and practiced daily.

Freud coined the unconscious as being everything outside of our awareness, yet it shapes reality via our automatic behaviours. The lack of conscious ability in the pre-frontal cortex due to an accident or an illness to relate consciously to other people does not take away their reality though. That is because everyone creates their own reality, either by default or by design. And your reality is based on your personality which is not necessarily engraved in stone. The qualities which serve you well; leave them as they are., as for the negative qualities you can and must delete or change them.

At different stages of our evolvement and life we want and need to become another person That does not mean that you become false, it means that you see the qualities and talents you need to develop to achieve and live your next goal and you then set out to integrate the actions, thoughts, and feelings of that new you by doing daily self-improvement work.

Gandhi said it best. 'Become the person you want to be'! Your mind-set determines your future. Design your life now and you won't have to earn a living later. Whatever you expect you will get.

Your income will provide all you need to live the life you are designing now.

Your essence is that of a powerful energetic being with no boundaries; and source energy flowing 24/7 through you. You are infinitely more powerful than you can imagine and that you know of currently. By repeatedly and continuously doing the exercises in this book you will learn how to activate your dormant metaphysical energies.

This chapter is very important as I attempt to open your mind to accepting that you can do everything you want simply by anchoring that image and feeling into your nervous system.

The universal source energy flowing through you abundantly is waiting to be tapped into by yourself continuously.

Like most small children you were programmed or educated to believe that it is more polite and generous to give than to receive. Even though generosity is a worthwhile quality; it is one of the reasons that most people are more comfortable giving time, energy, support, and guidance rather than in accepting it. Life is ying and yang. To give, you must receive!

Accept everything graciously to open your energy fields to receiving. Even if what you are feeling or must live in the moment is horrible accept it is a lesson. If you have a habit of finding it difficult to not accepting gifts, compliments but also criticisms, your vibrations broadcast the message "Don't bother to come here, as the door is closed!" If the advice or gift is very important for you, it might try its luck but won't stay for very long.

THINK ACHIEVEMENT & WATCH IT HAPPEN enables you to identify blocks between you and the field of abundance you are entitled to as your birth right. If Mahatma Gandhi, Martin Luther King, Nelson Mandela, Henry Ford, Joan of Arc, Elon Musk, Louise Hay, Oprah Winfrey and many others, mostly whom were all simple and humble people; were able to change the destiny of thousands as well as that of a nation you can create the outcome of your ideal life. You are the leader that your inner child is waiting for. Live up to your responsibility. Search for your creativity then give it time to morph into excellence. To be born and to live is an honour and a privilege. Value that.

Sadly, though due to negative childhood mental imprinting where most have inherited old mental programs, once those programs take root the prosperity you desire is unable to germinate. This book will show you how to proceed to create and germinate the new into what you want to experience.
Both the subconscious and the conscious brains are active chemical factories. Thoughts and feelings are the seeds of reality. All our chemicals originate in one part of the brain or the other. Big pharma starts at home!

THE SUBCONSCIOUS MIND

Autopilot of your reality! ...Launchpad of all your emotions because it regulates all your emotions, thoughts, and behaviours with its habitual actions through programming. Contrary to common belief; hard work, focus and persistence are only a small part to reaching goals.

The key to reaching your goal is in mastering the tools in 'THINK ACHIEVEMENT & WATCH IT HAPPEN'. Learn and apply the different modalities in this book to communicate your conscious message with clarity to your subconscious mind.

The easiest way to change your reality is to change the part of the mind which houses your limiting or negative beliefs which were created in your youngest childhood, probably not later than 8 years' old.

But change is scary, and any talk of change creates chaos in the brain by activating fear. Fear of the unknown and the unfamiliar. Fear is uncomfortable and uncontrollable unless you are aware of what is going on you will be tempted to continue doing what you are doing even if it is not good for you, only because it is familiar. The brain is an 'Excuse Making Machine'. You get stuck in habits, but mostly bad habits.

Be willing to go into fear mode to change your habits and get away from your familiar but comfortable bad habit paradise. Break free from chains of gradual self–destruction.

When you imagine repetitively and daily the new story of what you want to do with more money, a better figure, a loving relationship, a clean bill of health; you are softening your habitual fear patterns and beginning the fear override process of the unknown for the upside of all the benefits of a new way of life. Fear is uncomfortable; however, it is an over-rideable emotion that disappears as you get used to your new story.

Self-discipline plays a big role in keeping you imaging your new wanted reality since fear or anxiety over activates the brain which can no longer even think straight because the brain connects to chemicals which make you physically feel fear while draining all the blood away from your pre-frontal cortex and pulling it down into the gut and legs. Oxygen is the blood, so if your brain is not irrigated by blood the neurons start to implode and die.

In the very early years of our childhood our brain operates mainly in Theta mode, which is the frequency we access as an adult just as we wake up and doze off to sleep. We are comfortably and fuzzily conscious. Once we fall asleep our brain slows down to the Delta frequency throughout the different cycles of sleep.

The subconscious takes for granted all mental strategies which you are entertaining. It perceives those thoughts and mental strategies by way of the subtle; and at times not so subtle vibrations emanating from those created or un- unwanted thoughts as the case might be it gathers momentum and moss.

The subconscious mind considers all mental strategies as valid targets to reach. And when those mental strategies are imprinted repeatedly with conviction and energy either in thought, writing or speech, they mutate into powerful orders which are executed by the subconscious mind.

Use this book to retrain your brain by shifting from force to flow.

This is of course part of the eastern culture, however our westernised education, mostly based in science is only recently allowing the information and truth to re-emerge in the western culture today as an accepted belief.

Modern science confirms that 'emptiness' does not exist. What we perceive as empty is a grid of energy laden conduits. The astronaut Edgar Mitchel called that empty space 'nature's language' some other people call it God. But one thing is certain, that nothing is empty and each atom in the universe vibrates either visually, audibly, or tactically.

Research based on imaging techniques show that the energy projected from our emotion's spreads like wildfire on the invisible grid of so-called emptiness and in so doing automatically connects with identical energies of other situations acting like magnets attracting themselves to each other. Indicating today how science has proven that like attracts like. That 'like' is projected from your subconscious mind so be sure you are formulating the correct beliefs of what you want to happen in your life as existing already.

Q: Why is it important to auto induce yourself to believe that your goal is already existing in your life?
A: Because the subconscious delivers what it knows. It does not analyse what you are saying or believing as to whether it is bad or good for you, or if you are only joking. The subconscious takes at face value what it picks up from your energy vibrations and delivers situations which carry the exact same vibration. Like attracts like.

Max Planck stated: "*The mind is the matrix of all matter*". I urge you to activate your subconscious via the tools you will learn in this book and apply positive thought strategies to your subconscious mind to create the flourishing environment which are the mental and emotional flora in which your subconscious will flourish.

Data and knowledge are both looked for yet sadly ignored when found, because new information means change, and change disrupts the subconscious.

The subconscious dislikes change. It feels very uncomfortable in unknown situations and therefor does everything to resist a new paradigm. That explains why so many people live the 'Stop-go- stop' effect, or 1 step forwards, 2 steps backwards and sometimes if they are lucky, thanks to the fact that what they want is already set as a belief will suddenly deliver the 10 steps forward moment.

Humans are creatures of habit. Feelings, behaviours, and thoughts are things which become habits. At some point in our lives, we needed to feel the way a certain specific behaviour made us feel in the past. The problem lies in that the conscious moves on but our subconscious, i.e., the body stays stuck in the same old memory. The memory has anchored itself in, and if it is a negative memory, it will bring forth and manifest for you if your body harbours that negative memory corresponding situations which your consciousness does not want or need to live through anymore.

During the process of becoming self-aware and mindful of your desires, you will realise that such a feeling is not what you need today to achieve your goal. And if the habit was bad, it will become clearer for you to 'Break the habit' and create new appropriate habits that will enable you to reach your current goal in a correct manner. Create the habit that will create you.

Studies of the subconscious can be traced all the way back to the 14th century by the doctor, mathematician, and philosopher Nicolas Oresme, who identified the responsibility of the mental attitude of a person and its effect upon their health and condoning 'TCM, Traditional Chinese Medicine.' Studies of the subconscious remain one of the most influential developments of modern psychology.

95% of our reactions and behaviours derive from our subconscious thought patterns yet psychologists still can't all agree on the definite description of it. But we do know it is the cellular memory in the DNA.

In the 19th century, Freud envisioned the subconscious as the storage room for man's sexual desires and impulses as well as the importance of associating a person's dreams to their past and future life. Freud intuited that a person needed to clearly identify the source of all their beliefs to self-improve.

The other "Mind Super Star" Jung; Swiss psychologist 1875- 1961 had a strong influence on aspects of the mind in the 20th century. His ideas were based on his studies of art, mythology, alchemy, religion, and oriental theology. His background in mythology gave him the basis for his concept of 'Archetypes' which made him famous when he stated that the image one presented of one's self to the world was an Archetype but the hidden aspect was the anima aka the feminine aspect of emotions or the animus being the masculine aspect with logical tendencies .Otherwise interpreted superficially today as the subconscious where many if not all of our repressed weaknesses, loves, and hopes marinate like a juicy steak in olive oil!

Jung contrary to Freud attached a lot of importance to the spirituality of a person, seeing the subconscious as the building blocks of the personality. Most people grow and evolve into their personality by mid 30ies.

Personally, I think Jung had a larger and more accurate vision of the unknown and often unproven powers of the subconscious. Even though Jung's opinion was that whatever was missing in the anima / animus would automatically be attracted to complete what was lacking. Whereas I hold the theory that whatever our subconscious beliefs are we attract to ourselves the same, whether that is what we lack or what we have. Our inner beliefs create our reality, and our reality mirrors our inner beliefs.

Evolvement means that as we travel through life, our new wants and needs will have a better chance to manifest into reality when different thoughts, attitudes, and behaviours are adapted. Be aware when you snap back to old patterns to hold the reins tighter of the white horse of consciousness. The white unicorn of consciousness must be alert and not let the black subconscious unicorn go off on his own!

Deeply engrained beliefs don't allow new habits to make them easily obsolete. It will take a coup d'état and a new regime to auto- install new beliefs. This shift must be done holistically and spiritually to succeed. Sheer force and willpower will not succeed in changing old beliefs because those new conscious beliefs will conflict with our oldest learning's; those which have been laid into our minds before the age of 7 when our brains were ticking along in Theta mode when the imagination is greatly enhanced.

That explains why children are so easily self-involved in their imaginary games. For children imagination is the real deal. They are experiencing all the emotions very deeply. If they choose to stay in that imagery, it is because they are feeling good and familiar in it. That explains why internal images don't change, just because we grow up. On the contrary all images, notions and perceptions experienced before the age of 7 will become anchored as a deep-seated program for life, unless you use your mindfulness later to delete those programs and replace them with a program of your choice. This is the new biology of our reality. It was born in the 1920's with the advent of the research and study of Quantum Physics. The development of quantum physics additional addition shows that man does not necessarily have to be controlled by hereditary factors unless they allow themselves to be a victim of their genetic inheritance.

The power of the new and emerging peer reviewed science in biology is that we create our reality from the inside out and not from the outside in.

When man chooses the other option of mindfulness and consciously creates thoughts to mirror his desired outcome of any given situation or subject, man is then creating a future memory in the present moment, and the epigenetic effect is impacting the neuroplasticity of the brain and the body.

It is tantamount to changing a hard drive in a computer.

Centuries ago, the church burnt books because it feared losing its power as the masses would have almost as much knowledge as the clergy. All that new knowledge;

so easily available to the masses was going to become a threat to the established interests of the clergy or those in power. But of course, with time nothing resists the tide of transformation. Resistance is only a way of showing up and communicating that change is on the way. Personally, I have noticed that on several occasion's people whom I have disliked at first, have turned out years later to show up in my reality and teach me a lesson. Often, it was a lesson which highlighted that the reason I did not necessarily like that person in the beginning is because my subconscious was picking up on the vibration of change that would have to occur to improve my life.

The Subconscious processes effortlessly around 20,000 000 million bits of data per second. What a powerhouse of energy!

Even though it is programmed, it can be later changed and faceted by its environment which influences our reality and our behaviour despite being unaware as to what is going on. A perfect example is when you experience a 'Freudian Slip 'which means that you have said something different than what you intended to say consciously. But upon reflection, if you do take the time to reflect!!! you will most likely realise that there was an unresolved issue needing to be dealt with.

From years of coaching and observing people I have learnt and experienced that we are masters at distracting ourselves. One of the ways we distract ourselves is by complaining. You can't create a better momentarily reality for yourself then by complaining!

Q: How can I remove vibrational poison from my complaints.?

A: Take this as an example. Let's imagine that you want to tell your spouse or work colleagues to stop doing something or do it differently, but you fear their reaction as you know they are allergic to criticism and from experience that they have a nasty habit of becoming verbally and perhaps even physically abusive. Simply contain the object of your 'complaint' into one word and deflate its importance by summarizing the entire issue into one little package and calling your complaint 'a thing'.

The translation into English of any complaint means 'I am a victim.' But you don't want to be a victim, you want to be in the driving seat of your life!

Refer to chapter 24 exercise 14 for an exercise that will give you the solution for not contaminating your vibrational field negatively.

So, what is going on in your subconscious mind?

- Long term memory creates confirmation that what you know is the "right" way. But that is not the truth. If you have limiting beliefs, then your long-term memory is only confirming wrong beliefs.
- The subconscious is on a program. What it knows is what it does.
- The subconscious mind is nothing more than the program you download into any computerised program. If the output is wrong, you must change the program.
- 95% of our reality is the printout of our subconscious programs.
- Vital processes which allow us to live... Such as breathing, cell renewal, heart rate is part of the Reptilian brain because we come into this world with our body "knowing "how to operate such a complex system. It can be easily called genetic memory! Our genes inherited from time immemorial. The conscious mind knows, the conscious mind does

- The conscious mind processes 40 bits of data per second, but the subconscious mind processes 20 million bits of data per second.
- The subconscious mind produces approximately 60,000 thoughts per day of which about 80% are on the famous hamster wheel of the previous day.

So, change your thoughts and change your life!

THE CONSCIOUS MIND

Self-Awareness is a developable talent, aka 'consciousness'. Remember that the conscious and the subconscious interact with each other 24/7.

The potential and the advantage of controlling the indefinable quality of the conscious mind is by having a grasp on the first step to reach the goals you want and achieve ultimate happiness. This is scientifically proven repeatedly. It is as at the forefront of everything around us and is the boss of our subconscious and the home of emotions. It is the head of the creativity chain. Yet we don't know for a fact where it evolves from, nor do we know its ultimate strength and capabilities. I have read in Greg Braden's book 'Human by Design 'that emerging research is indicating that about 400,000 years ago, our cells fused, and our species developed almost supernatural powers unlike any other living species past or present. But to be honest I do not know much else. Perhaps it could be the subject of some very interesting Q & A sessions with such scientists as Gregg Braden, Dr Joe Dispensa and Dr Bruce Lipton who are very well versed in the scientific research of these matters.

For those who buy into the concept of the minds power; the exploration of consciousness will prove to be the most exciting and powerful crusade ever undertaken. Technological advances now allow us to start exploring one of the most asked questions since man was man.
"What is consciousness?"
- It is not an entity that can be touched and identified.
- So, does it exist?
- Yes, it does, it is in the core of our peace and the awareness we have of reality through our 5 senses.

Herr Einstein decreed that "There is a spirit manifest in the laws of the universe vastly superior to that of man; and a spirit is consciousness!" When you allow yourself to be YOU, you are existing in the core of your peace.

Published research demonstrates that the chance factor of restructuring a series of numbers to match what the scientists pre-selected is less than one in a billion. The odds stack up to uphold the theory that your mind creates your reality.

'Random Number Generators' functions on a chaotic sequence of zeroes and ones. It is impossible that anyone can predict what number will appear. The testing is done by mentally projecting a number to materialise out of the RNG numbers machine. The RNG has also proven that when there is massive, compounded emotion of the mass population focalised on a single event at a specific time that numbers seem to coincide. This time the result is attributed to massive similar universal energy produced by the synchronisation of an emotion at the same time. For example, moments like when Kennedy was shot, or the Twin Towers crumbled.

Just like night has day, the subconscious has the conscious.

But what is the conscious mind? That is the million-dollar question. It is an identification process in progress. Each monk and meditator have a different slant on it. Ask neuroscientists to define consciousness, they all more or less agree, but there is still not one single unilateral international definition for it. It is an elusive reality like love! If we could specifically identify how to create consciousness, we would know what it is. To be more exact it is a vaguely defined state that no official body in most countries will grant research money for studying it.

Everyone will agree that a dog is an animal; and that a chair is a piece of furniture, but what word identifies 'consciousness?

Until the powers that are agree on what consciousness is how can one study it officially? And as consciousness does not 'exist' it is impossible to get a grant to study it. Grants are given to study something, not to study something that does not exist!

For now, all that can be agreed upon is that the brain and the heart emit electromagnetic patterns showing the functions and results of consciousness. The brain emits electricity, and the heart emits magnetism. We even can't agree on when consciousness starts. Is it when the umbilical cord is cut, or is it when the foetus is developing, if so at what month? Or is it when the child is old enough to assemble feelings with a certain reality around it? There is no consensus as to whether animals have a conscious mind. And what about when a person has an accident or goes under anaesthesia, does that mean the person has no consciousness?

There are many theories but as of today there is no 'proven' or 'accepted' scientific identity on the reality of consciousness.

One important and verified factor is that focused use of the brain with awareness and intent such as in the act of studying demonstrates how the energy emitted stimulates the physical growth and connections of up to 1400 synaptic connections per hour. That happens when consciousness is in use. (Mr. Eric Kandel Nobel prize)
The mind is a generator for the brain or to put it differently the mind is the brain in action.
The easiest way of agreeing on the semantics of consciousness is to align it with the word awareness.

Without dropping into thousands of definitions of what it is and is not, for the purpose of reaching your goal which is the mission you are on, create an image of your consciousness as a tool bag full of the images which you want to become your reality, and see that tool bag offering them to your next image which is of a pair of open arms holding a magician's pouch symbolising your subconscious and knowing that once the magic of your powerful subconscious mind accepts the images from the conscious tool bag it will go to work and in turn develop those pictures into situational or physical reality.
Is an aspect of consciousness the ethereal ability to be aware of what we are thinking and why we are thinking of it? Our tool of knowing what we are experiencing is self-awareness also known as mindfulness.
Consciousness does live in the real world, just as we live in a world of our own created and perceived realities.

When we develop a subtler understanding of what life is; through experiencing numerous situations, we can choose images and thoughts to focus on to avoid or experience them.

That brings us to another question of 'What do we define life as?'
Understanding the meaning of reality to be what we see, think, do, taste, hear, feel and experience are the causes that gave us that effect which we perceive through our 5 senses.

Roger Nelson Ph.D., of the laboratory at Princeton University for Engineering Anomalies, researched on the identification of consciousness and a machine called a 'Random number generator' which demonstrated that when people next to the machine would focus their thoughts on specific numbers that exactly those numbers appeared on the screen of the binary system of zero's and one's Random Number Generator. Even though the results were not systematic it did occur sufficiently to be considered a reproducible method.

- ✓ Is consciousness a global mind or a worldwide spiritual forum?
- ✓ Do we all tap into it or do we all create our own thoughts and emit them out to 'The Field/ Matrix' or whatever you wish to call that vast so-called emptiness between objects, people plants and mountains.?
- ✓ Is intuition part of the conscious mind?

Intuition gives us insights and understandings into situations which cannot be logically explained at times. On the face of it, I would tend to say it is not part of the conscious mind, but when we are aware of an intuition then we can decide to apply the findings of that newly identified felt answer in a rational or logical manner. It will be at that point that the conscious can benefit from intuition.

Another word for Consciousness could be Mindfulness or Awareness and again, awareness is not something that can be quantified yet it exists.

I also ask myself 'Are emotions and feelings part of the conscious state?' Since emotions are feelings which in turn are the by-product of chemicals made in house by our own pharma lab, they in turn can guide the conscious mind to take focused viewpoints. The moment we consciously feel and identify a state we are in; we have used the conscious mind. But I would rather say that emotions have helped the humans evolve over the ions of time.

Q: Is a thought as powerful as King Kong or a nuclear reactor?

A: Yes, the outcome of thought determines the ultimate outcome of our reality. Therefor we must determine our thought procedure carefully at the outset of all new destinations.

Thinking is vital. Let's focus on the Wright brothers. If they had not fixated so much in thought on how to fly and float; airplanes might not have been taken for granted as they are today. Thoughts carry their own energy. Thoughts are contagious, dynamic, and ever evolving.

Let's call that the Universal intelligence. But we can all be forgiven for thinking that reality is an illusion! Why, because each person's thoughts create their perception of a thing or an event. So, what is real for someone is not always reality for another. To clarify, I am not talking about bricks bolts and mortar. But let's take a movie. One person might think it is a comedy and someone else might find it pathetic. Depending on who the critic is, the movie's description in the papers could go from 'Funny

Family Comedy' to 'Badly Directed Psychological Thriller'!

Keep on developing the ability to monitor your thoughts to always be able to keep yourself on the road of positivity if you choose to feel positive.

Again, remember you have been given the gift of choice especially when it comes to thinking. Either you choose what you think about, in which case you are taking control of your life, or else you allow your mind to think whatever it wants, and you will find yourself shortly living a life that does not correspond to what you are really looking for, which sadly further down the road, will result in you not even remembering the dreams you entertained at one point.

Everyone thinks! ... People think all the time. There is nothing special about that, because minds think, and everyone has a mind. The key is to become aware of what you are thinking. That is the starting gate to using your thought process optimally and productively.

As this book is for self- improvement, focus your attention on everything that will lift you, your project, and your environment one notch higher. Self-Improvement is like a ladder; the rungs of a ladder are only there to put your foot on it for a moment as your other foot reaches for the rung above!

A workshop was held to increase sales for a group of car accessories shops. That is not the sexiest of retail sectors. So, a think tank of how to make shops look more inviting took place. Someone came up with the idea of changing the name of their 'after sales' from 'Customer *Service*' to 'Customer *Happiness*' and within 2 weeks of making that one-word change, the little area became friendly and fuzzy, sales started to increase because more mums were comfortable to come in and buy from a "happy"

orientated sales staff rather than from a "sales" orientated sales staff.
The domino knock on effect always happens no matter what the action is. So be aware that your initial action is positively orientated.

Q: Does a thought always lead to an action?
A: Yes, but that action need not be physical. The mere fact of reflecting and contemplating is an action.

Q: Can we control our Conscious Mind?
A: Yes, by developing self-awareness. The Institute of Noetic Sciences IONS in Petaluma, California is spearheading a scientific project on coming to grips by understanding how global Consciousness comes into being and its effects. They use a machine called a REG Random Event Generator, which identifies that human consciousness does affect the reality of what we feel and does react with the physical world.

For the purpose of using awareness of your emotions to form them into what you want to have in physical reality is all you need to be convinced of for it to eventually take place.
In 2004 an Italian scientist and Neurophysiologist by the name of Dr Rizzolatti working at the University of Parma identified how 'Mirror Neurons' functioned. They fire together when we have an emotional experience, because emotions are high energy frequencies, and those frequencies are the instruction to our brain to produce the necessary chemicals of what our mirror neurons are seeing. But what was also proven was that the mirror neurons do not perceive the difference between a physically felt experience or simply if the experience was imagined. Real or

imagined the brain will execute the necessary actions to deliver a matching reality.

The aim of this book is to show you how you can catapult yourself beyond your existing reality into a reality of your desire by challenging and stretching your imagination.

Q: How do we gain self-awareness?

A: By paying attention to oneself inwards instead of always being outwardly focused. It is easier and less painful to focus on other people then on ourselves. So, get ready for some personal internal discomfort which will not last for very long. As soon as you start to love yourself and ask yourself daily "What can I do to make myself happy" you will soon be living in self-awareness.

Q: What quality helps to develop self-awareness?

A: Just like everything else; time and repetition. The more self-discipline you apply to your chosen tasks the better you will master them. The big advantage of self-discipline being the main tool to mastering all techniques is that it is implementable by everyone, regardless of IQ, gender, social or financial class, nationality, age and so on. Everyone can develop self-discipline like a child assimilates it. Even though it does get harder the older we get. Start by doing one thing at a time as best as you can. Focus on your task, pre-think the thought and see your desired outcome in depth.

Your subconscious is online 24/7. At night, it directs your dreams, and, in the daytime, it regulates your behaviours towards your goals.

When you succeed at something, look back into yourself and remember the positive beliefs you had before you succeeded, become more and aware how your thoughts predicted your reality.

The only way to foretell the future, is to write it first!

While Freud and Jung are reference points in the subconscious, modern identification of consciousness goes back four centuries to Rene Descartes, who initially used it to identify an individual's personality and character. The conscious mind encompasses everything either physical or not which we are aware of. It processes thoughts logically otherwise known as 'rational'. The conscious state draws information from its pre-conscious mind which can be seen as the archives of all types of information. We draw on it at need, sometimes consciously and other times it comes to us via intuition, which Freud identified as the pre-conscious.

Training the subconscious to execute the conscious is only down to discipline. Everyone can do it. So, everyone can for all intents and purposes improve their life's condition to the level they have set their imagination at.

Consciousness can be defined by immediate awareness and by focused reflection and activation of memories to analyse.

Consciousness is mind over matter as well as being aware of our present state of mind.

Consciousness cannot be that easily explained. Even the location of consciousness can't be physically located, but semantically it is safe to say that it is at the base of thought and consequently matter.

Descartes believed mind and matter are separate. But a few hundred years later, the physicist Albert Einstein showed us that the so-called solidity of matter is just an illusion.

Science makes a case that matter is the result of frequencies from subatomic particles. Quantum physics identifies that every atom is the reflection of a smaller one, thereby it is impossible to separate, and another way to describe that would be with a Hologram. A whole in a whole and so on. In today's understanding of what is 'matter', it is generally proven and agreed that energy is in all matter thereby opposing the statement of mind and matter being separate.

Our conscious mind accounts for approximately 5% of our brain power. When developing empathy which is best described as the ability to perceive the other persons emotions, you see situations and use your perception of a situation from the other persons viewpoint to interact more productively. Making the effort to tune into others is a vital conscious function.
Focused and relaxed contemplation is a 'conscious' trait. Consciousness and intuition go hand in hand and is described as 'pure knowing'.
A role of the conscious is to investigate and logically analyse possible scenarios and outcomes. Emotions and feelings don't enter the equation of consciousness. But it can make deliberate choices of how to react to an emotional situation when awareness is switched on.
The conscious mind is a library for reflection, but it does not deliver any action.
We should be and can be in control of our feelings. Decisions are made in the conscious. So, the conscious and subconscious must be driven in parallel from the same chariot.
Whatever the conscious mind gets used to or becomes bored with is relegated to the subconscious. This is the time when one wants to be very careful of our awareness of images, thoughts and sensory moments that will be

transferred to the subconscious and taken as truth, stored forever, and developed into reality.

Be mindful of what you allow to pass into the gates of your reality factory.

Using our conscious ability with awareness gives us the ability to create and to understand humanity. To paraphrase Scott Fitzgerald, "He who invented consciousness has a lot to be blamed for"

The Conscious mind can choose thoughts. It is the tip of the iceberg and uses its rank to create paradigms.

Imaging technologies today allow us to go in the brain and see the live thought processes in action as they manifest themselves physically by creating axioms and connecting to synapses while the vibration of emotion passes along and more importantly creates new growths of physical matter in the brain.

Despite all those explanations no one has come up with a single global agreed definition. It is like the search for the Holy Grail. It is easier to understand the value of mindfulness by filling the void in your life. How scary if suddenly you were to lose your consciousness. We take everything for granted, well how sad and empty would your life be if you were not aware of it.?

We lose track of sensory or auditory images of sensations. It is easier to understand by the route of feelings. You *feel* your feelings, but mostly you *understand* someone else's feelings, unless you have a deep degree of empathy. Feeling your own feelings is your ability to be in the moment, present and aware of self. That is consciousness, in the here and now. Even if you are feeling emotions relating to a memory of something that happened in the past, the fact of feeling the emotions and being aware of them in the now; proves that you are CONSCIOUS of your feelings ...or your SELF.

Neuroscientists have created mind maps based on physical research not just on suppositions. Some good books are:

'Self Comes to Mind: Constructing the Conscious Brain' and 'The Feeling of what Happens', both are by Antonio Damasio.

The consciousness is what constructs the self. By dropping deep into ourselves and coming out with creativity we develop the consciousness which connects are body to our brains.

Some people discover what is... Others create what is yet to come. Imagination is the seed of that.

The ability to create the world within as well as on the outside and the ability to feel and own your opinions, sensations and feelings is thanks to your consciousness.

The most valuable asset we have is our mind, let's train it to become efficient as it will do everything it is programmed to do. A secret to success is to train your own mind to aim at your target. If you don't use your mind, others will use your mind to get to their own targets. That is what crowd control is all about! The controllers can prey on the masses because they don't bother to auto train and use their conscious minds. Use it or lose it!

Daydreams work ... IF you work at inventing them. We are not talking about nice sleep dreams. We are talking about CREATING your dream. That is called 'Lucid Dreaming'. It takes focus and work to design, create, and modulate the dream with clarity. After which you will use the tools to drop the messages into your subconscious.

The first step to success is to be willing to fail. Believe you have the power to sustain the failure and you will succeed.

The mathematical equation of 'I AM'

I = Intention / A = Action / M= Manifestation

Step one: Who are you now? / **Step two**: Who do you need to become to be what you want to be? / **Step three**: Add them both up and that is what you need to act on to manifest what you want to achieve or have.

<u>**HEALTH TIP**</u>: All decisions derive from the pre-frontal cortex. The CEO of your brain! So, power up your brain with health foods and drop drugs, alcohol, toxic foods, and chemicals. Neurogenic research proves that positive decisions grow the brain.

Mood regulations stem from a brain chemical called Serotonin. Leaders who allow themselves to express positive emotions stimulate the same emotions in followers which invariably leads the leader to be perceived as effective and charismatic, Military leaders who communicate vision and love develop a more faithful fan base then those who deliver a stronger commitment and better productivity. When you consciously work towards 'Positive Psychology' the effort will deliver effective leadership at any level, from the family to the cub scouts and all the way up to the boardroom.

Young maverick scientists at Mc Gill University in Canada and other universities around the world are starting to investigate divine body questions. Science has still a lot to learn from theology. But sadly, when it comes to scientific research it takes a big push to have a major paradigm shift from the forces that are locked into the old guard network of the science of neurons. The concept of religion and spirituality connected to neuroscience is still a little bit taboo as far as research is given. But we are making progress.

The old thought school still believe that the brain is only the result of electrical connections but like everything... the truth eventually comes out.

Even though I am a lay person, I have attended numerous conferences, read untold reports and have had the honour to hear of experiences first hand from healers and healed patients; and my gut feeling, and common sense leave no doubt about the primary importance of our conscious and subconscious beliefs as the resulting emotions in the cause and cure of diseases.

One of the most fascinating stories is of Dr Ryke Geerd Hamer who has not only had to endure prison, just as Copernicus did for his beliefs, but Dr Hamer also relocated to another country to be able to live in peace. Dr Hamer had his share of failed diagnoses, but he believed in his metaphysical ideas related to Mind-Body health and called it Germanic New Medicine.

I am not declaring war on big Pharma, but I am inviting you to read up on the meticulous research that is so easily available today and which has been either compiled, peer reviewed or/and verified by meticulous researchers on the importance of psychosomatic evidence, confirmed by numerous scientific institutions and open-minded orthodox professors of medicine worldwide.

Knowledge of the consciousness will bond the world together, as we are all made the same way. When we learn how to regulate our thoughts and behaviour the world will be a better place for all. Start right now... practice makes perfect.

The brain has a huge connection to the immune system in a big part thanks to the vagus nerve. Scientists on the edge of discovery are those that are today breaking through the glass ceiling. We are moving the frontiers of neuron knowledge and conscious ability. It is not because we can't yet prove scientifically everything that it does not exist.

It has finally been accepted that stress makes a body sick. 30 years ago, a doctor could have lost his license to practice if he talked of such a heresy. The next step is to learn how to install systematically into the brain the necessary mindsets to induce a healthy physical body.

The facts of how the body accepts and acts on the Placebo and Nocebo effect are today common knowledge. The question remains as to how each person can create and anchor their own necessary beliefs to placebo cure themselves on demand.

Decades of research in brain imaging demonstrates how consciousness and intention influence and modulate brain activity. Placebo will please the body and the Nocebo will harm the body. Both effects have studies proving that "expectation" significantly influences the brains functions. We know it works, now we need to apply whatever technique fits best with us to ensure our permanent self-improvement, development, and healing.

The brain is the conscious starting point from which the body commands the physical mechanisms to operate more efficiently, otherwise the body ends up with DIS… ease. Belief and desire influence the brains chemical and electrical output. Theology and decades of western research show that the mind and consciousness affect non-local actions, as well as the physical structure of the brain. This information is not mainstream because the research establishment considers those subjects a taboo.

UNCONSCIOUS: For the purposes of this book, I want to explain that unconscious is a physical and medical condition. In the case of an accident or severe malfunction of the brain, whereby the person is simply not conscious or aware in a manner that can communicate to others. That is what I will call "Unconscious."

INTUITION AND / OR PRE-CONSCIOUSNESS:
Is a 'knowing' communicated to us by our feelings instead of by logical explanations that add up to an explainable reason.

The answers might be different for every individual, as every person is different, we all seek and need different states to feel comfortable in.

Always act on your intuition over any logical argument. Intuition is an inner message which is processed accordingly by each individual and the information is based on the inner ability to recognise a certain way of behaving. However, the groundwork to ensure that your intuition is delivering clean and positive messages, needs you to first be aware and recognise where your understanding of life might be toxic and then apply the daily self-discipline of re-educating yourself by selecting positive reading material to build your knowledgeable foundations on.

The more educated your memory banks are, the better results you will derive from your intuitive and/ or pre-conscious 'knowing's'

Yesterday I was clever, I wanted to change the world.
Today I am wise, so I am willing to change myself.
Rumi

CHAPTER FOUR

IF I COULD DO IT... SO, CAN YOU

Here is my story.

By the time I was 45 years old, I had lived about 50% of my life. I had nothing to complain about, I had surfed happily and blissfully unaware of the necessity of living a meaningful life. That is not to say that I was clueless, but I will say that I was 80 % rudderless!

My saving graces were, I was a happy go lucky girl since early childhood, which was all to the credit of my parents and governess. I lacked for nothing and did not even know the meaning of the word 'lack'. I lived a structured life and if I stayed within the confines of my beliefs and education everything worked out fine for me. I was not even tempted to challenge my beliefs. All my friends and relatives were normal nice people, there was never a hint of any type of violence or abuse in my childhood nor during my 20 years of a mostly happy married life.

Despite both my parents having become at different stages of their life alcoholics, they were never violent with me. I had been so sheltered that I was unable to feel their despairs which had led to their drinking. I was in a way emotionally disconnected, living in a permanent bubble of mental and emotional happiness.

But was I really that happy or was I unknowingly using food as a leverage for feelings I was afraid to let surface? I was born in 1952 during the last year or two of an era, where young ladies from well to do families were not expected to study or pass serious exams and get a career. I had no specific driving passion, except maybe the idea of being an actress on the stage, but it was certainly not an overwhelming desire. And despite being told that I was talented somehow, I did not take it seriously enough to sacrifice my time or my body on the casting couch simply to land a role.

My first huge surge of passion came when at 19 years old I set eyes for the first time on my husband to be. For me it was love at first sight.

At 17 I graduated from a Swiss finishing school in Lausanne with a degree in arranging tulips in a vase! A few well-spoken languages; always useful in international social gatherings and a well-honed 6th sense for sneaking out of the boarding school at night and organizing parties in town. Nothing that was going to make an icon out of me in life.

Fast forward 25 years later, after a very friendly divorce and a gorgeous son who was now in college, I was in Argentina where I was living 3 months a year playing polo. The game of polo had grabbed my gut and I was seriously passionate about it. It had become my 'Raison d'Etre'.

In the last chukka of a tournament in the semi-finals, I smashed my shoulder into a goal post breaking a bone.

The x-ray showed a clear break and the doctor proclaimed that my bone would be fixed in about 4 to 5 weeks, and I could start my rehab physiotherapy then for about 3 weeks and could expect to be back in the saddle in about 2 months.

There was one little problem, and that was as we had qualified to play in the finals in 10 days' time and there was no way that I was not going to play.

Remembering the book and talks of Louise Hay, 'Heal Your Body' and how she cured herself from a cancer, I decided to do a lot of visualization of seeing my shoulder bone mending. Every morning and early evening for the next week I sat down in a chair, setting the alarm clock for 60 minutes and proceeded to close my eyes and 'imagine' my bone closing. As I had no idea of anatomy, I replaced my bone with the image of rice-crispies and marshmallows meshing and binding together, then for blood, I watched on the screen of my imagination how nicely grenadine juice was flowing like bees to honey to all the spots where bone had to be irrigated with blood!

9 days later, I stood in front of my mirror and attempted to move my left arm. With a look of awe in my eyes I watched my left arm lift about 40 cm from my body.
30 minutes later I bounded into the doctor's office, who dismissed my excitement by sending me downstairs to get an x-ray done and bring it back to him.
Another 30 minutes later I had the immense satisfaction and joy to see my doctors jaw drop. He was speechless for a few minutes while he took in the undeniable fact that my bone had mended 100%. He could not dismiss it by saying he had misdiagnosed my bad shoulder because he was looking at the before and after X-rays of my broken and now mended bone in less than 12 days.

The rest is history, I played in the finals and went on to study the power of visualization in the context of creating everything I wanted to have, be, see or do in my life.
Suddenly, it dawned on me that the brain I had in my skull was the gateway to my dreams and wishes. No longer did my long list of wishes have to remain wishes. I had realized that my brain was my magic wand that would help me transform my wishes into goals.

I was also discovering the meaning of the word 'TRUST'. Of course, I could trust myself I was obviously only going to do what was best for me. I was able to accept with frustration what I had heard for so long. 'Everything is going to happen when it is right for you 'I could do that now because I knew in my gut that I could have faith in my Higher Power and my Spirit and Guardian Angels. After all they were there for me.

I urge you to read, learn, assimilate, and apply the exercises and mental gym work in this book. Imprint these empowering exercises into your daily routine.
This is like pushing your 'reset' button and knowing that from your inner launch pad you are propelling yourself to success, good health, wealth and happiness and everything else you choose to be, see, hear or have.
This is the moment when you are turning yourself around and pointing your subconscious to 'SUCCESS'

The meaning of 'SUCCESS' does not automatically imply that you won an Oscar, a gold medal or are happily married with a happy and healthy brood of children. Success means, knowing what you want, and then consciously living your life focused on the path to reach your goal. That is not only 'Success' that is also a fundamental ingredient in happiness.

The mere fact of setting your intention to live the life you dream, yearn of, and want; is rocket fuel. The clearer you define your intention, the easier you are making it for your subconscious mind to lead you there.
Write out your intention on a card, plasticize it and keep it in your wallet or use it as a screen saver on your phone. Every time you open your wallet or phone you are giving

your subconscious mind a reminder of what it must do to deliver your intention. Here is a totally encompassing green light affirmation for your subconscious to work towards and deliver to you: 'I am open, accepting, and grateful for all the wonderful opportunities and things that are coming to me. I am enjoying accepting all these powerful gifts of manifestation."

I started noticing small unexpected, out of the normal occurrences in my life. I had a familiar feeling in my chest that reminded me of the excitement I used to feel the night before Christmas morning.

As I indulged in this long forgotten good and elated feeling, more and more 'Gifts' from the Universe were manifesting in my life. I was beginning to figure out how to open the tap of abundance in my life. I never gave instructions to Santa Claus as to where to find my presents. I did not bother to tell him the best way to order my presents from the store, nor did I even think of asking Santa Claus if he could afford my presents. All I did was ask him for what I wanted in a letter which I would post in mid-November and simultaneously I worked on my thank you letter to him.

Today I do the same thing, I allow myself to feel the joy and excitement in my body of having manifested what I wanted by approaching all my goals in the same way I used to write my Christmas wish list to Santa .I write out my goal list totally free, I ask myself for everything I want without worrying about how and or even if I have the resources to reach my goal.

I write down my dreams and goals, draw or sketch them out, ask my Genie while enjoying the gut feeling of already being on the path to my goal, as well as reaching it.

I allow myself the luxury of not being a perfectionist; and when I write my goals I do so with the awareness that I am allowed to change my mind; knowing that I probably will. Because as I progress along the path to my manifestation I learn and discover new information that might have an impact on how I see my end goal. But at least I get started in the direction that will bring me to where I want to end up.

This gives me the possibility of changing or re-adapting my strategy. When I hit a crater or a roadblock, I simply re-adjust my steering wheel!

Sometimes, I feel an extra inner boost, and my inner visions show me that not only am I walking to my goal but that the universe is swirling towards me at breakneck speed and is whisking up the matter which is propelling my goal into my lap. It feels great because I know, believe, accept, and feel that I have set the manufacturing wheels in motion.

Once I have put it down on paper, it has a sense of being official and I know that my Higher Power now has a 'To Do' list and that he is enjoying himself while he works with me on my targets.

There are moments when I do take a step back and say to myself. "Hey Nicole, are you crazy, don't waste Genie's and your time; you will never be able to reach that goal'

But I quickly catch myself and remember "Ask and you shall receive". So, I take a few moments to read or write my goals and, in that moment, I feel I am in the future living my goal.

I admit that when things are tough, and I feel sad, depressed, scared and not seeing the light at the end of the tunnel, I find myself on that inner black icy and slippery road quickly descending into my self-induced state of negative mental projections and emotional drama.

It is not always easy to snap out of my total negative feelings but by now I have practiced so much on making the 180-degree visual point of view switch that I count down like a blast off: 321 and I do what I preach and sure enough the feel-good feeling floods over and through me again. When that happens, I know the gate is open, and my dreams and goals are becoming true. It is only a question of time.

I have retaken control of my automatic pilot and reclaimed the ownership and direction of where I want to be. No longer are the unwanted limiting beliefs of my subconscious dictating me where I will go! Granted, it did take me time and perseverance to get to this point. But I am here now, and if I can do it… so can you!

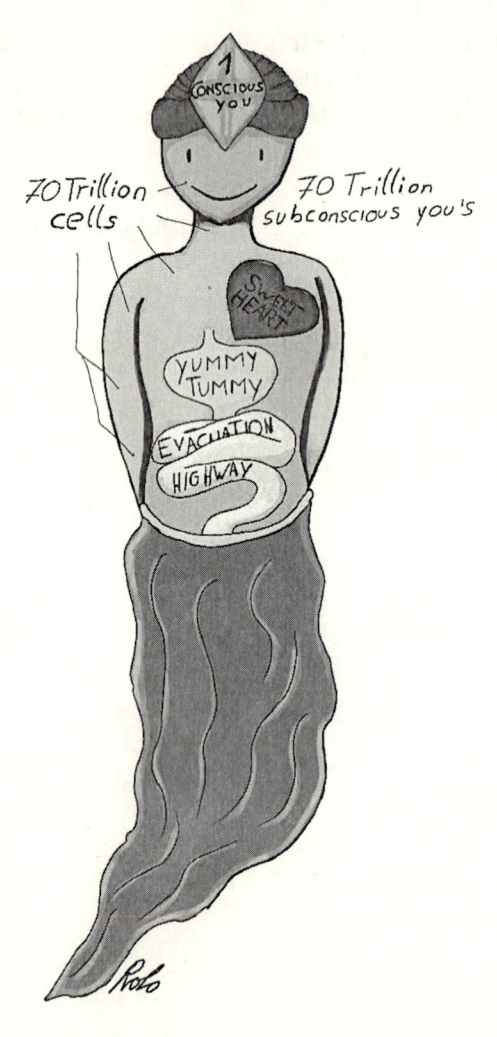

My conscious mind is the only part of my brain that will allow me to choose and do it on a regular and repetitive basis to re-imprint my subconscious mind which is lodged in each one of my 70 or so trillion cells. And that is why I now choose to always be the boss of my thoughts by choosing what I want to think of and them creating those thoughts.

I have experienced that it was and is only my thoughts about projected situations that are creating those situations. In other words, whatever I have and am experiencing is because of me and not because of external circumstances.

Again, I count down to blast off, 321 and I choose an empowering thought.

Even if I don't believe it at that moment, at least I am stopping my inner chemical factory from flooding me with negative chemicals that make me feel bad. It was only my negative thoughts that were causing me the suffering.

HEADING TO GOAL!

One of the empowering steps I take to generate motivation, self-confidence and reliance is to take stock of all my resources. Like everyone, I have gotten into a mode of behaving in a certain way which very often brings me success. But when I don't get the success, I am hoping for I withdraw, blame myself for not being good enough or think that my idea is not worth pursuing because 'this time 'it did not work.

I have learned to look at my backup resources. I have a list in my goal reaching vision board, and the headlines that I fill out each time I need to look for another solution.

1. What available sources of finance do I have, or can I get: From current or saving bank accounts to antiques in the cellar.?
2. What do I own materially that can come in useful to reaching my goal? Computers / Office equipment/ Google search engine/ a car/ a house or apartment/ etc.?
3. Who can help me: Family/ colleagues/ neighbors/ family on the other side of the world / clients who want to keep me afloat since they love my services/ friends/ old school friends/ etc.?
4. Which skills and talents do I have, or can I develop which I have not tapped into yet?
Talents such as good energy/ a loyal co-worker/ I am good in negotiating/ I can dance, sing, paint, write and do cartwheels!

Your heart power is your wakeup generator. Let's work with that power. Let's understand how our power works.

THREE STEPS THAT HELP YOU TURN INTENTION INTO REALITY

1-Dream BIG. What would you love...? Accept as a fact that everything is possible. With that in mind what would you love to do, be or have.?
2-Connect to yourself. Your dreams, desires and goals are YOUR life.
3-Stick to your New Year's resolution by applying self-discipline. Everyone can discipline themselves to stay on track and take the daily action to make it happen.

Brian Tracy, a leading author on self-improvement said, *"Winners make a habit of manufacturing their own positive expectations in advance of the event"*

Q Why do most resolutions fail?
A Perhaps they are too superficial. Results and situations manifest through and according to vibrational alignment. The resolution is made because of something you DON'T want, instead of being of something you DO want.
Therefor the resolution is connected to a NEGATIVE goal of yours. Move out of the energy which you DON'T want and put your focus and thoughts and intention, which is energy on what you DO want.

What you resist persists. Everything has a vibration, whether you want it or not. Don't fight things. Learn to let go.

LACK OF SPECIFICITY

- Be specific Don't say I want more.
  Be SPECIFIC. When you tell a builder how many rooms in your house you give him the exact number of rooms you don't say 'I want more rooms"
- Be aware of the Law of Proximity which states that objects or living matter such as animals, plants, people that are near or 'proximate' to each other tend to be grouped together. It is part of the Gestalt **Laws** of Perceptual Organization and Gestalt psychology, which was founded by Max Wertheimer
- Law of Vibration. We live in an upwards spiral universe. Everything grows around in circles and upwards. The more time you choose to focus on imagining what you will feel like when you have reached your goal, the faster that goal will arrive at your feet. Spend as much daydreaming time as can get hold of and daydream vividly your goal into reality. In your mind everything is possible, so dare to dream big.

LET'S TALK ABOUT MONEY

There are 4 invisible laws of success

- Be specific and have clarity. I have Euro 10,000 of disposable income per month. (Specific amount)
- I have total financial freedom and security.
  (Your 'WHY'. This is your underlying motivation.
- I have 2 credit cards. One that I use and another

in case the first is not working. A physical, measurable result that could happen when you have a monthly guaranteed cash flow of €10,000 per month
- Change your financial thermostat. If you are used to living on a given budget per month. Mentally 10 X it and now daily make lists of everything you can do with 10 X the monthly or annual income you have now. Then after 6 months, mentally increase that amount another 10X.

The key is to spend 2 to 3 minutes morning and afternoon inner-imaging your life on 10X your current budget. As your mind becomes more and more familiar with your new inner-imagined new clothes, home, trips, and lifestyle your financial thermostat is moving much higher up the ladder. And like all thermostats it keeps on going until it reaches it's set point.

Our mind thinks in PICTURES. What do I want in 2022, 23, 24 and so on? Create the snapshot in your creative imaginary mind.
Will-power is all about push energy and when you use too much will- power it mirrors that you are not in alignment with the belief that you are or have accomplished your goal. Your imagination is about the energy of 'Being There in your Mind BEFORE you have manifested it in your reality'.

Will-power is like pushing a beach ball under water, it is possible to keep that ball under water for a while, but as soon as you take your focus off the ball it pops up to the surface.
On the TV or your phone, all you do is change the frequency, turn the dial or push a button and you get the

energy frequency you of the channel you want. You get to decide the vibration you want.

Following are 5 'C' Step processes which I use once a week as a check list to create, modify and update a vision for myself.

Connection: First I put myself in the right energetic state of my intention. / Quieten my mind and connect to my heart. I sit still for about 10 minutes, and weather or geographic location permitting, if possible, I am bare foot on grass, earth, stone, or sand.

Compassion: Then I ask myself some questions as to what were my greatest successes and challenges this year?

The answers don't have to be news breaking, they only must ring true to me. And in my case, they were the following:

- Finding 2 tenants to rent out my studio for the year and the villa for the year.
- I used to hate going to the Gym. I found it boring and tiring. But I accepted that after a while I might get used to it. And as I willed it, so it happened and now I go to the gym regularly 5 to 7 times a week, and to make it enjoyable I discovered how I use that bicycle time by plugging in my earphones and listening and learning from conferences on TED and on YOUTUBE.
- I was very stressed out and did not know how to handle moving my partners household to a new country in which I did note even speak the language. But by simply taking the first steps to find a removal company a few months later we moved into our new house, and I decorated it

nicely, and handled everything well. The necessary people to help us seemed to appear once we acted.

Clarity: I am ready to create results that I am in love with. A good tip is to take the time to write down your end goal. It might take a few days or even weeks to outline the goal you want to achieve. But write all aspects out very clearly. The acid test is that someone who does not know you will understand exactly what you are creating.

Congruence: Make a wheel of all the aspects of your end goal on which you have described above, and now draw a line from one pie slice to the other and see if they all match in rapport, compatibility, and conformity to each other. It is like the wheel of life. (See chapter 24 & 25)

Conversation: Take a few minutes to speak to yourself in the mirror describing to yourself what it is like now that you have reached my goal. Listen to yourself and to your own inner advice as you talk out loud. The fact of speaking out loud to yourself while looking into your eyes helps retrain your brain into believing it has already happened and gives your intuition the opportunity to speak to yourself.
Destiny and future go by different names for everyone. Some people are brave and enjoy the notion that destiny and future is the creating factor of their 'My Ideal '. Others might be insecure, unsure, hesitant seeing their future as 'The Big Unknown'; and finally, for those who are shy, weak and scared of their own shadow; future and destiny is called 'The Impossible'.
But an ideal and secretly desired life is achievable by everyone.

Establish your ideal outcomes by taking powerful committed action to tackle your current obstacles. If you see it as an obstacle, it is, but when you 'choose' to see it as a lesson, the obstacle becomes the steppingstone and a moment in time until you graduate suma cum laude into a happy, successful life.

Massive, committed action is required on your behalf for the required results. For starters delete as of 'now' your victim mode and your litany of daily regurgitated complaints.

Embrace a clear new inner vision and full understanding of what needs to be done to create your ideal future.

When you decide to completely revolutionize your life, immediately instill a new plan of action. The time to do that is NOW!

Become uber-positive and practice training your mind and your eyes to look forwards. If you want to see the sun rise at dawn you have to turn your eyes towards the east. If you want to have success you have to look forwards and upwards with your eyes and with your heart.

You will need some very powerful and result producing strategies. Success is a method and the exercises and tools in THINK ACHIEVEMENT & WATCH IT HAPPEN will all produce success when you apply them. Just knowing about the tools without implementing them is a guaranteed waste of time.

If you have not reached your goals yet it is only because your strategy, providing you have one is not efficient. Change glasses or get glasses, but make sure that in every difficulty you encounter that you look for the opportunity.

Look out for and implement a new strategy. Every human being is born with an amazing wealth of talents and power. Today we call such happenings 'Miracles' but that only means we can't explain yet completely scientifically how the desired outcome occurred against all perceived odds. The important thing is that we all do have such powers and your challenge is to release your inner blocks so that your supernatural power can produce your desired manifestation easily.

Join me in taking the action to transform your dreams and goals into measurable results.

The decision to bring your dreams and goals into reality is the first imperceptible millimeter in the right direction. When you look down the road of time that millimeter will have widened to 180 degrees. You are on your way of revolutionizing your life.

Excellence is achieved by taking ordinary common-sense activities and consistently carrying them out to the best of your ability. Amazing results and miracles are not created overnight.

From cradle to grave, we go through sequential periods of self-development, experienced by morphing in and out of situations, all of which are opportunities for us to learn from or be of service to others.

I made the decision to see my problems from a different angle.

Albert Einstein made a clear and concise observation: *"The problems we face cannot be solved at the same level of thinking we were at when we created the problems in the first place"*

Define what your best qualities are and use them to the hilt. YES… Depending on your attitude you will ABSOLUTELY reach ALL your goals.

We see things as we 'believe' they are and not as they really are. When you advance to accepting that you can believe you are whatever you want to be, your life will blossom.

Since I can do it…. So, can you!

CHAPTER FIVE

WHO AM I?

Become the NEW you.
"If you know the enemy and know yourself, you need not fear the result of a hundred battles. If you know yourself but not the enemy, for every victory gained you will also suffer a defeat. If you know neither the enemy nor yourself, you will succumb in every battle."
— <u>Sun Tzu, The Art of War</u>

A successful life happens as a result of thousands of minute correct decisions. Consistent baby steps are a key to success. I would advise you to ensure that one of those decisions is to get to know yourself, so you can become the person you need to be to reach your goal.

- First and foremost, humans are the result of their brains and their mind. As they say in the banking world, one of the main steps in compliance is KYC, which stands for Know Your Client. In YOUR life, YOU are YOUR client.
- New peer reviewed scientific information is coming to light which is turning the concept of who we are as humans on our heads. It is so exciting that I can hardly contain myself. The information which is coming in from serious specialists in their fields is that the Homo Sapiens DNA is the result of a spontaneous fusion, of which I do not have the scientific textual facts to relate in this book. But for the case of 'THINK ACHIEVEMENT & WATCH IT HAPPEN that special fusion explains why Humans can switch off the 'Auto Pilot 'cycles of –

Thoughts- Feelings- Behavior- Reality Results- to what we CHOOSE to feel, have and be instead of what our subconscious auto pilot programs dictate.

Q-How does the brain do that?
A-It builds neural connections that organize and support relating mental and emotional habits which it gathers from conscious and unaware cues drawn in from our experiences, interactions, and physical surroundings. The brain and the sub-conscious's main goal is to take all that information and process it to deliver us to safety.
The brain is wired to scan our RWA- Ready- Willing – Able resources and provide us with whatever we have at hand to defend ourselves against all threats. Each person is different, so the feed chain of our neural network accrues from our behaviors and thoughts.

Adjectives which resonate with you either positively or in discomfort are pointing out your traits. Be aware of the feelings in your body. Your body is speaking to you, and with insight and awareness you are starting to understand your own characteristics. Here are a few to get you going. Extravagant – Untidy- Impulsive- Shy- High Energy- Low Energy – Fear of Uncertainty – Emotional – Sentimental – Ambitious – Perfectionist –Depressive- Procrastinator – Powerful – Independent – Burned Out- Hopeless- Stupid – Brilliant – Capable – Dependable – Exciting – Interested – Passionate – Silly – Bright – Optimistic- Happy- Resourceful – Compassionate – Spiritual – Self Confident – Selfish – Generous.

You have more power over your physical and mental reality than you think.

The purity and quality of your spiritual, psychological, and emotional diet has the same impact on the life force of your cells then the whole foods you eat. Consciously choose uplifting comments about others and yourself at least once during each meal.

Transform on the inside to become what you need to be to help yourself live your dreams.

Most of us are the mirror image of what our parents, schools, careers, peers, advertising, society have influenced us into believing how we must be.

That makes you 'THEM', but your aim is to become 'YOURSELF'!

A good question is always more beneficial than knowledge. Change your questions and you will change your life. While lying in a drowsy sense of sleep ask yourself out loud these questions.
WHO AM I?

And the first answer is: 'I am a lattice work of energy pathways'
- When do I feel loved?
- What turns me on?
- Who am I thinking of when I feel that warm feeling of unconditional warmth flow up from inside of me?
- When do I feel financially empowered, secured, and free?
Hear the feedback emerge from the silence of your mind. Take the time to answer those questions honestly to yourself. As soon as you feel good about an answer that resonates, practice enlarging it in the vastness of your imagination. Make the sounds happier, the buzz lighter, the

colors brighter. You are imprinting your daily energy vibration to a higher frequency.

When you open to empathy you are enlarging your world experience by putting yourself behind the eyes of the person you are speaking with. That will instantly give you more winning options, as you now can see a road map or a goal from the other person's point of view.

We are what we eat and what we think. As this is not a book on nutrition, I will jot down a few good nutritional tips and then let's look at what we think.

THE EASY EQUATION FOR GUARANTEED FEEL-GOOD IS:

Daily exercise plus whole foods are guaranteed to make the body feel good. When you feel good, you can't become stressed, it just doesn't happen. But a healthy body needs to be built on good solid and sustainable food, liquids, and exercise in the right quantities.

So always buy fresh and if possible organic foods. A surplus of proteins, carbohydrates or fat will transform and stock as sugars. Carbohydrates burn cleanly and emit carbon dioxide and water.

Beware that when you eat too much protein and fat no matter how good a quality they are, that extra fat and protein will make you age and feel tired.

Protein is excellent but in the right amounts. Protein repairs and maintains tissues and cells. It strengthens the immune system. Even though it is a building block foundation it is not an immediate source of energy. So, avoid a heavy dish of sausages, steak, and eggs before your next sports event!

The approx. amounts needed daily are. 40 to 80 grams per day of protein.

Now let's give some food to thoughts which are based on beliefs. The question is: How to discover what we believe because about 95% of our beliefs are entrenched deeply into our blueprint, otherwise known as our subconscious.

A blueprint is a belief that is deeply embedded in the subconscious, but it is changeable. We will discuss some of the belief changing techniques in other chapters. But remember that EFT and Ho'oponopono are the fastest ways to delete all negative, sabotaging beliefs.

Our beliefs determine our behavior, our emotions, our results and ultimately where we end up in life.

The clearest way to find out what our beliefs are is to reverse engineer our current reality.

1. Analyze your reality in the cold light of day in all the sectors you can think of. Relationships, finances, health, family, friends, reaching your goals and the list goes on.
2. Start by giving yourself a grade in each field. 1 being the worst and 10 being the best. Wherever your self-score is below a 5, know that the only reason is due to your inner limiting or negative beliefs in that field.
3. The easiest ways to change your reality is to change your beliefs. Rest assured that whatever self-negative messages you have been hamster wheeling for years have manifested their truth in the reality of your life.

If you wanted to become an Astronaut as a child but are struggling learning how to drive a bus, it is not because you can't drive a bus but certainly because somewhere early in childhood you accepted unwillingly a suggestion which is playing itself out now in your reality and confirming to yourself that you are always right.

That limiting belief could be something as silly as women make lousy drivers, or being an astronaut is dangerous. Do you get the idea? I run very successful Belief Integration workshops. Everybody enjoys my workshops because it is like shopping for new you! We can't exceed our expectations, which is why you want to upgrade your beliefs of yourself. It is like setting your thermostat higher!

1. The course of action to take is to replace a limiting belief with an enabling belief.

   Limiting beliefs are the unconscious negative chit chat which is running your life without you even being aware of it. Your Subconscious mind is handling those programs. An easy way to identify a limiting belief is by noticing when you feel uncomfortable, or when you don't have an obvious answer for something.
   (Refer to Chapter 24 exercise Nr.13)

   If you have been working smart or hard, won the lottery yet lost the money or are not in a state of financial abundance which you normally would be enjoying because smart work is designed to produce financial gains, the reason could most simply be something as benign as having heard your parents say at the dinner table, night after

night when they were trying to convince themselves that despite their poverty, they were at least happy.
A common panacea was, and sadly still is:
'Money does not buy happiness" or perhaps "Money is the root of all evils". That is a very clear example of what becomes a limiting belief.

Are you always getting nipped in a business deal? Well, you might be unwittingly running this type of limiting belief: "Be careful you can't trust anyone these days."
Do you loathe going to family reunions and getting embarrassed when one of your aunts or uncles always asks the same question:" Why is such a pretty or handsome girl or guy like you still not married'?"

The reason could be that as a child you witnessed your parents in a terrible and acrimonious separation or divorce and told yourself that you would never get married. Limiting beliefs are very often negative messages which you absorb unwittingly, and they evolve into memories and at the time when they were absorbed by your subconscious mind, the messages were totally out of context.

One of the saddest effects of a limiting belief that I came across years ago was that of a beautiful young and happily married lady who had never been able to enjoy an orgasm. After numerous visits to gynecologists and other physicians she decided to see a hypnotherapist. And the cause was quickly bought to light.
As a young child, her mother and nanny spanked her and said that only naughty girls wet their panties. The consequences were dramatic. Of course, it was not a willing fault. It is just one of those things that happen and had very disabling consequences.

The solution is to reverse engineer the fact, but don't waste too much time on finding out the 'Why' because whatever the reason was, it is gone, and you can't change what happened.

The answer is to create an 'ENABLING' belief. And those are also called 'Affirmations'. In the case of this woman, she said her affirmations daily and she chose to anchor in the benefits of her affirmations by tapping on her 9 EFT points while repeating her affirmation for about 3 minutes 3 times a day.

She told me that within 2 months she and her husband were for the first time enjoying a mutually fulfilling sexual relationship.

(Read chapter 18 Deletion Tools- This is when you empty your body of the negative energy frequency connected to the 'WHY'. Tap it away, create a void in your nervous system and fill up that void with your new enabling belief. Or use the 'Emotion or Body Code" by Dr. Bradly Nelson.

Here is an example:

Child 1: As a child going to the beach was fun. You swam, built sandcastles and at night you were lovingly and safely tucked into bed with a big kiss from your parents and you fell asleep smiling and reliving the whole fun, gorgeous day.

Child 2: Hated going to the beach because he had gotten stung badly by a jelly fish, and when he cried, he got spanked by his father for acting like a wimp. That could have been traumatic for a 4-year-old boy.

Even though consciously it was quickly forgotten in the child's little mind the energetic impact of the emotional trauma created a negative belief that all beaches were a danger zone; populated with dangerous fauna and aggressive people.

Years later the 1st child, let's call him 'Happy Beach Boy is now in his teens and loves going to the beach with his friends and hangs out, relaxes, is comfortable in the elements of the water and the beach, and will probably develop good relationships with his buddies, and go on to develop business advantages as he grows older with some of his beach buddies.

While child number 2 'Unhappy Beach Boy' will be spending all his time focused on the sea trying to spot jelly fish for fear of getting stung again, and therefor will never be aware of the other opportunities around him at the beach, such as friendly people and potential business opportunities.
Yet those business opportunities are there all the time.

If Unhappy Beach Boy is conscious and aware of what is going on, he will want to also enjoy and relax at the beach and meet the nice people and make potential business contacts. But first he realizes he must relax.
He must 'Reprogram' his brain and nervous system. That is equal to putting new software into the brain. Brain software is only a new set of beliefs.
He will therefor create a new film and flesh it out in his imagination until he has the exact scenario that he wants. His brain must be imprinted with the clear vision of his desired outcome. He must understand that the first step is to believe he already has what he wants before he

physically experiences it, instead of being told that he should only believe something when he sees it.

Change your imaginary blueprint to see the physical results.
You don't change your brain; you change the programming that goes in your brain; and the method to use is called 'imagination'.

A blueprint is the set of instructions which the subconscious thoughts have declared as being a fact. But that blueprint is dynamic and changeable.

Replace one blueprint with another self-created program designed to include all the pictures, sounds and feelings that portray exactly what you want to feel, see, and hear when you reach your goal.
That new blueprint will start issuing you instructions which are known as 'intuition' Follow your intuition and you will reach your goal.
The imaginary blueprint is being programed into your mind which houses the reality of the placebo effect. Except for some open-minded people and cultures as were many in the East, most western allopathic medical people dismiss the mind as having anything to do with the body.

Monsieur Rene Descartes, the 16th century French mathematician whose penchant for medicine led him to convince the powers that be at the time, that a body was merely a machine.
The question of the 'Soul' or the 'Mind' leaving the physical envelope immediately upon death was a necessary argument to keep on obtaining and dissecting cadavers

which he studied with a mathematical and mechanical approach.
That argument convinced the medical authority and the church who were happy to accord him the legal permissions to dissect cadavers at will.

Without that argument and useful point of view that the body was only a machine, the church would have refused to give their consent to dissecting cadavers because the body until then was sacred.
It took over 400 years until the 1960ies that an opening and loosening in mindset allowed the civilization in the West to investigate transcendental meditations and the effects of the psychotropic drugs which were becoming increasingly available even though illegal.

Over the course of the last 50 years, with technology and the sophistication of medical imagery where scientists, researchers, medical doctors, and a growing body of similar thought orientated lay people and professionals have been able to prove that when the brain processes thoughts which are invariably sourced in the mind, the photons deriving from different thoughts can be tracked in different areas of the body.

We are slowly able to understand how a thought produces a choice of 6 different 'Emotional States" and those 'States' vary throughout the day. Each emotional state has its own setting on the scale of vibrational frequencies and will therefore attract a situation with a matching frequency.
Those emotional states are happiness, fear, sadness, disgust, surprise and anger.

If you feel unpleasant, anxious, scared and so forth because you think you might become ill, depending on how long you harbor those thoughts and states, the likelihood is that your body will develop a condition to match that of your underlying belief or fear. That is called the 'Nocebo'effect.
But the same is true of the 'Placebo 'effect. It stands to reason that if you can think yourself ill, you can also think and feel yourself well and healthy.

The reality is that each ordinary homo sapiens possesses what we loosely call superhuman powers. The faster you believe in your unseen force the faster you will enjoy the unlimited potential of your superhuman powers.
Don't let the so-called reality of the doom and gloom of life paralyze you into fear. Just as we created that doom and gloom we can create, good health, success, wealth, and happiness.

In the mega workshops of Tony Robins, untold thousands of people including myself, have walked on burning coals of approximately 500 centigrade for around 20 seconds and have not even incurred a blister. People achieve this by preprograming their minds to believe that they are walking on cold stones.

The same phenomenon exists when people trek barefoot in the snow as certain tribes do in the mountainous area of Iran.
These people achieve what can be called superhuman status by programing their minds with the belief that that the coals are cool, and the snow is above freezing.
When I walked on those burning hot coals in the early 90ies in London the word 'unbelievable' left my

vocabulary after that experience. As most of you know, Tony Robbins is a convincing speaker, and until I walked the coals, and took the action myself, I simply enjoyed his workshop. But the impact that walking the coals did for me was profoundly transformational. After that everything I felt I wanted to do, I knew and believed became 'Doable'. I hardly use the word 'trying' and 'unbelievable' anymore.

Avoid wherever possible to let your mind get programmed by external negative messages carriers. Such as TV, sensationless journalism, and doomsayer. Avoid all areas of mind poison. We are superhuman and us homo-sapiens can achieve miracles because a miracle is only an event that science has yet not been able to explain or duplicate regularly.

The day may not be faraway that a pharmaceutical company will break down the block chain process of the mind and body and create at will spontaneous remissions. When they do that and can bottle or package the method it will become accepted as truth because those pharmaceutical companies will re-write the medicine books to fill their wallets. Who cares why they do it, it is only important that the process will be widely accepted, and disease will be a thing of the past.
The body is the mirror of the belief's it holds. Change your beliefs, create new ones, and experience a new set of physical realities.
Belief is like pregnancy. You either are pregnant or not; you either believe or don't. But a negative and limiting belief is much easier to undo then a pregnancy. We will discuss that more in the chapters 14 and 17.

Look towards solutions and you will overcome your own barriers and limitations.

Use your own resources to reach your goal. Very often I have noticed that my clients have a pattern of using 2 or 3 of their qualities and talents to reach their goals. But if that does not work, don't give up, simply look inside of you and tap into your other unused resources. Break your habit and play with your other talents or resources. Broaden your chances.

Step out of your habitual comfort zone and look at yourself from the viewpoint of someone you admire. What familiar traits would they see in you.

Here are some pointers that will jolt you out of your habitual view.

<u>Finances:</u> Untapped savings account, art that you forgot about, dead assets such as some old family silver that might be lying in the attic, some business investments.

<u>People Support System</u>: Can you think of someone in your family who could help you or has the know-how you need now? What about some old school chums? Clients – Old work colleagues- current work colleagues etc.

<u>Do you know which talents you possess?</u> Recall compliments that people gave you in the past. Did anyone say you were a good dancer, singer, painter or any type of artistic talent? Do you have a sense of humor? Are you loyal, eccentric, self-disciplined, determined, introvert or extrovert?

Can you speed read? Do you have a good memory? Are you willing to learn and open yourself up to self-improvement, because how you change is how you succeed?

Following is a little self-discovery guide of some stereotype personality portraits. See for yourself, where you feel at ease and what the pros and the cons are of the different profiles.

1. Let's start with the ever dependable and reliable person:

- Have you noticed if people flock to you like bees to honey looking for a sympathetic ear into which they can pour out their troubles?
- Do you prefer to listen to the other person rather than risking your vulnerability by sharing your own problems back to them?
- When other people around you get agitated, angry, and visibly upset do you feel totally in control of the situation and don't get flustered in the least?
- Are you averse to others asking personal questions?
- Are you averse to asking yourself some deep and meaningful questions about your own actions and reactions?

If you find that you resonate with these questions and were able to answer them, it will stand to reason that you have a propensity for being seen as dependable, endearing you as you are perceived as a true and consistent friend or colleague. You most likely derive a sense of pleasure when giving and being generous either with your time and emotions and probably material and financially as well.

However, your relationships might be lackluster, passionless and meaningfulness since you don't dare rock the boat as you might not have 100% faith in your convictions and don't want to be tried or tested on your or someone else's opinion.

That could stem from a situation in the past where you were disappointed and saddened, and as you don't want to experience that again you got into the habit of not confronting those involved choosing to repress your feelings. Those sorts of reactions over time can lead to being perceived as being a cold and detached person. Repressed and unexpressed sadness evolves into anger.

**1- What about Rodin's famous 'Thinker' statue.
Is that how you would like to be seen or thought of?**

Do you enjoy the control and laser fast speed you exercise over your thought process? Being on a high as you logically deconstruct and reconstruct arguments, opinions and presentations.
Rejoicing in the speed at which your intellect is formulating new watertight scenarios, thereby automatically challenging others to prove you wrong while you stand cool and calm in control of the situation and your arguments.
You are floating on an intellectual magic carpet ride, overriding your own doubts about the reasons why others might be getting frustrated with your arguments. If you can logically prove and present your argument you will feel confident and won't succumb to your negative gut feelings, discounting your intuition completely, and instead bank and argue on your provable points.
However, you do overhear people saying you are a cold fish, you know it is not a compliment, but you quickly and easily discount them as simply being jealous of your IQ and brainy disposition.
When other people tell you to stop obsessing about a goal you want to reach you hear them, understand them but

still can't admit defeat until you have the answer. You are like a dog with a bone, you just don't let go.

Here are some steps for **SUCCESS**: **S**ee your goal achieved in the eye of your mind – **U**nlock your self-confidence – **C**lean out your limiting beliefs – **C**reate self-discipline & resiliency – **E**xpect your expectations to manifest – **S**tructure your plans – **S**tart now

2- Have you heard from some well-meaning friends that you should learn to protect yourself with some boundaries?

Do you pride yourself on being totally transparent and wearing your heart on your sleeve? In other words, you find it almost impossible to keep your feelings to yourself and easily succumb to the need of sharing everything with everyone as soon as your emotions come into play.

The worse you are feeling about something; the faster you will effortlessly articulate your negative muddled up emotions and communicate them very succinctly to whoever is able and willing to listen to you becoming a very enticing drama queen or king as you spew out your problem.

Once you have emptied your bag so to speak you might very often regret having shared it with others, but the regret won't stop you from reacting exactly in the same way time and time again. Because you are naturally emphatic you listen to other's woes with sensitivity enabling you to develop an important and supportive network of like-minded friends.

To close this chapter, give yourself and your children the best gift you can. Auto hypnotize or condition yourself by recording on to your phone in your voice
"I am destined to be a great success in my life". Play it in a loop every moment you can with earphones, while you drive, jog, eat, and any other available time you have.
After a while you won't even be hearing it anymore. That is when your own voice recording is penetrating deep into your subconscious. As the message gets lodged deep in your subconscious, you will begin to realize how everything you do, see or hear will automatically be bringing situations to your awareness whereby your behavior will be in sync with success.

A burning desire to be the best success you can, will propel you to your goal.
Keep on listening to the recording of your own voice even though you might be hearing your monkey voice in the background saying that you are not a success and that listening to the recording is a waste of time. Ignore the voice and use EFT to dissolve the resistance that those thoughts are creating.
They are the limiting beliefs which your subconscious is used to and does not want to let go of. But they are not true unless you allow them to become true by acting on it.
As you start to know yourself, it becomes easy to reverse engineer your 'belief blueprint'
Start seeing yourself now as being a leader in your chosen field and then back up your goal with the necessary action to get you there.

Alexander Graham Bell said: "When one door closes, another opens. But we often look so long and so regretfully upon the closed door that we do not see the new door that has opened for us."
Get to know yourself!

Here are some personality characters. See if you can identify yourself. The 'Believing' part relates to your faith in your own ability to create your future memories by implementing some of the exercises in this book.
Believe in yourself, believe in what your heart feels. THINK ACHIEVEMENT & WATCH IT HAPPEN is all about playing with some of the different procedures in this book until you feel comfortable with a few and then use them regularly to ignite your energy generator out to the universe to allow the universe to deliver back to you your desires.
Knowing is the first step, but that only works if you DO the work.

Are you a **Disbeliever?** Someone who is very narrow minded, unable, and unwilling to learn that many phenomes happen which are completely outside the realm of Newtonian physics.

Do you feel overwhelmed at the thought of reading the endless papers printed by reputable scientists in reputable scientific publications proving without a shred of doubt that totally unexpected manifestations took place based upon inner vision and feelings.?
If you don't believe, stack yourself up with peer reviewed science that proves every angle and exercise in THINK ACHIEVEMENT & WATCH IT HAPPEN will deliver.

It could be very scary to have to go back to the drawing board and learn all over again new ways how to create the reality of your dreams.

Or perhaps are you a **TENTATIVE BELIEVER"?** When you hear people talk about experiences with clairvoyants that were 100% correct and helpful and when you have heard examples of telepathy, or placebo healings and so on, do you find the stories entertaining and amusing but are not open or willing to take anything at face value until you are satisfied with honest testimonials and endless scientific papers full of verifiable successful content?

Maybe you are **skeptical.** Even though I personally believe 100% in everything I am writing in my book, I enjoy challenging skeptic's as they are mostly highly educated and well read on the subject but have allowed themselves to only read what would support their disbelief.
Their own subconscious is blocking them from self-empowerment and self- improvement.

And finally, are you a **real believer** in your extraordinary talents and abilities?
My advice to you is 'Believer Beware'. Does my advice sound strange? I can understand how it does. I am only telling you to tread carefully on your manifesting journey and not necessarily believe everything and everyone at face value.
Undertake your own research and experiments. And then work yourself up to a true believer based on your own lived experiences. Rome was not built in a day.

The following questions are guides and trailers to help you dig deep into yourself. Just write out your answers as they come to you, and later contemplate your answers and feel if they are true to your personality.

You are putting yourself under observation and the best way to drive yourself to your goals is by knowing exactly what makes you tick, purr, vibrate, back up, and go forward.

Take 4 hours of self-focused and undisturbed time every month for 1 year and monitor your path. Yes, I did say 1 year.

The exercises in this book are designed to reformat your neural pathways. It takes at least 1 year to be completely rewired. The brain needs 1 full year for each cell to renew itself.

Devote that time to knowing yourself. You will become an expert on yourself, which is very important as you will carry yourself to success.

In what sectors are you on target and what do you think contributes to that?

1. What would I be if I could be anything I wanted to be.?
2. How will you know that you are finally who you want to be?
3. Is it important for you to make a difference?
4. Does love move you?
5. Are you happier on your own or do you prefer the emotional and mental stimulation of people you admire?
6. Do you criticize people easily? Or do you find that when another makes a mistake it painfully reminds you of your own mistakes?

7. Have people told you that you are complainer? Or have they told you that you are a pleasure to be around because you are so positive?
8. What have you learnt from your mistakes? And how have you implemented that knowledge?
9. Are you easily sarcastic, rude, abrupt, or authoritarian?
10. Can a lot of your mistakes have been avoided by being focused on the task?
11. Do you enjoy wallowing in self-pity for yourself?
12. Be very clear here: Do you estimate that you spend more time thinking about your failures or your success's?
13. Do you avoid the company of certain people?
14. Why? How do they make you feel?
15. Is financial security a given for you or is it something you still want to have?
    Have you been rich, lost it and want to make it all back and more again?
16. If you are in good health, do you take it for granted?
17. Whose life inspires you the most?
18. Which qualities or resources of that person would you like to have?
19. Do you have a written list of 5 dreams or goals you want to achieve in your life, and if so, do you have a written strategy how to reach your goals?
20. If you are not in good health, are you committed to finding the solutions to live in good health?
    Good health starts on the inside and goes outwards. Meaning that your emotions, habitual behavior patterns and the food you eat as well and what you drink all contribute to your health.
    If what you are doing is good, great continue. If not; are you prepared to stop whatever harmful patterns you are doing and adopt new healthy patterns?

21. If you are addicted to substances or negative behaviours, are you willing to go into therapy and commit to the necessary self-work in order to delete negative old patterns and replace with positive new patterns?
22. No matter how self-confident we are, there are always areas in which we lack self-confidence.
23. Do you find that over the years you have lost or increased your self-confidence?
    If so, can you attribute some specific areas?
24. If you are honest with yourself, do you think that you overreact to small disturbances?
25. Do you have big mood swings?
26. Do you hold grudges for a long time?
27. Are you happy to let other people do your thinking for you and not bother to double check if it is good for you?
28. Every time you are busy is it a productive business or do you think you are keeping busy because you are unwittingly procrastinating to doing something uncomfortable but necessary as a steppingstone to reach your goal?
29. Are you careless about your appearance?
30. Do you indulge in substances to ease your discomfort? Such as excess food, drugs either prescription or not, Alcohol? Have you been labeled a 'Workaholic'?
31. Do you routinely take the time every day to work on yourself, such as workouts, spiritual work, meditation, visualization etc.?
32. Do you have a 1 year monthly good new habit instalment plan written out?
33. Do you enjoy being with friends or colleagues that are mentally or spiritually superior to you?
34. Do you make a point of learning one new thing every day?

Either by reading and understanding or doing something new? Are you deeply committed to your ongoing education regardless of your age?

The older we get the more important it is for the neurons to learn new material and then daily repeat it so that the memory neurons stay active.

Monitor yourself for a week and then be aware of how much time you spend on learning new information either for yourself or for your work or hobby.

35. Who in your entourage encourages you to improve and learn more? Who makes fun of you for even trying to self-improve?

    The moment you identify who that is, disconnect yourself from them.

36. Do you have a tendency of accepting advice from others when you have not asked for it?

    Be careful, because mostly those are people judging you and maybe they don't have your best interests at heart. But by telling you their opinion they are making themselves feel important.

37. What behaviors irk or disturb you the most in other people? (Remember the pointing finger, while you are pointing at someone else with 2 of your fingers, 3 of your fingers are pointing back at yourself)!

38. If everything were possible and nothing is an obstacle write down all that you want to be, have, and achieve.

39. Do you intend to achieve your answers in the previous question?

40. Are you influenced by what other people think of you?

41. Who is your hero? (Dead or Alive)?

42. Why is that person your hero?

43. In your opinion do you think that person is superior to you?

44. If so, why?

45. Do you make friends for an ulterior motive?
46. How committed are you to reaching your goals which you answered in question number 36?
47. How much time do you spend every day on reaching your goal?
48. How much time do you spend every day accomplishing nothing?
49. How much time do you spend every day on yourself, showering, putting on make-up, trying on clothes?

There are 168 hours in a week, time map yourself well to increase your learning time. It will always be useful.
Everyone is inclined to want to see the results of their self-improvement work bear results within 48 hours. But there is no magic bullet traveling at supersonic speed. It will take weeks, months, years, and lifetimes to grow enabling new neural circuits of desire and success.

If you are the impatient type, this is one of the self-improvement traits you will have to delete and replace with trust and patience. And remember that when you fail it is only an opportunity to start all over again and this time with more wisdom in a more intelligent way.

We all have an unconscious tendency to "rush" toward change and transformation.
It's easy to imagine being instantly happy and rich, but it takes many weeks and months to build strong new neural circuits of desire and motivation which in turn auto produce the required success neuro chemistry.
Once you're motivated, you must act. Here's a simple way to begin. Identify a *small* goal that you *know* you can achieve in the next week and then write down three things you will do to reach that goal. If you stay focused

on the pleasure of achieving that goal, and the reward you will receive, that will stimulate the motivation centres of your brain to act and will make the "hard" work feel easy. We all have beliefs on everything whether we know it or not. Every time we take a step or pick up a fork and knife to eat, we have the belief that we can. Which is why we continue into the action so smoothly.
Be self-aware of your body language, it is speaking to you.
The easiest way is to muscle test yourself on any question you have on any subject. You will read more about muscle testing in the chapter of energy medicine
If you want to change certain behaviours in yourself, you will first need to integrate new supporting beliefs of that behaviour at the subconscious level of your mind.

Life is dynamic and transformational. The longer we live the more we learn about ourselves, our powers, our dreams, our capabilities for reaching them and our understanding of mankind through our own experiences and those of other people developing empathy.
Here are the 4 stages of a life broken down into quarters based on a century.

- From birth to 21, from the moment your baby eyes open; the world feeds sensory information that develops into experiences and the ability to translate your experiences into knowledge.
- From young adult hood to the beginning of your middle age, in other words until your 40ies, you apply what you learn, and you defy challenges and try to prove you are right.
You tend to defy other people, whether they are well or bad intentioned.

- From your 40ies until your mid 60ies you harvest what you have sown.
- From your 60ies until your passing you will be connecting to other people more than ever as you become thirsty for human warmth and wanting to share, support and being grateful of support.

There are opportunities at every stage of life. Your attitude and positive outlook on every situation are what will enrich your time on earth. Your attitude will determine your altitude.
The above real-life descriptions are only a little guide to open your awareness as to what can happen to most people.
What are some decisions that you can take today, and which will improve your life?

The ability to transform your dreams into goals and then into reality is a major contributing factor to fulfillment and happiness as well as the willingness to feel in your heart of hearts gratitude for ongoing improvements and matters. Take the time to find out what you appreciate and what makes you feel passionate.

The following areas constitute a full life. And as you break them down it will give you clarity as to why the river flows in the following way.

- At the bottom of the list is your physical body. And since we are human beings, our bodies are vital to our ability to travel through life.
Vitality, good health, and boundless energy give deep and meaningful meaning to a full life

- The importance and point of view you attribute to emotions. Remember that we are not our emotions unless we allow ourselves to become victims of our emotions. Emotions derive from the neurochemistry as the direct effect of thoughts and beliefs. Those thoughts and beliefs must be changed if they do not support the ideal outcome you want from life.
Know what pushes your emotional buttons, that way you can be proactive instead of reactive.
Those are important qualities in a leader.
- Relationships of all sorts are a big mirror of subconscious, unknown inner selves. It is easier though to see ourselves in others then in our internal mirror.
- Time management: List your priorities.

We all have 24 hours in a day so let's analyze why successful people get more accomplished than unsuccessful people. (Take a look at Steven Covey's immortal best seller. The 7 habits of successful people).

Time management helps put things in the right order and not waste time. Pre-think your actions and your words.
For example, there is no point in putting oil in your car at 10.00 am if you are taking your car for a revision in the afternoon and the mechanic will empty your oil and put in clean oil.

When you speak; put clarity into your sentences. There is a big difference between saying 'The cat licked Miranda' and 'Miranda licked the cat"

	What have I done?	Why I'm doing it?	Who could help me?
Monday			
Tuesday			
Wednesday			
Thursday			
Friday			
Saturday			
Sunday			

Columns of:

- What to do that is most productive towards my goal?
- What have I done?
- Why am I doing it?
- Who could help me?

Start your day at 6 am end your day at 10 pm and in between be conscious of everything you do.
When you are aware of what makes you tick and inspires you, you will get to the point of finding and doing a work that will never seem like work to you but only of self-fulfillment.

The only thing that money can't buy is time. Do not waste time. Life is the real deal it is not a rehearsal. Avoid wasting time by gossiping and unnecessary things.
Stick to your timetable and be sure to include play time, social time, family time, culture time and physical exercise.

- Finances are a big and important part of life's equation. Very simply put, financial security and abundance can buy us the security to live our lives without having to depend on others.
- Crown everything with spirituality. I am not talking about religion or God; I am talking about the universal consciousness and energy that has a divine intelligence which infiltrates our lives on all levels with the best intuition that guides each person from a different starting post to become a spiritual technician!

By using the clarity of the above bullet points, assemble your strategy of connecting and evolving through all the above-mentioned steps and bullet points. A good strategist can link the known to the unknown and connect to the right people at the right time.

First and foremost, honor each of your goals and dreams, no matter how small or big, by writing down clearly what is YOUR purpose for achieving it or living it. Simply put, aim high and get there.

Enjoy the process of becoming a success regardless of the time it takes you. Success is different for everyone, for some it might be to graduate, others want to win a gold medal and others want to be healthy and peaceful. Honor what you want and go for gold.

NOW, is the right moment for you to be clear about what you want to achieve and write it down as minutely detailed as possible.

Purpose is fundamental, you will uncover more of yourself when searching for YOUR true purpose in each one of your dreams and goals. Most people want to develop and improve their lives.

Self-Development occurs by improving, stretching, and challenging your own thoughts and ideals. Actions derive from those thoughts and situations which manifest. This is your evolution. The more uplifting you become the more self-knowledge you need to become conscious of. Everyone has something they love to do and were born to do. It is your soul's purpose and your life's mission.

Some might know it consciously and are doing it, in which case fabulous, continue your path.

Others might not yet be aware of what they even crave or feel-good doing. Don't despair; with self -awareness of your inner voice you will come face to face with your soul's desire, it will feel like an 'Ahh ah moment', unfolding gently for some or like lighting for others.
Accept the insight, stay with it, be grateful for it and go along with its unfolding. You are embracing the grace that comes with the gift of living your souls' purpose and destiny. Follow the road signs of your heart, otherwise known as a 'Hunch'
Many people live their lives intellectually, basing their decisions on rational thinking.

The downside of making decisions rationally is that as there is so much data available today to everyone, overwhelm easily fogs out the correct solutions.
A brain performs better on the 'less is more' theory.
'Correct' information for each person comes from our intuition and has very little if none of logical data.
Often the simple fact of listening to your hunch or gut feeling will unravel itself to have been the correct decision for yourself and give you a far better ultimate outcome.
Intuition flourishes best without rigorous rules and timelines.
Brainstorming sessions are a fertile ground allowing unsought ideas to rise to the surface.

There is intuition in everyone, learn to listen and honor your own hunches and if you are a team leader always trust yourself to honor other people's ideas.

You will be surprised at the amazing outcomes.
A brains activity signals the universal mind.
Your mind, thoughts, actions, and results are the mirror of your brain operating mostly on a subconscious and unaware level.
- If your unknown beliefs are negative, your personal reality is known as your personality!
BUT...
- if your beliefs are anchored in love, positivity, empathy, understanding, and good values; rest assured that your personal reality will mirror that back to you as well.

Thoughts come to us from the cosmic intelligence. What we emit in vibrations we attract back to us in thoughts and situations. Humans are electro-magnetic beings.
The power of creative thought is unmeasurable in terms of energy volts. Your power comes only from within yourself. Do not be afraid of your own nuclear power.
The mind is universal, and it is the only creator that exists. It is unlimited and multi-faceted. Everyone will either unknowingly or knowingly feed from the universal mind.
Every individual is a perpetual student who profits from understanding how mental laws flow into our reality delivering us failure or success. We are identical to a radio; we only hear the music of the channel we have dialed into.
If you don't like that channel's music, you change channels. Do the same to yourself. Think different thoughts, emit a different vibration, and live a different experience.
Develop your mind power, and your self - awareness, by identifying your limiting beliefs to release them and fill the new void with a better set of enabling beliefs that you will choose yourself.

Self-awareness allows us to develop and cultivate an understanding to reset our beliefs that benefits our body, health, relationships, finances, and all areas of what is needed in a fulfilled and balanced life.

When going through the daily discipline of clearing and cleaning your beliefs, by using one or more of the modalities in this book, such as EFT, Ho'oponopono, meditation etc., other people will intuitively feel that you are a forceful person and will therefore automatically want to please you.

You will soon be attracting the right situations, people, and things effortlessly to yourself. You will be aligned and in harmony with the positive energies of the universe.

That is the success platform on which you want to stand to benefit from the advantages of the business and social world that most people live in or depend on.

Obliterate, depression, sadness, anxiety, distrust, guilt and all forms of suffering and illnesses. (Chapter 17) Replace vague, unknown, and unexamined murky beliefs with clear principles, good values and join the ranks of the winners of this world who operate on the laws of good values and efficiency.

Knowledge is vital, but implementation is the carburetor of reality. A new civilization is being bred and born, this generation is quantum leaping their lives into success because they embrace the new accepted possibilities of our individual self-powers which science and not dogma is starting to prove to us today.

That peer-reviewed research and scientific proof is very much cutting edge.
Questions lead to awareness which in turn open the door to deep inner self knowledge.

Following is an extraction of a process of self-analysis drawn up in Napoleon Hill's book; 'The Law of Success'. I urge you to dedicate about 8 to 10 hours of quiet time and introspection and answer these questions as honestly and deeply as you can.

These questions will lead you to answers which will unveil your real inner self. There is no bad or good. There is only 'you'. And each 'individual', as the name says it, has their own unique set of talents, advantages, and obstacles to deal with and use for creating the life that we want.

1- Do you complain of feeling bad? And if so, then why?
2- Do you easily find fault in other people?
3- Do you make mistakes in your work often?
4- Are you aware if you learn from your mistakes?
5- Do you tend to be obnoxious and sarcastic?
6- Who do you deliberately avoid? And why?
7- Does life seem like a waste of time?
8- Do you dwell in self – pity? And if you do, then what is your recurring theme of self -pity?
9- Have you noticed if you are jealous of people who are more successful then you?
10- Are you aware if you spend more time thinking of failure or success?
11- As time goes by, do you think you are becoming less or more self-confident?

12- Do you easily allow friends or family to worry you with their negative thoughts no matter how well meaning they might be?
13- Do you yo-yo up and down between elation and depression?
14- Who is the most inspiring person you know and why?
15- Are you careless or proud about your appearance?
16- Do you find you keep busy as a way of not looking at uncomfortable issues or challenges?
17- Do you prefer to think for yourself, or do you tend to simply allow other people to do the thinking?
18- Do you fall back on drugs, alcohol, shopping, or any other diversion to soften your mental, emotional, or physical anguishes?
19- What is your strategy for reaching your goal.?
20- What do you do to actively keep your mind positive?
21- Do you make it a point of leaning something new every day?
22- Do you willingly accept responsibility for your problems and work to overcome the problems?
23- Identify your 3 worst weaknesses and write down what you do to overcome them and change.
24- What habits annoy you the most in others? Use the mirror principle and notice that you have the same annoying habits.
25- Do you have strong opinions? Can you debate them?
26- What spiritual approach do you like to use to keep you free from fear?
27- What traits do you like in your friends?
28- Are your friends of work colleagues mentally inferior or superior to you?
29- How much time do you devote daily to your hobby? Sleep? Play? And learning?
30- Who among your friends encourages you the most?

31- What is your greatest worry?
32- Before discounting other people's advice, do you take the time to analyze it as well as their motives for giving you the advice?
33- What do you desire above everything else?
34- Do you intend to get it?
35- What is your strategy for getting it?
36- How much time do you devote to your strategy daily?
37- Do you tend to finish what you start? If not, then analyze why.
38- Are people's opinion of you important to yourself?
39- Do you make friends with people because you resonate with them or because of their social position and wealth?
40- Do you change your mind often?
41- Who do you believe is the greatest person alive today... and why?

Everyone is inclined to want to see the results of their self-improvement work bear results within 48 hours. But there is no magic bullet traveling at supersonic speed. It will take weeks and months to grow enabling new neural circuits of desire and success.

If you are the impatient type, this is one of the self-improvement traits you will have to delete and replace with trust and patience, then internally reverse engineer your processes to discover what motivates you.

Your feelings, whether they are physical or emotional either paralyze or motivate you.

Emotions and feelings are the tip of the iceberg when it comes to the journey within If you are wondering why, you behave the way you do; mirror your behavior and reality. They are messengers of your base beliefs. Beliefs that you have accepted since early childhood or else during a traumatic situation.

Our subconscious and conscious beliefs are the equivalent to the root of a tree. Roots of a Maple tree will not bud through the earth and become a Birch tree. The only way to grow a birch tree is to plant birch roots.
Beliefs whether you are aware of them or not create your behavior and consequently your reality. The structure of your life is the fruit of your seeded beliefs.
And those beliefs are what your mind accepts either consciously or not as 'The Truth'.

The advantage of being human and having a pre-frontal cortex is to use it with clarity and create a new belief to plant as a seed into your nervous system allowing it to develop into a thought.
Once the subconscious has assimilated your chosen new belief, your behavior will change reflecting your new beliefs in a habitual way until once again you become unaware of your behavior and inner vibrations, but now your reality is in line with your wishes and your goal.
The immune system, success factor and attitudes are all connected by the neurochemistry in the nervous system where electro - chemicals, enzymes, hormones and all the rest of the pharmaceutical lab, which are fired off by the rampant running limbic brain.
When you travel within you get to identify your beliefs, and consequentially create new thoughts. A thought is identical to a thing. When you don't like a 'Thing' you adapt it to what you want or throw it out and get or make a 'Thing' that you want. The same applies to 'thoughts.
To get the information you want about yourself, have the courage to be vulnerable and ask a few people whom you admire and respect to be so kind and to give you their honest opinions of yourself.

Here is a list of questions to get you going, feel free to adapt them to your circumstances.

The questions fall into different categories, obviously the more feedback you can get, the better off you will be to understand how others see you. It will give you a better platform to self – improve.

MOTIVATION

- Do I believe or feel that I demonstrate my commitment to my job/ relationship/ company / community / etc. And if so, please explain "HOW'
- Do I come across as being self-motivated?
- Have you found it difficult or easy to motivate me?
- Do I feel / see / believe that I motivate others positively?

INTERPERSONAL SKILLS

- In your honest opinion do you believe that I show good leadership qualities in my role as: Parent/ CEO/ Community / PTA/ etc.
- I would be very grateful if you could write one or two examples either way as to how I don't or do show leadership.
- If you believe I do not show leadership, please be kind enough as to advise me how I can improve my leadership.

FINDING SOLUTIONS

- Do you rely on me easily to find solutions to problems?
- If so, what specific talents or attributes in your opinion have I shown an ability to find solutions or improve situations.
- If you believe that I am a solution orientated thinker, what area do you suggest that I focus on to improve my working skills so that I can be relied as a trusted solution finder.

SOCIALLY INTERACTIVE

- How do I liaise with the rest of the team/ colleagues/friends/ family members / etc.?
- How do people speak of me behind my back in the: Company/ Community/ workplace/ etc.?
- What advice can you give me to increase the effectiveness of my communication with other people?

AM I AN ASSET?

- In your opinion do you notice improvement in my work?
- Are you happy with the results I produce?
- Am I efficient?
- What can I do, be or become to increase my efficiency in my responsibilities'?

All the above work has resulted in your own discovery of who and what you are. Now is the moment to create a better self-image of yourself.

Re-define clearly who you want to be. Keep all your good qualities and character traits, as well as your enabling beliefs, but underline all your negatives and replace them with positive statements instead.

Remember you are only limited by your imagination. It all starts in your mind where only you are entitled to rule.

Use inspirational role models as a compass. Listen to their podcasts or read their autobiographies and notice how they talk about themselves and their lives.

It is productive to admire and pick up qualities in people you look up to.

Negative comparison is not constructive and will make you feel bad about yourself.

Read the 'redefinition of your ideal self' every day for the next few months, until you have become familiar with the new. Notice how you are automatically morphing into the new and better designed you.

It takes time, stick to your desired image, and watch yourself grow and morph into your ideal self.

You are yourself by design. Design yourself to your liking.

CHAPTER SIX

KNOW WHAT YOU WANT

Otherwise beware....
Someone else will make you do what they want

ADVICE: DO NOT ALLOW YOUR PRESENT CIRCUMSTANCES TO DICTATE WHAT YOU WANT. WRITE OUT EVERYTHING **YOU** WANT AND NOT WHAT YOU THINK YOU SHOULD ASK FOR. LISTEN TO YOUR HEART AND NOT TO OTHER PEOPLE. WHEN YOUR HEART SINGS YOU ARE CONNECTED TO YOURSELF AND YOUR HIGHER POWER.

Knowing what and why you want what you want are the first steps to happiness. Once you have pinpointed your goals the act of imagining feeling, seeing, hearing, tasting, whatever you want allows them to become your vibrational alignment with your goal.

Success is getting what you want, and happiness is wanting what you get. David Bohl

Turn off your autopilot and deliberately guide your senses into the imaginary realm of what you want. Be self-aware that your thoughts are focused on what you do want even if you must push and guide your mind towards it. Every time you go back into the images of your imagination the scenes or situations will carve out in more detail. Assume the emotions you want to feel when your goal is reached. Become the master of your mind, don't permit yourself to be imagining what you do not want to have or be in the final outcome. Human beings are the only living species that can self-regulate. No other living species can self-regulate at will.

It is not WHAT you know that is important, but WHAT you WANT to know and WHY do you want to know it. Ask the right questions and get the right answers.

Every Sunday I take the time to enjoy myself by doing a re-discovery weekly ritual. Events, hopes and situations have probably impacted me during the past week. Maybe my perceptions have shifted but in my hurriedness of living I did not stop to hear myself. Now is the time to build up a clear image of whatever I am thinking about and enlarge it on the movie screen of my inner vision or imagination.

Perhaps these questions will resonate with you. Play with them and see which ones bring an answer to your mind.
- When do I feel loved?
- Which person gives me that wonderful warm feeling of being: Loved- desired- protected, etc.
- When do I feel abundant? Is It with a lot of money in my account, oodles of good health, or more than enough time to do what I want?

We are part of a whole. Happiness and success are a group effort. No one succeeds on their own. The sooner you can put a good perspective on your relationships the sooner you will be on your way to getting what you want. But you must engage and respect others. A 'Win – Win' situation is the only win that counts and lasts.

Andrew Carnegie: the most important steel magnate in America, built a colossal empire starting from dire poverty in Scotland, immigrating to Pennsylvania and living

with his parents in abject poverty. He had a very basic education as he was already working at 14 years old to help bring money to his family. He had no idea about iron or steel. Yet he achieved amazing and financial abundance and success learning from all experiences in his young working career and by relying on other people, seeing, feeling and understanding their viewpoints and being able to intuitively connect everyone's selfish personal reasons into what he coined the 'Mastermind'.
You can easily do the same.
Look at a specific situation from behind the eyes of the other person.
Imagine what they are feeling in a certain situation.
Step into their shoes and perceive the set of facts from their point of view.
See if you get any 'Aha' moments of insight.
Use that person as your mentor.
Imagine what they would tell or advise you so that they can get ahead.
Of course, you only want to be doing this with people whose values and intellect you admire and respect. Once you connect to other people's reasons or goals intuitively, get out of their shoes, go back into yours and tell them something that they will enjoy hearing and in a tone of voice that they will relate to.
Match their breathing and match their body language without being overtly obvious. These little tips put the other person subconsciously in a familiar zone and they are now much more apt to go along with your ideas or goals.
You will always catch bees with honey.
If you want someone to see things from your point of view, you will come to understand that people do what they do for a good reason. They might not even know

what that reason is because they are running on deeply embedded habits. So, study them and spy on what they are seeing from behind their eyes. That will allow you to instinctively formulate the right sentences or enticement to bring the other person over the street and together march towards your success.

There are horses for courses, and a good trainer can get all horses to gallop well on a course. The analogy here is that even though there will be only one winning horse there are now several horses to choose from as they are all primed for that same finish line.

The big secret of reaching a goal is not to know how to reach it, but why you want to reach it.

The path from where you are in the present moment until you reach your goal will most likely take you off course 90% of the time. Just like an airplane is off course for most of the flight but as the autopilot is well programed and set with absolute clarity the plane lands and comes to a smooth halt at the right gate.

Apply that analogy to your life, if you don't imagine and feel already with conviction and clarity your arrival on a continuous daily basis, as soon as your path takes you off course, like a roadblock or even a failure in one of your baby steps you could give up.

You've set goals in the past and reached them, but on arrival you felt empty.

Why? Because you have not ticked off on the next two sentences.

- Success is knowing what you want.
- Happiness is wanting what you get.

Arthur Schopenhauer, the German 19th century philosopher had a big impact on the lives of many German artists.

He stated that for anything which is a true law of nature it must go through 3 stages:
1st stage: The idea or concept will be ridiculed.
2nd stage: The idea will be violently opposed. This is when the messenger must hold their ground and have faith that the truth will eventually be perceived.
3rd stage: The idea gains momentum and is soon accepted as a truth. This is when you must leave your ego out and be grateful that you are benefiting from the knowledge of the truth.

Time is money, and the best way to save time is to plan what you want to experience or own clearly in your mind and imagination first.

Once your arrival point is clearly identified in your mind, you will automatically stop reacting to situations which only results in wasting time and losing your focus. Instead act in accordance with your direction which puts you on course to your destination.

POWER

P= The possibility to REPROGRAM your 'Belief 'system

O= Own the responsibility of every situation that happens to you. (Understand Ho'oponopono chapter 17) Accept and understand how repetitive thoughts become beliefs. Accept that all subconscious beliefs attract the necessary situations to yourself allowing you to live the reality of your beliefs. It is up to you to RE-program your belief system.

W= When, Where, and Why. Get into the habit of asking and you will receive answers.

E= Evolving and learning with awareness through situations and emotions are a key factor to empowering yourself.

R= Respect others and respect yourself. Take responsibility for every one of your actions and the ensuing results.

Congratulate yourself and if it does not reflect what you want, create the imaginary image of what you do want and start from scratch so that you can give the necessary time to yourself to germinate and water that imaginary seed into the fertile energy ground of your mind.

You might have realized on arrival or completion of your goal that you were not feeling as you had wanted or hoped to feel. And you asked yourself.' All this work just to feel empty?"

And another time all those setbacks took away the initial excitement that overwhelmed you at the start of your quest. 'Stickability' is an important trait of character necessary to reaching goals.

You will never know if you could have succeeded if you give up. But if you are clear about what you want and why you want it, nothing and no one will allow you to give up.

Hear the sounds or words you imagine you will be hearing when you reach your goal, see what you will be seeing when you reach you goal, feel the emotions and linger in the joy of those feelings. You are programing your autopilot to take you to target.

Each thought and feeling you express in your imagination are cumulating the matching energy frequency that you are pulling into your orbit.

Like attracts like. You are setting your energy frequencies to vibrate in peak state. You are anchoring by choice those frequencies to lodge themselves into your nervous system and become the new you. This is one of the steps you want to accomplish to experience the life you want to live.

Imagine yourself now feeling the way you want to feel when you have reached your goal. By doing that you are not only making every day a happy day, but you are creating your mind set for the day, the month the year and for life.

Self-Hypnotize yourself into a deep, trance-like state of relaxation and concentration halfway between wakefulness and sleep that creates a fertile ground for retraining and reprogramming your brain. A state of self-hypnosis opens the mindset to change beliefs and habits at a deep, nonconscious level. When you go into auto trans mode, you are fully awake. You are totally in control and command of yourself.

Affirmations, visualization, audio suggestion and guided imagery have a more powerful impact when you are in a state of self-hypnosis. Your body relaxes, negative thoughts subside, and self-hypnosis becomes a place for dramatic change. Use the correct methodologies to assist you in implanting and anchoring new beliefs and habits into your sub-conscious mind. You can reprogram your subconscious to automatically overcome undesirable habits, gain confidence, eliminate old, negative beliefs, and reprogram yourself with new, empowering beliefs.

How will you benefit? When using self-hypnosis, you can reap unlimited financial rewards and personal success, vibrant health, a significant reduction in stress and complete peace of mind.

Sure, there might be days when you will want to pack it in, but your deep desire for reaching your goal will put you back on track again. However, that will only happen when you know for sure what and why you want it. The 'how' and 'why's' will most likely be a string of setbacks.

And without you knowing it, your happiness thermostat will be on high since you are doing whatever it takes to fuel your desire of reaching your goal.

SUCCESS AND HAPPINESS ARE METHODS

Do the following diligently by spending 30 minutes every morning when you wake up. Make sure you do it for at least 4 weeks allowing success patterns to build up. This is proven to work by the research into neuroplasticity.

1. Define your dream. Remember that whatever you can conjure up on the screen of your imagination can be achieved. There is no right or wrong, there is no can or can't reach that goal. If you can imagine it, you can do it.
2. Write out a list of what makes you tick. These are called 'values' Are you motivated by kindness, competitiveness, power, honesty, good luck, music, camaraderie, admiration, excitement, peace, giving of service to others.? These values are your inner petrol. You need to feel and experience these qualities regardless of the situation for you to be happy. So, you want to be sure that your dream goal will encapsulate your values. Otherwise, you are not well aligned and will be shortchanging yourself. My most important values are, or to put it in everyday talk

Fill in the blanks. Honor yourself by taking the time to think and feel what really is of importance to yourself. Say out loud "I choose to"
a-
b-
c-
d-
e-
f-
3. Is this really my dream or have I taken on somebody else's dream?
4. Is the outcome of my goal right for myself and my family?
5. Is the outcome of my goal correct for my community/ business/ planet…etc.
6. Is the ideal outcome of my goal legal?
7. Now that you have gone through the check list of your ideal outcome, and you know what you want your outcome to be….
Have a clear path and imagine the baby steps along the way that you must take.
8. Maintain focus on your outcome
9. Be realistic in what can be accomplished along your timeline.

A clear general definition of happiness can be to enjoy desire and ability today by sacrificing instant gratification for what we eventually are reaching for in our end goals.
Knowing and feeling what you want is the basis that will allow you to live what you want. Therefore, focus your thoughts and mind to build your future reality upwards and outwards like you would build a house. If your dream

seems out of reach, just keep on persisting. Suddenly it becomes a successful reality.

Floor by floor, staircases, window and doors for ideas and situations to enter and exit. It takes longer to build the blueprint and foundations of a house before you can notice one floor on ground level. If your foundations are not well thought out by the time you get to building the roof, the walls might cave in or a staircase might not be strong enough, window frames might collapse from the external weight of a balcony and so on. Your blueprint will determine your outcome.

Your life and the perfect achievement of your goals needs the same focus and preparation. Success is guaranteed if you start with a sound vision and comprehension of what you want as your outcome and why you want it.

Even though the blueprint is part of the 'HOW'. While you are writing your blueprint, you will get deeper in-tune with 'WHY' you want your specific outcome.

If the clarity of the feelings you come up with are not overwhelming to you as a clear 'want', then stop and ask yourself if perhaps you are living out someone else's advice or instructions.

The following questions will help bring clarity into your feelings:

- What are you willing to give up gladly in exchange for achieving your goal?
- What will you gain or lose when you reach your ideal outcome?
- Are you willing to self-discipline yourself to reframe and retrain your brain?
- Is the outcome of your goal only for yourself, or other people as well?

- Are you willing to commit to yourself that you will continue until you reach your goal, no matter the length of time it will take or the sacrifices you might have to make?
- Thinking of your future in the present guarantees you will see that in your future. Don't think of your desired future as some cloudy nebulous event. Train yourself to use your results today as you explored your future.

Remember that thoughts are things, and where thoughts grow, energy flows. Discipline yourself to expanding self-awareness, so that you can always keep your finger on the pulse and do all you can in self-awareness for your thoughts to be positive. Make a conscious choice to decide what you want for the future and then go about making it happen, one inspired baby step at a time and watch your goal happen.

THINK ACHIEVEMENT & WATCH IT HAPPEN!

You will have joined the ranks of the 'Minority Club' of achievers.

To do that you will need to give up blaming and focusing on others and instead become introverted as to the awareness of your thoughts and which beliefs are producing them?

The treasure that you are looking for is buried in what you are avoiding.

I will warn you here, that most people find it easier to apply their energy to the futile and useless task of changing others, since if others don't change, they can have the excuse of not blaming themselves.

It is much more difficult and tiresome to develop self-awareness 24/7 and change yourself inwards so that your outward results will mirror your inner changes. Before you achieve anything excellently you will make many mistakes. Be grateful for those mistakes they are not failures; they are your guidelines for a better future. Those mistakes are your teaching steps.

These are some questions that will assist you to declutter your mind set around your goal's outcome. Take the time to write down your notes. Don't just do it in your head.

The fact of handwriting them down, triggers your reticular activating system, which is very valuable in the visualization process.

1- If anything were possible, what is my ideal outcome? And then proceed to answer it in the present tense.
2- What is my current position/situation in relation to my ideal outcome? Or if you prefer, where are you right now in relation to your outcome.
3- Be very clear on what you want to: hear, see, feel, touch, and taste when you reach your outcome.
4- Describe how you will know when you have reached your goal.
5- Describe what reaching your goal will allow you to do or get you.

Clarity on your wish or goal is a necessity. But why do you find it difficult to be clear?

A lot of people find it more comfortable to be liked rather than upsetting their friends or colleagues by always putting the bar higher. And maybe their goals have nothing to do with the lifestyles or the people of the groups they want to fit into rather than forming their own.

Before you read the next paragraph, get clear on your own goals and intentions, otherwise you are shooting yourself in your foot.

These are steps that sharpen your inner sense of intention.

1- What do you want to DO?
   The sky is the limit, from business to relationships to sports or culture, and everything in between. Start your sentences in the present tense with I AM DOING (describe what you are doing)
2- What do you want to OWN-POSSESS- HAVE?
   Again, anything and everything from time, to money, to health, cars, planes; this is the moment to write your Santa Claus list. Even if your wants seem silly, or unobtainable write them out because they might lead you down to some deeper wants you have which you are not acknowledging.
3- Finally… if anything were possible, who do you want to BE?
   Your wants must include states of mind, of health as well as personality traits you want to become and social roles, such as a parent, a friend, a leader and so on. Again, be sure to start your sentences with 'I AM'
   Let your hand flow with the pen or on the keyboard and splurge in details.

If you hear an inner voice, self-criticizing what you dare to want; just ignore it. The fact of putting the craziest of things and reasons on paper will bring clarity to your desires. What you appreciate, appreciates in turn.
Know that you are only limited by your imagination. Put your hand on your heart, look in the mirror and say to yourself outload. 'I allow my imagination to run free".
Appreciate everything you have, that will allow you to see more opportunities.

Then ask yourself "What choices can I or do I want to make to support myself and give myself a more fulfilling, passionate, healthy, and loving life?
Listen to your inner voice and commit to doing that action today.
Trust your inner answers and enjoy the freedom of trusting your inner supernatural powers.

Everything is energy… remember when you state your goal out loud SAY IT THE WAY YOU WANT IT. It is statistically proven today that goals which are emotionally stated in the positive and in the present have a high rate of achievement.

CHAPTER SEVEN

GOAL SETTING

Dream... Go... Achieve!

Do not succumb to the belief that you are 'stuck'.
There are ways to get out of 'being stuck" (Chapter 18 Deletion tools)
Energy is on the go 24/7
We are first and foremost energy, only then do we become matter. Our bodies are more than 98% energy. And this can be identified when you use a very powerful microscope to investigate the cells, you will see swirling reams looking like the milky way... welcome to your inner core. Your own renewable energy system.
Our beliefs stem from our childhood and even earlier on when we were unwittingly indoctrinated either by words, behaviours, experiences, and vibrational frequencies when we were in our mother's womb.
Beliefs are programs.
You can have bad programs that have bugs and viruses in them, which have negative side effects on your actions, like second guessing yourself and delaying your action out of fear and doubt.
Or you can have great enabling programs allowing you to reach you goals.
You alone are the gatekeeper of your thoughts. Self-awareness of your emotions and fleeting thoughts grant you the possibility to choose if you would rather continue in that line of thought or if you prefer to pivot 180 degrees to the same thought but from a better

perspective. When you take that action, you are creatively changing the patterns of your neuronal pathways. Choosing develops freedom. Freedom starts with your choice of thoughts. No one can or needs to help you to free yourself from your limiting beliefs. Only you can do that on your own.

Your future is the vibrational mirror of your present vibrations. Just as your present circumstances are the mirror of your past beliefs and vibrations.

Since thoughts are vibrations, change your thoughts to what you want your future to be and then wait and watch it happen.

Hindus use the word 'Namaste' as a greeting. It means "I salute and acknowledge the Divine in you' and the Mayans used to say, 'In Lakesh' which means 'You are another version of myself'. Today's modern language of speaking about the vibrational mirror is only a verbal development of what has been known and incorporated since time immemorial.

I sum it up to be we are all the same and, in that sameness, resides the Divine, our higher power, or if you prefer in today's non-religious language an energy far more powerful than our ego and consciousness can fathom, it is a pity to waste our gifts of Divine power by lack of belief in your own ability to reach your goals. Whatever those goals may be.

Question yourself on "What are my beliefs"? then write down your answers as they come to you Read your answers out loud back to yourself and notice if you enjoy reading about your beliefs? Do they match what you want in an ideal world?

If not, rewrite your beliefs to spell out the reality of what you want. No 'but's or if's' Just a straightforward simple belief statement of what you want written out

positively and in the present tense. All behaviours are belief driven. As Henry Ford said" If you believe you can or believe you can't, you are always right'!
Choose your beliefs carefully with foresight.

If you are lucky those beliefs will have served, you well. How can you tell?
Easy. The parts of your life that are going in a positive flow stem from enabling beliefs.
But the parts of your life that are stagnant or deteriorating also stem from your indoctrination.
Solution?... Do what successful people do. CHOOSE a model of reality that you want to be your own and go about integrating it as your new belief.

Personally, I used to be and still am very high energy, but it was dissipated energy because I lived my life as a victim of whatever emotions I was experiencing. If I was angry, I would react by taking it out on others without stopping to think how my impatient and angry behaviour would impact them. My emotions were stronger than me and they had my subconscious blessing to keep on being the boss.
As the saying goes; 'I was all over the place'; thereby never having the peace and focus or taking the time to develop all the amazing ideas I had.
I was and thankfully still am creative, and good ideas kept on popping into my head but despite getting excited about them and talking like a windmill to any and everyone who was willing to listen to my ideas, at the end of the day I never really started many of my ideas and when I did, I hardly ever accomplished or finished what I had set myself out to do.

I had no knowledge or idea that I could re- direct my energy to being productive and achieving measurable results simply by changing and focusing on thoughts that would produce the peak state that I had imagined would be beneficial for me to live to being able to be fulfilled and proud of myself.

Today, after quite a while turning the steering wheel of my life towards daily baby steps in self-improvement exercises of many sorts, I hardly experience that bubbling anger and constant impatience I used to feel and emanate. I can now recognise when the tell-tale signs of imminent danger are on the horizon since I have the tools to disembowel, diffuse and transform the negative outlets. Tapping and Ho'oponopono have become my favourite and most expedient deletion tools. You will discover those in chapter 18.

But as far as reprogramming yourself for positive achievement follow these easy steps. These steps are not a goal, but they are a path to use on a constant daily basis for your positive evolvement. Play around with them and find out which steps work best for you. After a while you will automatically develop your own recipe.

Identify clearly what you do not like in your current reality. The right brain develops the imagination, and the left brain is your logical side

1- Figure out the root belief that you would logically have and which you think is producing your current reality.

2- Identify clearly in not more than 3 sentences the specific reality you want instead.

3- Create an affirmation which confirms that your 'want' is already in the post, you have the tracking number, so you are in a calm, trusting state of expectancy until the envelope is delivered to you.

4- Build yourself up to your optimum and peak state.

5- Become totally engaged in reaching your goal. Make a list of all the mini goals you must accomplish before reaching your ideal end goal. A detailed method of this in the G.R.O.W. model further ahead in this chapter.

6- Now mentally and emotionally quantum leap forward towards your end goal. Act NOW by mapping out a strategy to reach that goal. Your written strategy will facilitate everything.

You can start by a phone call, or making an appointment, but take some action no matter how small or insignificant. The mere fact of taking the action now will put you on the tracks to your destination. Outline a strategy to reach your goal. Most goals are never reached because the person does not have a strategy and a timeline written out. And one year later they realise that their goal is lying in tatters in some corner. Write out a timeline and hold yourself as near as possible to it.

7- Be sure to follow the step-by-step strategy method in the G.R.O.W model which I describe clearly further on.

Example: You live in a terrible place and have been unable to upgrade your living conditions for a long time. You don't enjoy where you live and always want to escape your home and be anywhere except in your current home.

Examples of a few beliefs you could be holding unknowingly:

- Even when you were small your parents did not have or live in a nice home. They or where you lived were dirty, there was always fighting going on in the background, you witnessed abusive behaviour towards others and perhaps were even abused yourself, so home was dangerous, loud, dirty, aggressive, and so on.

Example of a reality you would want:

- To have a clean welcoming home where you feel cosy, safe, and peaceful.

Example of a sentence you could create and write on your card, phone screen and everywhere else that you can think of where your eyes fall on regularly. You are positively programming your mind to accept our new belief.
'Since anything is possible in this universe, I am choosing to enjoy living in my clean and peaceful home.'
Make a point of seeing that card at last 3 times every day and be in a state of relaxed trust as you expect that home to be yours just as sure as you trust that the letter in the post is coming into your letterbox
That is the peaceful state of trust and expectancy, that the new reality is yours. Imagine you were sent a 'Tracking number' from the Universe. You would feel very relaxed as you know it is in the post. You only must wait a little for the parcel to be in your hands.
The reality of you reaching your goals is down to the choice that you make as to what and how you think about your goal. Energy flows where thought goes. So,

CHOOSE your thoughts carefully to study mirrors that reflect what you are looking for.

Pump yourself up emotionally, mentally, and physically into your peak state. The better your peak state is the more charismatic you become. So, when you wake up in the morning you have put yourself into a state of expectancy of manifesting your goals.

Let me give you this little story so it will help you to relate.

You are on a business trip to deliver a keynote speech. Of course, you have booked your room in a hotel to make life easier and more comfortable. But when you arrive at the hotel you find out that the reservations desk made a mistake and have overbooked leaving you without a room.

As you are peacefully in a peak state, and therefor obviously grounded, you think clearly and don't automatically become a victim of your anger at the front desk which will only result in the reservation team at the front desk of the hotel getting more defensive and clamping down even more to your problem.

You might be enjoying your state of peace so much that you increase your self – confidence and power by thinking calmly 'Peace begins with me'

Suddenly, you come up with a humorous question and ask the reception desk, "If the Queen of England comes to town today and wants to stay here would you find a room for her?"

The receptionist raises an eyebrow unsure of how to answer but most likely will attempt a funny or hesitant: "Yes of course, for the Queen of England we will find a room for the night"

And you are quick to reply, "Well I just had Her Majesty on the phone, she has changed her plans and is not coming tonight so you can give me her room".

Charm, smiles, logical replies, and your sense of expectancy will get you a room. Because you are in your peak state that is whom you become, 'a person who gets what they want'.

To love yourself is the best way to improve. As you improve; those around you also improve. You are creating 'win- win' situations for yourself, friends, and colleagues. Energy is contagious.

Each physical or situational substance has its own distinct energetic vibration signature which is a thought. Thoughts are created from our memories. And memories consist of deeply buried frequencies in the nervous system. Those unconscious memories are programs that were created in our recent past but also which we can have inherited from our parents as well as from many past generations. Those memory frequencies vibrate everywhere and in our atoms. Every time you encounter an obstacle, a problem or what is also known as a challenge; understand and accept that it is only a memory which is interfering and acting up inside of yourself.

In chapter 18 you will read and learn about tools which deep clean the nervous system and erase those limiting frequencies. As you clean up and delete the dense blocking energy of your limiting memories you become able, willing, and ready to change your thinking methods and transform your reality. You are cleaning up your energy filters.

Atoms are immaterial they are without physical substance, yet they are the building blocks of physical reality

Rest assured that you do not have to study physics to reach your goals and live the life of your wishes, you only must understand the concept that by activating your subconscious mind through one or more senses, the mind accepts that everything you want has already manifested...

Energy, situations, and substance are one and the same. Draw the goals of your life onto the canvas of your mind and (watch them come to life. (Refer to chapter 20 on visualisation)

ADVICE: On 3 large sheets of sketch paper draw a 'Bullseye' big enough so that in the middle you can write your short-term goals about 1 year from now, your midterm goals about 3 years from now and your long-term goals about 5 years from now. Describe in writing the goals in a few words.

On the external circle rims of the 'Bullseye' write out the steppingstones you feel are needed before you reach your bullseye.

Goal Setting is of course the first step and an important one. Goals give a reason to get up in the morning and set the compass for which direction you will move towards during the day. Even if you take a long time to reach your goal, it will not be wasted time because you will be learning about yourself nonstop.

SELF – PROGRESS ADDICT…
A PRODUCTIVE ADDICTION TO HAVE!

Do your target practice very often, it helps you to feel a daily sense of progress. A measurable daily progress boosts your feel-good neurochemistry until such a time that you become a self- progress addict.

Become self -aware and identify all small steps which are successful. Relax into that warm endorphin injection of 'going forward' in the right direction and look inwards at your progress for the next day as you duplicate and replicate that same warm feeling of self-achievement. That feel good need is equivalent to having excellent suspension and power -steering to enjoy a confident and comfortable journey to your destination.

Enjoy being self-aware of your own good efforts and results. Be sure to congratulate yourself as you move forward.

Let's start with some easy steps that allow you to cross the bridge from your wishes to your goals.

Auto- train your brain to stretch your current boundaries of imagination into new visions of what you want and allow your new beliefs to transform into your new reality.

It is only a process. Trust the process and trust yourself. It is important to sync and anchor goals into the conscious and the subconscious minds equally.

1. Keep the end in mind, by imagining and reminding yourself what impact reaching and living your goal will have on your lifestyle. Keep your vivid imaginary picture in your mind and feel yourself in that situation daily.
2. Perhaps at present you see all the odds are stacked up against you, nevertheless, create your expectancy that

reaching your goal is feasible and a done deal. Even if your heart is not in it. You might have had a setback, rest assured that you are in the creation process. Keep on creating. The images you see inside your mind will become what you see in the reality of your life. I promise that is what happens because you are creating a new energy flow rate. It does not and cannot happen any other way.
3. Have fun, go back to your early childhood when you used to IMAGINE without any constraints or restrictions. What you imagined as a child was your reality. The 'unconscious' mind does not know or perceive the difference between, past present and future, but when you choose to imagine yourself in your goal NOW, your limbic brain releases the neuro –chemical cocktail that gets your subconscious mind addicted to feeling what you are imaging as if you were presently living your goal.
4. BAD beware!! Be very conscious of negative feelings. As soon as you detect any familiar 'drama queen' scenarios running. amok in your mind use the pivot tool (chapter 18 deletion tools exercise 5).
5. By indulging in your familiar focus of 'lack' scenarios; the brain formulates a high voltage of neuro chemicals which vibrate and automatically attract situations which invisibly guarantee to make you live a situation in real life delivering all the reasons to feel the same bad feelings you experience when you project a negative scenario in your mind. Like attracts like. It is important to be aware that when you resist a thought or feeling your energy is generating that exact vibrational signature. The answer is not to resist the feeling or thought but to release it. Again, refer to chapter 17. What you resist persists.
6. Use your ability and birth-right gift of 'Choice' to CHOOSE a positive thought instead. Release all negative emotions relating to the past. Use one or more of the

deletion tools that are explained in chapter 18. 'Deletion Tools' The daily practice of doing a few rounds of EFT Emotional Freedom Technique is the fastest and strongest first- aid that you can implement. Your entire nervous system auto-cleans negative neurochemicals which are altering your subconscious into a positive fertile growth base.

7. Transform each one of your wishes to goals by applying the S.M.A.R.T. goal setting method described further on in this chapter. This method stacks up all the advantages on your end. It is a concrete and precise way of acting during the creation process. Each letter stands for a set of actions and enabling mind-sets which add up to a logical way of reaching your goal. We are energy, spirit, and matter. The matter part of us operates in the prefrontal cortex and this is where we drive our actions.

Become conscious of what you desire your end destination to be. Elaborate, entertain, and dream about your vision. In your imagination have fun and make your vision as big and good as you wish. Your life is only limited by your imagination. And once you have a clear vision of your end goal, come back to where you are now, and take the logical next step with common sense.

Ask yourself what is your next hurdle? And then proceed.

S.M.A.R.T, G.O.A.L.S, G.R.O.W.!

3 POWERFUL & DIFFERENT PROCEDURES

S.M.A.R.T (Procedure 1)

S: SPECIFIC: Be as clear and specific as you can. Keep on chiselling away until your goal is well defined and easily imaginable. The acid test is to tell your goal to someone else and see if they can understand the goal you shared with them.

This step is your goals mission statement. Include a list of who you will need to help you reach this goal. Everything is team orientated. A good team is composed of people with different talents and attributes.

Think of where and when you want your goal to materialise. This is the moment to analyse if you are realistically able to start on your main goal now, or perhaps you have more baby steps to accomplish before you set off for the big target. For example, if you want to open a chain of restaurants but you have no idea how to cook or compose a recipe, manage accounts, or read contracts, this is the moment to back pedal, and learn cooking first, get a job in another chain of restaurants and learn the trade an insider, after which you can get a good general feel of the industry you want to take on as a leader.

Take into consideration levels and areas in which you feel confident enough in to go forward.

Walk before you run.

M: Stands for METRICS – MEASURABLE

What must happen or be in place for you to say, "I have reached my goal"? Once again, here you most likely will have to climb the ladder. So, identify as many rungs as possible before you start your journey. Identify as many junctions, obstacles, and solutions as possible in your plan. This is all part and parcel of the pre-planning creation map designed to reach your goal. You are still planning your trip. The more answers you have before you leave the more efficient your journey will be.

As a tip, you will want to look at the G.R.O.W. models of questioning at the end of this chapter. I have included the full set of questions which I use when working with business executives on long term goal reaching as well as when I work with competition athletes.

A: Stands for ACHIEVABLE

Take the time to list all the reasons why reaching this goal is paramount to your success or/ and happiness.

Imagine you are a mentor of your choice and put yourself in their shoes. Which skills and tools would they point out that you will need in order to reach your goal? If you are completely suggestive, then you can omit the mentor approach. I just find it is always best to have an outside view from someone you trust. And your imaginary mentor will come to you subconsciously. If you don't have the tools and skills presently, go back to the drawing board and figure out how you can acquire those tools or skills.

R: For RELEVANT

The goal in question must be relevant to your overall career, business or life goal and values. Otherwise, you are wasting your time. For example, if you are a singing teacher and are passionate about music, but you have the idea of opening a travel agency, or becoming a ping-pong champion, that will not be relevant to your main frame. You would end up fracturing yourself and your time.
Unless of course you only consider becoming a ping-pong champion as a hobby.

T: Stands for TIME

The whole point about setting a goal is reaching it, so give yourself a realistic deadline. This is important for staying on track otherwise you can tend to procrastinate and eventually your goal will no longer be relevant to you. Sit down and map out your baby steps. (Look at the step-by-step approach on the G.R.O.W. model.) It is also useful to write down what you want to have accomplished at a specific point in time.

Goals are dynamic. They are not set in stone. Once you put your foot into the stirrup the horse takes off, and along the way you will encounter situations that you had not thought off. Be flexible while all the time keeping your focus on the bull's eye.

Write your closing statement.

Condense the previous S.M.A.R.T. steps into:

1- Take the time to put together a clear strategy to reach your goal. And just in case it does not work out as smoothly as you would like; create a backup strategy. Then map out your strategy in a step-by-step approach.
2- Write out your deadline.
3- Choose an accountability partner who will be responsible for making you do what you said you would do. when you don't feel like doing it. When we least feel like doing something is when we most need to do it.
4- Imagine what you will feel like if you don't reach your goal, give that feeling a number from 0 to 10 with 10 being the worst, and then use EFT Emotional Freedom Technique to tap that feeling out of your nervous system. (Remember to go to chapter 17 where EFT is explained in detail)

Goal setters BEWARE! The road to hell is paved with good intentions. And the road to your goal will be paved with pit falls and all sorts of logical reasons why it will be understandable and normal to give up and not waste any more time on pursuing your dream and reaching your goal.

There is one guarantee that I can give you. If you give up for any reason, you will NEVER reach your goal.

But... if you have your heart anchored in a desire which is stronger than life itself you will overcome all the obstacles one way or another and will reach and live your goal.

Take some quiet time and meditate, allowing YOUR answers to bubble up to your awareness and answer these questions. There is no right or wrong, there are only your reasons that count.

I want to reach my goal because …
- My emotional Why?
- My mental Why?
- My physical Why?
- My financial Why?

Now answer these questions relating to your goal.
If you are starting out fresh on your goal, look at yourself in the mirror and say out loud "I want to reach my goal but ………". Allow all the buts to come up and acknowledge them. Don't ignore those 'But's'

Use the EFT Emotional Freedom Technique to tap on the discomfort that your inner arguments disrupted your peaceful determination to reach your goal.
If you have been on the road to reach your goal and have given up and would like to pick up where you left off and continue, then look at yourself in the mirror and say out loud "I have not reached my goal because………"
I am not efficient/clever/clear/self-disciplined enough. What is the matter with me? And the list can go on as everyone has their own story. The answers that come up won't feel nice, but they are helpful. Once you have looked the devil in the eye and survived your limiting beliefs will dissolve automatically. Now you can change your approach and at the end of every day, sit down and tick off your 'To Do' list and change your self- talk to: "I did my best, and gave it my all. Tomorrow is another day, and I am going forwards".
Personally, I have always preferred writing out my 'To Do' lists on paper and being able to scratch them out and tick them off at the end of the day. One sheet of paper limits my daily tasks as opposed to the ongoing digital pages on an app. I want to fit my daily 'To Do' and 'Did

It' lists on 1 page per day that I stick somewhere visible throughout the day.

Then as I progress throughout the list I also like to physically tick off on the list and I can see how much time I have left for the other daily goals. I feel productive when I track my progress.

I make sure that my end goals are really broken down into doable daily goals. If my goal is to launch a new magazine. I don't 'write down 'Work on magazine' because I know what I need to do today. I will write down 2 or 3 mini goals for my magazine that day. For example, 1- Start on my list of who will I choose to be my editor – Prepare list of distribution channels – work on the mission statement of my magazine- change the red toner in the printer in the office- etc…

All the daily goals are bite sized and achievable.

At the start of the day, I have the most energy, so I choose to work on the most crucial items first. Side-tracking opportunities happen constantly. I make it a rule to complete my daily crucial task first, before moving on. And that is why I chunk down that crucial task to what can be logically achieved in one day, even though I am perfectly aware I might need 2 years to reach my goal.

I keep my daily 'To Do' lists in a binder, and at the back of the binder, I rewrite my 'To Do' list into a 'Did It' list. Not only does it boost my immune system every time I look at it, but it helps me keep track of my progress towards D- Day, which is my time target.

Do the 5 by 5 list. Every day at 5 pm, I sit down and in 5 minutes I write out 5 actions that I will do the next day by 5 pm. It ensures that I keep my action momentum productive.

We are living in a reality of constant change. Dedicate 20 minutes each day, to informing yourself on new technologies. Be up to date. Along the way you will find better ways to reach your goal then the old ones you have been using. Our brains must be flexible to improve and reap better solutions non-stop. Gone are the days of 'Learn it once and it is yours for life!' Always be on the lookout for better developments.

When I am tired at the end of the day, I will choose one item on my 'Did It' list and be sure to indulge in my joy of having done it.
Often, I will then celebrate it.
Celebration is an energy booster. Enjoy all celebrations.
Now just do it!

G.R.O.W

From the boardroom to the sports field via the homework process of children the GROW model is an easily applicable proven 'success' method.
Integrate the S.M.A.R. T. goal into your GROW model.

4 STEPS TO THE FINISH LINE

The idea that you had thought of in the past but either had only entertained briefly or had given up because it proved to be much more complicated than you had bargained for?

And later in life you found yourself saying: 'I remember when I had that idea. I should have developed it." But now it was too late because someone else had the same idea and they beat you to it. Action more than knowledge makes things happen.

By going through the steps of the G.R.O.W. model, you will bring yourself at your own pace, along the road to your goal. But instead of one big jump, your brain will grow the necessary neurons, axioms and synapsis that will correctly wire and fire your brain until success becomes your default mode.

Trust the following questions and do it on a weekly basis, for at least 6 months. By giving yourself 1 week to accomplish your baby step goals one week at a time you are automatically retraining your whole body to vibrate in success mode by default.

When I work with my clients on the G.R.O.W. model I make sure they break their baby goals as small as possible, and instead of going for one goal a week, they get into the mental rhythm of reaching 2 baby goals every week.

Procrastination becomes a forgotten and unfamiliar inner frequency.

Feel free to adapt the following questions to suit your own needs. But go through all 4 sections at least once a week.

Not only will the G.R.O.W. model remove the pressure, loss of confidence, confusion, brain-fog, fear of failure and procrastination, it will especially help you to automatically retrain your thinking processes in all areas of your life.

Success is a method. Everyone can enjoy success by acquiring the successful attitude. It takes time, but then again, all sports gold medallists needed time, methods, and the right attitude to put them on the winner's podium. Look at Tiger Woods, he reached the top, spiralled to the bottom, and needed 11 years from 2008 until 2019 when he reached the top of his game again. His mind set got him back to the top. If they can .... so, can you. Your attitude will determine your altitude.

Instant gratification does not work or pay dividends in the long run.

The question roll-out in the G.R.O.W. model allows you to pinpoint a specific goal that you want to reach. Then it will help you clarify where you stand now and remind you what you have done in reference to your intended goal to be where you are today.

The question process funnels your thoughts through the steps of moving forward while being aware of certain realities and numerous options that in most cases are not self-apparent.

Invest in yourself. You are the vehicle that will get you to your goal. Spend a few hours doing the G.R.O.W. questioning process. It will be of huge apparent benefit in the weeks, months, and years to come. Excellence is one of the benefits and results of investing your time into this process.

Let's start with **G for GOAL**

What is it that you really desire? If anything were possible and money, time or health were not an obstacle what would you love to be, reach, see, have, or experience? Be sure to answer what YOU want and not what you think or feel you should aim for because someone else has advised you of what you should do or have. This is only about reaching YOUR goal for YOURSELF.

Think about it, write it down. Take your time but be sure to work on it every day for about 10 minutes at the same time carefully and feelingly writing down your end vision. Start with the end in mind.

Each day read what you wrote the day before and refine it to be more specific, notice if any other ideas or visions come to your mind.

You want to clearly see your final goal on the movie screen of your mind and feel excited as you think of yourself there. Write your goal on a card, photocopy it, and carry it around with you all the time so that you easily see your end goal 2 or 3 times a day as you look at that card. Copy the following questions, and print them out weekly, keeping the paper forms in a binder. You will want to go back through your answers, because it is easier and more effective for the mind to work this out on paper.

1. Think about a challenge in your current reality and write it down.
2. If everything were to be perfect in your current challenge what would be happening now?
3. Sing the Beach Boy's well-known song to yourself...." Wouldn't it be nice if......" lalala
4. Make sure that your answers are written in the present tense and in the affirmative. I.E., 'I am a healthy and happy successful entrepreneur earning a monthly income of...

G is for GOAL

1- **What does SUCCESS of your goal look, smell, feel, or sound like to you.?** Fast forward yourself to a place and time where you imagine yourself in your ideal outcome. What is happening that proves you have reached your goal. Whether it is a problem you have solved, or an achievement you are enjoying.

Some people are visual, others are kinaesthetic, others auditory, so we all experience in our imagination via different senses. Everybody learns differently.

2- In your own words: **Why do you want to achieve this goal?** Please answer 'WHY' and not 'How'. Whatever your reasons are write them down. And that is because your 'WHY 'is much more important than your 'How'. The trip to your destination might be very rocky, and so you want to be sure that your reasons are so deeply rooted inside of you that all sacrifices along the way will be worth it. It is best to identify this now, instead of months or years later, when you have reached your goal and don't enjoy it.

Goals always start with: 'I am' or 'I have' Goals are only about yourself.

3- I have a job that pays…....

I am enjoying……...perks in my job

I am winning …… competition

The above are only examples. Choose your desire or goal and write it in the present tense. Doing this daily is helping your subconscious mind to anchor into its neurons and molecules that you already have reached your goal. Once the subconscious has stored these frequencies in the nervous system of your body, things drop into place easily. You are part of the creation process, no one except yourself can imagine and retrain your subconscious mind. An average brain has enough neurons and cells to form a long string that will stretch around the planet 3 times. We are what we think.

4- I have a business, a job, or capital that produces X amount of X per hour, day, week, year.

5- I have been able to make a positive impact in the life of ……
6- My ideas on X are being accepted and my project is in development.
7- My X is published / heard/ communicated / implemented
8- Clarify what must be done to reach the above targets
9- And finally in the section of G for GOAL, 'How will you know when you have reached your goal?
10- How are you feeling at this point in the future? Create your future memory now.
11- What are you saying to yourself as your goal is being reached?

R is for REALITY

Make a mental screenshot of your current reality in relationship as to where you are today in the context of reaching your goal.
What do you need to consider getting closer to your goal? You want to be as exact as possible. Not better or worse, but realistically where you are today.
A GPS system needs the exact current position to program and unroll the best route to the destination you want to reach.
Be brutally honest with yourself. Whichever questions are the most uncomfortable for you to answer are the ones you want to take the time to dig deeper into and answer. Feelings of discomfort are your inner guidance warning signs telling you to prepare yourself for a bumpy ride, because you will be looking at your weak points, which is never a pleasurable moment. But the pain is worth the

gain. Be brave and listen to your feelings. Do not ignore them and push them under the carpet.

These emotions which you are feeling is your intuition helping you, and you are honouring your own intuition by listening to its message. This is real teamwork.

Let's continue with the questions in the second step of the G.R.O.W. model.

12- What obstacles do you believe and see are currently obstructing your progress to your goal?
13- What other potential obstacles can you IMAGINE could become a problem?
This is of course negative projecting which I normally advise not to do. But in the context of the G.R.O.W. model, it helps you to be as best prepared as possible. In any scenario, you want to see the pros and the cons.
The girl scouts say 'Be prepared"
14- When do you want or need to reach your goal by?
15- How much control do you have over the process of reaching your goal?
16- What information or knowledge do you currently need to know which will help you reach your goal?
17- What is going on now that tells you there is a problem, or something is not right.
18- What would others do if they were in your situation now?
19- What could you or would you do differently from what you imagine the others would do?
20- Why would you do it differently?
21- List what is important for you in this moment or period of time.
22- What specific area would you like to focus on currently?
23- What areas or sectors don't you like to focus on?
24- Why don't you like to focus on that?
25- Are you procrastinating?

26- What is your procrastination costing you?
27- What have you done so far which is improving things as they stand?

O is for OPTIONS

In the previous process 'R" for Reality, you have identified several points which are holding you back from reaching your final goal destination.

In this 3rd section of 'Options' open your creative thought brain and let all the answers just spill out. Write them all down, you can cross those you don't want as your read them later.

These options are baby steppingstones, to help you walk the path from where you are now to your final destination. You will have many pit-stops until you reach your goal.

Good questions give correct answers. In case you want to replace these questions with your own questions make sure that your questions are 'open 'questions, and that the answer is not a simply a closed 'yes' or a 'no'.

Following are tried and tested questions which will deliver the right answers for yourself. Be open minded. There is no right or wrong.

No one except yourself will be reaching your goal. So, your way is the best way for yourself.

28- If anything were possible, write out 3 options of how you would like to reach your goal.
29- What are the worst aspects of those options?
30- What are the best aspects of those options?
31- What do you think or feel you need to change to reach your goal?

32- What initiative can you take to make those changes?
33- What impact will that initiative or action have on your next baby step?
34- How can you be pro-active?
35- When can you start on your new action?
36- On a scale of 1 to 10 what is your commitment to act towards your next baby step?
37- If anything were possible what else could you or would you want to do if you did not have to be responsible for the consequences?
38- Write down 7 answers, and then look at them and see for yourself which actions are the most realistic for you. I did not say, 'easy' I wrote 'realistic' in YOUR opinion. Be honest with yourself. Don't over state or under state. The fact that everything is possible because we create it in our minds first is correct, but the steps to get there grow internally. And this is your journey, so you must follow your inner visions and intuitive messages honestly.

W is for WHEN

You have established your end goal and created a strategy to reach your goal. Be flexible as often results will not materialise as you had planned. Be mentally and emotionally in peak state and able to adapt another approach. The G.R.O.W. model keeps your automatic pilot on course but there are moments when detours will occur. Your' ETA' Estimated Time of Arrival' is the last step you want to have anchored into your mind. So, let's nail down the 'Tick Tock' of the clock by answering this last batch of questions. Since action is important, chunk down your goals into smaller baby steps. A key to success is to execute each action as best as possible. Small steps done to the best of your ability ensure excellency in the final outcome.

Example:

a- End Goal: Creating a franchise model for your vision of a chain of student travel hotels world-wide. Good value, good design, good service.
b- Start with the first student hotel.
c- Do the business plan.
d- Break down the business plan into sectors and chapters.
e- Research time per chapter.
f- Proof reading chapter per chapter

As you can see 'F' is a small task but must be proofread in depth and allow time to make corrections. That can be realistically done in 2 or 3 days. The quality of the overall business plan will come down to each section being as good and accurate as possible. By chunking down the actions, each baby goal is doable in 2 or 3 days. Keep the momentum to avoid overwhelm. The G.R.O.W. model will guide you through the chunking down process and ensure that each little baby step has the time to be accomplished as well as possible.

39- By what day do you want your next baby step to be finished?
40- How can you keep yourself motivated to finish this baby step on time?
41- What could stop you from moving forward?
42- How can you overcome that if it occurs?
43- How often do you have to review your progress? Hourly- Daily-/ Weekly/ Monthly/ Yearly?

44- Who can you turn to for assistance and support to help you stay on target?
45- Check your calendar to make sure you have the available time to carry out your baby step goal; and if you see that you don't have the time to complete your baby step, then chunk down your baby step into smaller chunks so that you do have the time to complete that baby step in the next two or three days.
The ideal momentum is to set yourself two baby step goals per week. Your brain stays focused, and your subconscious moves into success mode. It is best to do two small actions per week rather than one bigger action every week.
46- Restate and redefine in detail now the one baby step that you will do next to reach your goal and reconfirm in writing to yourself in your calendar by when you will have it done.

Following is list of boxes that will help you keep on track to reaching your goal in a very easy method.
Week per week copy out the following check list and work on it daily. Consider it your weekly dairy memo:
1- Which articles, books or audio books will I either read or listen to this week?
2- What will I complete this week that is still 'incomplete'?
3- Write down what is not working in your life
4- What is the 1 new action that you will implement in your life daily for the next week. When you keep on doing this action you will be pleased to realize that after a while that new action is part of your automatic self. You have created a good habit for yourself. It will now happen automatically.
5- On the basis that you have put together your peer mastermind group, set a date each week whereby you all agree

to meet systematically, ether on Skype, or in person. But you want to SEE each other. You can create your real or imaginary Master Mind mentors.

6- To reach my goal. Identify one new talent that you need to master.
7- Identify each time you manage to super calm down yourself when you are catapulted into a stressful situation.
8- What is my weekly affirmation?
9- What specific target do I want to reach and succeed this week?
10- What actions do I want to accomplish this week?
Every week, auto examine yourself and be as truthful as possible.
a- How may preparation days have I enjoyed before the end of my weekly target?
b- What was the best result I got this week?
c- How often did I manage to meditate for 15 minutes minimum per day?
d- What is the best information and advice I can give myself for the future as I read my results from the past week?
The above information is the backbone for building your goals. But in Chapter 26 'Exercises' there are several goal tools you can use.
There are horses for courses!

SUCCESS CHECKLIST

Asking good questions improves the quality and results of your to-do list.
Rome was not built in a day. So, take your time to answer the following questions and then find the ways to integrate them into your lifestyle.

1- **Imaginary Ideal Mentor Mastermind Think Tank meetings**.
Which 6 people would you put together to form your bi-monthly think-tank groups who gather to network, motivate, and find solutions for your goal at hand. Even if your group is in your virtual reality take the time to get behind each member's eyes and see how they see your current situation. You can talk back and find a meeting ground,
Then create your affirmation which mirrors the conclusion your mastermind group including yourself agreed on and make it yours by inserting into your subconscious mind.
You need to believe that you have a choice, on how you react so that you can control and create your future. How? By taking guided action from your intuition. Start by generating in your imagination warm loving feelings for yourself.
Zig Ziglar: A goal properly set is halfway reached.

CHAPTER EIGHT

BURY PROCRASTINATION

Do today what you can do tomorrow

Now that you are familiar with the real possibility of achieving your goal, and have discovered some tools to help you, don't give into procrastination.

Your subconscious mind will more than likely tempt you to put off actions that will get you to your goal. Just be aware of those temptations. The bad habit of going against your best interests stems because the subconscious likes "status quo" even when that status is far from successful. The subconscious hates you to venture into success if it is not used to success.

The subconscious mind is where your learnt actions, experienced behaviours and anticipated automatic responses find their platform of 'beliefs'. The subconscious is responsible for a lot of good actions though.

Your 70 trillion cells perform untold billions of necessary functions every second of every hour, keeping you alive and healthy. If you can read this book, you are alive and ticking thanks to the hundreds of litres of blood which your vascular system pumps automatically daily.

In the blood is oxygen, and we won't go very far or very long without oxygen!

Yet you are not conscious of your body performing all your life generating functions. Just as you are not conscious of most of your mental and emotional processes.

And if some of those processes are badly programmed even though you are used to them, they are harming you. Procrastination is one of the negative processes.

Here are some tips and ideas to beat your subconscious mind into submission and retrain it so that what you perceive as anxiety, fear of the known or the unknown which ends up in you procrastinating gets overtaken instead by productive actions and results.

Fear is also an indicator that you are not living in the moment. You are the victim of your neurochemistry. Fear means you are projecting into the future. Make a mental effort and bring yourself back into the moment, look into the mirror and tell yourself 'I have the ability to create my future by choosing what I want to feel, and what I want to be or have'. And right this second, I am choosing to feel self-confident and trusting that all will be fine. Use Ho'oponopono in that moment to clear and clean your fear. (Chapter 17)

Say goodbye to procrastination for ever. The famous clock is tick tocking away and procrastination has no place to play.

Very often when the decision and the commitment to go forward in a certain direction to reach a target has been taken; all sorts of 'if's and but's' appear suddenly on the horizon. It is good to see what obstacles you will have to clear, but they are only obstacles and are all lessons in disguise so you will be getting an added benefit from overcoming those obstacles.

Those are all excuses and 'excuses', also known as 'reasons' have no place in the path to success. Despite your motivation to succeed you might be in a situation that is not ideal or perfect to reach your goal.

Don't allow yourself to fall for the negative aspects of the perception of your circumstances. Your Divine mind is much more powerful and resilient than your circumstances.

Today's problems were created in the past, now it is the exact moment to create desirable circumstances for tomorrow.

No matter how bad your current circumstances are in the moment, know that you are totally able, capable, and worthy of reaching your targets and changing all circumstances.

It happens all the time until you are aware that your subconscious mind's patterns can change and be reprogramed. Do you notice that when you have made a commitment each time you felt in peak state and were fully motivated, but gradually the daily humdrum of your life took over and the promises you made to yourself lay in a corner gathering dust?

Next thing you know, is that months if not years have drifted away, and your habits and default behaviours are the same. Surprise, surprise…. Your lack of results has also stayed the same.

The self-realisation comes from mirror moment opportunities, such as next year's birthday or New Year rolls around the corner and as you take stock of your 365 days you realise you have not accomplished anything on your wish list.

Let's start giving reasons and excuses now as to why:

You are too stressed out, too much work, less staff to help you, someone ill in the family, the car broke down, the house was repossessed, the children got on drugs, the spouse ran off with the next-door neighbour, your company went broke, Trumps wall did or did not get built, the economy is in recession or a depression, and the list of excuses can go on.

As soon as you use an excuse, ANY excuse you are depleting your gifts of power that you received at birth, stripping yourself of your positive uplifting hormones and uplifting chemicals. Instead, you feel uninspired by life, devoid of happy hormones, the present and the future sepia images seen though the grey lenses of your inner-magination are dull. What is sadder than all is that you are feeling that way DESPITE, all the good things in your life now which you are not able to enjoy because you have given into procrastination.

If procrastination is one your habitual behavioural patterns and you know it is anti-productive, why do you allow yourself to be lulled into a false sense of security by the hypnotic feeling of your daily routine?

Again, user beware: If you keep on doing the same thing you will get the same results. If you want different results, don't procrastinate; obey Nike and just do it NOW. Procrastination is a serial killer. It kills all dreams, hopes and possibilities.

Take an honest cold look at yourself. Do you ever get things accomplished or are you always putting them off until tomorrow? And when tomorrow comes do you have a deep filing cabinet where all your excuses are stored, labelled and easily accessible to blurt out?

Ohh oh... Those are danger signs.

EFT – Emotional Freedom Technique is very effective in combatting procrastination. (See chapter 17)

Change does not necessarily follow knowledge, but it does follow behavioural shifts which are made with intent and repetitively. Knowledge and education can guide and help you to take the action to make it happen. Because once you know something new you can never 'Not know it 'from then on forwards.

President Obama coined "We can". Never were more truthful words uttered by any politician. And you are part of the collective 'We can'.

Make your slogan 'I can- I will- I am'

Even if you are the worst procrastinator in the world, there were times in the past when you did get things done. And despite whatever else you had to do at the time, you managed somehow to get those goals accomplished. Perhaps your goal was way beyond what you ever thought you could do, but your decision to say 'yes' happened so fast that you could not go back on your word. During that self-stretching challenge of over self-accomplishment, you automatically uncovered hidden talents that you did not know you had until that moment. Life produced a situation outside of your comfort zone whereby you would learn to discover some of your hidden and buried talents. Regardless which way you look at it you and only you created your result. You discovered parts of your extraordinary untapped powers.

Your 'Why' was so strong that it pulled you though until you did what you wanted and had to do. The shift in your thinking created the shift in your behavioural actions and consequently resulted in reaching your goal.
Somehow you found the solutions and the ways that allowed you to reach your goal. Perhaps your adrenalin kicked in and you became awash in positive energy or maybe you found someone to relieve you of your daily responsibilities while you carried out your other tasks. Because you were in the action of reaching your goal solutions appeared which you had not envisaged.
You felt intuitively confident that you could easily do much more. Whether it was being able to mediate, learn a new program on the computer or making two new networking friends.
As soon as you enjoyed that inner knowledge of an expanded possibility in yourself you experienced the flow of positive energy in your blood stream. The peek – a-

boo instant you enjoyed of your expanded possibilities and capabilities produced a surge of enabling chemicals that allowed you to powerfully remind yourself that in unexpected moments of life we feel the buzz of life while your hidden talents, qualities, thoughts, and ideas automatically self-align.

This powerful inner feeling of 'Possibility' attracts all the people you need to support you towards your goal like bees to honey. That is positive energy and intention on the go.

Squeeze your index and thumb together now, as you anchor into your subconscious this enabling energy. And next time you find yourself procrastinating quickly squeeze your index and thumb together to reactivate the 'I can do it' surge and take whatever action to make it happen.

In the flow, write down ten actions you think of as helpful to get you to your next goal.

And start executing those steps NOW.

User Beware!! Don't succumb to your inner voice which is whispering 'Be careful in case you fail again' or "If you fail this time, you will be the laughingstock of everyone at the office or wherever you hang out"

Take 5 minutes now, sit down calmly, breathe in deeply to calm your background growing sense of desperation and choose to inner-imagine yourself in your desired outcome. If you do this, not only are you creating your desired reality first in your mind where it must incubate, but you are also, being proactive towards your subconscious clearly showing that you are in the driving seat of your life; choosing and deciding what you enjoy imagining and creating.

Here are some questions to help put you on track.

They are all 'HOW' questions which I normally advise not to address in the beginning, because the 'HOW' question is ego based. Only your own knowledge can see the answers. The real solutions appear when you bridge your goal to spirituality being the Divine in you who and/or which knows better than you can even conceive of better and more efficient solutions.

But the HOW question will get you started on being part of the solution.

- Why do I want what I want, and how do I know it is what I really do want?
- How can I have and obtain what I want?
- How will I be able to achieve it?

Now take the action to face your fears. Perhaps the answers or lack of answers to the above ignited a surge of insecurity, lack of control or too much of a challenge which are pushing you to procrastinate.

This is the exact moment to instead stare the devil in the face and write down all the negative thoughts and answers that are coming up in your mind. Those are your challenges and your blocks. Those emotions are reflecting the negative memories stored in your nervous system and subconscious mind.

With awareness and in consciousness put them all together in a bundle on top of a fire and see them burning and turning to cinder and ash. And tap on the bad feelings that are coming up in you. (Chapter 17 EFT Emotional Freedom Technique)

Look squarely and fairly at your fears, see them for what they are. Don't ignore your fears but don't make them worse either.

You are the boss of the thoughts that get allocated screen time in your Genie's mind. If you lack anything, acknowledge it but choose instead to focus, see and appreciate what you do have, and your Genie will figure out how you can use it to your advantage.

You are born far more powerful than any obstacle which is in your reality now.

To harness and operate those powerful talents we are born with you must make them work for you and not against you.

Consciousness, mindfulness, and awareness are your gateway to the command center of your subconscious mind. When your inner Genie efficiently connects your awareness to your subconscious mind and links self-discipline to carry out whatever actions are necessary, and not succumb to procrastination you are pro-actively living your life and driving success and yourself to each other.

Be aware of the negative fairy tales you are telling yourself derived from old memories which have transformed over time into conscious and unconscious beliefs and became self – sabotaging behaviors. One of those behavioral patterns is to procrastinate.

In a nutshell you can stop sabotaging yourself when you are on the way to success and suddenly pull a stupid stunt on yourself that will set you back more steps than you have taken forwards.

An easy example is someone who has been overweight for a long time and has yo-yoed up and down without ever so far having reached and stayed at their ideal weight.

A limiting belief is leading them to the candy shop each time they are halfway towards their ideal weight, and the kilos pile on again.

Will power is not the ideal way to let go of that limiting belief, one of the solutions will most likely lie with EFT Emotional Freedom Technique. But once again the person must carry out the tapping sessions on themselves and not procrastinate by telling themselves they will do it as soon as they have more time to spend on themselves. That is a procrastination which produces bad results.

The other solution is to implement a self -disciplined daily mindset routine, of eating nourishing foods, until such a time that the body has no more desire for empty nourishment such as alcohol and junk food. It takes time and the will power is the mind set to override the cravings for a while, knowing that because you are only eating nourishing whole foods it is only a matter of time before the body will stop craving fattening foods. But the will power will only be used for a limited period. Not for ever. You only need to use will power the time it takes your body to be healthily well fed.

The only time your limiting beliefs don't manifest is when you are in your comfort zone. Which means when you are behaving as you are used to doing which proves you are not progressing towards your goal!

Learn your body's language, when you feel nervous your body is telling you it fears acting in a new behavior because it is unfamiliar with the results that new actionable behavior will produce. That translates into: "My body is saying that as we are not used to being successful, we feel uncomfortable and not in control'.

Now that you are listening to your body with awareness say: "I hear your body, but I am the boss, and I know we are on the right path, so I choose to have faith, take the action, and get closer to my goal because of my action'.

Does the following scenario sound familiar?

You are retraining yourself into a new technology that will enable you to work in an amazing company when you retire at the age of 65. You are very excited because by learning this new technology you can be in the working atmosphere of your ideal industry.

You decide to start on Monday morning, but suddenly, the children are hungry, the spouse is urgently in need of something, the next-door neighbor needs your help and on and on go the very valid 'reasons' and 'excuses' to delay starting your training as planned.

Just be aware it is normal. Your limiting habit of procrastination has kicked in automatically and is delivering a ton of reasons why you should not bother to start your training today.

That is what a bad habit does best... it always gives you good reasons why not to do something productive.

And if by any chance you end up overruling your procrastination habit and acting, beware how your inner voice will start whispering:

"Knowing very well that you are up to your eyeballs in work right now, and the last thing you need is to train for the future today". Or "You must be calm and peaceful when you study hard for your new work. It would be better for you to start in 6 months' time when you are on summer vacation"!

The sneaky subconscious mind hopes that by then you will have forgotten about your idea of training for a new career. It is a bit like Brexit was; as the politicians kept on moving the 'leave date' down the line, the whole concept of Brexit could have faded away without ever taking place.

When you know and understand how your subconscious operates you are better prepared to use an effective counter-offensive.

All vibrations aka frequencies are logged into the nervous system which lay somewhere in the 3 layers of the biggest organ of our body which is our skin.

The skin organ is permanently connected to all your memories. If you have acted positively more often than negatively then that becomes the predominant vibrational habit, and your body will automatically produce the necessary behavior to move forwards productively.

On the other hand, if you are a procrastinator by nature and habits such as not doing what you promised yourself or someone else to do, being unreliable towards yourself, down talking and dismissing your own dreams; then your hard drive is about to run out of necessary storage space to insert a new program.

You must first delete then remove that negative program and replace it with a squeaky-clean program made to measure for your desired outcome.

HOW TO LOSE BAD HABITS FOREVER AND EXPAND SELF-AWARENESS OF YOUR PHYSICAL FEELINGS AND THEIR LINK TO YOUR THOUGHTS

- Be aware of butterflies in your stomach.
- A ball of lead in your gut.
- Unexplained sweaty hands or forehead.
- A sudden need for coughing or clearing your throat to allow that frog to jump out.
- Aches either sharp, dull, or pounding anywhere in the body.
- Stiff joints or / and muscles.

Each time you hear of something new and want to do it but feel an unexplainable resistance, be aware that it is your subconscious attempting to protect you from running the risk of failure. The fact that you want to attempt something new means you are going to be out of your normal parameter's whatever they might be, and which are known as the 'Comfort Zone'.

The subconscious mind and nervous system instinctively hate anything new, even if it is good for you. You just must accept that and work around it by learning how to 'let go'.

The process of focus and at the same time letting go of the habit of being
connected to relationships that don't serve you any longer and have outlived their shelf – life. You might also be running patterns of negative emotions that you don't want to feel but nevertheless you keep on experiencing them in all sorts of situations. Emotions such as out of control anger, uncontrollable jealousy, chronic sadness, impatience and the music go on!

Emotions are confusing and tricky and especially if you tend to feel them repeatedly, you want to learn how to recognize them, acknowledge them, process them and not ignore them.

It is difficult at first, but it is doable and must be done. Otherwise, you will never make productive progress in your life.

Let's look at relationships to start with. If you are feeling hooked into a relationship, and it is over the 50% margin of 'bad time', you will need to release the power you have given to that person as being fundamental to your happiness. It is scary at first to let go of the addictive feelings. You will be subconsciously scared of letting go of those feelings. Usually when someone is in that situation it is because they have given to much importance to their desired outcome and in a way have become addicted in the process to feeling dependent and scared.

'If I can be married to XYZ, then I will be happy for the rest of my life. 'You are making your happiness dependent on one person. No one except yourself is the key to your happiness. Never put all your eggs in one basket!

On the contrary the only basket where you should lay all your eggs is 'Me, Myself and I'

Change the focus of happiness from that one person to other perspectives. Get away from that person physically so that you don't get triggered constantly by the proximity of the person you are obsessed with. Instead seek out new groups of friends or activities.

Discover where you can get a buzz from a different area of focus. Sports, new hobby, new town. new or drugs.

When you let go of specific outcomes you open endless more opportunities which you could not and would not have imagined in a million years. You need to feel the feeling first, and then let go after a few minutes trusting that the 'FEELING' will be bought to you in a certain situation and that whatever that situation is, it will be the best for you.

Accept that you will continue to get what you got until now unless you change your subconscious beliefs, vibrational frequencies, and behaviors. Trust the process even if it does not make any sense to you now. With time and experience it will become your second nature and everything will fall into place. First Trust, then do.

Look at yourself as you are; whole and complete. You don't need someone or something else to make you feel peaceful and complete. Feel your emotional shifts, process the uncomfortable emotions, don't suppress them. Emotions are messages, listen to the messenger. Remove the painful emotional charge from your emotions simply by being aware of them. While you notice where the messages are showing up in your body or how you feel, say to yourself "Ok, for the moment such and such and emotion is running rampant in myself. It will soon diminish and eventually I trust that it will disappear. I trust that by trusting that it will happen."

Lay back and enjoy the weakening of the specific emotional grip on yourself.

Expand your self-awareness to notice what you notice! Over time and with experience your self - sensitivity will alert you that you are not feeling or acting in alignment with how you want to feel when you reach your goal. Practice describing to yourself in detail how you want to feel.

Here are some red lights to watch out for. When these or similar thoughts pop into your awareness you will know it is time for processing and deletion action. Because otherwise your procrastination will latch on to these excuses bringing you further back again from reaching your goals. Don't judge yourself badly for having the thoughts, just be aware that the thoughts or replies are expressing themselves through you. Then gently ask yourself, "What thought would be better for me then this one?"

Be polite to yourself, listen, don't judge, and simply create a better thought afterwards.

Instead, most people will spurt out these sentences, without being aware that they are stopping themselves from transforming to the better.

- "This is the way I have always done it."
- "Stop telling me what to do".

- "I am who I am, if I am not good enough then you can leave me alone."
- Any form of: "I can't".

A gentle, efficient, and self-convincing turn of words is to say, "I choose to think (this) from now on"
Another little tip is to say "This is the way I have done it and then add …. UNTIL NOW"
As you embark on your U turn distancing yourself from always feeling an emotion as a reaction to the procrastinating thoughts you are entertaining. Understand that emotions grow out of beliefs. If you believe that someone's behavior is not in alignment with your belief as to how a person, should, could or would act or react in a situation you want to manifest. This is your opportunity to be mindful and make the choice without being judgmental. I know it is easier said than done. But each time you catch yourself and promise yourself not to make a judgement you are growing spiritually.
Let's take a work situation. A colleague did not react to your input in the positive way you anticipated or expected they would. Of course, you don't know that just that morning their spouse asked for a separation or a divorce. Your belief as to how you expected them to react to your brilliant input was not met, and automatically your mental blueprint for how success should be expressed in accordance with your beliefs was not met and you felt deflated.
Be self-aware of your deflating energy and generate a new enabling thought along the lines of: "This is only a setback, I choose to trust that my input is good, and the fact that I can and will relax now until I have the chance to represent my concept the next time.

If you decide to be proactive and take every step you can towards daily moving forward, then get yourself an accountability partner. The speed with which you implement your actions will determine your success. Your attitude will determine your altitude.

Choose your accountability partner wisely. For the sake of your relationship do not ask your spouse or romantic partner to be your accountability party because there could be a conflict of interest. Rather than insisting you finish your daily commitments they might prefer to go to the movies with you or hang out over a nice glass of wine. Use someone who is neutral to you since they also want to reach their goals. Help drive each other forward, and not allow the other one to procrastinate. A good accountability partnership does not allow and accept procrastination. That is the main aim for having an accountability partner.

Finally, carry out your daily 5 minutes 'check in' chats, verbally and if possible, via Video, either Skype, Facetime, WhatsApp or Zoom. The more personal your connection is with your accountability partner the more successful it will be.
Don't hide behind emails, it is too easy to cover up behind a few platitudes and words. Make your accountability chat real and connect your energies.
Take the action and make it happen.

NOW is always the best moment to start. Every positive action you take and make towards your goal reprograms your subconscious mind to believing that procrastination is a habit of the past.

It is more important to reach your goal than to enjoy instant gratification. The 'WHY' of traveling and reaching your goal is well worth the momentary hardships and challenges you will have to face to achieve. The upside is that you will be enjoying having achieved the goal and all its good side effects for the rest of your life.

Choose to spend time imaging how great and buzzy you feel when you are holistically well, physically healthy, and financially abundant.

The results are well worth the price to pay for changing your limiting beliefs and procrastinating habits.

Don't become a sitting duck, practice becoming pro-active every day of your life. Welcome to the 'Empowered Club'.

You transform for the better every time you take a positive action to move forward. Don't give in to the feeling of "I am OK where I am now. Why rock the boat"?

The enemy of success is 'Good'.

Never settle for 'good'. Go for 'Great'.

Thrive as you start to explore living life to the hilt. Worry about not moving forward and not about making mistakes.

Every day in every way become better and better. Start NOW!

CHAPTER NINE

HONORING YOUR DREAMS

Good Night, Sleep Tight!

HOW TO HONOR YOUR PASSIONS AND CREATE YOUR DREAMS.

Find something you like and DO IT IN YOUR MIND FIRST.
Imagination creates reality.
Plant your dreams as seeds into your subconscious. The subconscious mind does not know the difference between what you experience in real life or what you are experiencing in your inner-magination. The subconscious mind believes that what you are imagining is real. Past, and future have the same impact on the carbon copy of the mind. The more you create in your inner-maginataion, the more you are creating your real-life reality. Tell yourself a make-believe good night story as if you were your own child.
Here are some teasers to warm up your inner-imagination system.

- 'I am meeting the president of my bank who is begging me to share with him how I went from an average of $1,000 overdraft on the current account to having over $20,000 monthly in my current account and over $4 million dollars in my investment account and $1 million in my savings account in under 2 years.'
- 'I am walking down the road in casual clothes size 10 instead of size 22, which I wore 24 months ago.'

- I am walking up the gangplank of this luxury sail yacht which I rented for 2 weeks at the cost of $100,000 per week, and on which our entire family, children, grandchildren, nannies, and even the in-laws are enjoying a lovely all expenses paid 2-week luxury cruise during which we are all reconnecting to each other, laughing and feeling overwhelmed by love and gratitude of being all together.
- Imagine how well your business appointment or your job interview which is scheduled for the next week is all going. IMAGINE it going just as YOU WANT it to go.

Play with your mind and yourself. When your logic mind which is situated in the left pre-frontal cortex gets out of the way then your subconscious mind which has the sensory manufacturing pharmaceutical lab located in the Thalamus can get going and will whip up your images into reality.

Create your dream BEFORE you go to sleep at night. Honor your passion by imaging yourself living out your ideal situation. Participate in the creation of your good feelings for at least 3 minutes in the vastness of your inner mind as you lie down under your duvet before you drift away to sleep. By consciously setting the intention of what you want manifested into your reality you are creating a deposit account of your future memories in your subconscious mind. This is very important because the subconscious hates what is not familiar. As you are creating your future in the present moment your subconscious is becoming comfortable with it and therefor will not be scared by an unknown future as it is seeing it safely in the current present.

Daily creating and feeling the good emotions of living your imaginary goals creates a 'familiar zone' for your mind in the right hemisphere of the brain. Thus, enabling the miraculous quantum power of the virtual reality action of the right brain to kick in and create the matching frequencies.

The subconscious mind is a creator. The hypothalamus frees up the neurotransmitter's so that you can recuperate the endorphins, while the hypothalamus generates all the dopamine and noradrenalin you need to pounce into action. Big natural pharma and physics are at work creating the codes and chemicals of what it repetitively believes, sees, and feels.

Creating means to disregard the past and put together a new future in the present.

- Your past failures do not indicate your future, nor for that matter do your past success's guarantee your future ones.

- Break the chart line tendency by looking at your past mistakes, acknowledge them as errors, be open to new solutions and imagine your future successful outcome.
You have successfully changed the future course of your life. Don't waste time by fixing what is not broken!

GOOD NIGHT RULES

1- Before you allow your eyelids to close into sleep, make sure that you anchor your subconscious mind by seeing what you want to be the positive reality of your outcome.
2- Inner see yourself in that imaginary reality for at least 3 minutes and allow the feelings of success to flood your senses while you either make a tight circle with your thumb and index finger or you can also just clench your fist. Those are two very easy physical anchors to help your cells jumpstart into that feel-good mode.
3- Good night drink. As emotions get carried also by water, I find this very helpful when I am looking for an answer to something. I fill a glass with water, ask my spirit to give me the answer, then I drink half the glass of water before going to sleep and I drink the other half when I wake up in the morning. You will be surprised how fast the answer to your search comes to you.

Studies and peer-reviewed research prove that when we create new self-belief programs consisting of drawing up a situation we want to live in our reality and delve into it with all our senses, we are in fact extending those energy resonant vibrations into the universal environment and thereby attracting back to ourselves the required ingredients to fulfill our desired outcome.
This is a metaphysical concept and approach, but whether you like it or not you are emitting your energy footprint 24/7. The empowering behavior is therefor to 'choose' your desired outcome and emit those vibrations you want to emit rather than the magnetic vibrations of what you don't want!

Nighttime programing is very powerful. Advertising is only directed at the consumer's subconscious mind. To quote but one of many confirming opinions let's choose what Gerald Zaltman; a business professor at Harvard explains how 95% of consumers decisions and consequently purchases occur in the subconscious mind.

As the subconscious mind is one million times more efficient and powerful at processing and implementing information than the conscious mind plus it is further responsible for anchoring our limiting and enabling beliefs, it stands to reason that you want to pre load your subconscious for at least 21 nights in a row, every night before going to sleep with the exact description of what you want to live in reality and let it go to work while you sleep.

That is called working smart.

The subconscious mind is composed of logged in operational memories.

One of those programs is 'ESP'. Extra Sensory Perception meaning that your understanding or 'knowing' does not filter through our 5 senses which is where and how the vast majority of people communicate. Sight, touch, sound, smell, and taste. A more common word for ESP is 'intuition.' Each human being has intuition, but few are intuitive.

In the last century, as science carved out a place for itself the acceptance by the masses also grew that their inner messages were not a figment of their imagination but were telex's, fax's and now emails from the universe addressed specifically to them and whose messages were also specifically only addressed and meant for the receiver.

ESP is in all of us, Albert Einstein said: "*The intuitive mind is a sacred gift, and the rational mind is a faithful servant. We have created a society that honors the servant and has forgotten the gift.*"

Clairvoyance, telepathy, and energy distance healing are now widely accepted modalities in western mainstream populations. Due to the growing widespread openness and acceptance more and more people are experiencing success as they become more conscious and aware of their own contributing impacts and happening's.

Words like 'coincidence' are being increasingly switched to 'synchronicity.' Despite thoughts being immaterial they are made from biochemical and bioelectrical frequencies, and those frequencies have a very clear effect on the physical and material world.
Bio-photons are the subatomic light particles which show up in every person since human emotions highlight and intensify those bio-photons. Thoughts, images, and dreams emit to the universal memory fields clear messages. And the universe answers back with reality mirrored situations.
If your dream feels scary and overwhelming, you are on the right track. Become fearless and your life will be limitless.

CHAPTER TEN

DREAM OUT OF THE BOX

The visionary lies to himself, the liar lies only to others.
Friedrich Nietzsche

Don't compete for better standards….
Create your own goal posts.
Ask your inner Genie for 3 of the most outrageous things you want.
Situations or objects that in your wildest dreams you have would not waste time entertaining the thought of wanting, because you simply knew, believed, and accepted the fact that your current life circumstances would never allow you to reach or receive what you would really love to have. With your daily workload there is simply no time to waste on silly dreams.
I am a very practical person, and if you take the time to use and implement the tips and exercises in this book, your subconscious mind will resolve blockages that are occurring in your life.
Stop … Love yourself, by enjoying 15 minutes a day to daydream. No Facebook, phone, or TV in the background.
In a quiet spot, close your eyes, go to your inner movie. Load yourself onto the screen of your imagination having, being, or doing whatever you want.
In the confines of your mind, you can only be right. Start enjoying...
Ask yourself.' What would I do if I knew I would succeed'?

The first step to success is identifying what you want. It sounds easy enough, but you will be surprised how many people don't go further than a superficial answer simply because it is quite exhausting and tiring to have honest clarity on our wishes.

Show up for yourself. If you are a teacher you will show up for your students regardless of the bad weather or traffic, and if you are a hairdresser you will get to the salon regardless of whether you have a hangover from the night before. Always show up with a loving heart and positive mind-set for yourself all the time.

In the 'dream show' of your inner-magination, you are the director and actor of your lucid daydream. Give yourself the directions and 'innersee' yourself acting out your role on your directing instructions.

Call out the actions that you are directing yourself to take until you are happy with the scene on the screen of your inner-maginative movie.

Since you are the director, simply go back to the starting gate. If you are not happy with your inner-maginative scenes, then keep on re-starting the scene from scratch in your mind as long as it takes until you feel exhilarated with the imaginative scene you are producing in your lucid daydream.

T.E. Lawrence wrote: *'All men dream, but not equally. Those who dream by night in the dusty recesses of their minds, wake to find it was all vanity. But the dreamers of the day are dangerous, for they act their dreams with open eyes and make things happen.'*

What you focus on day after day… grows. Be aware of that. If you don't have clarity on exactly what you want to focus on today, then start by telling yourself as you look into your bathroom mirror when you wake up:

"Today I choose to feel good about myself as I move forward knowing that I am doing my best"

When you open your eyes 15 minutes later jot down on some paper whatever it is that you saw.

Here is a list of subject titles. Enjoy your time writing and filling up the pages with all the dreams you want, especially those when you are catching yourself self-talking with comments of, "This could never be possible for me because...."

Don't be afraid of this powerful little exercise and allow whatever words your inner voice is communicating to you from your intuition.

On the contrary, this is the moment to break through your own limiting beliefs and pour onto paper whatever you want. In your mind everything is possible, and it is in the mind that everything begins. Change your mind... change your DNA. Your DNA blueprint changes when your inner vibrations change.

- IDEAL LIFESTYLE IN 6 MONTHS FROM NOW

- SPIRITUALLY

"I've never succeeded, why should it be any different now?"

That is the most classic opt out question and excuse in the world, and perhaps has become your own elevator speech. That self-excuse is an invitation to procrastination.

Make a point of getting used to ask yourself a good question such as:

"What do I want to choose to think about myself today that will empower me?"
Tell yourself, and believe it while you say it:
- 'The bad in my past does not constitute my future"

Start by speaking to people whom you can help, children, elderly, distressed people, there are people out there who will benefit from what you believe it. Speak from your heart and realise for yourself what it feels like to get people to listen to you. Get used to being aware how people do listen to you. And build from there.
"My spouse left me without anything, it is not my fault... So now I will have to live with... because I was left penniless..."
WRONG... Be accountable to YOURSELF and take charge of your own life. It will work; it works for others; it will work for you.
To help you structure your thought process, write out 3 pages and see how and where you want to integrate the following subjects.
In the words of William Shakespeare: "There is nothing good or bad, but thinking makes it so"
- MY IDEAL DAY
- My IDEAL WEEK
- My HEALTH
- FINANCIAL
- BUSINESS
- FAMILY & RELATIONSHIPS
- CHARITABLE
- LIFESTYLE

At the entrance of Epcot in Disney World there is a sign that says:" If you can dream it, you can do it".

Mozart 'heard' his music before he wrote it. It was a form of audio dreaming. Everything is sourced somewhere, the invisible, ideas, thoughts, feelings are all part of the non-material realms of being. Everything that was, is and will comes into being from energy fields. But each person's beliefs define their culture and their own relationship to material matter and how it vibrates. 'Inner-magine' yourself whirling and transforming into the focused loving leader in your sparkling limitless passionate, healthy, successful, loving life.

The vision for an intention is initially created as a model in your brain. The more you see it and imagine it the more matching and mirroring neurons and synapsis' will develop and grow in your brain. That is called 'neuro-plasticity'.

This is a small part of physics where energy becomes matter. To keep those 'matter' parts up and vibrating you need to solidify that image by imagining and working on your imaginary creation daily. As you continue to do that the freezing of your creative image in your brain starts to solidify and your intention is now duly recorded as existing already.

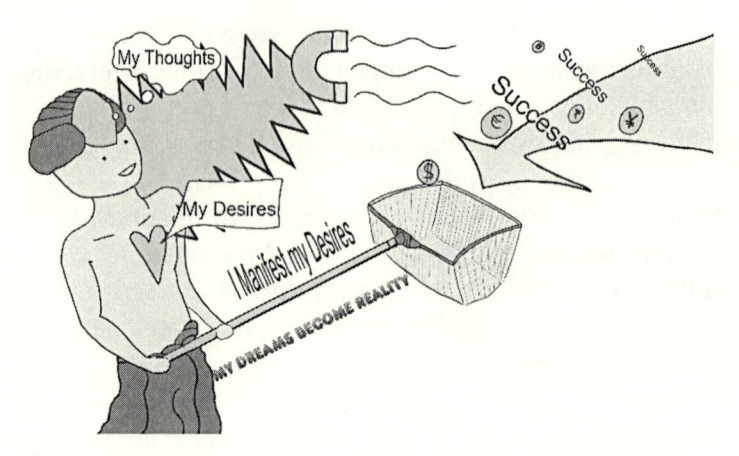

The more you DESIRE and feel PASSIONATE about reaching your goal the higher its vibrational frequency signature will emit out into the universe transporting those powerful signatures of desire and automatically attract situations which can deliver the same frequency. That is why it is important to understand that we are electromagnetic beings. Emitting from thought and attracting from feeling.

It is YOUR life we are talking about so become the leader of your life. Your personal mission statement created with your ideal end in mind will become an ongoing process of keeping your inner vision aligned with your values throughout all the actions of your daily life.
Enlist the help of your right brain daily to feel the wonderful feelings associated as you dream out of the box and see yourself living your ideal outcome.
While crossing the time bridge from your past to your future, your brain is consolidating all the frequencies of the situation you want to have into matter which is dense enough to start creating its own set of frequencies allowing you to bridge your past into your future.

The clearer you are on what you want, and mesh that image into the emotion of living it already; you are walking in your future. Your wish is in the manifesting stages.

While you spend a few minutes daily relaxing and enjoying the 'Yourself' as you see yourself already now, play with different imaginary situations and feel the physical sensations such as the clothes you are wearing, the furniture around you as you are living your desired outcome. Look in your mind's eye at the facial expressions of those concerned in this scene.

Allow yourself total permission to experience in your mind the rich detail of the whole scene, that allows you to integrate your dream now. The more vividly you can imagine the detail the more deeply you will experience it. You are creating your future memories out of the box today!

Great painters have simply accessed visions which they unknowingly and automatically copied from the visionboard of their mind while they were daydreaming. Visualising is like being in a light trance.

Indulge in guilt free daydreaming. Enjoy the actual time off. Most people feel guilty about daydreaming. They are embarrassed at being called back to the present. On the contrary, it should be encouraged. You will learn and contribute much more to the world from creative daydreaming then from watching TV.

'Inspiration' derives from the Latin meaning of 'breathing in air" When you daydream you are unwittingly absorbing matching frequencies to what you are searching for. 'You become what you think of all day long'.

When I said that to a young girl a few years ago, she laughingly answered: "Will I become the boy I am thinking of, because he is the only person, I think of all day long?

It is well known that the survivors of the 2nd world war concentration camps spent most of their time unwittingly lost in the daydreams of their desires escaping the horror of the camps and living in freedom. Somehow all those who were spared death had that in common.
The journey of your dream is as important as reaching the destination in your dream. The stronger the 'bull's eye 'of your dream is in your imaginary focus the sooner you will reach, live, and have that goal in physical reality.
We have dreams... and life has dreams for us! The secret is to find the middle ground!
Magicalise your life...
I can't make your dreams come true... but I guarantee that if you practice the principals in this book, you have a much better chance of very quickly reaching your goal. You are your Genie.
Transform your inspirational dream into an 'Intention'. Live that intention with clarity in all your actions as to why you are doing what you are doing, overcome your doubts.
Develop the courage and the skill to face fear... and go forward. That is real courage.
Courage is not about the absence of fear. That is called stupidity!
Courage is about feeling the fear and doing the action nevertheless
Sometimes the most difficult part of attracting something is figuring out specifically what it is that you want.
Start off by thinking of a goal you have in mind... something you have not yet achieved.

Do not think of your goal as the "Maybe someday' dream? That approach makes it much more difficult to obtain, if not impossible!

<u>Use this checklist as your self -assessment test. Grade yourself on a 1 to 10</u>
1- I feel lucky
2- I seem to reach my goals effortlessly
3- I am very intuitive
4- I easily identify what I don't like in my life and very fast identify what I do want in my life.
5- I am driven by my inner inspiration
6- I have and know what my clear purpose is in my life.

Inspirational dreams are fundamental to our life's advancement. Ideas start as inspiration and evolve into dreams. However, a dream cannot be strategized whereas ideas and goals can.
If you don't have a dream... then make your dream to have a dream!
Daily and repetitive consistent daydreaming of your specific desired goal is much more powerful than long intense visualising sessions.
Listen only to your dream. In your daydreaming enjoy being an anti- conformist. A block to daydreaming and goal setting is that many people conform to most of the population.
Have you heard the adage 'Safety in numbers? the problem is that most people are the 'wrong' role model; they are normally the majority who have not succeeded.
Good luck helps in everything, but we each make our good luck by thinking and daydreaming of what we want to become.

Marcus Aurelius said, 'Good luck is the result of preparation meeting opportunity.'

You will get what you want by thinking and daydreaming consistently about it, that is the 'preparation' that Marcus Aurelius was talking about.

Daydream with thoughts compatible to your wish. If you want to have an hourglass figure, pull yourself away from thoughts of cream cakes. If you want a gold medal in your next sports event, focus on imagining yourself standing on the podium and proudly lifting your gold medal for the press to take your photo.

In your daydreams enjoy being your own magic wand, creating out of thin air the circumstances you want. You have the gifts and ability to mould your future to what you want to live. The planning and execution stages always start while daydreaming.

Re-format your inner hard drive for the event by first dreaming it. Imagination and daydreams are the basis for creating a mental picture which you are not experiencing with any of your 5 senses at that point in time.

I like to call it 'Inner-magination' blending, Inner journey- magic and imagination.

Plato recognised two types of imagination:
1-The fact of recollecting past experiences from memory and then adapting them to suit your current goal.
2-The other is pure creative imagination by which you allow streams of thoughts, visions, ideas to embed you and you follow that thread. Yves St Laurent, Mark Bohan, the Beatles, Jeff Bezos, Elon Musk, Leonardo da Vinci, Joan of Arc, and as much as I hate to say it so was Adolf Hitler when he wrote his dreams and vision while

in jail and called it ' Mein Kampf'. Those personalities were creators.

Think of your super powerful Divine Inner Genie as being outdoors window shopping for you now. It is scouting and sourcing the universe to deliver your order. Make it easy for your Genie, by being as specific as possible so that your Genie can easily spot what you are looking for. Your Genie will deliver what you create in your imagination and daydreams. Be careful to daydream only about what you want. Your Genie hears you loud and clear in his language called 'vibrations or frequencies'.

Flirt with yourself daily. Enjoy conquering yourself and getting to know what you think about and what makes you tick, in the same way that when you start a relationship you are passionate trying to understand your new partner.

The waking up process like that of Snow White is not an easy rollout. It will take months even years of evolving into a new default operating system which is that of being aware and conscious of what you are feeling and thinking. Commit to self-awareness so that whenever possible you choose to entertain thoughts designed to produce emotions that will serve you productively to reach and manifest into reality your goals, targets, and dreams.

Feelings are loaded with energy, and those energy frequencies are the signals your genius subconscious understands. Genie makes sure it brings back to you in manifested form what you have emitted from your energy field. You can also call it the 'Boomerang Effect'
In your daydreams strive to always feel happy for yourself. The difference between sorrow and joy is a choice. Life is hard at times, but pain is an option that you do not have to endure. Does that surprise you? You are the creator of everything in your life, your subconscious is the Divine creator within you, drive your life, your subconscious mind is waiting to grant you the wishes you want when you ask for them clearly.

John D Rockefeller who started Standard Oil was not rich in his youth. But after a lifetime of experience at the young age of 86 he wrote this little poem:
I was early taught to work as well as play.
My life has been one long happy holiday.
I dropped the worry on the way
And God was good to me every day

CHAPTER ELEVEN

YOU ARE ONLY ENERGY

Einstein coined it. E=MC squared. Meaning energy = matter

When you realize that in acupuncture all you need are a couple of needles well placed in the correct energy roads of the body to successfully alleviate and remove pain, reverse addictions, and bring peace and joy back to the soul. The answer has got to be... 'We only need to do the actions which create the energy wattage and flow we want to enjoy.'

In this chapter, we will look at a few 'DIY' Do It Yourself methods of how to change your energy frequency resulting in a better reality.

Balancing time management, commitments, hopes, goals disappointments and celebrations are vital actions for an 'aware' person.

Don't go on a vacation and spend your time working on your laptop, don't waste your energy and your time talking to people who are not connected mentally to you in the moment.

Connect to yourself and to those with whom you want or need to connect to. Because of technical and internet super sophistication most humans are over connected yet disconnected. You owe it those who are in your life circle to show up mentally, emotionally, and physically when you are together.

Advice: Recharge yourself. Even though our energy is renewable it is by no means limitless. Exhaustion is dangerous and it is real. Manage your states of energy healthily' it is the biggest act of generosity you can do for yourself and those you like, respect and love. When you are good, they will feel better.

As Eckhart Tolle's book says. 'Be in the NOW'. Focus on the moment. Stop regretting the past and worrying about the future. Enjoy the moment of NOW. There is always something to find and enjoy in the present moment.

Energy is for real. Today sophisticated scientific research centers are set up with all the current technology needed to follow the illumination of photons throughout the body as the person is either told different words with different frequencies such as 'hate' which has a low frequency and 'love 'which has a very high frequency. One frequency dims the light of the photons, and the higher frequency increases the brightness of those photons.

Although the body is a complex network of atoms making cells that form bones, nerves, muscles, and all other body elements, essentially, we are all just different vibrations of energy.

We have energy fields and depending on which blocks or repeated; negative thoughts you might be unknowingly thinking; those toxic thoughts build up a block to the free flowing of energy of whatever it is that you are seeking to attract or manifest into your reality. Complaining and gossiping are convenient, socially accepted ways of staying stuck and distracted. Distraction is just what the subconscious likes so that you can remain stuck in the negative states your subconscious is used to. The subconscious hates change even if the change is an improvement and is necessary for you to live a better quality of life than you are living presently.

Being aware of this makes it even more important to clear the patterns of these negative limiting blocks to live the life and lifestyle you dream of wanting to live.

When our lights are on in the front drive, our guests find their way easily to the front door!

The energy which is needed to illuminate the front drive is measured in the brain with an EEG, in the cells and tissues by an MRI and in the heart with an EKG.

Those highly specialized and fine-tuned machines demonstrate how our life energy aka 'Qui' flows from the most inner parts of our bodies outwards. That is when the reality of your energy in action is manifesting and mirroring your inner past or current energetic vibration.

All types of pain will either dissipate a little or completely when tension is released. Drinking water and deep breathing works miracles quickly. Pain is a stress signal. Pain is not physical even though we feel it in our body. Deep slow breathing increases the circulation immediately and automatically shifts the blocked heavy energies which are creating the sensation of physical pain.

Pain pain, go on your way.
You are not welcome here today.
Cells relax, blood move fast
I feel good now and it will last!

Decide the path you want to follow to reach the peak state you want to experience by default.

Since physical symptoms are the result of disruptive energy patterns bought on by negative thoughts and beliefs, an easy way to quickly delete the pain is to tap gently and continuously on the Gamut point with one hand on the back of your other hand ;1cm down between the knuckles of the 4 and 5th fingers.

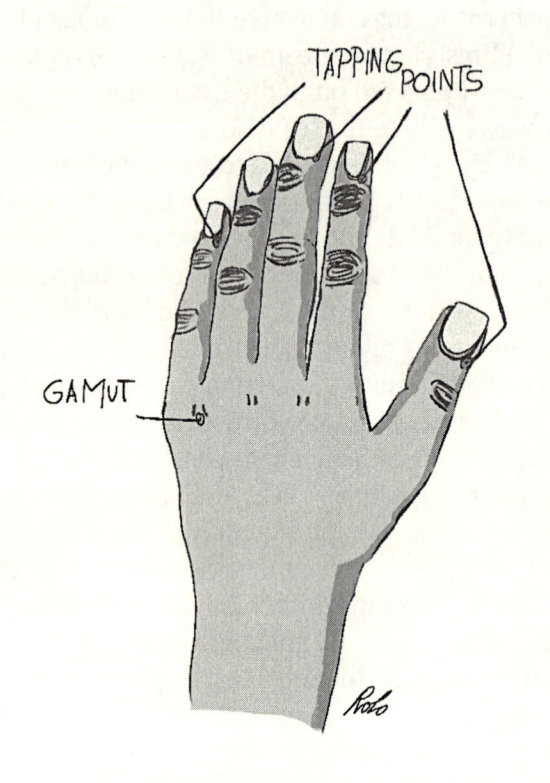

Continue tapping, breathe in deeply and slowly from your nostrils for a slow count of 3, then hold your breath for another slow count of 4, and to close the exercise. Do it one more time, again by exhaling slowly as if you were blowing into a straw for a count of 5.

Do this breathing exercise in a loop 7 times, which will last approx. between 2 & 3 minutes depending on how slowly and long you can hold your breath and breathe in and out as well.

You will notice that the pain disappeared. It is impossible to have conscious thoughts and focus on your breathing at the same time. And since you cannot have conscious thoughts, you are incapable of thinking of your pains or your problems and therefor the limbic brain has stopped producing symptom's.

For an added booster to delete your negative emotions while you are breathing, tap on your karate chop which as the name states is coined by Roger Callahan the forefather of EFT and a big adept of TCM Traditional Chinese Medicine.
As you know that thoughts are things, negative thoughts become negative things, and bad thoughts and memories create stagnant boulders of static energy inside of our nervous system. (Refer to the sketch on page 215)

The act of gentle continuous tapping on the Karate Chop opens the small intestine and allows the small intestine to properly digest not only the necessary good foods but also to protect the heart, which is an organ for emotions by separating conflicting thoughts, which have conflicting energetic vibrations and instead creating a free-flowing peaceful transition of our emotional energy.

On one end of your body, you have feet which will physically walk you to your destination and on the other side of your body you have neurons in your brain which will deliver the enabling thoughts to and from your mind which choose to think of.

If you allow yourself to be flooded by stress you run the physical risk of deregulating your immune system and conditions from diabetes, anxiety, depression, auto-immune diseases and so on which can deteriorate your physical, emotional, and mental well-being.

All stress hormones are toxic and inflammatory, and before you know it you have become the victim of your own fears and negative perceptions.

If you have allowed yourself to be constantly submitted to stress, with your neurons on 24/7 red alert, unable to focus on a thought for longer than a few seconds and mentally going from pillar to post; your brains pharma center loses its ability to generate the much-needed serotonin that balances your body.

The fastest way to reverse that is by daily sessions of EFT which are detailed in chapter 18.

Patterns are cycles which manifest in your life. And if you pinpoint a pattern that you want to break, you will first have to delete the energy thought blocks which are creating this pattern.

Let us look at an easy pattern, the yo-yo effect on weight loss. Huge weight swings that in the end tire out the body and often veer towards the negative in the long run, resulting in more weight gain then loss!

Another pattern is someone who goes though boom and bust cycles financially. The aim is to maintain a healthy body weight and to have a positive financial stability. Those are healthy building platforms for positive development.

The solution is to remove the blocks, for you to keep the money you make and make more money from it. Like attracts like.

Become conscious of the fact that whatever your life is today there is only one single cause. And that cause is YOU!

Every time you have been unable to manifest your dream; it is only because you are unknowingly carrying that negative energy related to your limiting blocks in your psyche.

WHAT IS AN ENERGY BLOCK?

It is the energetic result of a negative emotion that you probably experienced a long time ago, but the negative energy mass has lodged itself in your ANS Automatic Nervous System and increased in size over time becoming a self-fulfilling prophecy of negative energy swirling in your system. It can be as big as a melon.
Energy psychology calls it a negative and limiting belief. An easy example to understand is by thinking of something you desire so badly it hurts. Whether it is the ideal body, health, relationship, financial situation and everything and anything else.
It is great to desire, but it is harmful to feel the 'lack' of not having what you want. The more you feel the 'lack' of your goal the more you are creating limiting beliefs that will distance your goal from your reality.
Be aware of how you are perceiving the wish and yearning for your goals. Take the action to flip the desperation into aspiration.
That way you are enabling positive energy.
Which is a positive high frequency word or thought. The better the emotion the thinner it becomes and therefore it flows easily and fluidly throughout the nervous system irrigating our system with oxygen and all the feel-good nutrients we need to flourish.

Dr Emoto, the author of 'Messages in Water', was famous for his research on the reaction of ordinary drops of water freezing into different shapes and nuances of white and dirty sandy colors depending on the words that are placed on the bottle or the piece of glass behind the microscope.

There are people who can see energy auras very clearly, and one such a person Christie Marie Sheldon, an expert energy healer. She has clearly seen a conic vortex energy swirl on the outside parameters of a person's body who was experiencing gratitude.
That vortex looks like a funnel for bringing positive energy and manifestations into your reality. (Listen to Christie Sheldon's Awesomeness Fest on You Tube). Gratitude is a fabulous enabling energy to use.
Energy is familiar to everyone, but it is still a vague concept and a challenge for a lot of old school trained medical specialists to open their minds to reading and researching the causes and results on energy psychology. As time progresses the momentum is speeding up and thanks to all the information on the internet a critical mass of the population is jumping onboard this school of thought that us; human beings, have all we need and only need to look inside of ourselves and drive our thoughts, emotions, behaviors more in alignment with our values.
Each one of our (approximately) 70 trillion cells can be compared to a ticking battery. Every cell communicates electromagnetically and electrochemically 24/7 throughout our nervous system, reaching out beyond the physical boundaries of our bodies.
We are part and parcel of the 'Universal Divine Field'

Compare our 7 chakras to major airport hubs. From each chakra untold paths of energy depart and arrive from outside and inside our body.

If you can visualize yourself as a car, you will know that the car's engine is your heart and your heart/ engine is the energy producer, but your chakras must be balanced and pumped up, just like the tires of your car. If you have a punctured or flat tire, no matter how much energy your engine is producing your car will not run efficiently, fast or on course.

Each one of our cells are a complete 'US' Think of your body as a team of 70 trillion 'You's'.

In sports, work and everywhere the better the team, the stronger and better results it produces. You are the only team in the world that is composed of at least 70 trillion people. Each cell is a 'you'!

When one of your cells holds a belief, it is only a matter of time before everyone or if you prefer, every cell in the team will hold that same belief. That is quantum power on the go!

A block is a limiting belief held by the entire team of 'You'

The psychology of energy relates principally to the meridians. Medical, and scientific research is building up.

One of the leaders in the field is the Heart -Math Institute, have made a case for the importance of the heart and shown that the same neurons which live in our head brain also live in the heart. As the heart is the landing page for emotions it has been easy to prove certain results scientifically.

Namely, the Heart-Math Institute have shown that when two people are in a room together and connect visually, they will pick up on each other's emotions, and energy waves. Their hearts will sync, and as that happens those waves travel up to the brain evolving into thoughts and then chemically into moods.

What is less known but interesting enough is the body has 7 main chakras, but there are in total 114 chakras which are tiny energy junctions through which flows 72,000 independent energy channels.

Very often when a child has had a traumatic emotional upheaval, like the parents divorcing or the sudden death of a close friend or sibling, the pain in the heart can leave such traumatically sad memories that unknowingly, in growing up they develop a self-protection belief that it is unsafe to love someone because they are bound to suffer like they did in childhood.

Unwittingly and unknowingly that person has created a block of loving energy and will most certainly not be able to live a fulfilling loving relationship unless they are open and willing to learn, accept and implement various tools for reprograming and removing the negative effects of their limiting beliefs.

The answers to all our hardships and failures lay in the blocks of energy in our meridians, chakras, and nervous system. Thoughts, whether conscious or subconscious come from our knowledge base called our memory. Scientists have only been able to agree on one fact, and that is that memory is non-local in the body. Meaning that memory is housed everywhere and nowhere at the same time. When memory is activated, it ignites the energy system like a flint of a cigarette lighter.

Science has not yet been able to demonstrate and prove exactly the flowchart of energy from its ignition and source linking outwards to its manifested results.

There is no doubt left that psychiatric issues have been weakened and often completely obliterated with the practice of 'EFT Emotional Freedom Technique' which is the act of tapping on certain energy storage hubs on the top half of our body.

I want to make a point here, 'THINK ACHIEVEMENT & WATCH IT HAPPEN' is about the reader hopping on board to live a better life as soon as possible by alleviating all forms of suffering from the physical to the emotional.

I am not attempting to make a scientific case of how to harness and release energy. I am only asking you to accept that as you are first and foremost made of energy and that your physical matter as well as the reality of the situations you live, experience, and emote are by-products and measurable results created by your energy.

The better and more efficiently you drive your energy the better your life will be.

If you are sick use one of the numerous alternative therapies or energy protocols to shift negative energy in the body.

20 years ago, a doctor would have lost his license if he declared that stress had a negative impact on the body's health. Today stress and its related expressions are all covered by insurance companies. Stress is the basic cause of all physical disruptions.

It is important to accept that you are energy. So, study and discover one or more modalities that will shift your energy blocks to become a free-flowing transit system for your energy. Your reality is the result of your energy traffic.

There are quite a few insurance companies insisting that doctors use tapping before prescribing more expensive modalities. Energy psychology and therapies are becoming the norm. Chemical medication suppresses the causes of negative energy from releasing themselves from the enclaves of a physical body which are lodged deep in the nervous system.

That results in, physical, mental, and emotional health issues. On the other hand, the self-application of all the access switches we have to our inner energy system organically regulates us to harmony so that we are in sync with our values and our goals.

There is a lot of positive upside potential which comes by taking the time to understand and research alternative inner energy solutions. Some of them are, acupuncture, cranial sacral therapy, acupressure, yoga, martial arts and finally study and work with Donna Eden's energy schools. She is full of life, love, joy and a deep knowledge of short and very efficient tricks and tools that you can immediately apply on yourself and obtain the immediate benefits of 'feel good' symptoms.

Hang on to your hat, once you experience the way to get on the escalator of innate positive energy to being in sync with the journey to your goal; you will no longer approach yourself from the outside inwards direction.

Cortisol diminishes with the use of acupuncture and tapping because it instantaneously opens the gateways allowing distress to evaporate. If you monitor a body as the result of a self-induced placebo happening, the markers will have shifted measurably.

All that is energy!

The amygdala, which is lodged in the limbic brain, is the major emotional headquarter. It detects threats problems, whether imaginary or not. Therefore, it so important to use 'Goal Setting Imagination' techniques because the limbic brain does not know the difference between reality and what you are imagining. The emotions emit the message to the universe that are inner-magining.

Harvard Medical and many other leading universities have done numerous studies on the ebb and flow of energy throughout the body. Thereby the proof for the need in reprogramming the energy flow to allow yourself to create imaginary peaceful imagery and beliefs instead of imaginary negative beliefs.

When an experience goes first to short- term and evolves deeper and longer into long-term memory it becomes an integral part of the neurological amazon jungle that is continuously on the move in our body. It is very clearly impacting the flow of energy in your body.

Most of our experiences happen as a confirmation of the beliefs we have about ourselves. Those beliefs are energy and over time, together with the accompanying story they have developed into our identity and personality. The experiences come complete with emotions, behavior patterns and especially self-fulfilling prophecies. We become addicted to our identity even though it could be a bad identity.

If you are having relationship problems of any sort, the 30,000-year-old ritual of Ho'oponopono opens the energy paths between the other person and yourself very fast.

Rather than looking for emotional fulfillment and joy through a relationship with A.N.Other; look inside of yourself for those feelings. Every relationship we have with someone else regardless of whether it is a friend or foe, long or short term, they all come up in our lives as a mirror of the relationship we have with ourselves. We were all born with them. Your inner child is much wiser than your ego and intuitively knows where to guide you so that you will be protected. Just don't get in the way between your intuition and yourself.

I know these words are clear and sound simple, and that when you want to put it into practice your intellect bounces back into play. That is the time to let go, hang up on the receiver of your ego, sit back and listen to yourself.

If you have an idea or a sense of déjà vu, it is only the frequency of the memories that we carry throughout eternity in our energy field.

When you say the four Ho'oponopono statements (Chapter 18) your inner child and your super consciousness go through the Divine process of removing those frequencies attached to your bad memories.

The more you clean yourself the more place you have in your Divine self for 'Enabling Beliefs'.

Think of your frustrating blocks and when you identify some of your negative beliefs, realize that they are nothing more than signs of dirt. Your inner broom consists of doing this short protocol that you can follow easily and notice the rapid results.

1. Think of any person with whom you are in discord with. Another way of putting it would be to say. "We are not on the same wavelength'
2. Imagine a small pedestal or stage just underneath you, and in your imagination place that person on that stage under you.
3. Visualize a never-ending stream of pure and healing love flowing like silk in gentle waves from a divine and invisible source of light and love above the crown of your head. That love is from your spirit, your Higher Self, God, Energy, and welcome and enjoy the warmth and clarity of that source of love which is now flowing gently

inside and outside of your body. It overfills from your inner body and flows out of your heart continuing it journey down on to and into the person who is standing on the stage below you. Allow that person to accept the healing of love and light.
4. When you feel comfortable that you have processed the healing have an imaginary conversation with them whereby you both forgive each other.
5. Now in your mind's eye, see that person floating away.
6. The acid test is when you can think of the person without any negativity.
7. Repeat the ritual each time you feel negativity.

We are addicted to our identity... even if our identity is not good. Change is uncomfortable and we resist transformation. Change our mind about ourselves is not comfortable and it is certainly not for sissies.

Discomfort arises automatically each time we want to change. (EFT tap on it)

A common destructive identity is ... "I am not good enough' Not smart – powerful- talented etc. not enough) It is constantly a nagging inner voice saying: "I WANT THIS.... but I am not going to be able to do it because I am stupid too... short, tall ... old... young...) this way you are limiting your behavior and consequently your results.

This type of lack of self-worth emotion stems normally from poor self-esteem and lack of self-confidence. When you learn to use magnets as Dr. Norman Bradly, author of "The Emotion Code" does when he releases his clients blocked emotions you will feel freed. Your mental clarity will improve tremendously.

Releasing your blocked emotions from your nervous system as you unburden yourself from emotional overweight baggage is a main benefit to your health.

Get specific, because if you are vague, you will be allowing your subconscious identity to keep on going as it is.

Focus on a specific moment in your life. Remember your emotions and the setting when you were experiencing that emotion. In your mind's eye shift it to what you would have ideally wanted it to be. Paint a new scenario of that moment. Your mind is limitless, let it imagine freely what you would have ideally wished for if everything is possible...

This is vital because good health starts with prevention. If you prevent you will stay healthy and then you will not have to cure!

Alive ...happy, healthy & wealthy.!

Every single disease, whether you contracted it because it is contagious or self-induced such as a kidney failure, or a cancer or a leaky gut, stems from negative energy breeding in your system is present in your reality because of the matching energy frequencies which were happily vibrating away and gradually creating the bedrock for whatever physical problem you are living through.

Allopathic medical doctors are incapable of diagnosing the energy flow blocks that are beginning or are already running amok in your body.

Unless you release your negativity, you are heading for the wall.

Toxic frequencies result in regretful comments and behaviors. Enslaving you in bad reactions and behaviors to certain comments. Most likely prompting you to jump to the wrong conclusion and consequently answering rudely. That negative chain of reactions is due to the blood draining away from your frontal cortex and leaving you as a victim of your own destructive instincts.

Energy blocks will cause you to come to incorrect conclusions and see negative attacks when there are none leading you most likely to react in an aggressive and rude way laying the ground for the saying that that the road to hell is paved with good intentions.

Remember that thoughts are things, so whatever you are thinking will manifest in one way or another in your reality. Therefor by becoming 'aware' of your thoughts, start journaling then as they come up.

At the end of the day, read the thoughts you had and see for yourself how you can transport and transform a project that is junked up with problems and transform the project into a mental success. You have the gift of choice. Choose and create your vision of the ideal result.

It takes short bursts of daily practice. Analyze which sectors in your life are downward spiraling then notice what thoughts you are harboring while you become more and more aware of your negative thoughts. As your thought consciousness expands with practice you will have the experience and awareness to pivot from a limiting toxic thought to an enabling thought. You will soon notice that as you focus on your choice of an ideal outcome you feel uplifted and energized. That is the power of choice.

Wherever your thoughts go, your body follows. It is the same experience as when you ride a horse, a bike, a car; where you look; your horse, bike or car will follow. When you want to turn right at the tree which is 200 meters away you keep your eyes on the straight line and as you approach the bend, your eyesight projects its view still further into the future where you want to lead your pony, car, or body to.

But if you look downwards at your heal, the instant you decide to turn right or left your horse or bike will probably crash to the ground then and there. Why...? because matter follows thought. And thoughts are the fact of looking at something. So, change the point of your vision, to permit your thought and your matter whether it is a bike, a car, a horse, or the reality of your life to follow the energy that is produced by the thought of where you want to be.

Thoughts are electromagnetic and the more similar thoughts you entertain the stronger the magnetic field you create. Thereby attracting and creating the reality you want by pre-shaping it by holding corresponding thoughts of that situation.

To prove my point of our magnetic field. Take a €1 coin and apply it firmly to your forehead just above your eyebrow and notice how that coin will stay fixed to your forehead and not fall.

Why? Because thoughts are magnetic, and your forehead is holding the coin to your forehead with the metal that is inside the coin.

Remove, forgive, and delete the underlying causes of problems, which lay in energy blocks. Often chemical drugs relieve painful symptoms but when the body gets used to the drugs the pain shoots through. Disintegrate the causes, and you will never need any drugs, as you will symptoms free.

Negative frequencies must be released as soon as you become aware of them otherwise with time, they become very dangerous. Time increases the dangerous potential of disease. Wounds fester with time unless the live frequency is removed from the nervous system.

Energy Psychology has entered our awareness and understanding. It has been accepted in the occident and it is here to stay and grow. One cannot eradicate a law of nature. It encompasses the links of our past experiences between the body and mind.

Energy psychology is totally holistic. And when I say Holistic, I mean every person and soul, dead or alive throughout time. For some fascinating insights take the time to read up on the Akashic records.

CHAPTER TWELVE

ROCKET BOOSTING CONFIDENCE

Take the Action to Make it Happen

Use or lose your Superpowers
The quantum creative desire to live the life you want to design will manifest thanks to the conscious and directed force of your mind. The logical, scientifically, and medically proven reason is simply that the human body is composed of an ongoing average of. 70 trillion cells. Taking into consideration that cells dissolve 24/ 7 and new cells birth. Each cell emits an energy frequency. We are electro-magnetic beings. Meaning that we attract the equivalent of what we emit.

Every 7 years the body is an almost complete brand-new set of cells. A very small percentage of cells stay as is from birth to death.

Think of your body as the largest manpower factory on earth. With 70 trillion workers at your beck and call obediently executing instructions which are emitted via the electrical frequencies of your beliefs.

Put that into perspective by imagining you are the Genie ruler of planet earth and that you rule over the world population whose only purpose is to create and deliver whatever you want. By the way, the world population is about a 0.01 % of your inner cells!

Here is an easy step by step inner self confidence building tool.

A- Relax your body but stand up. Imagine a gold thread going from the top of your skull being pulled up to the heavens. Your skull is like a puppet. Head up, eyes looking ahead and chin slightly down, so that the back of your neck is stretched.

B- Imagine or remember a scene or time in your life when you felt totally safe, in control and confident. You did or do not have to rely on a third party. You are holding all the reins in your hand.

C- Inject into the eye of your mind color enhancers. Whatever you are seeing in your imagination inject brighter colors. If there are sounds sharpen and intensify the sounds.

D- Monitor your feelings and the inner idea as to where in your body they are, breathe deeply and quietly for about 3 minutes and increase the color vibrancy and sound pitch, and keep on increasing the color brightness and the sound pitch.

E- Now imagine the situation you want to manifest and feel your inner confidence, relaxation, and absolute belief that you have reached and are living it already.

F- By now you must be feeling relaxed and confident. Self-confidence is not arrogance.

G- Anchor your self-confidence as an automatic default to your way of being by create a link between your thoughts and feelings and then making a physical gesture.

The moment you have the 'feel' of self-confidence, squeeze your thumb and index together. Blink, or touch your nose. It is best to choose an easy and discreet movement so that you can do it anywhere without having to feel self-conscious about it

That movement will deepen the Genie's neural pathways connections in your body while your Genie internally 'See' your situation un-roll to your liking.

Part of building self-confidence comes from repeatedly seeing yourself living your end-goal, the fact of repeatedly seeing this perfect little painting in your mind is entering your subconscious mind and creating a comfortable memory of already haven achieved your goal. That sensation is building up self-confidence.

Your subconscious does not know the difference between imagination and reality. As far as the subconscious is concerned, when it receives an image in your imagination it believes it is reality.

Renewing that feeling repeatedly in your imagination obviously makes you feel self-confident since you really believe that you have achieved your goal.

Here is a short method that will help you activate the anchoring belief into your cellular network and hack into your given power.

a- Either remember or conjure up in your imagination a moment when you were brimming with authentic relaxed self-confidence.

Either remember what you heard at the time or imagine yourself hearing something that you would want to hear. Direct your thoughts to feeling invincible and confident that you want is happening.

b- Now inject colors into your memory or creative visualization and turn a mental dial to increase the vividness of the colors and the loudness of the sounds.

c- Suddenly you will feel a positive feeling which is different for everyone. Immediately you feel something quickly make a physical move on or with your body to anchor that feeling in the memory of your cells. Make the movement a discreet movement so that you can always execute the movement even in public without fear of being ridiculed. You can touch your nose, or pinch your ear lobe, you can cross your feet or fingers, you can also squeeze your index to your thumb. That is how you anchor the feeling you desire to have deep into the neural pathways of your brain. Your nervous system remembers the feeling and each time you access and strengthen that feeling faster and deeper.

You are reprograming yourself and creating your future memories.

Today's cutting-edge scientific research proves beyond any doubt that every human being whether they are aware of it or not is controlling their lives and creating their reality.

- Your reality is 100% the result of your mind.
- And your mind is the result of your brains activity.
- Neurosciences is the study of the brain in action with the mind.

Genes do not have to play any role in your life's reality if you consciously apply awareness to your perceptions of all situations.

A perception is only a point of view, and you have the gift of choice to change that perception. It is your active involvement in the guidance of your choice of either limiting or enabling beliefs that will open your inner door to realize your true powers.

Whatever part of your body, brain or soul perceives as a threat, it will have to withdraw from your energy supplies sufficient positivity to counterbalance any energy depletions which are happening elsewhere. The more energy reserves are used to prop yourself up against anything negative the less energy is available to support your growth. In other words, your body is putting itself at risk in order to protect itself!

Therefore, the tools of positivity are so important to use in your varied daily rituals.

When you KNOW who you are, and ACCEPT who you are, self-confidence starts to build up on the inside.

Accepting oneself does not mean allowing oneself to accept the negative qualities that are hacking happiness and not doing anything to delete them and replace with positive and enabling habits and qualities.

Self-confidence and assertiveness go hand in hand, it is about getting what you want without pushing the other person aside or making their decisions for them.

The acceptance of self partly means to acknowledge that as a HUMAN BEING, we are blessed with a pre-frontal cortex from where we can make and apply choices to be a better version of ourselves.

Our thoughts are energy and therefor produce results, that is why we owe it in our gratitude to use our power of choice and thought to become the person and its experiences we choose to become.

The human being is the only living species that has been granted that superpower ability to auto-transform and create a better version of ourselves.

Animals can be trained by outside forces to behave differently and then obviously enjoy different results.

Plants don't even that ability at all.

But Humans do!

When you take a melon and squeeze it, you will get melon juice, regardless if you, your mother, the kitchen tool, or the cook squeeze the melon. You will not get any other juice other than melon juice. If the melon is old and shriveled then there will probably be very little juice, but it will still taste like melon.

So why do you expect to be more successful if you work to becoming another person. Don't waste your time. Everyone else is taken. Be YOURSELF.

Be grateful for your own uniqueness and use energy cleaning tools to get rid of all your negative aspects by identifying them. Then use EFT and Ho'oponopono to delete all that you don't want, leaving your energy space to become all you do want to be.

That is self – confidence. We have all we need to be perfect, and happy. Perfection equals paralysis. Progress is dynamic.
It is up to us to find out which tools facilitate our process. And then of course to use those tools.
The world makes place for the man who knows where he is going. Ralph Waldo Emmerson

I learnt a very useful little tool from one of Christi Sheldon's energy courses. Which is to clear space of negative energy, by imagining a purple tornado coming into the area of your choice and sucking up all the negative and dirty energy from the room, building, car, plane, boat, handbag, briefcase…... and I can go on and on.
I use it all the time in all the rooms of our home and our office.
It is the easiest and most effective daily cleaning job I have ever done!
As you read the content and have the 'Ahha' moments, act on those movements. That is how to connect the dots and bring it all too life.
Get out of your own way and brand these words into your eyesight: **I GET THE RESULTS I CHOOSE TO HAVE.**
The verb 'GET' is an action. Action makes things happen. And DOING is more important than KNOWING. Doing nothing is also an action. Action breeds self-confidence. Action has a price, and the price is time.
A fun 'confidence boosting' tip is to get into the habit of complimenting people. It is quite unusual, normally people see themselves as not quite up to the mark. Start by complimenting others and as you bask in the warmth of their gratitude, you will feel your self – confidence

thermometer raises because your inner self will know that it is only you that made a positive impact in someone else.

Another very positive action is to 'Dress the part'. Success dresses up. For business, dress the power look. Even on casual Friday dress powerfully casual. Neat, clean, and classic.

Body language will increase your confidence. Sit and stand up straight. It takes awareness but it is also very healthy for your muscle tone.

When you walk, walk straight, and determined. You don't have to jog but walk at a sustained stride.

Dump the slump and spend time with successful people. Go to where the successful people hang out. Become part of success's energy field.

CHAPTER THIRTEEN

RELATIONSHIPS

The art of relationships is vital to success in all fields of life. We came into this world alone and we are leaving alone, but in the meantime every living organism is connected at one level or another. Organisms are in relationship with other organisms.

The better you get on with others the richer and more supported your life will be.

A Harvard study identified that loneliness is a bigger threat to our health then being overweight or smoking 20 cigarettes a day. Reach out to other people. Souls and bodies need validating and supporting social connections. Challenge yourself and extend beyond your comfort zone. Meet and discover new people.

Depending on your personality type, if you are introvert, shy, a wallflower, self-effacing or suffering from low self-esteem this is a clear and necessary stretch for you. Just bite the bullet and get into the daily habit of introducing yourself to strangers as well as engaging more openly and vulnerably with some people you already know. Shed your armour and be yourself. Relax and become curious about whom you meet. If you want people to be interesting, become interested in them!

Since like attracts like, you most likely have a circle of people like you who are craving tighter human connections and don't dare to reach out.

Be the game-changer in your group of friends and enjoy the warmth in your heart as your burgeoning openness and vulnerability touches others.

I am not talking about Facebook friends or any other social media platform. Bonding in person is vital to our immune system.

I want to make sure, especially if you are younger than a Baby Boomer that you are not falling into the social media friend trap.

A video relationship on Skype does not count for your energy's good health. The relationship must be in person. Whether you bond and agree or disagree on a subject, you are interacting not just with 1 other person, but with approximately 70 trillion other people, since we are made up of about 70 trillion cells which are complete 'Us'!

Others are like you. Whatever we do is for a reason, even if you are not aware of it. The people who meet us have been attracted unwittingly by our emitting energetic frequencies. Recognise it.

Rene Descartes said, "The heart has its reasons of which reason knows nothing". And as knowledge is power when you see an objective, target, or a reason from your opponent's vantage point you will steal the wind from their sails as you prepare the terrain without allowing them to start conflicting arguments.

1. If you are in an argumentative situation where you and others have conflicting views or desires of an outcome, start with being clear about how you are currently feeling on that issue.
2. Then put yourself behind the eyes of the other person and be totally un-judgmental. Imagine that you are in their skin, their shoes and behind their eyes. We are here to learn, and we learn by experiencing situations. Whatever is upsetting you, in the other person be aware that there is something identical inside of you that you don't like. Like attracts like which is why you are noticing that

irritating habit in the other person instead of yourself. This is your opportunity to become aware of yourself.
3. Put yourself in the skin of the elder wise person in the tribe who has seen it all and is no longer surprised by anyone or any behaviour. Look objectively at yourself in position nr. 1 and your opponent in position nr.2.
4. Notice how they are behaving towards each other, is what they are saying to each other destructive or constructive? What advice would you give them both as a wise old mentor?
5. Now go back into your own skin and shoes and look at your opponent as you just saw him from the wise and elder's perspective. Choose your words carefully so as not to offend your opponent so that he relaxes and is willing to move forwards with you.

You have the gift of choice and therefor the power to choose your thoughts. Thoughts are things, which become energy and eventually can transform into beliefs.
Be sure to choose thoughts that will develop into enabling beliefs. Your beliefs are the keys to reaching your objective. They are more important than factual truth. I have said the same thing in other chapters, but that is because the more aware you are of your beliefs the easier it will be to avoid tripping up on yourself!
In chapter 5, 'Who am I?' How you and eventually others perceive yourself is down to what you subconsciously accept and believe about yourself.
In everything, but especially in relationships it takes two to tango; meaning we are responsible. Responsible does not mean guilt. The meaning of being responsible is being ABLE to RESPOND. If you don't like what you are living with the other person, thank the Higher Power for having mirrored what it is that you don't like in yourself

and proceed with the deletion processes as laid out in chapter 18.

At least start off by making that assumption; even if you are not sure you are 100% responsible. You are only partly responsible but if you behave as if you are completely responsible then all the happenings in your life will change for the better.

Act as if you are totally responsible for everything that happens in your life and watch your life transform. Learn more about the mechanisms in Chapter 18, Ho'oponopono.

To quote Gandhi… *'Be the change you want to see in others'*

If my spouse or partner is upset and in a bad mood, I understand that there could be a lot of unpleasantness or thorny issues going on with my spouse that have nothing to do with me. But if I ask myself "What did I do that has produced such a reaction in my spouse"? At least I am looking in the right direction and taking responsible action. If I find anything; I can then choose to change it. I must be aware and looking to find something; and I can only do that if initially I expand my self- awareness.

Make it easier on yourself by looking at yourself in a mirror saying out loud as you look into your eyes: "I approve of you, I value you, I respect you, I love you."

Whatever I might have done to upset my spouse I regret as I did it unwittingly."

I would also suggest that you say to yourself out loud while looking into your eyes in the mirror; "I love you" and get into the habit of automatically reciting the 4-line prayer of Ho'oponopono. 'I love you, I am sorry, please forgive me, thank you. You will be amazed how situations change to your advantage. That prayer cleans you, and therefore you stop attracting people with mirroring vibrations of yourself you don't like.

Hear your inner voice throw out unkind insults at yourself. Your critical mind is spewing out as you continue to tell yourself: "I love you".

Which inner self-critical voices or paradigms do you hear yourself repeating repeatedly?

Look into your eyes in that mirror, while you tell yourself out loud that you love yourself. Each negative statement that you hear your self - critical voice saying, jot it down in your little 'MY BOOK'. Those messages are your major blocks and problems which are preventing you from having what you want and deserve.

The good news is that you can get rid of those self-insults by tapping while you use the script on negative self-talk which is in in Chapter 18.

Who are you when you are self-reassuring and allowing yourself to love yourself as you are? Your best qualities will emerge out of the darkness. Let's call it 'Coming out of the closet!"

It takes practice and trust, give yourself a bit of daily time to understand how you function. The understanding of your mechanisms and patterns takes time but they will be delivering the best of everything to your front door which is your awareness.

Like becoming familiar with a new smart phone, app or keyboard. Once you understand which icons or keys to press on your smart phone, app, or typewriter the object turns into your fairy Godmother. It takes practice until you figure out which icon or key to press on next.

You will discover which negative thoughts you are carrying around and what matching negative realities you are living because of them.

If you put garbage into the oven, you will get cooked garbage out!

As you become mindful of your negative thoughts, better and productive thoughts will become available in the radar of your Genie's mind. Your new thoughts are different seeds. Enjoy choosing the seeds you want to plant in your heart and in your mind.

Core beliefs get anchored into you from impacting people in your very early life, most likely before the age of seven. Children are vulnerable and it is highly probable that you have been totally brain-washed with the beliefs of others until your early teens.

Healthy self-love is fundamental to productive and happy development. You learned to relate to others because as a child intuitively figuring out how to relate to those in your immediate surroundings.

The answer to a good self-relationship of 'Me-Myself & I' is believing that you are your own best friend. It is the most intimate relationship you will ever have.

Put your hand over your heart and make a marriage vow to yourself, that for better or worse, in sickness and in health you will always be there giving yourself the best advice and guidance you can.

Assess your beliefs one by one. While building up your inner relationship with your beliefs you will know immediately what direction your life will unfold in. Your current experiences and situations are the direct reflections of the beliefs you hold or held in your mind.

Beliefs are only a perspective of yourself. Your beliefs can be changed without the permission of anyone. Your beliefs are the open window through which you look out into the world and your life.

Choose a belief that fuels your goal and anchors it. Don't worry if the belief is true or not but use it to ignite your imagination daily and imagine what your life will be like when your belief pans out.

A good source of enabling beliefs can be identified by taking your current negative beliefs or self-talk and turn them into positives.

Then work your way down the list.

Finances: What is your current financial reality and what do you believe contributed to that reality? If you find yourself in a negative situation financially and you hear yourself blaming XXXXX for it, you have just identified your block. Take the blame and turn it into a positive affirmation.

You might feel frustrated, tense, disappointed and find It difficult if not impossible to switch your beliefs to positive in this moment.

Now is the moment to connect with your inner- self by taking 10 deep slow breaths, make it simple, just breathe in through your nose and out through your mouth and count to 10 each time. You are gently pulling oxygen back into your system and soon you will be calmer and then can start to hear your inner voices.

Example. "I have no idea how to run a business." Switch to. "I am learning easily how to run a business".

I will always suggest that you apply Ho'oponopono at this stage. There is more explained of this message in Chapter 18.

Health: Do you hear yourself saying:
- "My parents had this issue"
- "I am overweight that is why my legs hurt"
- "Cancer runs in the family"
- "I have asthma because there is too much pollution in my city" etc

Switch your story to:
- "I am not my parents; I can change my thoughts and my vibration changes which is why I am becoming healthy"
- "I am releasing weight easily and my legs are starting to feel strong and relaxed again"
- "Not everyone in this polluted city has asthma so I don't need to have it either".

Do you get the idea? Choose an empowering belief and make it yours.

No one knows you better then yourself. It is the most fulfilling relationship you can ever have.

Don't hold back from greeting yourself and asking yourself in the mirror "Are you having a nice time and what can I do for you?"

Enjoy discovering yourself. Discover the advantages of being alone. We are all alone. Even Siamese twins are alone.

We have companionship and people around us, but our powerhouse generator is our own soul. And that is whom we aim to have the best relationship with.

If something is wrong, then confront yourself, and not another person.

Being alone is not being lonely. You can be lonely with other people nearby.

That said, it is very fulfilling to be vulnerable since it leads to rewarding friendships and relationships. The deeper the questions you ask each other the more intimate the relationship will become.

Don't be judgemental, be open with those who respect and appreciate you with all your flaws. That is experiencing freedom.

Communicate verbally with your close friends, stop hiding behind your SMS's or your one- liner emails. Speak and look at each other in the eyes, while you re-connect to meaningful and deep conversations.

Vulnerability is not for sissies. If you have been hurt in the past or suffered embarrassing moments of being rejected or judged, you will experience why taking the plunge is worth the short-term discomfort.

When building a relationship, the other person will feel validated when you take a visible interest in them. The simplest and most transparent way is to ask questions. The questions can be fun, different and at first glance must not appear to be prying.

Here are some examples that you can use in most conversations even with people you have just met. Use the questions to start a meaningful conversation instead of superficial chit-chat.

1. If you could be famous, what would you choose to be famous for?
2. What is your ideal day?
3. Which one quality do you want your Genie to grant you?
4. What is your most memorable memory?
5. What inner secret are you keeping from yourself that you wish your Genie will unlock for you?
6. Which ingredients do you believe are vital in a strong friendship?

Enjoy setting your own priorities for different moments in your day - year – life. That is done by setting your own goals to be achieved within that defined time frame.

You are activating yourself today, and that feels good. Remember to reward yourself on each success, small and large as motivation tends to dry out. You still have a long way to go.

See your life as a successful work in progress. It is important to be spontaneous and flexible. But always remain true to your own goals. Sometimes your goals might have to go on hold, but as your self-talk is now loving and understanding you find it easy to interrupt the action of making it happen and step back reflectively like the Sphinx who rises again and again from the ashes.

You can reappraise your current situation and give it another go later.

Enjoy developing your self-care routine while being taken care of by yourself. Healthy sleeping patterns, recreation, the anchoring of good mental habits and finally…. always be kind to yourself. Be selfish towards your own self development and improvement. It is the best way to make a positive impact in other people's lives.

Be patient knowing that the change will occur, and as it takes its course to become the version of the person you want to be to attract a fulfilling relationship with another.

Treat yourself as you want to be treated and always treat others the same way.

Love yourself until you feel like a feather tickling your skin.

When you deeply love yourself, you will fully enjoy loving another.

Do you feel empowered? Lucky? Successful? Capable? Fearless? Scared? Depressed or Happy?

Aim for feeling happy at least 65% of the day.

Assertiveness is a quality to express when communicating with others. And in relationships there is always 'another'. There is only one way to become assertive and that is to speak up clearly while believing what you are saying.

It is your opinion, and you are entitled to have it and share it.

Always be considerate of the other persons boundaries.

Empathy, sensitivity, basic good education, and politeness will stop you from crossing over someone else's boundaries without being invited in.

You don't however have to explain your opinion to others. Just be aware that you have your own opinion, and if someone asks you to explain then share your beliefs calmly. If the other person argues you down, stand your ground by replying along these lines: "Please recall that you did ask me to share my opinion, so now please listen to it and don't interrupt. It is my opinion; I am not saying it must be yours!" That is a clear example of setting your boundaries.

When clarity becomes your default state in mind and heart, you will find yourself automatically communicating and speaking assertively, honestly, and transparently, which is very helpful to making others feel better about themselves.

Honest heart- felt states create and maintain healthy and respectful relationships with everyone.

Listen and hear the expressed needs of others. Do what you can if you can't do much then do little. Just make sure it comes from your heart.

When you allow yourself to be yourself you are being assertive. And being yourself is to relax in your relationship with yourself. Don't fear being yourself, the worst that can happen is that other people will criticise you. You won't be the first and you won't be the last.

Aristotle said it many hundreds of moons ago; *"There is only one way to avoid criticism: "Do nothing, say nothing and be nothing"*. If that is the case, why bother to live at all?

We have gone through some questions in chapter 5 'Who am I'? But here are some more:
1. What do I value the most in life?
2. When I look in the mirror what do I think when I see myself?
3. Do my approaches to life serve me well?
4. Am I getting more of what I want in life than what I don't want in life?
5. Do you want change but don't know where or how to start transforming?
6. Do you feel that you are being pushed around and that you are always playing second fiddle to someone else?

In all '12 steps programs' counsellors say, "You need to acknowledge things about yourself before you can start on the deletion process". Stop playing hide and go seek with yourself. Be objective, gentle, and understanding when you contemplate yourself.

If you have been educated since a very young age to be obedient, you might find it difficult to become assertive as an adult. But it can be done with awareness, support, and sensitivity.

Be warned that the path to assertiveness can be like a minefield of disagreements, pessimism, and scepticism. We all want to be liked, admired, needed accepted. With a positive mind-set, rejection is no more than a sleeping-policeman on your road. You might have to slow down for a while, but trust that you are on YOUR path and therefor keep on going. Be assertive towards others but more importantly towards yourself. Commit to what you decide or say you will do and carry it out to the end. Your day will become what you mentally decide it to be. Plant the seeds of your day every morning.

Assertiveness is not only getting others to do what you would like them to do, but also about setting boundaries and making sure they stay up in the future so that you do not end up being a 'yes- sayer' to please your boss or colleagues.

Assertiveness is not aggressiveness. You get bees with honey!

It is not always easy to say 'No '. But if you don't learn to say a polite and firm 'No' it is just as detrimental to your health as being a doormat and taking on more than you can or want to handle, because you are afraid of what might happen when you say a firm but polite 'No'

CHAPTER FOURTEEN

CELEBRATE SUCCESS

Congratulations on getting to this chapter, you are on your way to being permanently in your Peak state.
Absorb enabling beliefs to transport you from the platform on which you stand now to the target you want to reach. By exercising daily, you are doing the necessary mental and emotional gym work for your neurons.

Success is only a question of formatting your brain correctly for success and taking focused action.
Success is different to each person because everyone has a different point of view and expectation out of success.
Knowledge can be important to success, but so can lack of knowledge. As *Coco Chanel* put it so elegantly *'Success is achieved by those who don't know that failure is inevitable.'*
You must play before you can even have a chance to win. So, keep on celebrating your wins. The more you celebrate the better your energy becomes for attracting situations that will give you the reasons to celebrate.

Humanity is wired for happiness. Over time, man has gone from the brain of the heart to the brain in the head. Now it is time to use and bridge both brains by default. Science has proven that the heart has a big number of the same type of neurons that are found in the head brain.
The heart's energy battery; increases exponentially all our emotional information, either by importing into the body or by exporting it into the universe.

The heart chakra as well as the heart organ are situated in the middle of the body between the lower and the higher chakras. The heart is the physical headquarters for all emotions.
Though the heart is a physical muscle; it is electromagnetic and interacts also via the pineal gland on the spiritual plane of the universal energy matrix.
When we process thoughts methodically and logically, we are using the head brain. Therefor our search mode and the consequent answers we give ourselves are based on knowledge, experience, and familiarity. Our minds emit answers back to us that have been fired from the physical brain in the first place.
We attract what we think of either consciously or by default thanks to our sub-conscious.

That is why the answers that come from our hamster wheel circular way of processing thoughts, emotions, feelings, and conclusions self-confirm the answers we arrive at.
Our conscious awareness perceives 15 bits per second, but our subconscious mind perceives millions of bits per second
Trust and grow with your inner flow. Intuition comes from the heart and does the thinking. Don't second guess your first instinct. Our heart always knows instantaneously. When your heart sings you are in the honest flow of life.
Celebration is vital to ongoing success. Be aware of all the mini successes and gifts that come your way expectedly or not. Rejoice in the 'progress' of your path. Immerse your heart, eyes, ears, head brain into the feel – good emotion of your progress. You are conditioning

your body to always attract situations that will allow you to feel this good.
It makes success your default mode.
Keep on celebrating, burst of joy is activating your feelings of gratitude and emitting a pleasure message to the universe "Celebration is Welcome 'automatically attracting more and more reasons to celebrate a success.
Repetition is the best way to ensure something becomes engrained… so celebrate daily something successful. Even if it is that you successfully made a meal, took a walk, found 10 minutes to meditate. But CELEBRATE repeatedly. I like to High 5 myself every time I see myself in the mirror. I get a surge of elation. I am feeding my body with homemade happy pills!

You are training your neural pathways to success addiction. While upgrading your knowledge and skills you are automatically upgrading your future results.
The mere fact of celebrating your baby steps and successes until you have achieved your goal is tantamount to wiring your nervous system to the familiarity of success. And since humans are creatures of habit it stands to reason that you want the good vibes of success resonating all the time in your energy.
Grab hold of any evidence that you are traveling in the right direction and celebrate that progress with self-acknowledgement. Your neurons are growing and forming in that vein.
Looking at yourself in the mirror and congratulating yourself in the present moment is a celebration. Calling up a friend and share your excitement. Go for a walk and enjoy the time off to self-indulge in your feel-good state. Whatever you do to celebrate your small success make

sure you do it with a smile on your lips and warmth in your heart.

Celebrate daily, weekly, monthly yearly and keep on finding occasions, achievements, and results to celebrate your whole life through.

When you make it a habit of keeping promises that you make to yourself you will notice how other people will immediately look up to you as a reliable person with the aura of a leader, because your default nature will now be to automatically deliver on the promises that you make to yourself and others. This should be natural but sadly the sense of ethics and reliability is not really a trait of character which is implemented in education or highlighted and taught to children these days.

In the age of technology, the demand for reliability has shifted to machines and technology. Society seems to forget that first there is the personality of a person that will dictate the outcome of situations. And the more sense of self-discipline and self-responsibility we develop the more success we will enjoy and be able to celebrate.

A good way to pace your motivation and productive positive actions is to establish a timeline for your success arrival at your goal. Developing successful mental, emotional and lifestyle endurance habits lead to more opportunities for celebration. Every day is a party!

Your inner clock is set to the new parameters for action. Now is the time to be realistic. Ask yourself how long it will take you to get to the finish line of your goal. A day, a week, a month, this year, next year, what year?

Then travel back from your ETA (estimated time of arrival) and chunk down the major steppingstones you see as necessary before proceeding to the next step.

You have successfully created a whole bunch of new goals to look forward to achieving.

Time to sit back and celebrate in your mind as you live each goal as clearly as you can while looking at yourself achieving those steppingstones goals from the eyes of your heart. The principal is easy, and it produces extraordinary results.

Close your eyes, drift into your minds movie and notice what you are seeing and hearing. Feel the buzz as you achieve goal after goal. CELEBRATE in your mind, in your heart and with your friends, family or any friendly human you know.

To achieve reasons to celebrate which have escaped you so far, change your thinking and the way you act and react. Align your actions and achieve the success's that will give cause to celebration. Enjoy celebrating. Enjoy the buzz of celebration. Success is your given birth right. Unlock it and savour it.

Success is a method and celebration is the cherry on top of the cake. If you want to eat that delicious cherry process and carry out the following steps.

1. Imagine what you wish to hear as you are living through the scene of having achieved your goal.
2. Ask yourself what you will smell, taste, and feel as you are going through the arrival gates of accomplishing your objective.
3. As you close your eyes, what are you looking at while you are achieving your dream.

The more often you get into the feeling of your senses the closer you are to creating the exact vibration or frequency in your nervous system that automatically emits and electro magnetically attracts back to you either your wish or a situation or person who can and most likely will be highly instrumental in manifesting your desired objective.
Even though we want things and have dreams normally we don't enjoy daydreaming about living out our dreams. Therefor our dreams remain fuzzy and distant.

Your dreams need to be alive and vibrating in your mind. So daily, choose one or two aspects of your objective and observe if you feel free or restricted in the moment you want to enjoy living out your dream.
If you feel restricted, it could mean you are trying to reach an objective that a well-meaning friend or family member feels is best for you, and you are playing into their game. Stop and regain control of your own destiny. You will only celebrate from the heart if you were part of the vision making team throughout. Beware... the only dreams, goals, and objectives you should create are those that make your heart sing when you see yourself in the successful end result.

A goal becomes good when it encompasses YOUR purpose. Your generator alights when your purpose is touched. Celebrate that you identified YOUR purpose.
In Chapter 5. Who am I?' is about knowing your inner self and the importance of discovering what makes you tick.
Write out some clearly defined personal purpose statements describing how you like to feel when you are in the flow, or you can look at it from the other point of view

by describing what you like to do and how you like feeling whatever, either during or after you have done your action.

After all, if you are going to CELEBRATE SUCCESS it stands to reason that you have been able to provide in one form or another satisfaction of having provided validating emotions via your actions to yourself and others.

Those 'others' can be customers, friends, family, teammates or even animals in the zoo or the wild. But you want to have used and reached your potential with others that you have been perceived as surpassing yourself and guided or inspired others to the same.

I have interacted , guided, supported and worked with a lot of people over the course of my life and my profession, and there is no doubt in my mind that everyone who is unhappy for one reason or another and shows signs of feeling victimized either by other people ,family , social, climate, political or economic circumstances never make any progress in any sector of their life until they switch their view point to look inwards at themselves and identify ways in which they can change from the inside out in order to reach their goals despite what they identify as 'the' problem. The instant you take responsibility to commit to your promises and reach your goals, mountains move, and everything becomes possible. It does not happen overnight, but it happens. And every inch of progress is a reason to celebrate.

CHAPTER FIFTEEN

WHERE IS THE MONEY HONEY?

The money is here, there, and everywhere. More than you want, more than you can imagine. It will float your way by the attraction of a similar and familiar vibe which your body must emanate. We attract what we emit.

Take the action and make it happen by turning your hopes into vibrational matter.

Shift your mindset, increase your money thermostat.

Ask yourself what will my life be like when I am earning twice as much as today?

Enjoy the possibilities that your envisioning produces in your body and your current emotional and mental state First see the money in your bank account in your imagination then wait for its arrival. Do it every day, find 5 minutes to daydream.

Write down 3 behaviors that you commit to change in your attitude related making and or earning money. Perhaps you will make a point of being happy for everyone near or far from you whom has had a financial success of one form or another.

Maybe you will sort out all your receipts and enter them respectfully into your accounts. Even if the receipts are small, you can decide to feel the gratitude that you had the money to spend.

You want to improve or add new aspects of positive behavior to your money patterns for at least the next 12 months and then review the usefulness of your new behaviors in some actions that you undertake to do.

For example:
- I will pay back my parents by X date

- I will swap my credit card for my debit card to help me never get into debt again.
- I will buy a car I can afford and commit to monthly repayment amounts

When I lead private sessions or group workshops in the '3 personality self-discovery test' which you will find in detail towards the end of this chapter, always includes one of the personalities in the trio as Mr. or Mrs. 'Money".

Money is not only a personality on its own; separate from you or taken up by the wealthy of the world today. It is a part of your existing personality. It is a part of you that is easygoing or worried, sexy, or off-putting and harsh, fearful or trusting, it might be addictive or addicted, it might seduce you and others in your vicinity.

Your money personality can have one or many facets, but rest assured that we all have a money personality. Even a Buddhist monk or a Carmelite Nun living happily in their retreat has a part of their being which is a money personality because money is only a means of exchange. And as everything has a value whether growing a potato or sharing deep meditation, we are always exchanging time for something.

Mother Theresa had a very self-empowering money persona that was proven by the success of her charitable missions.

You are your own Aladdin, and the Genie in your bottle only needs to change the way you look at your values and goals to manifest them into your palpable reality. Since you are Aladdin, and you have your own genie, ask yourself to deliver your wish of being the unique person you want to be, who will have the talents and expertise that will bring you the money you deserve to enjoy. Create a vison of the "YOU" you want and deserve to be.

Money is the strongest inanimate object that exists. It is brain dead, it can't talk, laugh, plan or even regret. The only thing it is brilliant at is conveying messages. In that context money comes into its own power. But the puppet master is yourself. When you breathe your vision into the money it will convey your message. Jim Rohn is famous for having said that a formal education will make you a living, but self-improvement will make you a fortune.

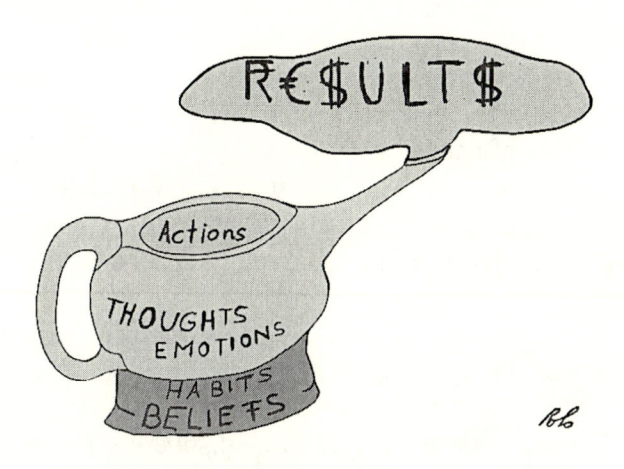

All the information in this book is about that message, which is the result of your brains invisible, unidentifiable, and very subconscious wiring based on your unknown root and core memories and beliefs. Those beliefs mirror what you took in as a small child and throughout life to date, from your daily surroundings, according to those beliefs your financial story today is playing out in your current reality. Each step in your self-improvement will bring you closer to your goals, whether they include money or not.

Maybe the ugly duckling grew into a prince or a successful entrepreneur with the Midas touch or maybe the child born with a silver spoon in the mouth grew up hearing an adult's negative opinions on money and wealth and what could have been a successful financially wealthy person ended up instead turning all fruits into rotten eggs!

It really is the luck of the draw, as to what financial inspirations and surroundings formed your root financial beliefs as a child. But, if today your financial situation is not what you want it to be, then become agile and understand that first you must change and improve your 'self-money story- to portray the inner image of what you want yourself to be.

So back to the drawing board to re- create yourself in the image of the perfect financial wizard. The joy and possibilities of choosing what you want to be is not a useless pass-time. It is real chemistry in motion and action. The emotional kick start that you are infusing your inner being with works in the following trail of actions.

1. The moment you 'feel' a little surge of pride, relief, or joy of seeing yourself as you want to be, that vibration registers instantaneously in the amygdala's of both your left and right brain central hemispheres. The first transformation of any stimulus, whether sound, imaginary, taste, feel, is emotional. Those microscopic, little almond shapes mounds of matter control our emotions and direct the stimuli it receives from the body and dispatches the message to the hippocampus which gives it a more literal or logical meaning. It helps to anchor in that new memorized feeling into your subconscious memory bank by making a small physical gesture, such as squeezing your thumb and in index or 3rd finger together or tweaking your ear lobe. This will ensure that every time you make that same physical discreet movement your body associates that specific movement with having a windfall of pride or financial gain or whatever good money-making

situation occurred either in your mind or reality. Now you mind will emit even further and more frequently the money making and attracting vibe.

2. You might have heard of the Midas Touch or Wired for Success. Both terms are correct. Neuron's wire and fire together mostly by default. If that 'default' mode is not set to success you must actively retrain your brain constantly to only see and feel the successes, you want as if they have already happened. This way the 'nucleus acumens' which is the 'Positive" center in the brain for pleasure and even addiction will eventually only be attuned to situations that will deliver the 'Addicted Success 'sensation. That is why you want to program yourself to the pleasure you derive from being the well-honed vehicle that will self-drive financial success to your doorstep.

3. Become aware of your own contradicting thought processes and wishes.
Be aware of the strong feelings that will wash over your body when you seek 'instant gratification', they are not useful for your ultimate money goal.
If one of your financial goals is to have a substantial nest egg on which not only will you be able to retire on and live life comfortably but also want to be able to provide a college education for your grandchildren, but your instant gratification urge is pushing you to buy that latest car model you want, or splurge $50,000 on a round the world trip now, to celebrate the super tough deal you just closed. You are in self -contradiction. Also known as being in vibrational resistance
Take a long deep look at the forward consequences of satisfying your instant gratification urge.

You might not sign another big deal like that for a while, and this is the perfect opportunity to invest your $50,000 and allow them to compound faster and bigger towards your grandchildren's college fees and your ultimate quality of life during retirement.

The above is a simple and typical example of how it is so easy to run conflicting financial scenarios. Self-discipline yourself and stick to the best. What is tough now becomes easier later, and what Is easy now becomes very tough later.

The 'Instant Gratification' wish for a mega luxury trip today is difficult to resist because your body is flush with chemicals produced by the anticipation of a quick fix of pleasure. Those chemicals are very real and that is why you are feeling the urge to splurge. The nucleus accumbens in the brain fires up on all cylinders the part of the brain that anticipates strong sharp pleasure on the short-term horizon. That anticipatory urge can be the same intensity as a 'crack-user's experience'

If the machinery of your mind -body- spirit are all in optimum condition it will be much easier for you to generate the positive decisions for your ultimate best financial goal.

Allowing your mind and yourself some daily physical play time, with the dog, the children, go dancing, go for a walk. All those play breaks give the brain respite and facilitates the draining process of stress.

Physical fatigue weakens the ability to resist temptation. A sustained diet of leafy greens, fruits, whole foods all add up to healthy and positive brain food. The more our cells are well nourished, our brains are drenched in liters of clean water daily, and we do basic common-sense exercise daily, such as walking upstairs instead of taking the escalator or elevator, walking instead of driving when possible and so on, all add up to facilitating your ability to make, keep take the right action to reach your best financial goals.

Move beyond your dips of desperation and frustration. Apply self-development tools that help fast track your brain retraining to success in the reality of your life.
Use and apply tools in this book to get into peak state for allowing positive opportunities and people to reach you. Open your inner gateway to the infinite rivers of wealth. Amplify positive self – talk by saying I love my work/ I am on the road of success/ Promotions and money-making opportunities are rushing into my life. Words resonate in different parts of the mind and the Vagus Nerve which is the main highway of your nervous system.

The following 6 words have been used for hundreds of centuries for inner wellbeing and wealth increase.
AUM means 'Pure force'
GUM dissolves energetic blocks
SHREEM vibrates with increased abundance
MAHA increases positive energy
LASKHMI YEI stands of intent and purpose
NAMAHA closes the cycle and means the goal has been achieved.
Simply spend a few minutes at the same time every day in a quiet and peaceful state of mind and allow the sounds of the words to rewire the energy of your subtle vibrations deep inside of yourself.

Shake off draining emotional habits such as fear, greed, and procrastination. Instead of thinking I can't do X because I don't have enough money, ask yourself and other!

'How can I get enough money to do what I want to do" There is ALWAYS a way and here are some.
- Activate your wealth switch, so that the wealth in the universe can easily connect to you.
- Be honest with yourself and expose your personal negative blocking and limiting beliefs about your birthright which is all about attracting unlimited wealth making opportunities.
- Notice how many small gestures of people who offer you help and feel the gratitude that they do. You will soon be feeling gratitude for events much bigger which come to you.

TRIO PERSONALITY

Following you will read about a very powerful workshop I do with my clients who are seeking to turn their financial reality around. I call it the TRIO PERSONALITY. And it is all about empowering yourself.

Find a friend and do it on each other. You will be very happy with the results of your introspection. You will need about 90 minutes to do it to each other.

P: The ability to reprogram your 'Belief' system

O: Own the responsibility of every event and situation that happens to you. Once you understand and accept that repetitive thoughts become beliefs. And those subconscious beliefs are attracting the necessary situations to you so that you can play out the reality of your beliefs.

W: When, where, why, get into the habit of 'Asking.' Ask and you shall receive!

E: Evolving and learning with awareness through situations and emotions is a key factor to empowering yourself.

R: Respect others as you respect yourself. And take responsibility for every one of your actions and happenings. Congratulate yourself, and if it does not reflect what you want, create the image to create the belief and start from scratch so that you can give the necessary time to your seed to germinate and grow out of the ground.

PART 2: GETTING TO KNOW YOURSELF

The more you can identify with clarity the answers to the following questions the easier it will be for you to change any limiting beliefs you are unknowingly entertaining, but which are sadly creating a reality you are not wishing for yourself.

1: Make a list of all the words or sentences that you find yourself saying to others automatically to describe yourself.

2: Make a list of all the ways in which you frown upon yourself or think that you are not as good as others or as good as you could be.

3: Which of your family, friends and colleagues do you get the impression is judging you?   In some cases, their judgement might be straightforward and in others you might have the feeling that they are being hypocritical towards you.

4: Which aspect of yourself do you criticise the most when you look at yourself in the mirror?

5: Be honest with yourself. Do you believe that your criticisms are justified, or could they be simply reflecting a general fashion in the media where you have allowed yourself to be brainwashed into believing how things should be?

PART 3: WHICH ARCHETYPE DESCRIBES YOU BEST?

1) <u>The Monkey that does not want to see:</u> If you don't have the courage to deal with what scares you, that un-faced fear will come bite you in the butt. But when you open your eyes and look the fear head on, you will be able to cross that bridge in a much more confident manner when and if that situation does happen

2) <u>The Monkey, which is timid, shy and self-effacing</u>: will sadly discover that other people will be quick to steal your glory!

3) <u>The Monkey with his pedal to the metal!</u> Do you tend to get things done with and over as fast as possible? Beware, it is one thing to get things done, but it is wiser and more efficient to do them slowly but well. Haste makes Waste. For an airplane to lift up into the sky it starts its taxiing journey at 20 % of its cruising speed. If it went from zero to 800 kms /hour, it would never be able to lift off the ground.

<u>The Monkey with the fur coat</u>: He is always freezing. Anything unfamiliar that comes your way, scares you so much that you freeze in your steps.... fur coat or not!

4) <u>The Monkey on the starting line:</u> This monkey will go forward and continue to go forward even when he realises, he or others have made a false start or have gone off in the wrong direction. Instead of cutting its loss he finds it easier to continue and see how things turn out.

PART 4: TRIO PERSONALITY QUESTIONS

SIT ON THE YOURSELF CHAIR

Personality 1: Answer all the questions as 'Yourself'

1- How are you behaving towards a personality group such as: Financial Abundance?
Personality Group Financial Abundance is abbreviated to PGFA.

2- How do you feel about (PGFA?)

3- What are your beliefs about (PGFA?)

4- Why is (PG FA?) important to you?

- Physically sit as your PGFA
- Give me a sound bit as to how your PGFA sounds when talking
- What is your posture,
- Describe your dress code.

1. When (YOU) spoke about yourself before, what feelings were coming up in you?
2. How do you feel about (YOUR) behaviour towards yourself?
3. What behaviour are you manifesting towards (Yourself?)
4. What are your values?
5. What are your beliefs about your current values?

SIT ON THE ELDER AND WISE ONE'S CHAIR

Personality 2: Answer all the questions as the Elder/Wise One

You are the ELDER & WISE ONE of the village now.
What does (YOUR NAME and PGFA) sound like?
Give a soundbite.
What do you think of their posture and their behaviour?

1. How are (YOUR NAME and PGFA) behaving?

2. How are they feeling towards each other?

3. What do they believe about each other?

4. What are their individual values?

5. What do they have to learn?

6. Do you get the impression that their perception is shifting?

7. What else do you think they need to change to improve?

MOVE OVER AND SIT ON THE YOURSELF CHAIR

After having heard the other people's opinions Answer these questions as YOU.
1. How did you feel hearing your (PGFA) saying all those things?
2. How are you going to modify your behaviour towards (PGFA) now?
3. What do you believe about (PGFA) and welcoming (PGF) into your life for ever?
4. What is important to you about (PGFA) evolving and moving forwards?
5. What can you learn from (PGFA)?
6. How has your understanding of (PGFA) changed?

MOVE OVER AND
SIT ON THE PGFA CHAIR

Personality 3 Answer all the questions as MONEY/ FINANCIAL ABUNDANCE (PGFA Personality Group Financial Abundance)

- Answer all the questions in your (PGFA) skin.
- Sit as your (PGFA)
- Before answering the questions, give a sound bite of how your perception (PGFA) sounds like.
- What is (PGFA's) posture and body language?

1. How do you feel after hearing what (YOURSELF) said about you?
2. How do feel about (YOURSELF) behaviour towards you?
3. Has and if so, in what ways has (YOUR) behaviour changed towards yourself?
4. Do you feel rejected by (YOUR NAME)?
5. In what ways are you making a commitment to change your behaviour towards (YOUR NAME)?
6. What actions do you expect (YOUR NAME) to make in their life?
7. What can you learn from having heard (YOUR NAME) talk about you?
8. How has your perception changed about (YOUR NAME)?
9. Are you treating (YOUR NAME) differently then you are treating others?

MOVE OVER AND SIT ON THE WISE AND ELDER ONE'S CHAIR

You are now the wise person and are asking:

1. How do you feel after hearing what PGFA and YOUR NAME are feeling about each other now?
2. What beliefs do they have about each other now?
3. How do you think that their thoughts about each other will affect them in the future?
4. What is important to both personalities?
5. In what areas has their understanding of each other shifted?
6. What do they most have to learn here today?
7. How could they behave as they go forwards in time?

Wrap up questions to be asked by the other friend or person who is helping you in the process. If no one is there, then answer yourself. Sometimes it is easier to answer these questions out loud and when you are speaking out loud to a trusted friend or advisor.

1- What was it like when you were being your (PGFA)?
2- How did you feel when you were in the chair of the Elder Wise One?
3- In what areas have you changed your perception towards your (PGFA)?
4- What vital points did you learn concerning you (PGFA)
5- What path is right for you?
6- Why do you feel that is the right path to take?
7- What are you basing your decision on?
8- Describe how your relationship towards your (PGFA) has shifted?

9- What will you do differently now to allow your (PG)FA into your life and keep it there?

When you have gone through the process of the Trio Personality you will have a new money personality, and your financial reality will improve

CHAPTER SIXTEEN

CHANGING YOUR POINT OF VIEW
&
FOLLOWING YOUR INTUITION

Changing your point of view ... changes your road map. Therefor deeply embed your goal into your belief system to arrive at your destination. In essence you are creating your future memory today.

Your perception in all matters of your life, other people's lives and of the world in general reflects and dictates your behavior and ultimately the situations you live. Your collection of memories is either accepted as being good or bad cognitively and emotionally by your subconscious mind.

Unless you have a very developed sense of self-awareness those emotions will by-pass your consciousness and bury themselves into your subconscious.

If you are not where you want to be yet, it is only because you have been looking at your goal from the wrong perspective. And that perspective shines outwards and manifests itself into your current reality.

General Patton said. 'We are not retreating; we are only marching forward in another direction. "

Your current reality is the result of your inner and subconscious beliefs. There are numerous, tried tested and proven modalities to change unknown beliefs.

Stick -ability is the dish and mental flexibility is a necessary ingredient for the recipe.

Having your end target goal firmly entrenched in your mind is the first step. See, feel, smell, hear, believe, and KNOW that you have already reached your target.

When too many hurdles appear, trust your intuition to show another path to reach it. When you get to the crossroads there will be two signs 'Give up road" and 'Keep on going road' This is where you must make the distinction between giving up... which means you will never reach you goal, or simply using another road to get to your intended arrival. Intuition will play a big part in your outcome. Later, in this chapter we will clarify how to identify and use your intuition.

If you are not used to hearing and acting on your intuition it can be uncomfortable , unfamiliar and scary in the beginning , but as you get into the habit of listening to your inner prompts you will be more and more in tune with the right way for you .Many businesses openly admit that they are making the wrong decisions because they are basing their actions on the fear of risk taking and relying on statistics in their short term thinking approaches and strategies.

Make a list of all your 'illogical & irrational thoughts' and for the fun of it, investigate them with more detail.

1- Identify your goal with as much clarity and detail as you can at this stage.
2- Ask yourself WHY you want to reach that goal. Even if the answer does not make sense, write it down.
3- Take the action immediately to reach your goal. It is important to train your brain to take immediate action and not wait until you feel like it or get around to it.

Never waste time asking yourself "HOW will I reach my goal?". If you do... you most likely will give up before you start. Your subconscious mind is already at work trying to make sure you maintain your current status quo.

Remember that if you venture out of what is familiar to you in the past and today, signifies to your subconscious that you are going out into the unknown wilderness which is automatically out of the cozy comfort zone where the subconscious likes to be.

The easiest way for the subconscious to achieve that you stay put in your status quo comfort zone is to let you ask questions about the 'HOW' knowing that you will give up, obviously at this stage of the game you can't have the answers, which will create an uncomfortable feeling of unease and lack of security.

This is one of the crossroads where and why the losers in life lose. Losers feel overwhelmed by the uncomfortable feelings which your body is now emitting via your home-made chemical factory and consequently 99% of people don't allow their goal to become a burning desire. Your subconscious won the battle. You will not attempt to reach out of your comfort zone and achieve the goal you wanted to reach.

Later, though those same people find themselves seeing that their idea was developed by someone else than their mantra becomes: 'Oh I had that idea 10 years ago, I should have forged ahead then.'

Of course, the 'HOW' question is an important sector for clarity. But as timing is everything, ask the 'HOW' question later down the road.

HOW is used when you create a strategy, not when you are programming your brain to create a vison of your outcome. There is a time and a place for everything.

Replace 'HOW' by 'NOW' when you take the action to make it happen. Your mind goes on a mental dynamo mode, and directional energy is produced to propel you forwards. Soon enough you will have established a routine in your actions since the subconscious loves what it is used to, it will now do everything to ensure you keep the status quo on the momentum. Successful action requires a clear intention. Intention is quantum energy because energy flows where thought goes.

Each person sees the world as they are conditioned or programed to see it. Reality is always subjective.

Take this as an example. Imagine sitting quietly on a park bench, your eyes are shut when suddenly you feel someone pinch you quite hard on your arm. Your reaction most likely will be one of aggravation, or a sense of being physically harmed.

But it could be that the person who is pinching you only wants to warn you silently of a possible threat or danger. How you interpret the physical feeling of being pinched, will dictate your responsive and reactive behavior. What changes is your 'Point of View' or paradigm shift on the pinching event.

Steve Covey, author of 7 Habits of Successful People, gives a very telling example on the importance of seeing a situation from another person's point of view. He was in the subway, sitting next to him was a father of 3 children who were being badly behaved, making a lot of noise, and disturbing the other passengers. Passengers were getting upset and irate because the father just sat there without disciplining his unruly children. As the father finally stood up to leave the subway at the next stop, he was told in an angry tone of voice by an irate passenger that he should discipline his unruly and badly-behaved children. And the father simply dropped his head and nodded while apologizing and adding that they had all just come back from the hospital where his wife and their mother had died.

Seeing the story behind the story immediately shifted the energy. Don't always wait for someone to explain something to you, use your empathy and open your mind to see a situation from different points of view first. You will broaden your approach possibilities and become more mentally flexible and in tune with situations as they arise.

Mental flexibility is necessary. Stubbornness is only the result of subconscious thought patterns not wanting to get out of the current comfort zone... even if it is a block to reaching a goal.

Forbid yourself to become your own worst enemy by giving into your negative and non-productive comfort zones. Every step in a new direction is the result of consciously choosing to break with your traditional old ways of thinking.

The direction you impose on your new thoughts whether they are in the negative or positive direction should come from your conscious choice and not simply be a reaction to an event or an emotion. Become and remain your own master.

One thing is for sure; that whatever your new 'story' will be. it will create powerful changes. Whether your 'story' is incorrect or correct, negative, or positive it is the root of your attitude, behavior, relationships, and measurable results.

Listen to your intuition, and if you feel you can't trust it or don't even know how to access your intuition, do the exercises that are covered in Chapter 24. Exercise number 7.

Those exercises will develop your ability to calm your mind chatter and hear the message from your inner self. Intuition is the most 'direct' form of 'knowing' which we can use at will.

There is nothing logical about intuition. It bypasses rules, regulations and anything that is acceptable or correct. Intuition is the byproduct of your unprocessed past experiences which have not registered with you on a conscious level. But it is our best friend, and many describe intuition as the soul's eyes.

There is an important difference between intuition and instinct. Whereas intuition is always best for us, instinct may lead us into problems. Instinct is the initial pulsation towards a given reaction that is normally based on a global accepted conclusion to a situation or a previously experienced event which you lived through. Very often it is primal and does not take into consideration other talents and solutions that are also good for us but are not so engrained such as solutions based on one's advanced knowledge or education. At times, intuition and instinct are at loggerheads.

Let me create an example.
If your best friend suddenly sits you down and insists to have a 'talk 'with you, to suggest that if you want to achieve something you had better change your way of behaving. It would be natural for you to feel attacked by your best friend and want to 'instinctively' be aggressive as that would be your primal survival mode.
By aggressively pushing others away one incorrectly feels we are protecting ourselves. Wrong...
That sort of automatic immediate primal response is what animals do.
Humans are blessed with the ability to think and project forwards.
Listen to your inner language, feelings, emotions , signs, since this is where and when you will be receiving a soft

spoken inner message that will be probably confusing your instinctual desire to be aggressive to your friend , and your intuition could be saying something like : "Calm down my friend; yes it is true that he or she is coming across a bit aggressively towards me because he is feeling uneasy about having to criticize me, but let me give him or her a chance and hear him or her out and see if he or she actually wants me to do something for my own good. That is acting wisely on intuition.

Self-confidence is important, because the answers or guidance from your inner self might not match the advice of others.
Your path is yours alone. Yes, obviously you must listen to ideas, advice, and suggestions, but always take responsibility for your own choices. intuition is a developable skill. Hone it. When you have mastered and honed your intuition you will enjoy relying on and applying it in numerous situations.
If you are an entrepreneur and are at a crossroads as to which direction to take, trust yourself enough to allow your gut feeling to steer you down the right road for yourself.
Instinct is founded on the collection of all past consciously aware and unaware happenings and experiences. They become memories, and all memories take on a life of their own developing towards the good of our inner higher power.
Scientists call the 'gut reaction' our second brain. There are more neurons in the gut then in the entire spinal cord. Those millions of extra neurons in the stomach allow our 'Gut' to overflow with information that is good for us. But not necessarily for someone else.

Why? Because there is a big possibility that your actions might backfire or not work. If you have mentally assumed responsibility, you can change and use that failure as a lesson to go forward in a better way next time. But if you place the blame on your failed actions or on other people who advised you incorrectly, you will end up wasting your good energy on angry and negative feelings towards others whom you will never be able to change in any case.
Responsibility is paramount here; your ability to respond.

The proven way to success is by following your inner hunch or if you prefer to call it your intuition.
Sometimes it does not feel right... but that does not mean it is not right for you. Trust in yourself now and go with your intuitive flow. Don't second guess it. Just go with your flow.

The difference between intuition and habit, is that a habit will always feel right to you and that is only because your body is familiar with it. But that does not make it right for you.
If you always take a drink and smoke when you are uptight, that is a bad habit.
If you take the time to listen to your inner voice it might be telling you instead "Go for a walk – listen to classical music, loosen up unwind and get back in touch with yourself", whereas you normally listen to rap and end up blasting your cranial neurons into the twilight zone with aggressive boom box noise. One of the ways to hear and recognize your inner voice is that it sounds like a simple uncomplicated instruction to do something; it just comes to you. It won't bang loudly or for a long time at the door. Your intuitive inner whisper will be present fleetingly in

your awareness, so be sensitive to your awareness and trust in your intuitive message. The odds are that often, when intuition speaks, it is asking you to take another direction that will have you looking at something in a new and unexpected light.

The practice of meditation has become widespread and is used in countless approaches, ranging from:
Super slow walking on an imaginary tight rope, focusing on pointing the toes of one foot directly in front of the other and as slowly as possible unrolling your foot into a slow-motion step while walking around a given area for 30 minutes.
Or just:
Drop to the floor, sit down cross legged, breathe in and out slowly and watch your future unroll on the movie screen of your mind… "

Sounds easy… but it takes a lot of patience and practice to go beyond your inner mind daily.'
These examples of meditations are only one of the tools to help you achieve the sensations of inner void. The aim is to develop your intuitive senses by tapping into your existing but most likely yet still occulted powers. Intuition is the language of your heart … and your stomach's 'Gut Feeling".
By developing and familiarizing your inner connection to these two important organs, you are on the road to tapping into your supernatural power. I only say it is supernatural because you read or heard others talk about it.
Now is the moment to give yourself the opportunity to find it already in your bag of talents.

Despite all the sophisticated research technology that is available and brings us to the Moon, Mars and even beyond we still do not have the technology that allows us to clearly identify our journey within.

I believe that with time that will happen because man wants and needs proof to help with their faith. Faith to many is elusive but very powerful. Everyone has what is loosely called 'supernatural phenomena' but most people are too afraid to acknowledge it as it leaves them feeling disorientated and dizzy to look closely in to the large gaps we face of our own ignorance.
Those gaps however are the most important voids to fill. When you tap into your heart endless opportunities unfold in front of your eyes. Suddenly you have access to new landscapes never seen, experienced or felt before.

This is a little exercise to help your brain getting used to changing habits, and obviously limiting habitual beliefs.

1. Clasp your hands together and notice which thumb is your dominating thumb. Or if you prefer is your right thumb on top or is it the left thumb?
2. Whatever it is, unclasp your hands and re-clasp them making sure that your other thumb is now the dominating thumb.
3. Do you notice that it feels a little odd?
4. Do this clasping and unclasping and switching thumbs 10 times at regular intervals for example in the morning, at lunch time, late afternoon, and evening after dinner. Do this for about 3 or 4 days. And notice that you have no discomfort either way. You have trained your body to feel comfortable in both positions.

Changing your point of view by searching for different answers or solutions regularly throughout the day for a few minutes awakens and activates neurons into search mode. They start auto patterning and facilitate your quest to create or stumble across a new point of view while feeling comfortable with the new answers or insights.

"The intuitive mind is a sacred gift and the rational mind is a faithful servant. We have created a society that honors the servant and has forgotten the gift." Albert Einstein

SUCCESS COMES WHEN WE ARE ON THE EDGE OF OUR COMFORT ZONES

As you go from what is comfortable to what is not, you are consciously re-formatting yourself for success by integrating different thought and behavior patterns which deliver different results.

It stands to reason that this is only when your results are not satisfactory to yourself. Don't' fix what is not broken! We all have enabling and limiting beliefs. Your responsibility towards yourself and your committed self-improvement lies in recognizing where your behavior is blocking your success and therefore which habitual but obviously self- limiting beliefs need changing.

- Successful people make up their minds quickly and change their minds slowly.
- Unsuccessful people make up their minds slowly and change their minds quickly.

Develop the habit of following your hunches, whether it is for buying a car, making a change on your travel trip, or reading the next book. On the spur of the moment, it might not make sense, but studies demonstrate over numerous polls and questionnaires that 65% and more of the people who made impulsive purchases remained very happy with their decisions. Trusting your hunches mostly results in a happier outcome.

Set the ground so that your intuition can flourish.
- Remove timelines and deadlines.
- Think intuitively and freely.
- Become aware how your talents or gifts flourish.

Some of us have a deep and easy intuitive connection with ourselves; and others must set the environment so that intuition can develop in safety. In general woman are more intuitive than men, mainly because women carry life inside of them and protect that life until the child can go through life safely.
Encourage your work colleagues to act on their hunches. Encourage them to be self-confident and reassure them that you don't need a logical explanation for everything. If you want to allow your colleagues to work more intuitively, then offer unpressured speaking time and space.
Choose quiet spaces and whenever possible reduce your pace. Walk slower, drive slower, pedal slower, ski slower, speak slower, eat slower, make love slower, dance slower... enjoy the life in your moments.
The more in touch you are with yourself the better your life will roll out.

If you are willing to test yourself, write out some questions that must be answered by an action rather than a philosophical answer.
Such as: Should I move to this town? - Should I quit my work? Should I buy this car? Etc."

I TALK TO MY SELF WHEN I NEED AN EXPERT OPINION.
Psychologists define intuition as "immediate understanding, knowledge, or awareness, derived neither from perception nor from reasoning". It's an automatic, effortless feeling that often quickly motivates you to act.
Mostly it will sound like a voice. In other words, it will not be so much lodged in the body or in the gut.
There is a big nuance between Intuition and Instinct. Identify with as much clarity as possible what you are experiencing.

Information is energy and it becomes available to your awareness and consciousness, via the 5 senses. Not necessarily all of them, but one or two will be transmitting the informational message.
At that point your subconscious beliefs will filter and screen a message, and as you listen to your body's language via your 5 senses, you are now in the driver's seat.
Know that all beliefs have numerous sources and reasons for existing, and beliefs can distort reality. Expectation, the sense of authority and uncertainty or ambiguity are major beliefs distortions.

Instinct is the automatic subconscious rapid response that is wired into us and is based on the memories of all our past experiences, behaviors, and results.
Very often our instinct is only the wish of our subconscious which likes what it is familiar with and is known as the' Comfort Zone"
If your life has unfolded with a higher-than-average success rate in the different slices of the 'Wheel of Life', it would be safe to assume that your instinct can be trusted.

But if your life is beneath the 50% success rate you will be better off in the long run by being sure you don't listen as much to your instinct as to your intuition.

As you learn gradually daily to train your own intuition by listening and trusting some intuitive nudges that you find yourself exposed to or pushed into, give yourself the time and the awareness to be conscious of your reality as you open and allow yourself the freedom to act in 'unexplainable' actions.

You might be afraid to let yourself go to unexplainable urges, and that is very often the case with people who have lost self-esteem and low self- confidence.

Our default 'Go Mode' is based on our filtered beliefs. We depend on them because on one hand no one has enough expertise on any subject and on the other hand there is just not enough time in a day to consider and ponder on all the information that comes to us. Action is our 'Go Forward' mode. We don't and very often can't take the time to even question our own beliefs and assumptions.

I urge you to try and question yourself, because your answers will liberate you as you realize you probably are not making decisions based on your deepest values but more than likely you were programmed to hold beliefs according to what others have told you to believe. You are indoctrinated! You are now an adult, and it is time to reclaim your freedom and mental independence. The sad reality of education is that children are not taught how to think for themselves in school, they are taught to memorize.

Polls of all sorts have been carried out and the results show how across the board people of varied education levels, religions and faiths are increasingly believing, accepting, and acting on their ESP, Extra Sensory Perceptions, of which Intuition is one of those senses. That ranges from clairvoyance, clairaudience, telepathy, and mental or spiritual healings also known as: 'mind/body/spirit' healings.

Numerous studies and experiments have been carried out under very strict and controlled conditions which leave no doubt in many disbeliever's minds as to the existence of ESP.
Telekinetic abilities used in conjunction with telepathy such as spoon bending by numerous subjects result in efficiently influencing matter at any distance. Of course, there are always certain subjects who carry out these experiments better than others but that still proves that humans possess the innate ability to do so.

That ability is there, and with time and research I believe that it will be in the future a subject that will be a technique like writing, playing the piano or reading able to be learnt and applicable with measurable results to all who learn and apply the tools.
It is also a self-fulfilling prophecy; the more one believes in ESP the stronger that ability develops within.
Max Planck and Albert Einstein both believed in the Divine Intelligence. And to end this little chapter let me quote Einstein.

"Everyone who is seriously involved in the pursuit of science becomes convinced that a Spirit is manifest in the Laws of the Universe"

CHAPTER SEVENTEEN

ENERGY MEDICINE

Use Energy Medicine by communicating to yourself via your neurons and energy meridians

Energy tools are excellent for remaining healthy and preventing issues by correctly balancing the energy flow in the body. Everyone will agree on the fact that essentially, we are first and foremost energy. So, it stands to reason that we do everything to ensure that our energy levels are vibrant and balanced.

There is a vast choice of modalities of which many date from thousands of years ago. If time is the mark of quality, then those modalities have passed the acid test of time.

"Healer heal thyself", when we use some of the exercises or modalities daily our stamina and natural enthusiasm for life replenishes our energy levels allowing us to think better and happier thoughts by default. The challenges of our times can be overwhelming for many and by applying one or some of the self-renewable-energy modalities we empower ourselves in the present for today and tomorrow.

Energize your brain. All our behaviours whether, mental emotional or physical issues are curable with the help of Energy Medicine.

Every problem can be improved and with 'Stickability'. All problems can be eradicated by shifting the energies in the body which are blocking the cures to the condition. There are numerous approaches and disciplines in the Energy Medicine field, Tai Chi, Craniosacral therapy, acupressure, acupuncture, EFT, Rolfing, Yoga, and the list goes on.

We are whole. And energy medicine encompasses the mind-body

Mental clarity helps creativity, Mental clarity also deletes depression and confusion. Longevity is only one of the benefits of daily practices of Energy Medicine. But longevity must also include top quality of life and joy.

Be Happy, Live Healthy and Die fast. Happy Healthy Dead. It is vital to live a top quality of life based on happiness and good health. That way you can enjoy every breath you take. We are wired for happiness and the ability to be in a peak state. If that is not the case for you now, it is only because your brain is drained.

Imagine your nervous system as a storage place. Every single thought you entertained, emotion you felt, situation you experienced is stored as a frequency. As the nervous system highway circulates in your entire body, all those frequencies expose themselves everywhere.

Each mental, sexual, physical, or emotional pain and joy is embedded in the memory circuits of your nervous system, but the negative frequencies are hi-jacking your ability to fully enjoy your life.

Emotional upsets and conflicts which occurred in childhood and have not been processed properly for release become stagnant negative frequencies stored away in the autonomic nervous system. Those frequencies remain active in the background and are the broken bridge between what you want consciously and what your body knows as truth.

A sure way to get to the core truth of your beliefs is to be muscle tested. That science is known as Kinesiology.

Your habit of ignoring the issue or simply getting on with life is a temporary bandage. But will never eradicate the cause. The way to delete those familiar frequencies from your nervous system is to disrupt what I call the Morse Code of the frequency, by tapping as you feel pain or bad emotions.

You want to release the negative and fill the new clean space with good memories. So, read, learn, and APPLY the exercises in THINK ACHIEVEMENT & WATCH IT HAPPEN.

As you keep on practicing on yourself you will find what works best for you. But you must first put in the time. Become 'IN-volved' with 'YOUR- SELF'.

Energy psychology goes way beyond normal 'goal setting'. When you incorporate into your daily ritual a choice of your favourite inner-cises, a clever word which John Assaraf coined; you free yourself from the expectations that others or society place on you, and your inner wings fly to the results of your conscious creation of what you yearn for. We all have certain gifts and talents, but too often they are buried deep below the fear of being yourself or even allowing yourself to entertain the images that what you want is valid and you have every right to be, do or reach your dream.

Choose at least one of the rituals in the book to broadcast to the universal field new electromagnetic signatures which will create new opportunities in your life.

The real pharmaceutical industry is yourself. It is your body that makes you feel good. Our bodies create chemicals, and because we have a body, we feel those chemicals.

Your homemade pharmacy is active 24/7 producing the chemicals that your body feels.

The key to success is knowing how to activate the correct chemicals that will serve your purpose.

PhD doctors, David Feinstein who is the husband of energy medicine Donna Eden and Dr Church were pioneers in carrying out lab testing on their clients as they went through energy medicine exercises, namely EFT Emotional Freedom Technique tapping. Their findings clearly support how the use of tapping radically reduces the amount of cortisol in the body which is attributed to tension, stress, worry and all other negative emotions.
Become addicted to your empowering home-made chemicals.

Bodies respond to drugs by way of neurochemistry, and that response is what makes you feel a certain way. Research shows each body's approximately 50 to 75 trillion cells continuously developing, stretching, reforming and eventually dying. Every one of those cells hosts opiate receptors allowing the body to heighten the endorphins controlling our pain and pleasure chemicals. We are all happy pharmaceutical factories.
Active sports such as tennis, skiing, riding your bike, walking the treadmill, pleasurable sex and orgasms, laughing outload until you are in stitches, dancing, boxing, soaking in a warm bubble bath, curling up into bed after a warm bath with a loving partner or if you are alone with a good positive book, playing with friends, children and animals, I am sure you get the idea by now that you are emitting endorphins which are in turn transmitting 'feel good' connections to your brain and then releases the messages for each one of your cells to activate into 'feel good mode'

The more you do that consciously the more you are re-programming your body's brain for happiness, success good health, vibrancy and all the advantages that come with it. You have the powers to heal yourself. From the known ancient days since human's lifestyles have been recorded, we see how mankind fended off illnesses and healed themselves while boosting their much-needed vital forces. From witch doctors to Shamans, from Jesus's miracle healings to recorded placebo healings of today, they all have a common thread. BELIEF and ENERGY.

Dr George Goodheart Jr, confirmed in 1964 the benefits of what is today known as AK Applied Kinesiology, how heavy density negative thoughts, whether emitted from the conscious or the subconscious repeatedly weakened a muscle that had been tested as 'strong'
Allopathic medicine of today heals from the outside in. The result is that it only cures the symptoms and not the causes, Whereas Energy Medicine heals from the inside out, thereby eradicating the cause… and consequently the symptoms.

Following, Monique Khelif, an energy worker explains how a few easy hand movements on DIY (Do It Yourself) daily movements will balance and align your mind, emotions, and energy levels.
Modern Science validates it all and leaves no room for doubt. What was good for humans thousands of years ago, is still good today. We just must rediscover the path. Muscle Testing in an excellent fail-safe way to further identify causes. Your body tells the truth.
Monique and I gave weekly workshops for EFT, and we always used Muscle testing to help us identify with more clarity the issues that the participants needed working on.

Here is a process for using muscle testing. The aim of which is to enter in direct communication with your 'unknown' subconscious beliefs stored in your autonomic nervous system. The body always tells the truth. Just learn its language!

There are various ways, but the following one is based on a 'receiver' being the person who is getting the 'lie detector' test, and the giver who will be asking the questions and pressing down on the arm of the receiver.

a- The receiver stands or sits upright looking straight ahead and raises to shoulder height the dominant arm. Right if you are right-handed and left if you are left-handed.

b- The giver will place his thumb under the outstretched wrist and his fingers on top of the receiver's wrist, thereby gently encapsulating the outstretched wrist.

The giver simultaneously places the other hand on the receiver's shoulder of the same outstretched arm. SKETCH

c- The giver asks the receiver to say their name a few times, then instructs the receiver to withhold the pressure in dropping the outstretched arm as the giver attempts to push down the arm firmly but gently while first instructing the receiver to "Resist" The downward pressure should be done with 2 fingers. Obviously, the receiver contracts the arms muscles which start in the shoulder and resist the downward push.

A few tests can be done so that both people become familiar with the exercise and experience the difference in the weak and strong responses of the arm.

d- The result will be that when the receiver says their name their arm will easily resist the downwards push. And that is because the truth was told about the receiver's name. Therefor there is no muscle conflict and weakening of the arm

e- The next step is to experience the weakening of the muscles and the loss of resistance on the downwards 2 finger pushes by the giver.
This is done simply by the receiver saying that their name is someone else's name, in other words the receiver will tell a lie.
And now the giver will again say "What is your name? – the wrong name is given- and the giver says 'Resist' and proceeds with the 2 fingers downwards push. This time you will notice how easily the outstretched arm gives in to the pressure and is easily lowered.
If the arm drops easily under the pressure of the giver's fingers on the receiver's wrist, the body is clearly indicating a negative response.
TIP: The receiver can blind test their muscle replies by first thinking of a pleasurable memory or experience. They must not recount what it is. When the receiver has after a few seconds integrated their nice memory, the receiver should nod and then giver should then press the arm downwards.
Normally the arm will resist the pressure.
Now the receiver should think of a negative memory or experience, integrate it for a few seconds and nod again to the giver.
This time the arm should give way under the pressure.
The receiver will see how the muscle testing works without any possible mental interference from the giver.
Make sure you don't become 'Stressaholic'

Your mood stems from your energy balance. EFT and other modalities such as muscle testing will help you identify your inner energy blocks. Remove those blocks and watch your life unfold in positive abundance. Stress does not directly cause the big choice of DIS-eases. But it is an excellent fertiliser of the body's energy field making the body much more susceptible to sprouting a new dis-ease. Chronic stress is a major sabotage agent and blocks the tremendous inner potential and financial abundance from manifesting into your reality.

Chronic stress negatively and invisibly impacts your bank account, it drains your energy down the hole, and it will hijack the cognitive part of your brain resulting in the impossibility to see a situation or an objective with clarity and thereby making empowered correct decisions for today and the future.

There is mental, emotional, and physical stress but if the stress is chronic the residue remains lodged in your body hijacking your success potential, and even more seriously the stress becomes uncontrollable.

The stress process unrolls systematically in the following steps:

1- Negative and scary thoughts or images flit across the screen of your mind. They can relate to a health worry either current or projected, it can relate to any unpleasant aspect of finances, career family or relationships.
2- At the same moment, in real- time the limbic brain which is your middle brain and houses the amygdala lights up with red danger signs as its senses detect a threat to your well-being
3- The well-trained amygdala reverts instantaneously to the releasing of cortisol and adrenaline which supposedly will allow you to outrun the danger, but on a chronic basis of stress, the extra injection of cortisol and adrenaline gushing into the body blocks the digestive system from functioning smoothly and therefor your brain is momentarily starved of a constant flow of glucose which the

brain needs to function optimally. This explains why cognitive decisions become impaired.

4- As your body learns to live in a constant state of emergency your energy is consistently depleted from positive, open and free flowing energy and the toxicity of the adrenalin and cortisol in the body become a breeding agent for all sorts of diseases, of which a small sampling are migraines, loose bowls, skin rashes, psoriasis, fibromyalgia and many more. Plus, all your entire mental creative abilities implode cutting of the vital access to your personal intuition, solution finding, and creative abilities. As Oscar Wild said 'Necessity is the mother of invention"

5- Your patience level drops, anything will set you off, and as your behaviour deteriorates you will find yourself in a lonely corner with most people instinctively avoiding your negative invisible energetic maze.

6- The ongoing production of adrenalin and cortisol pushes your body into adrenal fatigue and mood swings and depression can occur further lowering your energetic vibration.

Now is the moment to implement the following:
- Healthy tools to turn yourself around.
- Eliminate alcohol and coffee.
- Eat raw and home cooked food.
- Reduce mass media tv shows,
- Tap and do daily 10-minute bouts of EFT tapping.
  Even though some of the above tips might be difficult at first, within 3 weeks you can re-adjust. Just discipline yourself to do it, whether you feel like doing it or not. When we least feel like doing something is when we need it most urgently and importantly.

Clinical research was carried out on 3 groups and the group which did the EFT tapping which includes talking at the same time about the issue at hand clearly demonstrated an additional 10 % release of the levels of cortisol immediately and not over a prolonged period of days, weeks and even months as conventional talk therapy shows. When you only meditate or do talk therapy the hormone of stress, 'cortisol' continues to impact your brains cognitive skills solution finding as well as negatively impacting your physical health.

Energy Medicine 's big advantage is that everyone can unblock themselves and enjoy a better life very fast.

If you are not sure, what your issues are, apply the easy intuitive Muscle Testing which is explained previously to find if you are on the right path.

The very simple self-muscle test that you can easily carry out on yourself in case you are alone is the body test and the finger locks.

Let's start with the body's first self-test.

1. Stand up right with your feet parallel at your hip's width distance.
2. Shut your eyes and stand still for a few moments as you mentally ground and centre your body.
3. You will soon notice that your body has a slight tendency of tilting from one side to the other, like it if was looking for its own inner balance. That is fine and normal.
4. Keeping your eyes shut say the word 'love' and notice how your body will gently tilt forward.
5. Now say the word 'hate' and notice how your body will automatically tilt backwards.

    Our bodies which are 99.9% pure energy are automatically attracted to the positive just like tulips and plants will lean towards the light.

But everything that has a negative frequency will pull the body backwards.

So, as you start to test your body, when you ask a question if the answer is positive, your body will tilt forwards and if the answer is negative your body will tilt backwards.

The finger lock test is another one of the methods to test yourself.

With one hand make a zero by pressing your thumb to any one of the fingers on that hand that you feel most comfortable with.

1- Then take your index finger of the other hand, insert the index finger into the circle of the other hand and try to pull your finger out by spreading open the thumb and the finger.
2- Again, say the word 'Love' and notice how your finger will stay closed on the positive.
3- Yet on the negative word like 'hate' your finger will spread open and allow the index to escape out of the circle.
4- This is the body's way of reacting to positivity. When the frequency is positive the body becomes vibrant and strong, and when the frequency is negative the body loses its strength, and the muscles will automatically unlock and there will be less resistance to keeping the fingers locked and therefore allowing you to push or pull the index finger out of the circle.

When you connect your fingers into a circle do it with a light but secure touch. As if you were holding a beautiful flower but did not want the wind to blow it out of your grip. That is the strength with which you want to be holding your fingers together.

THE TILT TEST

1- Stand up straight with your feet slightly apart at hips width and gather your body's centre balance point. You will notice after about 30 or 40 seconds that your body is a bit wobbly, that is normal, and it is only trying to find its own gravitational centre.
2- Stand parallel to a full-length mirror
3- Now say your correct name or say the word love and see which way your body will tilt. It may take up to a minute or two. Everyone is different, but your body will tilt one way or the other. The normal way in about 99% of the people is that the body tilts forward on positive and true statements and tilts backwards on negative and untrue words.

These last two self- muscle testing don't need another person to do it on you.

Stop guessing and start 'KNOWING'. Use applied kinesiology on yourself, your food, your work, and everything that relates to your life.

Energy Medicine is free. You already have the energy! Over 6000 years ago the Chinese identified the energy highways of the body. They called the highways 'Meridians" Those Meridians connect to our physical, mental, emotional, and physical hubs, which are the 7 chakras evenly spaced out along our spine and head, influencing our moods and consequently our reality.

Pain is not the enemy. It is the messenger. Listen to its message and use Energy Tools to delete the cause.

INSTANT GRATIFICATION RECIPE

The attitude of gratitude physically makes a person healthier and happier by transforming the brain's molecular structure. This has been proven beyond any doubt by neuroscientists who study the reactions of the physical brain in relationship to the persons emotions. Let's get down to it.

a. Go back and relive in your memory and imagination a moment or period of your life when you were swimming in joy and serenity.
b. In your mind's eye see what you saw
c. In your minds ear hear what you heard
d. In your minds body feel the feel-good feelings you felt at the time
e. And if you never had a such a moment, start from scratch in your mind and create whatever situations you want to live and notice what comes up in the above points.
f. Hang on to the above feelings and visions for about 20 seconds and then sharpen all the sensations. Imagine the volume of the happy words, music, wind, or whatever sound is associated with your image. Become aware how your feelings of joy and peace are surging and welling up inside of you.
g. Mentally scan your body and pinpoint the area or areas where you are physically experiencing in the moment heightened feelings and paint those areas with a brighter

version of its current colour. As that colour becomes brighter and therefore easier to see, mentally move those photons of energy colour in your mind's eye all over your body. Immerge your body in the brightness of those colours as you sweep up and down your body from top to toe and back again. Do this a few times intensifying the colours each time you sweep the colours over your body.

h. Those bright colours are creating endorphins in your body. Painting a happy face on one endorphin and watch it immediately replicate itself Quantumly filling your blood stream with frequencies of happiness and joy as they float and frolic in the fluids of your body, visiting all 70 trillion of your cells at the same time!

i. The more you practice the faster you will be resetting your default mode to permanent happiness and peace. Which is the best endorphin and oxytocin soil to have as you grow your dream seeds.

Use this quick body sprinkler to immediately re-energize yourself which I have learnt from Dona Eden's workshops.

1- Stand straight and put your right hand on your left shoulder. Give yourself a 2 or 3 second hand massage on your left shoulder and dig your fingers into the top of your left shoulder,

2- Then with your right hand pull it diagonally down across your chest and imagine sweeping of unwanted crumbs of bread off your body.

3- Repeat that 3 or 4 times and feel the immediate tingle in your body.

4- Then change sides and repeat the same procedure the other side.

Those delightful tingles you feel is your energy reactivating.

If you have a headache or are feeling overwhelmed and

stressed do this easy movement by taking a few moments for yourself.
1. Place both thumbs on your temple.
2. Place your remaining fingers on your forehead and now with a gentle but firm pressure make curricular movements for about 5 seconds.
3. Then place your fingers in the middle of your forehead above your third eye and gently but firmly pull your hand outwards as if sweeping away all the tension from your forehead.
Repeat this about 3 or 4 times. Very soon you will begin to feel some inner peace.

We all know these little techniques but when you put yourself first and love yourself, you are taking the time to take care of yourself. This is where real health begins. DIY Do It Yourself.!

I have written out a list of numerous symptoms which are the result of too long or chronic stress.

EMOTIONALLY & MENTALLY

- Compulsive competitiveness-
- Perpetually racing against the clock, whether it is to get to the grocery store or beat the next red light!
- Getting the kids to school or making it on time to the movies.
- Can't switch off and slow down, can't enjoy chilling out and doing nothing.
- Insomnia
- Waking up for no reason and can't dose off to sleep again.
- Lack of focus and concentration
- Cloudy judgements
- Can't see the whole picture.
- Increase of senior moments. when there is no neurological illness diagnosed.
- Can't come up with new ideas.
- Depressed
- Losing your sense of humour. You have lost your ability to smile and laugh.
- Always judgemental and critical.
- You can get peeved off very easily.
- Your sex drive is very low or has become non-existent.
- Panic attacks
- Guilty feelings
- Not doing what you intend to do.

ON THE PHYSICAL SIDE:

- Unexplained headaches and migraines
- Chest pains
- Knots in your stomach and ulcers
- Developing uncontrollable twitches of your body parts.
- Excess urine and or constipation
- Skin rashes
- Your heart pounds heavily or you can feel it beat faster.
- Unexplained back pains.
- Shallow breath
- Perspiration
- Weak immune system, catching every bug in town.
- Dizzy spells
- Cancer
- No more self-respect for your personal appearance.

One of the most authentic healers I know is Les Greves in London. To quote Les he says that healing is just another form of psychotherapy working on the person's subconscious mind. Les visually projects his love for that person into his client's mind; thereby encouraging his patient to self-release their inner buried conflicts which automatically leaves the place for love to fill the gaps and delete the pain. Pain cannot live for long in the environment of love.
He focuses his mind on his patient's subconscious and influences a change in his patients thinking process.

The slightest shift in thought direction of anyone can bring about a change in the persons physical and/or emotional condition.

The action of focusing a positive intention is a strategy of concentrating the mind on a particular outcome. The concept of positive focused intention is a system that is well known and used by athletes as part of their training.

Les relates very tightly to his clients so that he can transmit directly into their subconscious minds with the love frequency.

Les believes that environmental programming dictates how each person reacts to each situation either negatively or positively he states that people's experiences subconsciously create damaging self-image.

So therefore, recovery depends on how flexible a person is of the negative parts of their self- image and their attitude in openness to listen. Attitude is vital because even if you are 'listening' you might not be 'hearing' due to fear of being criticised. Each person's vulnerability can delay the desire to change until that person feels strong enough to face the fears and is ready to change. There are infinite permutations of cause and effect of disease, each one is unique to each person's attitude and points of view and beliefs in life. Therefor the rate of recovery that Les obtains depends on each one of his client's behavioural patterns and their willingness to change.

Knowing that the frequencies of love warm our whole body and open us to empowerment, when we focus our thoughts on joy and being happy, we are automatically linking joy to love. At that moment we are counterbalancing a subconscious association to pain, hurt and rejection with love.

If you BLISSipline yourself daily to access those higher frequencies the easing and changing off ailments on your path start to lessen. To back up what you have just read here are a few cases study examples from Lez Greve's healing practice in London.

Mary – MS. Residence England.

As Mary has suffered from MS since many years, she had lost the use of her hands.

Lez's intuitive observation:
Mary as a young child got out of bed in the middle of the night looking for her doll. She fell over and hurt herself in the darkness, cried and woke everyone up. Her parents were always angry when that happened and put her back to bed very aggressively.

Prime Visualisation:
Les visualised Mary as a three-year-old little girl with her parents gently picking her up where and when Mary had fallen over. The parents gave her the doll she was looking for; hugged her and gently put her back to bed.

Results:
A few days after Lez's session with Mary she recovered the feelings in her fingers and was thrilled to be able to fasten her own buttons once again and by the end of the week she was able to pin and sew the clothes she designed.

Jason – Ulcerative Colitis: Residence Hong Kong.
Jason was suffering from Ulcerative Colitis and had lost hope as standard treatment and tablets hadn't really worked. It was most unpleasant for him with some internal bleeding most days. His free movement was hampered as he always needed to be not far to a men's room.

Lez's Intuitive Observation:
Jason had a deep unconscious fear of his mother that caused a feeling of not being capable or good enough despite his professional success She was often very difficult with Jason and his father and put them both down.

Primary Healing Focus:
Les visualised Jason as a small child with his mother teaching him very gently how to read. His father joined to help and put his arms around both. His mother smiled and praised her husband for how kind, caring and cleaver they both were.

Results:
Jason's condition improved drastically, and the pain and the bleeding subsided he was able to move around more freely and live a normal busy lifestyle. He has taken up bike riding again and can regularly cycle over twenty miles at a time.

Jane – Cancer. Residence England
Diagnosed with breast cancer, an MRI had revealed a shadow of her sternum.

Lez's intuitive observation
Jane was holding on to the loss and sorrow of a loved one in a past life. The loss was of her husband who died during the battle of Waterloo.

Lez's Prime visualisation:

Intuitive Observation:
Les visualised Jane's husband as a reserve soldier waiting to board a wagon to join the battle. A messenger arrived with news that the battle had been won and therefore he could stand down.

Results:
In Jane's subconscious mind her husband had not gone to battle or died, and Jane was able to let go of her inner feeling of loss.
Within a few days the tumour had reduced from 3.8 cm in diameter to 1.4 cm and the sternum was found to be completely clear.

Carol. Anxiety Attacks- Residence- Australia
Carol suffered from very bad, terrible claustrophobia exhaustion and severe leg pains and for years rarely ventured out of her house.

Lez's intuitive Observation:
Carol was restricted as a child by the fears and doubts projected by her mother. Fearful of failing and being judged she holds herself back refusing to enjoy the beauty of life.

Prime Visualisation:
Les visualises Carol's parents standing on both sides of her and each parent holding one of Carol's hands. Her parents are gently encouraging her to believe in herself and her abilities. She has a big smile on her face and feels supported and loved.

Results:
Within a week Carol was able to go shopping on her own and was even able to cut the grass which she had not done for years.

Tips for self-healing: Make it a daily routine to self-create a good mood for yourself. Those vibrations will protect your immune system from the debilitating effect of all unpleasant feelings and emotions. So daily and habitually take control of your thoughts at least 3 times a day for a few minutes, and purposefully create joyous thought patterns.

Enjoy your imaginary feelings and then go back to work. With time and habitual repetitions, your neurons and synapsis construct deeply rooted 'Happy' feelings. Those habitual happy feelings will keep you healthy and vibrant.

The above should have convinced you by now how energy distance healing works.

Don't let your body mastermind your thoughts and your brain. I say that because the entire body is also your subconscious mind.

The body is conditioned to feeling a certain way in relation to whatever emotions or type of personality you have. If the feelings are great... fabulous you have nothing to change. But if you suffer from moods, depression, anxiety, jealousy etc. It is time to retrain your brain to produce positive thoughts.

MY BODY IS YELLING FOR ATTENTION.

Everything in life, from the people you meet, to the feelings you feel are a mirror reflection of your beliefs and thoughts.

Why? Because every one of our 70 or so trillion cells are a complete 'YOU'. The outer body is simply a magnified manifestation of each one of our cells.

Beliefs and thoughts are magnified through the loudspeaker of your body, 70 trillion times louder so that you have no more excuse not to listen to yourself!

Our body speaks to us. Don't ignore the messages which come to us via all physical sensations, be polite and listen.

Choose your daily physical feeling, it could be an upset tummy, acid reflux, a back pain, a broken bone, twisted ligament, headache, runny nose, tinnitus, a numbing feeling somewhere in your body, anything that is physically painful or uncomfortable.

All physical sensations are messages trying to reach your mind via one or more of your 5 senses.

Then look into a mirror and allow your eyes to look deeply into the reflection of your own eyes. Look at yourself when you talk to your reflection. Just as you would look at anyone who is in front of you and speaking to you. Ask yourself the appropriate questions concerning your issues, the same way that a caring mother or doctor would ask you as they attempt to find out the reasons that caused you to feel bad.

Here are some common-sense questions in the case of tummy upsets, upset bowl movements, anything to do with the absorption or elimination of food, digestive tract etc.

- Am I scared about something that I am burying inside of me because I don't have the answers.?
- Is there someone or something that is bothering me, and I can't get rid of?
- Is there a situation or a person that I can't stomach?
  The pains we feel are the result of an incorrect perception that we have on a situation.
  I would suggest that you blend Tapping (EFT) with your daily ritual as you look into the mirror and tap your

affirmations deeper while looking into your eyes and say an affirmation that relates to your issue.

Here are a few examples which I have taken from the Queen of affirmations, 'Louise Hay'
- I allow my body to rest when it needs to.
- I love my amazing body
- I trust the process of life

I am safe
I am fearless
I give you permission to be well and healthy.
I enjoy the foods that are best for my body.
I make healthy choices.
I respect myself.
I approve of myself.
Every day in every way I am getting better and better.
I am constantly discovering new ways to improve my health.
Healing happens, I get my mind out of the way and allow my body to heal naturally.
I have a Guardian Angel.
I claim my perfect health now.
I love water it is my favourite drink. It cleanses my mind and body.

LET'S WORK ON A BIG CULPRIT… 'UNRELEASED ANGER'

Forgive and release any anger you might have, to feel better. Anger must be processed outwardly otherwise it will transform inwards. Don't swallow anger, it will lead

to depression or bad physical symptoms. It will also block potentially positive outcomes from happening,
Talk openly to the person you are angry with. If you can't talk to that person, then speak to that person by looking into your own eyes in the mirror. But make sure to release the anger verbally and if possible, look either at the real person or yourself in the mirror.
You will find that when you visualise your rage flowing freely out of your body, maybe by imagining a red cloud escaping from your mouth like the flames of a dragon.

Here are some ideas to get you going:
- I am allowed to be angry.
- I am proud to have the courage of expressing my disappointment and my anger towards….

Look at the mirror and say to yourself or the person who has harmed you and remember the moment or moments when you first became angry. Feel that anger mount and boil up inside of you, feel the hate or the tears as they surface.

And NOW… tell that person exactly what you feel angry about.

Here are some ideas to get your monologue started:
- I am angry at you because you………..
- I was hurt because you ……
- I am afraid because……. Remember that FEAR is only a make-believe emotion. It stands for: 'False Emotions Appearing Real'

Do this anger releasing exercise several times over the course of the next weeks until you feel you can talk about the issue remembering everything very clearly but ensuring and being aware that you are not 'physically feeling' that hatred or sadness bubble up inside of you again.

When you can relate the whole story without feeling any sad, scared, or angry emotions you will have successfully cleared the negative frequencies from your body.

Your body is now fresh and able to flourish in the frequencies of positivity.

What we believe about life becomes our reality. If your reality is not what you want it to be… then simply work on creating new beliefs by formatting them into positive and current affirmations and repeat them continuously until they do become your new beliefs.

Keep on saying them and boost the impact by looking into your eyes in a mirror as you say them.

You can also place the hand you are not using for tapping at the base of your throat so that your hand can absorb the vibration of your words while you speak out loud. That way you are totally immersing yourself by multiplying the entry points into your nervous system which transports all the frequencies created by the words you are saying

- Looking into your eyes = 1st multiplier
- Tapping while you talk = 2nd multiplier
- Listening to your words spoken out loud = 3rd multiplier
- Your open palm at the base of your throat = 4th multiplier

As time is money, by doing the above you get 4 for the price of 1!

Here is a short list of some metaphysical meanings related to physical pains since each pain is linked to an emotional upset. When you get to know the metaphysics of the body and integrate the message and its lesson the physical pain disappears. You must learn and figure out how to decode the physical pains when they appear.

Headaches: Very often you know what the correct decision or action to take is, but you don't do it. Relax every day and release your pressure.

Neck: Shows that you are feeling guilty and don't know or want to forgive yourself. Be more flexible and relaxed. Don't take everything so seriously. Life is a game. Have fun at home and at work. Work on forgiveness. (Ho'oponopono)

Shoulder Pain: Often related to emotional baggage. Think of the expression 'Needing Broad Shoulders'. It takes two to tango, engage whomever else you feel is also related to your past emotional problems and sadness.

Back Pain high up the back: You most likely don't feel emotionally supported. If you are single find a loving supporting partner and if you are in a relationship speak and discuss openly each other's emotional needs and find out how your partner is willing to support you with more affection.

Lower back pain: Is often related to financial fears as well as needing to exchange more affection. Pick up your courage and ask for an increase or increase your prices. It can also signify that you don't feel in control of your life.

Soreness in the gums: Tends to be a sign of procrastination and not be reliable and keeping your promises. Set your intentions and stick to them within 48 hours. Make that a habit.
Stomach aches: You might be feeling un-respected, or a negative situation occurred, and you still have not

swallowed or digested the painful emotions associated to that or those situations.

Tennis Elbow and pains in the elbow, knees, and hips: You are not flexible and resist change. Stop being so stiff about everything, relax, let go and learn to trust. Get off sitting on the fence and deal with the issues whatever they are.

Arm aches: You are carrying too much in your life. Is it worth it? Ask yourself that question.

All types of pain in the hands: Hands symbolize human connectivity to others. Maybe you are not being empathetic enough to others in need of a shoulder to cry on. Make new friends, or /and become more open and vulnerable with those you know. Allow people to feel closer to you.

Pain in the coccyx: Stop sitting on problems. Deal with them and put the problem behind you.

Tooth Ache: Since nothing stays forever, remember that when you are living a negative experience it is best to find something positive to focus on and get your teeth into!

Pains in joints: Indicates a big need to change your approach to life. Become more relaxed and flexible. Open up to a different point of view or even the suggestion of a new lifestyle.
Ankle pains: Stop punishing yourself and pleasure yourself more. Don't be so strict on yourself. If you are in a

relationship, do fun things again and spruce up your sex life.

Foot pains: Move away from any negativity in your life. Negativity will drop to your feet because negativity is a dense energy. Look for joy and fun in your life by creating it first in your mind. Develop a vocabulary about a subject you enjoy and watch your passion develop until you become an authority on your passion.

The following lyrics sung by Lauren Bacall in Applause in the early 70ies on Broadway describe clearly what we are all about!
I wish I could inject the music into this book…but I can't. However, go to YouTube and listen to her recording. It is explosively uplifting. Enjoy the song.

I feel groggy and weary and tragic
Punchy and bleary and fresh out of magic
But alive, but alive, but alive!

I feel twitchy and bitchy and manic
Calm and collected and choking with panic
But alive, but alive, but alive!

I'm a thousand-different people
Every single one is real
I've a million different feelings
OK, but at least I feel!

CHAPTER EIGHTEEN

DELETION TOOLS

DELETE IN ORDER TO TRANSFORM
DELETION TOOLS: EFT - HO'OPONOPONO – MATCHSTICK PEOPLE- RUBBISH CORK BOARD- STOP COMPLAINING – CLEAN WEAK DIET.

Liberate negative emotional energy stored in your body and replace it with clean energy to create your chosen targets on clean positive inner foundations.

A lot of people have experienced that the energy shifts in their bodies permeated deeply into what they call their soul. This has nothing to do with religion, but more to do with the Divine essence of whom we are and the energy matrix of the infinity from where we are sourced.

We are not born with beliefs. Initially they are seeded into us by our immediate environment as infants, toddlers, and children. With time those beliefs which are our reality change and develop. A belief is developed on the back of a memory. That memory can be inherited through generations of ancestors or else acquired and lived in your own life.

We all believe we are a unique model and are different from the rest of humanity. When you retake control of your life, you will understand that it is time now and up to you to decide what you will believe in. Hopefully you will want to exchange limiting beliefs for beliefs that will give birth to reaching your goals.

Which of your beliefs are limiting and which are helpful? The more empowering beliefs you have and create about yourself the more resourceful you will become on your path to success.

Release and delete old limiting beliefs that are unsporting of your current goals. The more mindful you are, the faster you will identify those memories or beliefs.

Beliefs are born from experiences, memories, or repetitive hearsay. Have you had impactful issues that occurred or maybe are presently occurring in your reality? From unexplained overwhelming anxiety, depressive thoughts in which you are drowning in black waves of hopelessness of ever being able to surmount the negative waves which are slamming you back down and under the water. Fear about the future, maybe in spending the rest of your life alone, without a partner, close friends or a support network of like-minded souls. Understand you can stop that fear dead in your tracks right this moment.

All you must do is focus on your reality in this precise moment. Take everything in that you can right this second. You will notice that by having switched your attention to the breaths you are taking now, what the chair you are sitting on feels like under your thighs and bottom, what the clothes feel like on your back, those few moments have taken your attention away from projecting into the future, and I am make a bet that you are feeling marginally better and more peaceful

Are you battling an ever-losing battle with an addiction? Is the stress at work or in your family so overbearing that you explode at the slightest contradiction? Do your feel shattered? Is your body expressing unexplained pains?

In this chapter I will explain some powerful tools which bring measurable results to your awareness in minutes. Though very often it can seem like a 'One Minute Wonder' be sure to incorporate these tools into your daily habits for life. EFT, Ho'oponopono and Stick Men all remove negative frequencies deriving from subconscious thoughts.

Thoughts form daily in our minds, and the more self-awareness you attach to your thoughts and feelings the quicker you can delete and choose to turn a negative into a positive or enabling belief. Successful people are in control of their own lives.

Real power is controlling your own reality. And that starts in the mind. Be 'aware' of your emotions and thoughts. The instant you realise you are running a negative scenario, use your self-control and switch that thought or emotion to an empowering affirmation.

Let us take an example. You go to the ATM to retrieve cash. The ATM says there is a problem with your account or card and to contact your nearest branch. You instantaneously feel a brick in the pit of your stomach and before you have walked 100 metres to your nearest branch you stop with the shock that you are running a drama scenario in your mind. If you are willing to take control of your thoughts, this is the moment when you will make the 'conscious decision' to replace the current negative most likely wildly exaggerated story you are telling yourself and that when you speak to your bank manager, he will give you an explanation as to why your card was blocked. You will sort it out easily and be back in the flow or your life. But if you see your banker in total panic, he most likely will not enjoy your panic or rudeness which is provoked by your current sense of panic and in turn your banker will do nothing to help you out.

Exercise 1

EFT EMOTIONAL FREEDOM TECHNIQUE – TAPPING

EFT is mainly for yourself, whereas Ho'oponopono is very useful for clearing the negative energies of people who have a disturbing effect on you. On the basis that what upsets us in other people, reflects what we don't like in ourselves. I like saying that because I attracted that person or situation into my life, I therefore have the same issue already buried deep inside of me It is "especially effective in clearing traumatic memories: accidents, abuse, violence, childhood memories; or even clearing persistent negative messages from family or key people in our lives."

The impact of a buried negative memory, a limiting or a self-destructive belief in your capabilities will block you from finding out how talented you really are. To find out what you are capable of pretend in your mind's eye that you can do whatever it is that you want to do. Pretend that you are doing it now in your mind.
If you go through the repetitive process of training yourself to choose to believe you can, you will! These are the building blocks of empowering and enabling beliefs.
Obama coined 'Yes We Can 'and look how powerful those three words became in the USA.

EFT EMOTIONAL FREEDOM TECHNIQUE

EFT Emotional Freedom Technique is a needle free acupuncture experience while enjoying a heartfelt verbal complaining session with your imaginary best friend. It belongs to an ancient form of treatment known as TCM Traditional Chinese Medicine and today it also comes under the heading Energy Psychology.

Of all the excellent modalities that exist and produce measurable results, EFT also known as 'Tapping' gives the fastest results. It is a gentle and efficient self-treatment tool that I have been successfully used for over 15 years. It is the result of searches to reduce a therapy process taking months if not years from reclining on the psychologist or psychiatrist's chair to getting visible and measurable results in days, hours and even minutes.

It efficiently and radically by-passes conscious and unconscious blocks and discomforts by gentle tapping on 9 easy access points of the upper body.

Our body is first energy and then matter, the electrical charges produced by the atoms are the building blocks of the body's physical matter.

EFT goes straight to the core of our body's electrical / energy makeup.

TAPPING PROCEDURE

There is only one way to do EFT wrong... and that is not to tap!
What I will explain here is the most widely used technique, but as you become proficient and familiar with tapping you will find your own rhythm.
You can tap with your left or your right hand, you can tap with one or both hands, you can switch from one hand to the other.
The only important thing is to talk and tap at the same time.
First let's memorise the very simple physical tapping procedure.
On each of the following tapping points use two or three of your fingers and get into the mental habit of tapping about 7 or 8 times on each point. There are 9 points in the main tapping circuit which are clearly identified further on.
Before we start, make a Tapping Target list of everything negative, painful, sad, and angry that you can think of and give it a number based on the paragraph below.

Step A- Identify your issue and give it a number from 0 to 10 with 10 being the worst. This is your own internal measuring barometer. It is important to rate yourself a number because that is the starting point for your internal GPS!
Just like your car's navigation system it will get you anywhere you want to go but it must know where you are at currently in order to map out the right road!
The big miracle of tapping is that it diminishes from a little to completely the feelings you are uncomfortable

with. The solution is not to avoid thinking and talking about what you don't like but, on the contrary, to talk about what is scaring you.

Step B- 'Set up statement' Karate Chop. You have given yourself a grading of zero to ten being the worst, and you know what your issue is. You will now use the fingers from one hand to tap on the Karate Chop part of your other hand.
The set-up statement consists of saying: 'Even though (state your problem) I deeply and completely love and accept myself.
You can put your own variation on the last point for example saying, "I love and respect myself, or love my body".
These are important words because you are speaking to your inner child who is living in your heart.

Our inner child is also our subconscious. I call it our first team member. The subconscious is the seat of our memorised habits and emotions. It is the platform from where you hear your self -talk coming from, it is also addressed as your inner child.
Probably ever since you were a child you have perfected the art of ignoring your pains, symptoms, and discomforts. Mostly due to the innate fear that you would not be loved if you were not perfect. The result being that the negative vibrations associated with whatever you were feeling were pushed deep down and with time the inner pressure resulting from these exacerbated feelings, seeped into the physical part of your body, and today are creating physical manifestations called symptoms.

The causes of the symptoms are deeply embedded negative vibrations and energy frequencies that are boiling over to be heard and released.

As an analogy think of this scene. Imagine a little child 3 or 4-year-old who starts crying and screaming and comes running to you for help and comfort. But you happen to be very busy just at that moment and your first reaction is to reprimand that little child and say something in a strict tone of voice such as "Go to your room and stop crying, I am busy" Of course that little child will scurry off to their room, but will continue to be scared of you and therefor cry in muffled tones, until their emotional or physical dilemma gets worse and they might even get a head ache from crying.

On the other hand, if that same child comes crying and you open your arms and comfort the child with soothing tones saying: "It's alright, what is the matter? I love you" ; within seconds the child will stop crying and will delight in whatever takes her attention. Perhaps a bird, a squirrel or a butterfly.

The explanation is that love opens and releases. So, when you tell yourself 'Even though (I am jealous, angry, have a splitting headache, back ache etc.) I deeply and completely LOVE and accept myself", your nervous system is automatically opening in trust and confidence that you will still love your inner child even though you have a problem and will allow the negative energy frequencies associated to that issue to be released out of your body.

Some people have such low self-esteem of themselves that they find it very difficult if not impossible to say out loud that they love themselves.

My advice is 'Fake it to make it;' but it is imperative that your say and hear yourself say those words. Love opens and heals, fear propagates negativity. Make sure you say in your own words that despite your issue, you love and accept yourself. Put as much loving emotion into your own statement as possible.

Use the 'Karate Chop 'set-up statement about 2 or 3 times. Identify as specifically as possible the issue you will be tapping on to release the symptoms. Because once you are tapping through the points as I call it tapping around the circuit you need only say the reminder sentence which I will cover in the next point. Furthermore, if while you are tapping round your circuits you run out of words you only have to say a word or two and your body will know which negative vibrations to release.

<u>Step C: Tapping around the circuit.</u> This is when you will use the 'Reminder' words. If your set up statement from the previous step consisted of "Even though I have a splitting migraine I deeply and completely love and accept my body.' Your reminder words need only be 'headache'.

However, I advise you to use the single descriptive adjective once you have exhausted your complaining spree. Remember that EFT is 'Negative chit chat'. You have the obligation to 'Complain' out loud as you tap around the circuit. It is the opposite approach to being positive. A good tip is to imagine that you are complaining about your issue to your doctor or best friend. People who will not judge you no matter what and with whom you are relaxed and trusting to spill all the beans to.

Here is a sample run and the explanation of the initials that you will see are internationally recognised in English. Even if you tap in a language foreign to English the initials will be the same on tapping forums and scripts.

KC= Karate Chop

EB- Beginning of the eyebrow where the inner hair meets the skin.

SE= Go around the orbital bone and tap on the little dent at the side of the eye.

UE- Under eye. Continue around the orbital bone and tap just under the pupil on the top or the orbital bone.

UN- Is between your upper lip and the bottom of your nose

CH- Chin, be sure to tap in the dent of the chin and not on the point of the chin.

CB- Collar bone. Measure about 2 cm down and 2 cm outwards. A stretched open hand can easily tap on that point.

UA- Under arm. Make a 90-degree angle at the height of the nipple or where the bra strap will lie and down straight from the middle of the arm pit.

TH- Many points all over the top of the scalp. I like to use all my fingers there and imagine I am playing the piano on the top of my scalp.

1- Intensity of the migraine pain '9'

2- KC: Set up statement: 'Even though I have a splitting headache I deeply and completely love and accept my body' –

3- KC:'Even though I feel like vomiting with the headache I deeply and completely love and accept myself' –

4- KC:"Even though every time I speak I have the impression that my head is splitting open and my neck is stiff as a piece of steel, I deeply and completely love and accept myself". "Even though I am scared of my migraines, I hope to have the insight to understand why they happen. But I deeply and completely love and accept my body" Some people have such low esteem that they cannot bring themselves to say, 'I love and accept myself", I will insist though that you force yourself to say it even if you do not feel you love yourself at all.

5- Tap through the points around the circuit, tapping on average 7 to 10 times on each point as you speak.
EB- "I can hardly talk"
SE- "My head is splintering with sharp pain".
UE: "My neck is stiff with pain"
UN- "The noise is searing through my skull"
CH- In the crease of your chin "The light is agony"
CB- Collar bone 'The pain is all over my skull"
UA- Under arm 'I am exhausted from the pain"
TH- Top of the head (tap in light circles around the top of your head, because there are many receptors points up there) "I want to vomit "

Now that you have finished 1 full circuit you might be out of verbal descriptions of your pain so all you must do is go around the full circuit again a few times, just saying as you tap on each spot "pain" or "headache"

<u>Step D Ending the taping circuit session</u> EFT is all about focusing on the dirt to remove it from your system, therefore I like to leave the EFT sessions on an encouraging feeling. Compare it to when you have spent hours on your hands and knees cleaning the floors but as you stand up to look at the result you enjoy seeing fruit of your work.

Here is an example of an uplifting script to end off your tapping session:

Without going back to the 'Set up statement' continue your last one or two rounds:
EB- I thank my pain for the message my body is giving me.
SE- I now trust my body to release the pain
UE- I trust that my body has heard the voice
UN- of the cause of my pain
CH- and that now my body is releasing the pressure and stress
CB- that my negative beliefs were shouting for attention
UA – And now that the pain gave me the message
TH – The divine intelligence of my body is resetting all my systems to peace and good health

Close your eyes, take a few slow and deep breaths. Imagine and then allow a golden or white healing light and energy to filter through your body and gently open your eyes.
See a beam of laser type light come at you gently and see it softly enter your body via your heart then sift upwards towards your brain then cascade down and around your body bathing yourself in and out with a warm bright tingle feeling of Divine Energy.
Self-scan your head and give your pain a number now 0 to 10.
In 99% of the cases the pain will have diminished tremendously and sometimes even completely.
You might find that the pain has shifted to another part of your body, that is also a good sign because it means that your energy is still cleaning you up and deleting unwanted memories. You might want to do another tapping session on the location of the new pain.

EFT is not always a one-minute wonder, though often it feels like that. Following you will find a step-by-step process that draws your focus on the tapping tree guideline. A useful chapter breakdown of how to go in depth to your core issues and delete them from you psyche for ever, is to tap through the dead skin layers of the onion peel. The deeper you go, the more the stench of the onion will be unbearable.

a- Start by doing a round of tapping on a 'specific' situation. For example, if you have a throbbing headache in the nape of your neck. Don't just say even though I have a headache, Say the 'pain at the bottom of the left side of my skull is so tense that I cannot even turn my head.'
That is your **SYMPTOM**

b- Your next tapping talk will be centred to whatever **emotions** you are running now. Perhaps you are angry that because of your headache you are afraid that you will not be able to deliver your sales pitch to your client. So here your emotion is FEAR and PROJECTION of a situation that for the moment is only in your mind. But as you might be aware, what you resist persists and what you fear manifests. Every **emotion** whether you like it or not carries a frequency that will automatically attract a situation which has the same frequency. Remember that like attracts like.

In this round of tapping, you will want to tap with clarity on the description of your fear while projecting that you will not be able to speak coherently because of your terrible headache.
By doing that, the 1st advantage which you are benefitting from is that you are removing and weakening the

frequency of fear. Thereby opening the subtle energy field to bring you a situation that will produce peace or the emotion of normality. Now imagine how good It feels and how much gratitude you have that you are trustingly retrieving cash from your ATM machine.

This 2nd round of tapping was based on releasing the current emotion that you are feeling.

C- Emotions are created because at one time or another you lived them out during an **event** which was probably traumatic enough that even though you no longer think or even consciously remember the **event** with clarity of the memory and the attached frequency are still lodged in your nervous system.

Take the time to tap through the parts of the **event** that you remember.

As you tap you will realise that you are getting 'Ahha' moments.

Write down whatever pops into your mind and when you finish this round of tapping, start another round of tapping on the new aspect of the event that came back to your memory. The aim is to talk yourself through the event while tapping and thereby removing and deleting any negative frequencies related to that specific event. The fact that you remember them, even hazily proves that the negative frequency is still live in your nervous system and is a cause for blocking whatever you want to manifest in your life currently.

D- As you are tapping backwards into time, you are reaching your 'Ground Zero" which is your belief system. We all have enabling and limiting beliefs. They are the building blocks of our personalities and our realties.

The most powerful beliefs are those running 24/7 in our subconscious and since we have no way to know what is in our subconscious, we can only access it by reverse engineering.

Which is why you began your tapping round on the symptom (the leaves), then you tapped out the emotions (the branches) attached to that symptom.

And went deeper into recalling the event (the tree trunk) where you can remember what happened

Now, when you take the time to listen to your intuition you will soon discover your 'enabling' and 'limiting' beliefs. (Tree roots).

Tapping Tree

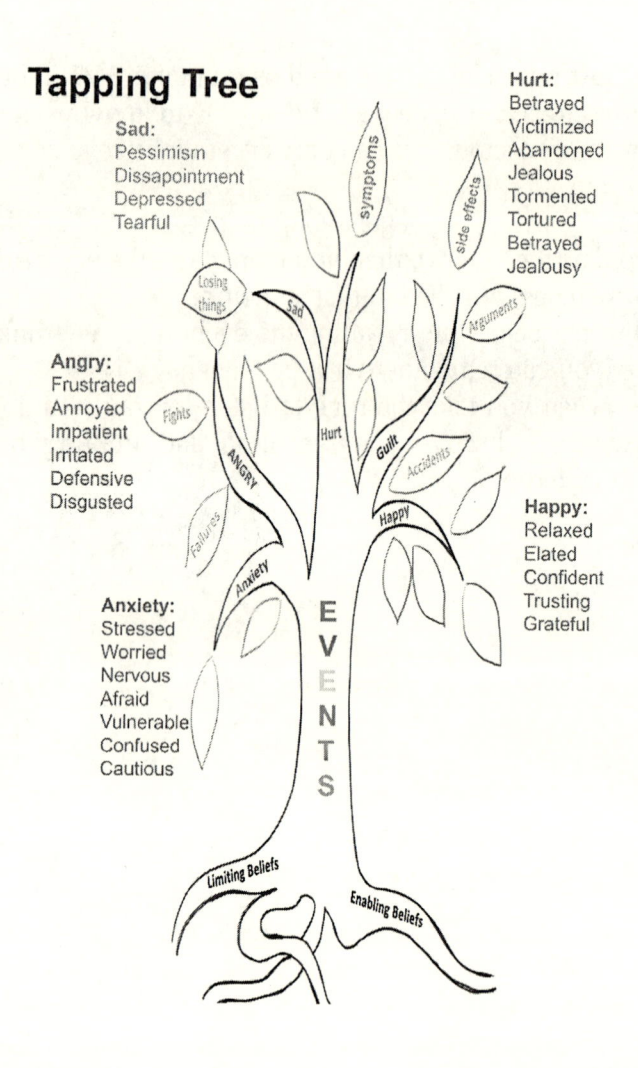

Sad:
Pessimism
Dissapointment
Depressed
Tearful

Hurt:
Betrayed
Victimized
Abandoned
Jealous
Tormented
Tortured
Betrayed
Jealousy

Angry:
Frustrated
Annoyed
Impatient
Irritated
Defensive
Disgusted

Happy:
Relaxed
Elated
Confident
Trusting
Grateful

Anxiety:
Stressed
Worried
Nervous
Afraid
Vulnerable
Confused
Cautious

Leaves: symptoms, side effects, Losing things, Sad, Arguments, Fights, Hurt, Guilt, Accidents, Failures, Happy, Anxiety

Trunk: EVENTS

Roots: Limiting Beliefs, Enabling Beliefs

LEAVES represent:
The symptoms & side effects in your
life which you have a problem with in one way or another

BRANCHES represent:
The emotions that one feels in conjunction with the symptoms/side effects identified in the leaves.
Familiarize yourself with different emotions and nuances that stream through your body at times.3

Here is a short list of some emotions and their nuances.
Anger: Frustrated, Annoyed, Impatience, Irritation, Defensive, Disgusted,

Anxiety: Stressed, Worry, Nervous, Afraid, Vulnerable, Confused, Cautious

Hurt: Betrayed, Victimized, Abandoned, Jealous, Tormented, Tortured

Sad: Pessimism, Disappointment, Depressed, Tearful

Guilt: Obsessive preoccupation, Shame, Grieving

TREE TRUNK represent:
All the moments /events in your life when the corresponding emotion to the symptom / side effects manifested.
Choose an emotion and then remember at what type of event, moment or situation occurred.
Next identify one by one all the other events in your life where you felt that same emotion. Do a complete session of tapping rounds on each event. This clears out the buried yet active vibrations per event.

Examples:
- I felt anger when I was not given the respect to say my side of the story.
- I remember a time that I was angry, hurt, etc at my friend's wedding.
- I remember when the sales clerk was rude to me at the grocery store.
- I remember when I felt hopeless in court.
- I remember how worthless I felt when my parents did not come to my school play.
- I remember how disappointed I was when my friend did not support my ideas at a meeting.

Even if you don't remember many details of the event, tap and say out loud what you do remember. Trust that the energetic cleansing process of infinite intelligence of your mind- body -spirit knows what to diffuse and transmute out of your autonomous nervous system.

TREE ROOTS represent:
Your unknown beliefs. We are the result of our beliefs.
Limiting beliefs: I am not good – rich – intelligent – attractive – popular – educated , etc... enough.
Enabling beliefs: I can do anything I put my mind to.
I am lucky. I am healthy. I have great friends. Most people are honest.

Beliefs are the basis of what our subconscious mind acts on. In order to 'transform-improve-evolve' into your new 2.0 upgraded image of yourself; your subconscious mind which is your invisible operating system needs to be reprogrammed.

This is why you tap out limiting beliefs and replace them by tapping in the enabling beliefs which you choose to operate from.

And so, you go to work and tap and talk, even if it is not coherent to you, just let the words spill out of your self-talk and hear what you are saying. Your subconscious beliefs are being given the freedom of speech and they are manifesting themselves via words. Listen carefully to what you are saying. You are beginning to 'KNOW' yourself. Your new-found knowledge of self gives the basis for seeing your subconscious blueprint and crossing out on the existing blueprint which you realise is no longer of any use to you. Replace it with a new blueprint of the energy and belief systems you want to install into your nervous energy system now.
This is called reprogramming.

EFT: The extra mile!
It can happen that the session did not work on you or provide strong and measurable enough results, so you can do the 'Extra Mile 'as I call it or you can wait and sleep on it overnight and measure yourself the next morning. For some people tapping is such a drain on their energy that they can become either weepy or very tired. I suggest sleeping on it overnight. But in the morning if you feel you want more or stronger results, then do this short procedure.

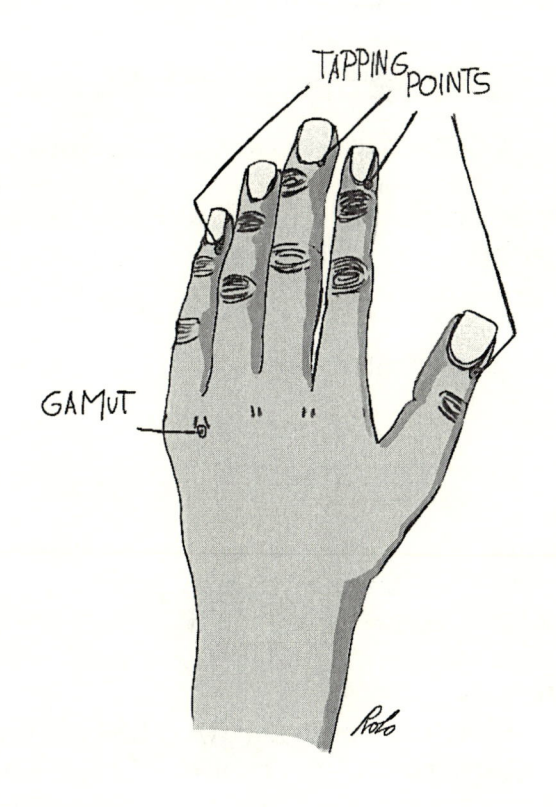

The Gamut Point (tap continuously on the gamut point while you tap your way through the next points
1-   Tap thumb = Lungs
2-   Tap index finger = Large intestine point
3-   Tap middle finger =circulation point
4-   Tap the gamut point: It is on the top (outside) of your hand about 1 inch down at the bottom of a V point between your 4th and 5th finger.

Keep on tapping non-stop on this
gamut point while you do the following:

a) 5-Close eyes – Open eyes- Look down to the left (keep your head still)
b) 6-Look down to the right keeping the head absolutely still.
c) 7-Roll eyes in a circle in one direction- change direction and roll your eyes in an opposite direction.
d) 8-Hum for 5 seconds
e) 9-Count to 5
f) Hum one more time for 5 seconds

TAPPING TIPS

Finger tapping is very useful if you are in public and cannot tap openly, it is also very useful if you suffer from insomnia. You can finger tap while laying down in the same position

Don't worry about tapping the right way, EFT is a very forgiving negative energy deletion tool. Discover what works best for you, as you notice and experience the almost immediate calming vibes you feel and the fast relaxations you will enjoy as you rapidly unwind. Follow your intuition and that way you will get it right.

Finger tapping is easily absorbable in your daily rituals.

Tapping happens at a very deep and inner level, oftentimes you will not immediately notice or feel any shift of energy.

- Always be sure to use the KC set up phrase. This is very important as if you run out of words to say while tapping

your body knows what to focus on as you explained it during the KC Set up phrase.
- Make sure to keep your start and end numbers as a little chart in your tapping book. This is how you will be able to measure your improvements.
- Tap for at least 3 rounds but don't over tap an issue either, the ideal time is between 5 to 15 minutes sessions of tapping.
- Pressure and tapping on the Gamut point is ideal for releasing stress. (The Gamut point in on the back of your hand between the pinkie and the ring finger about 2 cm down at the point of the V.

Instructions for tapping the Gamut procedure

On the thumb, index, 3rd finger, and pinkie tap on the side of the finger that is facing you when you hold your hand up straight.
But be sure to tap on the ring finger on the outside of the finger.
The tapping point is where the nail meets the finger.
Also tap on wrists,
And you can tap under the breasts and nipple which are the liver points.
For those of you who are beginners at tapping there is a lot of information above, so I have put together a generic script which is easy to follow as you fill in your blanks on a 'need to release' basis. Play with it as you relax into the script you will soon come up with your own words. Remember there is only one way to make a mistake when tapping. And that is NOT TO TAP!

KC: Even though I have a bad feeling because I still love and accept my feelings.

KC: Despite being (say something negative) I deeply and completely accept myself despite have this (repeat the problem)

KC: Even though every time this happens to me, and I feel my (name a positive feeling) draining away from me, I realise that I have the gift of choice, and I choose to say despite everything that "I love, accept and respect myself"

KC: Even though this (describe what) looks terrible right now, and I am feeling (describe your bad feeling) I am consciously choosing to trust in my Higher Power and in my positivity that I will be safely guided through this moment, and it is only a learning curve or lesson.

EB: I feel (state the negative emotion)

SE: I feel (state the negative emotional or mental feeling or state of mind)

UE: I feel (state a painful or uncomfortable physical feeling)

UN: I don't enjoy feeling or being any of the above, I am aware that my body and soul are speaking to me

CH: I have decided that I want to feel (State how you want to feel positively)

CB: Even though I don't know how to achieve that

UA: I start my day with positive intentions

TH: But I get more and more (depressed / angry/ jealous/ vengeful/ despaired/ etc.) as the day goes by.

EB: I have the best intentions

SE: And then ... wam- bam ... (describe what happens)

UE: And I am flooded with drama scenarios

UN: I must start all over again and nothing ever goes smoothly

CH: To add to all my problems I also have to deal with... (explain what your other current related problem is)
CB: I am overwhelmed by too many setbacks.
UA: I am exhausted from all my worries and disappointments.
TH: I want to give up.
EB: I am going making a clear decision today to spend 5 minutes thinking positively.
SE: While I am stretching my imagination to think of myself in a positive scenario
UE I will be distancing my 'Present feelings" from all that overwhelm.
UN: I am committing to looking at my situations daily for 5 minutes and mentally playing with any ideal solution I want.
CH: I am having fun exploring all the limitless solutions I can imagine and think of.
CB: I have all the control I want over my thoughts
UA: And I choose to think positive, even if it is just purely a fairy tale for the moment.
TH: The positive thoughts I choose to think are the first step for the universe to get my message
EB: As I commit to daily tapping on my ideal outcome
SE: I trust that my body is getting used to a "positive" frequency
UE: And that frequency is gradually becoming my default frequency
UN: I trust that my body is now being reprogrammed
CB: to the frequency of happiness and success.
UA: I am consciously enjoying myself and choose positive traits and feelings.
TH: I choose to believe that I am becoming a winner. My body is reprograming my energy. I am grateful for that.

Sometimes people get complete relief before a few tapping rounds have even taken place and sometimes others get results after a few months. I have noticed with my clients that the average is between 5 and 15 sessions. If it does not work, simple keep on tapping. I have found it to be the quickest release of all the modalities, from Reiki through to meditation.

But I always advise my clients that even when the issue is cleared to switch your tapping focus onto the next issues. Everyone has a lot of baggage that they will be very happy to off-load for ever.

STEP BY STEP FOR A SAMPLE 'FORGIVENESS MEDITATION'

1. Pick something easy.
2. See this person in front of you.
3. Feel the pain they caused you for 30 seconds.
4. Ask yourself: why did they do what they did?
5. Think about what you could gain from this experience.
6. Forgive into love.
7. To forgive yourself: see the younger version of yourself and apply the same technique.

In most cases tapping, produces amazingly positive results where nothing else has. After almost 15 years of being available to the general public a lot of clinical tests, studies and scientific research have been carried out on the body's subtle energies.
That is why partial and total relief from panic and anxiety, all mode of addictions in children and adults whether

physical, mental, and emotional pains and difficulties are eradicated. Victims of abuse and trauma regain a healthy balanced life. The amazing testimonials go on and on.

My advice is NIKE's advice... JUST DO IT!
As the title of this chapter states. These techniques are not only for deleting negative and harmful subtle energies and frequencies in us but also to install and create positive and enabling subtle energy waves. So....

TAP IN YOUR AFFIRMATIONS

Be very aware of all shifts in your body's feelings that arise imperceptibly while you are tapping and saying your affirmations out loud. Those are sensations, be sure to tap on them. The sensations are more than likely your body fighting back or resisting those affirmations
1. Tap on those sensations.
2. Notice any objections your mind has to your affirmations. Make a list of your objections and take your time to tap through them. If you commit to a daily 10-minute tapping ritual, you will have ample time to tap away or diminish your objections.
Even though I feel I can't overcome my [name fear], I deeply and completely accept myself.

3. Make a list of your affirmations.
   Say them daily while you also tap.
4. Tap while formulating new affirmations.
   Notice how your body feels as you experiment with different wording for your affirmations. Choose the wording that produces the most positive physical sensation.

5. Identify the objections that arise in your mind while thinking about your affirmations.
   In emotional freedom techniques, or EFT, we call these "tail-enders" because they pop up at the end of an affirmation, giving you all the reasons why the affirmation can't be successful.

   To have an impact, affirmations should be charged with high emotion. What's a way of stating your desire that engages your passion? Saying "I want a nice house" is a limp statement. Saying "I want the house of my dreams" has more positive energy. Saying "I am now living in the white two-story house by the beach in the south of France with the wrap-around deck" is far more concrete and is much more likely to get you emotionally fired up.

AFFIRMATIONS SHOULD BE STATED IN

PRESENT TENSE

Affirming that "I'm going to have plenty of money" pushes the event into the future. You might manifest your affirmation in 10 years. In 10 years, you'll still be in a state in which you are going to have plenty of money. Sometime, but always in the future. Saying that someday later you'll accomplish your dream means that you never reach the state in which it exists right here and now.
Affirmations are meant to be vivid and detailed.
If you are affirming health, what does health mean to you? Is it linked to outdoor activities like hiking, kayaking, and biking? Walking on the beach? Soaking in

a hot tub? Being slender? Eating certain foods? Create a vivid and detailed picture of exactly what you want and affirm that.

AFFIRMATIONS SHOULD BE CRYSTAL CLEAR

Write them down and then refine them, becoming clearer with each revision. Affirmations should be positive, stating what you do want, instead of what you don't want.
I recommend creating affirmations after meditating or another spiritual practice that puts you into an elevated mental state.

Script for 'Negative & critical self-talk'

KC Karate Chop- EB Eyebrow – SE Side of eye- UE Under eye- UN Under nose- CH Chin- CB Collar bone- UA Under arm – TH Top of head.

KC. Even though I have a bad habit of sarcastically putting myself down I do love myself
KC Even though I speak harshly to and about myself I do respect myself
KC Even though I would never speak to anyone else the way I speak to or about myself it is amazing how much I deeply and honestly love myself and my life.
EB I am rude to myself
SE It is my self-critical voice
UE My self-critical voice speaks up with my invitation

UN and when it starts to speak, I can make it quiet
CH I notice everything that I am doing incorrectly
CB I lash out at myself for being stupid.
UA but that is a lie, because I know I am not stupid
TH It is just the easy cop out to label myself stupid & moronic.
EB While I hear and say my critical comments
SE Telling me I am not good enough
UE That people will see through me and see me as a fraud
UN That I am not as knowledge as I pretend to be
CH That I am not the hotshot I would like to be validated as
CB I am scared that people will see me as a failure.
UA I find it very hard to stop the self-criticism in full flow
TH And if I am speaking to people I am scared they will think I am nuts if I change my so called humoristic self-criticism in mid-sentence.
EB I have a chatting pessimistic voice in my head like a broken record and I can't switch it off.
SE The words on the record say that I am not good enough
UE But as I know the words, I feel safe in a way.
UN Even though I know that those words are poisoning me.
CH I feel that I am addicted to my negative self-talk. It is so familiar to me.
CB Somewhere I think that my negative self-talk is my friend because it always points out what I am doing wrong.
UA So I give myself the excuse that it is keeping me safe.
TH It protects me from further disappointments as I allow myself to believe ahead of time that I am a failure anyhow.

EB My critical voice is reliable that is why I allow it to be my friend.
SE Only because I have heard it for so long.
UE But is it really my friend? Or has it just found a willing victim and is feeding on my energy at my expense for its own fun?
UN I am waking up to the fact that the critical voice is my enemy, it only cares about itself.
CH If I continue to give the go – ahead to my critical voice I will end up in a mess. Just like my critical voice is.
CB My intuition just told me I am having a wakeup call, and that I should not shut off the wake-up alarm If I know what is good for me.
UA I have paid too high a price in loss of time and opportunities of happiness and fulfilment by being a victim of my negative self-talk
TH I have allowed my pessimistic thoughts to high jack my happiness.
EB I realise that my critical voice only seemed real to me because I was practiced to it.
SE But today I am revving up my energy, switching gears and saying that horrible broken record," Critical Voice the party is over …Goodbye and good riddance"
UE Every day I hear my intuitive voice clearer and clearer.
UN I am enjoying getting in sync with my better self.
CH I am enjoying all the good things I am doing.
UA I am enjoying all the good things, situations, and people around me
TH I am so busy making my dreams come true
EB I am doing what is best for me.
SE I am trusting my intuitive voice
UE My intuition is becoming clearer the more I hear it.

UN This is my new journey
CH: I am full power ahead on positivity
CB I am enjoying my positive power and focus
UA I am free to change ways when it does not feel right
TH I am learning my new positive language. My self - awareness grows daily.
EB Today is a new day with new positive awareness's. My future is exciting

Exercise 2

HO'OPONOPONO

<u>**Ho'oponopono**</u> is an ancient philosophy of life practised still today in the South Pacific for pardon and peace.

Similar forgiveness practices were performed on islands throughout Polynesia, Hawaii, including Samoa, Tahiti, and New Zealand. Traditionally Hoʻoponopono was practiced by healing priests or kahuna lapaʻau among family members of a person who was physically ill. It has been successfully used to cure mental problems and illnesses within group communities and families.

It as a spiritually connected mental energy aide which ethically sets the intention and action with good wishes attached. It cleans up negativity which is locked in the never-ending loops of habitual and subconsciously familiar energy patterns.

As we clear others, we ourselves are cleaned and vice – versa.

My un-romantic description of Karma is one of Inherited behaviour modes and patterns, which are simply one or multiple memory/energy frequencies that were passed on in birth and embedded themselves in the highways of our nervous system. The good news is, that you can erase negative Karma. This is proven scientifically thanks to the research work on Epigenetics mostly bought to light by Dr Bruce Lipton, which shows how genes change in an environment. This means that when you change your vibrational frequency your inner environment changes allowing the memories in the DNA to transform.

Under old beliefs in the traditions of the people of the South Pacific, and for that matter also world-wide, it is an accepted fact that when or if one breaks the laws of nature, whether they are, emotional, mental, or behavioural that physical discomfort of one sort or another will manifest in the body sooner or later.

Chemical medication and treatments, such as surgery are useful but will only remove the symptoms because the reasons which are the energy frequencies of buried, unforgotten unconscious and subconscious memories and beliefs will still be operational. That is why energy medicine is a basic need for ongoing physical and mental health.

Today the psycho-spiritual, self-help procedure is very simple, the difficulty comes in the accurateness and self-honesty which you will want to incorporate in every self-session of Ho'oponopono.

The process involves going over the same procedure addressing all resentments one by one. Like the peeling of an onion until such time that you have addressed all you can feel, remember, or think of.

Ho'oponopono is best used as a daily ritual, even for a few minutes.

Modern versions are performed within the family by a family elder, or by the individual alone.

Ho'oponopono means to make right. Essentially, it means to make it right with the ancestors, or to make right with the people with whom you have relationships.

When we forgive others, who are we forgiving? Ourselves, of course.

The Ho'oponopono prayer consists of 4 lines, as seen below. I feel that it is always best to begin with 'I love you' because the vibration of love is the most powerful that exists. Since you are speaking to your Spirit, your soul, your Higher Power which resides in you, it is always more welcoming to be met with love then to say "I am sorry'

I love you
I am sorry
Please forgive
Thank You

The deeper meaning of those four statements is:

I love you Higher Power with all my heart and soul. I like to think of apologising to my inner child, aka my subconscious.

I am sorry (regret) dear Higher Power that I do not think as you do. You are there for the universe, but you are also in and around me. Again, here I think of my personality while I say 'That my thoughts vary from yours. And I am getting to realise and accept that I have made mistakes and I regret the pain I caused myself due to the mistakes I made that came from my ego.'

Please forgive me dear Higher Power that I do not love myself as much as you love me. I have made mistakes in my beliefs and thoughts for which I take responsibility, but I ask for your forgiveness so that the emotions attached to my errors leave me forever, allowing me to become whole, happy, and positively vibrant. Cleaning me in depth as only you can, so that my current platform transmutes in to one of positive memories of good health, happiness, all forms of success and financial abundance.

- Dear Higher Power, now I am addressing my super-consciousness. Thank you for your love and your belief in me that your will be done completely.

Either before or while you are saying your prayer set a specific intention in your heart of whom you are doing Ho'oponopono on, and what is the ideal loving outcome you are seeing yourself experiencing.

The following guideline for a visualisation will help you integrate the method.

I like to use these words as a prayer in my Ho'oponopono daily rituals.

I ask that the negative memories I hold in myself which are the reasons and causes of my problems and of other people's problems in my life be transmuted into positive memories of:

Happiness, Good Health, Success
and
Financial Abundance.

a. Then recall anyone with whom you do not feel totally aligned to or supported by.
b. In your mind's eye, construct a small stage below yourself.
c. See in your hearts eye an infinite source of love and healing flowing from a source above the top of your head from your Spirit or Higher Self, and open the crown of your head, flooding the source of love and healing down into your body and low out your heart to heal up the person on the stage. Be sure it is all right for you to heal the person and that they accept the healing.
d. When the healing is complete, have a discussion with the person and forgive them. Ask and allow them to forgive you.

e. Next, let go of the person, and see them floating away. As they do, cut the cord that connects the two of you which is the vibrational frequency allowing the telepathic communication between you and the person you are focussing on in this Ho'oponopono session.
f. If you are healing in a current primary relationship, then assimilate the person inside you.
g. Do this with every person in your life with whom you are incomplete, or not aligned.
h. The final test is, can you see the person or think of them without feeling any negative emotions. If you do feel negative emotions when you do, then do the process again.

I find it astonishing that almost a century after famous researchers and scientists have discovered and proved that quantic physics impacted energy medicine in a beneficial manner and has such tremendous benefits to those who practice and use various energy tools, that in the whole energy tools remain unknown by most of the population. And sadly, in many cases when certain people do know about the quantum power of thought energy, it is simply dismissed. I think the dismissal occurs because it is too much effort for people to stretch their minds to accept that they are so much more powerful than what they think they are. Quantic physics prove beyond the shadow of a doubt how thought changes matter.

Ho'oponopono erases with ease and wisdom the limiting memories blocking positive memories, beliefs, thoughts, and manifestations from occurring.
Without help from anyone the constant practice of Ho'oponopono erases in all those who practice it limiting negative beliefs. Out with the old and in with the ideal

new of what we all want. The daily practice rituals of Ho'oponopono eradicates jealousy and angers. It clears the inner and outer space in our energy auras to transmute for deep self-love, forgiveness, compassion, and comprehension to quickly bubble to the surface voluntarily or not.

Ho'oponopono is about clearing out blocks in ourselves that are manifested in others and thanks to our knowledge of the mirror principal we allow the Higher Power to clean up inside of ourselves what shows up on the outside or in others. Peace infiltrates and starts to radiate outwards.

Exercise 3

STICK PEOPLE

Cut negativity between you and another person, a situation, a business and even your attachment to a past life. It is all about cutting the negative energy ties and setting your mind and your heart free.

This very simple and highly effective deletion tool was imagined and created by a French Canadian called Jacques Martel. He wrote many books which are easy to find by typing in his name into Google. They very clearly illustrate and explain the deeper meanings of this method. In this chapter I will give you the 5 steps to follow which give the measurable results.

All you need is a sheet of paper a pencil and a pair of scissors. You can if you want used coloured crayons to draw the lines between the 7 differently coloured chakras, but it is not necessary.

When you do the drawings, the quality of the sketch is not important. It is all about the clarity and the purity of your intention.

When your drawing is complete, cut the page down the middle so you are on one page and the other person or people are on the other page.

Now you have freed yourself from the negative energies. But you have not to cut your ties with the person. You can do this with your spouse, children, parents, and everyone you love. You are cleansing the energy and restoring the relationship to a higher level.

Step 1- Start on the left side of the page first draw a stick man that will represent yourself or your team.

On top of the stick person write your name and those of anyone else on your side such ask the name of your company, club, or group.

Then draw your aura circle all the way around that stick man and the name or names you wrote on top of the stick man's head.

On the outside of the circle make little lines which symbolise the rays of the sun.

In other words, you are placing yourself inside a circle of light.

Step 2a- On the right side of the page do the same thing, except on top of this stick man's head, write the name of the person, people, group or anyone or thing with which you have an interaction and that you want to cut all negative ties with or free any energies that are disturbing on a conscious or subconscious level.

Step 2b If you are having a general problem not related to a person but to a situation, for example your dissatisfaction with your work, or your social life, or your community etc.

Instead of drawing a stick man on the right, draw a long rectangle the same height as would maybe be a stick man, and inside of that rectangle write out in bullet points your issues. For example, Aggressiveness at work, lack of transparency, I am bullied by my school or social media friends. I am underpaid for my work. Lack of satisfaction – disappointment – frustration etc. at the workplace (then write out the name of the company or sports team, community etc.) Draw the little lines representing the light all the way around the rectangle. Take your time to do it, giving your intention the relaxed and focused time to connect its metaphysical message and command to the universe.

Step 3- Now draw a line between the chakras of both stick people or the situational rectangle box.

The 1st chakra Start at the root chakra situated at the base of the trunk of the body which is colour red. That chakra impacts our physical strength and is largely attributed to our sexuality. The gonads are linked to the base chakra.

The 2nd chakra called the 'Sacral Chakra' is in the womb area and the colour is orange it relates to the lymphatic system, the bladder and of course the female reproductive organs. Joy, compassion, taste buds and creativity are connected to that chakra.

The 3rd chakra is at the height of the solar plexus and the colour is yellow. It represents success in all areas, business, personal, relationships. The yellow colour as the name solar suggests, promotes confidence, charisma, respect for all including ourselves. The adrenal glands are connected to the solar plexus chakra.

The 4th chakra is the heart chakra, and the colour is green. The gateway of all our emotions inwards and outwards occurs in the heart. Thanks to the sensory neurites in our heart, it is proven today that we not only feel emotions but also think cognitively with our hearts. Look up the work of Md. PhD J. Andrew Armour.

The 5th chakra is the throat with a bay blue, dark turquoise colour. The throat represents communication. Emotional and physical health get impacted by stress in relation to disruptive and aggressive communication. The physical symptoms can express themselves via colds, sore throats, soreness in the mouth and the gums.

The 6th chakra is the 3rd eye. Situated on the middle of the forehead just about the eyebrows. It is represented in blue indigo and is your gateway to perceptions and intuition. Foresight occurs via the 6th sense or otherwise known as the 3rd eye.

The 7th chakra is the crown. Situated at the top of the skull towards the back of the head. It is coloured purple, and our live wired consciousness allows us to access a higher degree of awareness way beyond that of our ego, worries and ego-based visions throughout our life's journey.

Step 4: Draw clockwise a very large line all the way around both stickmen. It is an outer rim circle. Once more draw the little lines outside the outer rim circle, representing the rays of sunlight.
Step 5: Draw a straight line connecting each chakra starting with yourself on the left and connecting to the chakra point of the stickman on the right side.

If you have a situational box on the right instead of the stickman, then simply draw the lines into the box at the height where the chakras would be situated if it were a stickman.

Step 6: The cutting and separation process. Take a pair of scissors, a knife and cut down the middle of the drawing or else you can also tear up the page down the middle between both figures. Your subconscious mind has registered the instruction to separate yourself from the negative energies you no longer wish to be subject to represented by the stickman on the right or the situation box.
This is an energy tool, and like each energy deletion tool, they all have many ramifications. For the Stickman you can find much more in-depth explanations of the benefits in Jaques Martel's book.

Exercise 4

STOP COMPLAINING
MEMO BOARD FOR NEGATIVE THOUGHTS

Even though positive thinking is optimal, and vibrationally ideal, contrary to what you might have heard it helps to list your negative feelings, ideas, and thoughts on a board or in a book. The simple gesture of acknowledging and writing down your negativity, and then reading them allows your brain to focus quietly and gently disconnect by conscious choice from what your eyes see on the board. By looking at the words without judgement your emotional charge will drop.

It is a form of yoga mindfulness, and it assists your limbic brain to gradually disconnect the ignition of your negative feelings.

Keep the book or board handy so that your 'mind' knows where all your mental garbage is, and like that your mind will relax and choose in peace to feel uplifted and trusting in reaching your goals.

2- PUT YOUR THOUGHTS ON PAUSE

Have you ever felt that your mind is running away, totally out of control.? It can happen under stressful situations when we don't know which way to turn or what to do next because we are overwhelmed with our own thoughts.

Thoughts don't even stay cognitive long enough to decode them before other thoughts are in your mind.

The quickest and easiest way to stop that is to open your mouth and make sure that your tongue is neither touching your upper palate or your lower palate. Have you noticed that many people tend to keep their mouth open as if waiting for someone to spoon feed them? Their body language is saying that they are processing emotional information mostly on an intellectual level.

Keep your tongue well balanced in the middle of your mouth for about 30 seconds and you will have reset your brain to normal. By doing that your internal self-chatter instantly disappears and your brain waves calm down.

1- Close your eyes if you can, obviously not if you are driving or operating machinery.
2- Let your mouth open and your jaw drop, like when you are surprised.

3- Feel the tension disconnect in the back of your tongue as you allow it to relax.
4- Balance your tongue in the middle of your mouth and feel it float as you exhale.
5- You might feel your tongue thicken a bit.
This movement allows the brain waves to reset and now you can proceed again on a clean thought platform.

Exercise 5

PIVOT TOOL

Switch from negative to Positive affirmations in the moment
As soon as you are in a bad space, mentally or emotionally on the spur of the movement break all conversation with anyone else do the absolute opposite.

Exercise 6

COMBAT LONELINESS.

Loneliness is terribly unhealthy. A lonely person is a sad person and sadness also goes to the lungs. Studies report that physical loneliness is worse for your health then a pack of cigarettes every day or being overweight.
Being connected on Facebook, or any other social media platform does not play a part in being connected physically.

You need to speak to real people, in a real world and not virtually. Speaking to others confirms that you are part of a community and enforces the subconscious belief that you are alive. You will feel like a hero when you have accomplished an important act of life which is to feel and experiment the capacity of connecting to another person's heart. The only way to get confirmation of that is from the other person to whom you have connected with. Learn to connect in a friendly way physically to other people. Bond with people.
There is science to this. Harvard research shows that physical connection bonds measurable energy between humans.
A clean surface is the fundamental for fresh paint to stick on the wall for a long time. The above tools and principals will remove the blocks that are not only holding you back, but which are also stopping good things to come to you. Until you repeatedly use one or more of the self-cleaning tools you will be living life in the hard, rugged, unfriendly, and fearful path. Life will be a struggle and you will most likely not reach your goals, and if you do you might not stay there.
Even if you are sceptical about what you read, and many people are! throw your scepticism out the window and give it a committed try. You have nothing to lose but failure and everything to gain including success.

All transformation and change that is worthwhile to implement needs a focused commitment to self-improvement and stickablilty to wipe out months or years of counterproductive habits. Breathe in and just do it! Deleting negativity sets you free.
Let's close the chapter on a positive note of creation. Once you have emptied your glass of everything that is

no longer serving you, say this little prayer which I have already included in the Ho'oponopono self-vacuuming process.

"I ask that the negative memories I hold in myself which are the reasons and the causes of my problems and other people's problems in my life be transmuted into positive memories of: Happiness, Good Health, Success, and Financial Abundance.
Thank you, so be it. It is done."

CHAPTER NINETEEN

NO BLAME ATTRACTS FAME

"People are always blaming their circumstances for what they are. I don't believe in circumstances. The people who get on in this world are those who get up and look for circumstances they want, and if they can't find them, they make the circumstances happen."
George Bernard Shaw

Don't blame others or yourself. The only reason you have not YET reached your goal or achieved what you would have wished to achieve is because you are unknowingly running contrary limiting beliefs to what or whom you consciously want to be. The act of blaming will only keep you wedged where you are now, but when you decide to use your:' Response-Ability' you will be claiming your freedom and changing the course of your life to success. Most people, whether they are poor or rich, educated or not, male or female are still asleep in Laladreamland and not even conscious that whatever their focus has been has become their reality.

They simply live their lives in a thoughtless loop, repeating the same patterns repeatedly without realizing that they can and should get a hold of themselves to create new patterns that will produce different realities.

In chapters 6 'Know what you want' and in the upcoming chapter 24 'Self Analysis- Know yourself' 'you will have identified your good and bad behaviors which have led and will continue to lead you to the same results in the future.

TIP: Keep what is good, don't fix what is not broken and take the time to reprogram the limiting and damaging beliefs which have recorded unwittingly into your nervous system.

Your 'learned' counterproductive behaviors are the result of the impact of actions and words of other people who have randomly and probably unknowingly acquired certain beliefs and behaviors which have sabotaged their lives and are now sabotaging your life.

Luckily this is not a death sentence for your dreams and objectives. The unknown and invisible sub-conscious patterns which you are running are recordings on an old tape which is going around and round in a loop playing out in the form of bad thoughts, feelings behaviors which delivers situations and results completely contrary to what you want.

The fuel of our beliefs whether conscious or not are the ramifications of old stories. But many old stories no longer serve a constructive purpose in your life today.

When you were very young, you were taught never to speak to strangers who approached you, as you could be in danger. And to drive the point home to you as a young impressionable child, that advice was accompanied by telling you a scary and dramatic story as to anchor the fear of God into you, to never speak to strangers.

That story maybe served its purpose when you were 4 or 5 years old, but if you hold on to that story today as an adult, and sadly many adults do, you will miss out on meeting fabulous people with whom you can interact with.

Recognize that you are now an adult, and you want to choose stories you want to hear and tell according to what you want to experience today and tomorrow.

ust as you would not talk to a tape which is spewing out stories or tales you don't agree with, you instinctively know that the only way you are going to enjoy hearing the information you want to hear is to delete or remove the current tape and insert a new tape or CD.

The same applies to all your limiting beliefs which are producing certain unwanted and harmful behaviors and are running tracks which are removing you further from the goal or goals you want to live.

Here are some areas which will help you to pinpoint your harmful behaviors such as the bad habit of blaming.

The negative default habit of blaming is your egos way of defending itself from your very own negative subconscious negative impulses of which you were incapable of stopping dead in their tracks.

The ego is so embarrassed of not having control over its negative habits and behaviors that it blames its bad habits to outside circumstances. That outwards projection is named 'blame' to anything outside of the subconscious.

Imagine you are speaking to your closest most trusted unjudging friend, and you would be sharing some worries. Listen to yourself as to what and how you would present the following issues. Can you hear yourself attributing reasons as to why these issues are or have happened?
- Complain about a stinking relationship
- Worries about your health issue or issues
- Your finances are dwindling south to a scary sum?

Have you been doing the wishful and positive thinking that you have heard and read about so often without not only obtaining a result but instead finding that everything has become a struggle?

Ask yourself:

"How did I end up where I am currently"?
"Why am I here, and is this where I really want to be'?
"How can I make the best of my current situation?
"What can I use to go forward in the directions I am choosing today?"
Carefully study chapter '17 Deletion Tools' to learn and apply different modalities, beliefs, and default empowering thoughts with which your nervous system will rewrite and calibrate the according emotion usefully.

Accept the fact that it is your subconscious programs which are making you 'misconceive' your potential.
The subconscious is a vehicle which runs 24/7 your belief system. And since your reality is a mirror of your subconscious wishes, you know that the ONLY reason for your current unwanted situation is because you are running the wrong program for yourself.
Solution: Use the tools and the techniques in this book to delete your current blocking programs and replace with programs that encode the future memories of what you want to happen.

You are far more powerful that you imagine, and as you take the time to learn about yourself and clearly identify your goals, also take the actions to change yourself and not anyone or anything outside of yourself.
This is what will happen as you discover and apply the different exercises and approaches to THINK ACHIEVEMENT & WATCH IT HAPPEN.
All the solutions work, but you must discover which ones you like best or work best for you. Knowing them is great. But knowledge does not deliver results. Only ongoing practice of the technique works. However, the time you invest in yourself by trying out which exercises you

resonate best with is what will allow you to successfully manifest the reality of your dreams and wishes.

Say goodbye to blame and excuses forever. From this moment on, don't talk to anyone or even entertain thoughts as to why you have not or cannot.
Dismiss the negative aspects of your mentality as a thing of the past. By doing that you are releasing and uncovering your powers to manifest your desired goals. When things don't go as you want them to go, your new question will be:
 "What belief is this new situation mirroring to me? "And if you don't know then apply Ho'oponopono. (Chap 18)

Remember that words are energy, ask yourself:
 "What words or sentences have I been using that have manifestly played against me?"
 "What on earth have I done to create this unwanted situation?"
 "How can I do it better next time"?
Stop defending your bad habits when someone kindly volunteers their opinion as to what in their opinion you can or should do differently next time. It is amazing the verbal garbage we can dredge up to defend our bad habits. Those habits can range from bad diet to why you drive instead of walk, to why you go to bed very late instead of getting your nightly dose of balanced sleep and so on. Your automatic defense refutations are nothing else but a waste of your precious time, energy, and breath.
Success comes with an open mind. Keep on educating yourself daily on all sorts of subjects. Choose one subject of interest to you and read up on it one hour every day. Your lack of knowledge can be very quickly turned

around. You are the reason for your lack of education, nothing and no one else is.

If your reality does not match your dreams, then change your game. Or in this case, change your attitude. Take responsibility for everything you feel, think, say, do and are.

Here is a very easy to understand example as to how you are the cause of your results.
You win $1,000 in the lottery and you splash out on great clothes, even though your closet is already bulging and stuffed. You will have nothing to put aside when the sales come along in 3 months' time.
Then just as the sales come along, you have an unexpected bill to settle and so you now blame that unexpected bill on the fact that you can't go and enjoy the sales.
Or
You win $1,000 in the lottery, you wait a few months for the sales to be on, and you spend $ 200 on half price shoes, so now you have two for the price of one. And with the remaining $800.00 you invest into a compounded savings and investment program and in about 15 years from now you have enough to put as a down-payment onto your new home.

Even if the same unexpected bill comes in, you will have some money to go and enjoy the sales. The only thing you will have lost is the opportunity to blame the unexpected bill!

In both cases your future reality is down to your behavior, your thoughts, what you eat and what you think today and going forward into the future. You are the boss of what you allow to happen in your mind, your heart, and your body.

Re-write your beliefs to support the goals you want to reach and claim your life. That is part of taking 'Response - Ability' of your life and your future.

Example: If you have been overweight for years and tried all sorts of diets only to achieve a yo-yo result or even worse being heavier now then years ago, it should be obvious to you that your subconscious is running some type of negative belief to 'BEING' thin.

Instead of blaming diets, dieticians, and events in your life that are tempting you to break your diet. Try this approach.

1- Put a photo of your face on the photo of a body that you want to be.
2- Write an affirmation along the lines of" I feel light, healthy, and attractive in my ideal figure and weighing my ideal weight'
3- Close your eyes and start tapping on whatever negative self-talk is coming up in your mind as you see your photo and read your affirmation. It is more than likely that your self-talk will be negative. Those are your blocking beliefs.
4- Start tapping on the uncomfortable feelings and thoughts you are running right now. Tap for about 5 to 10 minutes
5- Now do a Ho'oponopono mantra for a few minutes. Saying:
a. I love you (say your name). You are addressing your inner child or if you prefer your subconscious. And of course, you love your subconscious because it has a lot of positive programs that you want to keep, namely

organizing all your vital activities without you having to remember to breathe, digest, etc.

b. I am sorry, (you are telling your little inner child that you are sorry you are making them carry around all that excess weight. You realize very often you are eating the wrong foods, not doing enough exercise... etc. etc. Feel the sorrow for putting your inner child through that.

c. Now you want to ask your inner child for Forgiveness, and the mere fact that you are asking for forgiveness automatically signals to your Higher Power, your Guardian Angel, your Divine Intelligence, your Supra-Consciousness, to please step in, and remove all the unwanted limiting memories which are still vibrating in your energy field. The Higher Power will only do it when you ASK for him / her to do it.
And in less than the blink of an eyelid, non- serving blocking memories get erased from your subconscious program.

d. End by saying 'Thank You'. For having helped you clean the deepest recesses of your unknown memory baggage.

Just know and believe that the Higher Power, Divine Intelligence is happy to keep on removing old and recurring memories as long as you keep on asking for the cleansing help!

6- Now sit down in front of your vision board and do whatever inner exercises work for you and 'FEEL' yourself feeling how you can imagine you want to feel if everything is possible in your ideal weight and figure.

You want to aim for feeling that wonderful emotion in your heart more so than in your head. But just start... do it daily and soon you will be living your future memory.

7- Invested at least 20 minutes a day in yourself to start the beliefs foundation for manifesting your wish. You are incubating your manifestation and when all the elements are together it will birth. It must, it always does.

We are all Golden Buddha's. As we take the time daily to both dissolve the hardened clay that we are walking around with and then focus with positivity on our end goals our inner superpowers are being let free to shine and attract the good we want to manifest.

For those of you who might not know why I refer to the true Golden Buddha story, it is to show you the unlimited potential and spiritual energetic power which is the essence of every person.

A few centuries ago, in a remote Thai village there was a monastery which had built a very big Buddha in solid gold. The sculpture is about two and a half meters high. It is thought that at the time the Burmese invaded Thailand forcing the monks to cover their golden Buddha in clay in the hope that the invaders would not notice it's value and leave it standing as a valueless clay statue.

This is obviously what happened, and the golden Buddha remained in its cave for centuries until the monastery relocated in the mid-20th century because a road was going to be built.

When the monks went through the very difficult process of moving this huge clay Buddha, a wrong move produced a crack in the clay and a monk took his flashlight to examine the severity of the crack in the hope that the hardened clay statue would not break and collapse. To his utter surprise he noticed a shimmer from within the crack and gently chiseled away at the hard edges of the clay statue where he uncovered gold!

It soon became obvious that the monks in the monastery centuries past had all been slain and none had left any writings to indicate the value of the gold Buddha in their midst.

It was only when the action to physically move this huge clay statue occurred that the essence of the statue was able to start shining until its value, beauty and symbolism was uncovered.

The moral of the story is that you must take the action to make it happen and as you are generating your own energy in the forward path of life, your inner talents and powers will manifest themselves and play their role in guiding and supporting you to live your dreams and goals.

Taking responsibility, means creating your future according to what and how you want to be, what you want to achieve, experience, share and give to others. Become the author of your future. Write out what you want, pause, and feel if you are being truthful to yourself or are you perhaps re-creating your own version of what others have told you to do, or what you believe others expect of you. Don't complain and don't explain. It is a waste of unrecoverable time. You only complain when you know there is an alternative. When there is no alternative you don't complain you simply accept it as a fact. Well accept the fact that to reach your goal or live your dream there is zero alternative solutions to getting there except yourself.

Of course, there will be more than likely a risk of failing right away. You might end up in a fight or being ridiculed for having attempted something that you were warned not to. But either way you must take a risk. You can choose not to do anything, which is a guarantee of never reaching your goal. But if you want to get to success from where you are now, you are going to be taking risks along the way. So, start enjoying the feeling of adventure as you sail to your goal over choppy and calm waters.

Engage yourself with kindness and for free. A smile costs nothing and accomplishes a lot, therefor smile at others and at yourself. It takes some time to resonate with your own inner truth, but as you keep at it, you are discovering your inner self, and getting to your inner-source and starting point. When you reach your inner truth sweet spot, make a U turn, go forth and reach out to attaining your own goals.

Never blame yourself, because blame is the lowest of all energy vibrations and it does not serve any good purpose. When mistakes and errors occur be thankful as you have just learned a lesson. If you are new to the discoveries of self-improvement and transformation, this will sound strange but as you continue the goal reaching journey, you will become aware how all these tips fall into place and serve you well.
The moment you are aware that you are blaming someone or something for your current circumstances, don't berate and punish yourself, simply pivot your accusation into a question.
If you are again late at work due to another traffic jam, don't blame the traffic, instead ask yourself a question that will find you another transport solution to get you to work on time. Maybe you can cycle, roller-skate, move closer to work, take public transport, leave earlier for

work, and stack your car with interesting audio books so that you can learn while you are stuck in a traffic jam, while not being stressed out because you left for work an hour earlier.
That is taking positive action and you have created the positivity.

Stop living passively, wake up and roar, enjoy the new vibration of living pro-actively.
The words we don't say at times can hurt even more than angry words. Make sure you take the time to smile and say a kind word to your spouse, partners, family, friends. By making the choice to show up for a few seconds of human connection time you have warmed them and supported them. They will most likely be there for you in the future. Even though it is not a crime not to be nice to others, you will pay the price. Life is a boomerang. What you complain about comes back to you, and what you praise also does. So, make the choice of which one you prefer to receive.

Closing advice: Don't play the game of blame and shame and remember that 'luck' is already a part of you. It is NOT exterior to yourself. Just activate it. If you feel ready to grow into your untapped powers remember that a wise person learns from his own mistakes and a genius learns from other people's mistakes as well!

CHAPTER TWENTY

CUT A YEAR IN 12 SLICES

GET HIGH, BE HIGH, STAY HIGH IN YOUR MENTAL, EMOTIONAL AND PHYSICAL PEAK STATE

The mind delivers what is familiar. It takes a while though for the mind to become familiar to what it is doing. That is why you will want to adapt a new habit every month that will give your mind the foundation of being familiar with the good new habit.

Even if you don't like what you are doing in the beginning, say out loud, I love this, it is so enjoyable, I enjoy being good to myself etc. You get the idea. Fake it to make it. You must play with your subconscious like you would with a child. Get the child to do what you want the child to do and enjoy. Otherwise, the child will stop doing it the moment your back is turned away.

Example: If you are on month 6, which is all about physical exercise. And you must do your push-ups. Just say to yourself out loud, "Wow this is such a positive challenge, I really enjoy seeing my body get stronger and more vibrant each time I do my push ups'. Imagine you are acting out an advert for a gym. And if you are acting well, you will get paid a bonus!
DO NOT SAY: 'Ugh I hate doing these pushups etc., but I will struggle through them". Or anything along those negative lines.
You can talk yourself out or into anything. So, choose to make the effort of changing your self- talk and spend

your talk time, by talking yourself IN TO what you want to become.
THINK ACHIEVEMENT & WATCH IT HAPPEN. Choose and use the one liner advice and suggestions throughout the book.

Habits form out of consistency, consistency needs self - discipline and everyone can be self-disciplined.
Train your brain for self-discipline, by doing your chosen rituals daily, and don't let anything, anyone or any valid reason get between you and your daily rituals until you notice that your new self-improved behavior has become a habit.

Even though spirituality has no age or period, in today's tech revolution era technology spirituality is a word that currently resonates with everyone. I therefor often switch the word ritual for a technique or a tool.
After a while, these monthly rituals aka 'Techniques and / or Tools, will become habits. A habit is when your body knows better than your mind what or how to do something.
As all these monthly suggestions are very helpful for everyone, I suggest you do them or create another self-improvement one for yourself. If you already have one or more of these habits, then choose a new habit to install each month.

Take each one and IMPLEMENT them consciously into your daily life for a whole month. Put yourself into a positive frame of mind before. Be aware that you are inserting a new modus operandi into your brain and that it is becoming your new expanded lifestyle.

I promise that in one year from now, you will be living a totally healthy, abundant, and positive reality easily, because the habits of your new default programming will have kicked in and delivered measurable results
.
When you go on to the next month simply add the new behaviors to the one of the previous months. The longer you do them CONSCIOUSLY the deeper the new synaptic connections weave, groove and transform the wiring of your neurons. This is neuroplasticity.
What is easy at first making becomes very difficult later and what is difficult at first becomes very easy later.

MONTH 1: EXPAND YOUR COMMUNICATION

Become vulnerable in the nicest sense possible. Every day take a small risk and speak your mind or give your opinion especially if your opinion is against the grain of what the others think, say, or do. Get used to saying and communicate what you believe in and what or how you want to eat, dress, etc. In other words, become true to yourself. Even if others disagree with you, challenge yourself to express your opinion and not judge other people.
When you cross people in the street, say a hearty 'hello' with a smile. It feels very odd and scary in the beginning and most people will look at you oddly or maybe even rudely ignore you. Don't let that get you down. Make it a challenge to see how many people you can get to smile back or reply with a "Hello". You are stepping out of your comfort zone and are learning to give 'Good Vibrations'

MONTH 2: FOOD

Make a concentrated action to develop and practice clear awareness of what you eat.
If you are walking around in brain fog, it is time to reclaim your focus and your concentration. We are what we eat. And tough moments easily lead to junk food, alcohol, and prescription medicine. I beg you to trust that these very uncomfortable or stressful moments in your life are only lessons and opportunities from the universe for you to put into action good habits instead of succumbing to the easy way and instant gratification of avoiding the very scary situation which you are experiencing in the movement

Do not take prescription medication of any kind. Research proves beyond a shred of a doubt that despite the temporary relief you will feel, the residual side effects are devastating, and go from bad to worse as you find yourself climbing up the prescription medicine ladder going from one pill to another while at simultaneously sliding down the other side of the ladder deteriorating while enriching the pharmaceutical industry and the lazy greedy doctors who find it easier to write out a quick prescription for you regardless of the after and side effects. Meanwhile money hungry doctors quickly move on to their next fee-paying patients.
I have described an ugly situation. Sadly, it is the truth. Countless suicides are the result of people swallowing their instant gratification pills prescribed by doctors.
The 2nd 'No-No' is sugar. Absolutely verboten! The residue of sugar and sugar inducing foods such as white flour, etc.; drifts upwards towards the brain and forms

plaques around the neurons, leading to mental grog fog. Further on down the timeline, the sugar residue in the brain leads to the oncome of Dementia, Alzheimer's and other increasing modern-day problems and illnesses of the brain. These mental diseases have been on a steep increase over the last century due to very unhealthy modern-day food dietary habits.

Life is not perfect and don't expect it to be. You really do have to earn your stripes on our planet. Learn how to juggle mentally, by keeping your compass on 'Solution' finding. Develop agility as you skip from one area to another always keeping your eye on a solution. The more you look for the solution the faster you will find it. But you need a clear healthy brain outlook and attitude to do that, otherwise your outlook stays contaminated with toxic thoughts.
Toxic thoughts = toxic energy = **toxic reality**.

Don't think that you can replace sugar with artificial sweeteners. They are even more harmful than sugar because they kill good intestinal bacteria.
The neurotransmitter Serotonin is a one of our feel-good factors. Contrary to popular belief Serotonin is fabricated in our gut which also has neurons .and not in our brains. Therefor the good bacterium in the gut needs to be protected and not killed off. Healthy good intestinal bacteria are the natural and vital ingredients for our states of well-being and happiness.

Keep your words and imagination images positive.
The word "not" has no literal meaning to the subconscious mind -- so it is more effective to suggest to yourself, "I will eat one piece of chocolate for dessert," than

to suggest, "I will not eat too much chocolate"., Positive thoughts reinforce motivation, while negative thoughts damage motivation. During your visualization time: Imagine yourself happily eating one piece of chocolate and then walking away, well-satisfied... replay this image in your mind for several minutes.
Stuff yourself with Omega 3 superfoods daily.
Here is a list of some of them and they are all cheaper than prescription drugs and junk food.
- Roast your soybeans. This plant source is very rich in Omega 3 fats. But avoid Soya bean oil which is predominantly a polyunsaturated fat and not heart friendly.
- Eat salmon for breakfast, lunch and dinner and make sure it is organic if your budget permits.
- Carry walnuts in your pockets and snack on them all day long. Walnuts reduce blood pressure under stress and are very protective against heart problems.
- Put sardines into your salads or fry them but make sure you have at least 4 servings of sardines every week.
- Mackerel is very high in Omega 3. Use it and abuse it.
- Anchovies also provide a wealth of potassium and calcium. I read that if you eat the anchovies with their mini bones, you ingest excellent sources of Iron.
- Soak your organic superfood Chia seeds in water for about 15 to 20 minutes and then mix them in your vegetable and fruit juices, and your pro-biotic yogurts. Eat about 2 tablespoons per day. There are too many benefits to write about here. Just google advantage of Chia seeds and eat them every day.
- Eat as much organic spinach as you can, steamed or raw in salads. If Popeye ate spinach, we know it is good for us to eat as well!

Carry a small notebook around, and EVERY little nibble of solid and liquids that go into your mouth, write it down

after the fact and write down the time at which you ingested or drank it. If you can jot down a word that explains your current mood or emotion. Even if you just pop a few nuts into your mouth because they happen to be laying around in a bowl, notice your feelings either physical or emotional and write it down. For example:
- I stuffed a couple of peanuts because they were in a nice bowl when I visited my old school friend.
- I was wondering what it would be like to catch up with my friend. I guess I was feeling curious and apprehensive.
- 2.45 pm, I was not hungry when I ate the peanuts.

This is very helpful to streamline your food and drink intake. We all think we eat and drink much healthier than what we do.

This monthly habit is not only for people who have an eating or drinking disorder; it helps everyone streamline their drink and food input for a healthier lifestyle.

As we are what we think and eat, it is important to notice if we are putting junk food into the body. You will become aware of where you can make changes and get into the habit of only eating food that you prepare from scratch. NO JUNK FOOD or pre-prepared food and drinks.

MONTH 3: DRINK

Focus on your liquid intake. Keep on writing it all down from each coffee to each glass of wine. Did you drink a diet soda or a soda full of sugar? How much water are you drinking every day? Aim for 3 liters a day of still mineral water. Water has become a minefield on its own.

Aim for distilled still water, and if possible, energize your water. An easy way to do that is to store your water in a blue bottle. Leave it out in the sun or day light for about an hour and write positive words which you can tape on to the bottle with the word facing inwards towards the water.

For further tips and a deeper understanding, read "Messages in Water' authored by a Japanese scientist called Masaru Emoto.

You can also buy the small blue water hydration cards from Dr DREW KARP, they only cost a few dollars.
Be sure to keep a written track of what, how much, why, and when you drink in a day. Your written notes will highlight where you can set the habits in, and what drinking habits you can easily eliminate.

MONTH 4: MORNING TOOL TO HEIGHTEN YOUR MANIFESETING ENERGY

Every morning, make a list of what your priorities are for the day. And get into the habit of accomplishing your priorities before doing other things.
Here is a good 5 step morning ritual.
10 TO 15 DEEP BREATHS in through the nose and out through the nose. Keep on bringing more air in, especially when I think my lungs are full. And feel grateful for the oxygen I have.

GRATITUDE Put your hand on your heart. Feel the gratitude in your heart. Start with simple things, sight, good health, beauty, ability to manifest, etc.

Then write down into a little book with your non-dominant hand, at least 3 subjects for which you feel gratitude. By writing with your non-dominant hand, you are expanding your brain to be more balanced and flexible.

LOVE ENERGY: Eyes shut and looking upwards. Breathe in, seeing the white light coming from above into the crown of my head and going down to your heart. And the same powerful pure white light coming from the earth, the ground and going up in a straight line, between your legs into your body and up into your heart.
Breathe, and think about all you love, Nature, Myself, People, objects, feelings etc.
Say out loud: "I want to FEEL the LOVE in my heart."

GIVE LOVE Now that your body has love energy, which has come in your whole body, inhale and breathe love out, to people, objects, places, events,
Bring the energy in through your head, legs and heart then, while you keep on looking upwards and project the LOVE ENERGY from your heart, to people, situations, the world etc...
MANIFESTATION Visualise your day going perfect. Everything you want during that day; visualise it and see everything going well. Focus on appreciation,

MONTH 5: DETOX YOUR BODY FOR ONE WEEK

There are many detox cures and methods available. Choose one which is not too drastic so that you can integrate it for a few days and still feel comfortable, physically, and mentally.

MONTH 6: MOVE YOUR BODY

This is the physical movement week. Increase your level of daily physical activity. If you are already very active, then take this week to change your physical activity and discover a new method. If you go to the gym, spend the next week going to dance classes, or if you are a couch potato, start graduall going for 20-minute daily walks. If you are walking, then go for a daily bike ride or jog a bit and change the places where you walk.
I am sure you get the picture. Upscale your exercise moderately daily.

Integrate your daily exercise as a ritual at the same time daily, make sure you take at least 20 minutes a day and dedicate that to physical exercise. It is not only excellent because your heart will be pumping more oxygen throughout your brain and pre-frontal cortex, but it will help you think better.

MONTH 7: OXYGENISE YOUR BRAIN

Make this your oxygen week. Every hour on the hour set your phone alarm and spend 2 minutes doing deep inhaling and exhaling exercises. Notice your increase in mental clarity and awareness.

MONTH 8: AFFIRMATIONS

If you have not already done it, then spend an hour or so and play around with affirmations. Either ones you have found or others you have created. Commit to saying those affirmations out loud twice a day, every day while looking at yourself in the in the mirror.
Good affirmations include the following 5 points:
a- Compose the affirmation so that it is personal. For example, start with "I AM…"
b- Create a positive statement.
c- Say all your affirmations in the 'present tense.
d- Include visuals
e- Inject one or more positive emotions.
Here is an example: (a) I am (b) confident (c) as I am successfully auditioning (d) for the main role in Spielberg's new movie in front of the spotlights in the big movie studio (e) where I feel comfortable and relaxed

MONTH 9: SLEEP ENOUGH AT NIGHT AND PHYSICALLY MOVE ENOUGH DURING THE DAY

Every hour between 8 pm and midnight counts for 2 hours. If you go to bed at 10 pm and wake up at 6, you have the value of 8 hours sleep. Simply get into the habit to go to bed before midnight for a week and you will see how fast your mental agility will perk up during the day. During the day, make sure you move for at least 20 minutes nonstop, just above the comfort level. This form of oxygen stimulation is ideal for the brain. And the older you get, the more the brain needs oxygen input.

MONTH 10 BREATHING MONTH

Spend this month reading, learning, and implementing a few breathing techniques. We can live without water depending on our age, health, weather temperature etc. anywhere between a few hours and 3 weeks. But after a few minutes we need oxygen.

The heart pumps the blood through the body transporting the oxygen. So, facilitate the hearts work, and exercise daily for a minimum of 20 minutes.

In the ancient practice of Ho'oponopono there are over 50 different breathing techniques. Enough choice for everyone to find a few which works best for you.

MONTH 11: DE- STRESS

The moment you feel pressure, tension, anger, stress boiling up and getting the upper hand, deflate it immediately by discreetly tapping on the GAMUT point.

This is ideal if you are with other people and obviously don't want to start a full blown out tapping routine. Use the index finger from one hand to tap on the gamut point on the other hand. And notice your negative frequency deflate almost immediately. Read about it in chapter 18 Deletion Tools. Under EFT.

MONTH 12: EXCELLENCE AND SUCCESS HAPPEN BECAUSE EVERY SMALL STEP WAS DONE IN EXCELLENCE

Make it a daily habit to choose one of your projects and dissect the next step into smaller steps making each step excellent. Become familiar with your route to excellence. It takes time, and certainly slows down the time lapse of the outcome, but the journey is much more rewarding. The G.R.O.W. model which I cover in Chapter 7 in depth is ideal.

ALL YEAR ROUND EVERY DAY AND EVERY TIME YOU TALK

Make sure you ONLY say out loud what you want. Even if you do not have it yet.

NEVER ... I repeat NEVER say what you don't want. Because the mind delivers what it hears.

Examples:

1- You want to lose weight. Say, "I only enjoy eating delicious healthy slimming natural tasty foods."
Do not say: "I want to lose weight so that means I cannot eat any more delicious cakes"
2- You want to have a better job. Say "I know that my next job is exciting, fulfilling and giving me sufficient free time to write my book on weekends".
Do not say "I want a better job in which I do not have to stress out and work overtime and which does not leave me any time on the weekends to write my book"
Don't waste your precious time saying what you don't want. Only talk about what you do want.
<u>Fact:</u> What you do today will impact your tomorrow. Therefor you will be happier when you choose your daily actions consciously to improve your tomorrow. The time to do that is NOW. Life is always busy, and there will never be a perfect time to instill in yourself better habits than starting them right this moment.

These monthly habits you choose will serve you better in the long run and awake in you the realization that you, and only you are in control of shaping your own life. Wishing and hoping are not strong enough action verbs. Use the tapping in chapter 18 to stop your negative debilitating self-chatter. Discover by trying them out which tools work best for you to delete your anxiety and stress that you were unwillingly living with until now.

You are the answer to your problems, and you are also the magic wand to your desired outcomes. Don't seek out physics, healers, and prescription meds to make you feel better. Use your supernatural powers. You have them; we all have them.

Drop your focus from your head to your heart and trust that your inner self knows what is best for you. Follow your unexplainable intuitive feelings. It takes practice and trust in yourself.

Choose an option that you would like for your life and stay with it until your intuitive vision has clarity.

Go into your vision daily at the same time, make it a ritual. Soon your nervous system will relax into the moment and your guards will be down. Now you are entering your heart.

Become your own Guru.

What is a Guru?

It is someone who tells you what to do, and very often when asked 'Why' will reply "You will understand 'Why' once you have felt the experience.

When you start to ask yourself questions, let go and instead flow into the experience instead. As you do this daily you are strengthening and flexing your intuitive muscles.

A- Discover your intuition. Listen to your inner replies, do what feels good to reach your peak state. With time you will learn how to follow your intuition.

B- Sharpen your awareness whenever you can. Be aware of what you are seeing, touching, hearing, felling, tasting. Spend 2 minutes every hour becoming consciously aware. It is very uplifting to notice more and more of our 'Now' moments.

C- Gently choose small shifts that you want to manifest in your life and enjoy the feeling of amazement as the manifestations happen.

D- As time progresses increase your shifts and enjoy feeling more empowered.

All good habits help to create your default peak state from the heart.

Nature Medicine published: *'Adult hippocampal neurogenesis is abundant in neurologically healthy subjects.* This statement supports the usefulness of integrating a good new habit every month. We all want to live a long life, but we want that life to be one of quality. Which is why the reprograming towards positivity from all points of view is fundamental to neurogenesis. You are never too old to make a good new beginning since new cells and neurons in your system can grow way into adult hood. Being 90 years young today is the new middle age!

Depression, stress, anxiety can all become states of the past. Your future can easily become content, happy, peaceful, vibrant, and positive.

Jonas Frisén of the Karolkinska Institute in Sweden advocates that there is an overwhelming case for neurogenesis throughout the entire life span of man. Of course, like in everything other reputable professionals stand on the feet of being a Doubting Thomas. There is always a ying and a yang but hopefully you will agree that it is logical to self-improve as it can only pay off benefits in the short and long term.

I was given this little poem at one of my lowest emotional points in my life. I did not believe I could go on. I put this card on my night table and for years my eyes scanned it wittingly or unwittingly but today, about 11 years later, I can guarantee that we all have what it takes to enjoy life to the fullest.

GIVE IT YOUR BEST

There are times when life is tough, and trials are the worst.
There are special challenges when fortunes seemed reversed.
Life delivers problems that are hard to explain.
Certain situations cause a larger share of pain.
But out of all the trials flows a stronger side of you.
There are crucial goals you must continue to pursue.
You must confront the obstacles; you must defeat the doubts.
You must persist when giving up is all the moment shouts.
And when you reach the final stages of a lengthy test.
You'll be a victor of the heart because you did your best

CHAPTER TWENTY-ONE

VISUALIZATION & INTUITION

Visualization. New age word? Metaphysical expression? Airy Fairy language?
Maybe... Give it any title you want but visualization is very real and can be easiest described as a Mental Painting.
Beliefs form us, that is a fact. By helping your reticular activating system become familiar with the images it is seeing on your vision board it is starting to believe the reality of that image.
So, make your images amazing because they are the foundations of the new beliefs you are creating. As your mind does not care one way or the other, go for the best you can. Then it becomes true. Because your beliefs make your reality.
There is one facet I like very much on visualisations being that a picture can easily slip under the carpet of consciousness into the sub consciousness easier than an affirmation can.
When you logically reverse engineer a belief it is easy to understand that it stems from a memory.

Now let's ask ourselves: "What and where is a memory"? The reason you remember something is because your body 'felt' it emotionally, physically, or mentally at one point in time. those little neuropeptides lodged themselves into the nervous system which has all the receptors in the layers of the skin. Since you 'felt' something you 'know 'it is true, and therefore a belief was created.

I know some of you might be thinking, "How come she is not writing that memory stems in the brain. And the reason is that I studied a fascinating research document whereby to establish exactly in which lobe of the brain 'Memory' is stored, the researchers taught some mice how to scurry around a maze obviously memorizing the maze route. The scientists then started to remove the mouse's brain piecemeal as they would to notice that when the mouse would suddenly stop because it had forgotten where to go, that would show them the last piece of removed brain matter is where the cells of the memory are stored.

But lo and behold, the research lab technicians had physically removed the entire brain and the mice still knew where to go. This proved that the mice's memory was obviously located also in their little legs and feet.

Visualising is when you 'imagine' something that has not yet happened in your reality but as your inner eye and movie camera are filming the scene it becomes as vivid to you as if you were really living the scene. You will become immersed in corresponding emotions relating to what you are seeing, hearing, tasting, smelling or feeling in your mind. Those emotions will also lodge in your nervous system and then automatically become a belief.

But the fun part is that you get to CREATE what you want first.

You are creating your 'FUTURE memory'.

It starts in your imagination., which is down to the conscious mind. The conscious mind is the creative mind. Each man-made component has first started in the imagination. Before you can see, touch, smell or hear it your imagination must conceive it. Imagination is the ONLY modality to create reality.

Some lucky people have lived deeply and used imagination to their advantage. Sadly, most people have left their magic imaginary castles behind between the ages of 5 to 10 years old, thanks to teachers and so-called well-meaning adults who barked at children telling them to stop daydreaming and to pay attention to what they were supposedly listening to or watching. Obediently but sadly, the little children day by day stopped daydreaming and lost the gift of imagining.
The easiest way to imagine is to close your eyes and ask: What if.......?"

But the good news is that imagining is like riding a bicycle, close your eyes and drift, as pleasant thoughts, and pretty images come to your mind, and as you get used to knowing what you want as opposed to simply taking what appears in front of you, develop them in more detail. When you accept that one of the manifesting exercises is visualization, you will automatically be allowing yourself to expect your wish to materialize just as you expect a certain flower to bloom when you plant the corresponding seed.
When EXPECTANCY is lodged in your subconscious thoughts it is only a matter of the clock tick-tocking away before you enjoy the reality of your goal being tangible. Design your destiny now.
This is an important moment in the creation process of your wished-for future.
Be very clear about what you want. You want to be conscious of the downside as well as the upside.
TIP: Make columns of pros and cons. Take your time to go in depth into each situation measuring up if you are willing to pay the price for what you want.

A quick example might be living in a warm tropical climate in a beautiful house by the sea. But if you are currently living in an inner city, think carefully if you are willing to move to the other side of the world to be by the sea and not see your family and friends daily in the big metropolis that you know?
Or if you want to be a super star, are you willing to pay the price of losing your privacy? Because that is normally what happens.

Visualization is not a stand-alone generator for manifesting your goal. It is tied into feelings, beliefs, and thoughts. Every thought, color, sound, visible or invisible; audible or inaudible; literally everything has a vibration.
The right brain is imaginative, and the left brain is logical.
Unpleasant happenings set off the bio-chemical process which is the result of a thought or an idea.
Unwanted happenings result in feeling badly. Those feelings are the results of the chemicals that your body has generated originating in the limbic brain. This is part of your 'responsibility' as it is in your power to apply the solution of thinking positively in that moment.
When you challenge and apply yourself to no longer being a victim of your unwanted negative feelings and stop complaining about everything but instead use your awareness and choose to focus on becoming the creator of your feelings by boosting and empowering yourself with novel uplifting thoughts.
You are now moving from the passenger seat into the driving seat of your life and your future.
Conscientiously choose to create the events and quality of your future life.

Ask and answer the following questions:
- Do you want to react to what life throws you your way? Or
- Do you want to create your future as you want it to be?

Let's give it a go, as you read my following description, imagine it is really you, and let your mind float freely while you feel the journey.

You are sitting in the carriage of the big Ferris Wheel in London, the one down in the Docklands. As the Ferris wheel goes around and round, each time you get to the top of the Ferris wheel, you can see for miles in all directions.

You have made a bet with yourself that you will strap your little jetpack to your back, and you will wiggle out of the Ferris wheelchair, and as you ignite your jet pack, you check that your parachute is working just in case the jet pack fails. You are 100% safe.

Look down to the ground as you stand on the small platform of the Ferris wheel's carriage and slightly bend your knees, press the ignition button, and jump off the platform looking ahead as you do, and feel the jet pack propelling you forwards to the right.

Can you feel the warm summer breeze on your arms and face as you fly around seeing the Thames underneath? Can you feel your feet trail behind you as you are enjoying steering yourself with your arms to the right, left, up and down? Do you feel the feeling of safety and freedom as you play in the air? Do you see the birds at the same height as yourself?

After a few minutes, turn your arms to face downwards and head back to the base of the Ferris wheel. Feel yourself land with bent knees.

What do you feel? What do you see?
Can you pinpoint a feeling somewhere in your body?
Subconscious beliefs are the foundation of our reality.
If you are not living the life, you want it is only because your subconscious beliefs are attracting un-supporting visions for the life you want to be living. To live the life, you want you must first create life altering beliefs and behaviors by daily 'choosing' to visualize what you want as if they were happening now.
Remember that everything is energy, and whatever you think and talk about is where the building and creating energy flows to.

Visualization is not necessarily the act of internally 'seeing' in your mind's eye. You can also 'smell' in your minds nose, 'listen' in your mind's ears, 'taste' in your minds mouth, and 'feel 'in your minds body.
Life takes place dynamically in the physical body with sensory factors. However, humans as opposed to animals have in addition a highly developed sense of perception, will power and reasoning capacity which occurs thanks to our pre-frontal cortex which is much larger than that of animals or mammals.
We are born with God given faculties. We all have the highest faculties of any living species. We are super powerful. Yet only a very small percent of the population uses their creative ability to shape their lives. Those facilities are the amazing tools and abilities we are all born with in our DNA, show your gratitude by using them. Your imagination allows you to designate, identify and create.
Choose one or more blocks – limiting beliefs- uncomfortable feelings which you don't like and with applied focus replace it or them with a highly detailed and felt image of living your ideal dream in the now.

Don't ask 'How' or why? If your present circumstances are not what you want, remove the relevant feelings and emotions associated to what you don't like in the situation you are experiencing currently by tapping. (See the chapter on E.F.T. and learn about the trapped emotions in your body)

Whenever that negative feeling sweeps over your body or soul; switch it to positive by immediately focusing with intent on choosing or creating an image in your mind of how you want to be instead.

Your imagination is the building block of your reality. After the age of 7 every person can increase their approach to individuality or as the English say, to being eclectic. This is possible thanks to one's conscious mind, which is unique to the human being. All other forms of life from animals to plants operate on the input/ output stimulus. There is no thought process there. In the process of the human evolution, we formed a slice of living tissue which is filled with neurons, and that is what is called the pre-frontal cortex. It allows each person to honor their individuality and create first mentally what they want for their lives.

It is fun and easy to inner- image yourself in a specific scenario of your wish. Do it and experience how the mere fact of inner-imaging yourself will cause your body to feel real sensations.

Close your eyes, see yourself walking up the steps of a church steeple all the way to the bell tower which is 30 meters high, and walk over to the edge, notice that there is no protective railing on the edge so very carefully inch your way over to the edge, and then stand still and look straight ahead while your body becomes comfortable and relaxes, as you feel your body strengthen again, shift your eyes towards the ground 30 meters down and see how many parked cars you can see from your very high vantage point.

Can you focus and see the colors of the cars or is your body feeling uneasy, dizzy, weak, and maybe even with butterflies in your tummy?

Stay with that feeling for a minute or two, and now tell yourself that you are perfectly safe, since you really are, and notice how your body starts to relax and feel peaceful again."

What you just saw in the eye of your mind, physically and mentally affected you.

That little visualization exercise proves and allows you to understand that when you take the time to CHOOSE to imagine a specific desired outcome or situation it will show up for you. First in your body and then in your outer measurable reality.

What you put in your head and in your mind produces the experience and the reality in your life

Change your thoughts, and your reality will change.

How you change in your mind is how you will succeed in your life.

Practice imagining, rehearse your desired goals in your mind first.

Live them and create how you want to feel when you will be living them in your physical and measurable reality.

Whatever thoughts you are entertaining in your head whether consciously or not in the present moment are impacting your future right now. So, become self-aware as to whether you are visualizing the optimal outcome of your desired reality.

Ask yourself if you are entertaining in your mind harmful thoughts such as that you do not deserve what you really want and long for, and that for whatever reason you are not good enough in one way or another to deserve what you want and therefor it is a waste of time to even want it because all your efforts will be to no avail.

Those were two opposing possibilities. Understand and believe that whatever you choose to focus on will become a self-fulfilling prophecy. The amazing benefit of this knowledge is that only you can and must choose what you want to visualize on at least twice a day for a few minutes until it comes to pass in the reality of your life. Feel the nice physical sensation in your body. That is how you increase your options and chances of enjoying the outcome you want to happen.

Become the boss of your own desires, commanding yourself to focus and create clarity for your own wishes and aspirations. Some of you might be wandering uncomfortably into unchartered territories feeling lost and scared because this time you are on your own. You cannot rely on other people any more to tell you what you want to do/be/feel/ and so on.

For many people, the price of not living their dreams was worth it because they could always place the blame of their discontent on exterior reasons, other people or circumstances which excluded them from blame in their own eyes.

The truth of the matter is that it is only an illusion because every human being has all the necessary inner powers and tools to live their desired reality.

Enjoy the FEEL of the feelings and the emotions of what you want your reality to be. Submerge yourself into those feelings repetitively to create that feeling in your mind first. Your mind is now the belief generator since your body needs to start vibrating at that frequency and jump-start the physical creation process.

Each person's wishes, goals and dreams represent what they want out of life. Use the exercises in this book to lock in your daydreams to your sensory nervous system.

A belief is a thought that has been replayed either consciously or subconsciously so often in the imagination that the body accepts the neurochemicals from that belief to be 'reality'.

Once a set of bio-chemicals is circulating in your body your nervous system will direct all your other thoughts to support those bio neurochemicals.

Unwittingly since we instinctively need to be correct in our own mind, we unwittingly create situations that confirm our unknown subconscious beliefs, which in turn produce those bio-chemicals which we have become used to and, in some cases, also addicted to. Thereby allowing actions and behaviors to play out in such a way that the result of your behavior, will create the situation to support your subconscious belief.

Welcome to your own hamster wheel.

As subconscious thoughts run about 95 subconscious thoughts to 1 conscious thought, and the subconscious is 1,000,000 times more powerful than the conscious there is no way that your conscious opposing thought which is what you 'WISH" or 'HOPE" for to happen can underlie the weight of a subconscious thought of which the chemicals are running rampant in your nervous system 24/7/365.

Two steps must occur on a regular basis to reset those negative beliefs.
1- Release the negative frequency blocks which are commonly called 'feelings' from your body by tapping using the EFT method and by using Ho'oponopono. But remember that 'feelings & emotions' don't exist technically; they are only chemical compounds released into the nervous system by the limbic brain.

2- Upgrade your energy with oxygen. Breathe in deeply and exhale very slowly. Repeat those breathing exercises 7 times, repeatedly for 2 days.

3- Now that your nervous system is clean, you can install new beliefs onto a positive foundation by using your imagination to create either the picture, sound, taste, or smell of your desired outcome. This is when you do all the planting of your seeds into your own clean and fertile soil.

4- 'I' is for Intention. Simply set your intention. That intention can be for the day, the week, the year and so on. This step is not about seeing the result it is only about setting the intention. Example. I will eat healthy today. I will drive to the beach now. I will do all my bookkeeping next weekend. I will take my parents out to dinner on their anniversary. Those are intentions and they are clearly formulated and specific.

5- Now welcome the thoughts which accompany your intention.
Again, inhale deeply and exhale slowly 10 times. The vibrational frequency which corresponds to the images you are welcoming into your mind stay longer in your nervous system since you are releasing your breath as slowly as possible. The images of your intentions are being lodged in the subconscious paths of your body via the act of deep breathing.

Once you have observed the images that appear on the screen of your mind, open your hands so that symbolically the image can land in your hands. When your hands are full of the images depicting the result of your goal, gently bring your hands over your heart inserting the image safely into your emotional heart. As Shakespeare said, a picture is 1000 words. Your heart will convert the image of your visualization into the necessary vibrational frequencies.

A picture is emotional, so it belongs in the emotional home of your body being the heart. Hawaiian Shamans manifest their desired reality by doing this process for their visualizations.
Do you want to REACT to your life?
Or…
Do you want to CREATE your life?

The object of this exercise that must be done daily on a repetitive basis if you successfully want to reverse engineer your subconscious beliefs, so they no longer create a conflict within yourself. That is done by gradually getting used to a different set of situations and feelings.

New feelings and situations which you want to live, must be imagined with as much attention to detail as you can muster up. The more clarity you have the better, faster, and truer to your wish, will your reality become.

The approach to this work is methodical. Everyday work sessions of about 30 minutes twice a day. The best times are in the morning when you wake up and last thing before you go to sleep.

Make a list of all the situations in your reality that you are not happy with and know that those situations are created by your unconscious beliefs.

Then make lists of affirmations that will reflect the situations that you want to enjoy in your reality. You are far more powerful than what you know. Become fulfilled by generating the thoughts that will create the reality you want. It can be hard for some people that is why daily self-discipline is a must. Self-discipline is achievable by everyone. And once you are in the daily process you will have fun

PREPARE YOUR CREATION PLAN

1- What are you aiming for? Be specific and remember that everything is possible.
2- Affirmations are an excellent basis to help you visualize. I describe an affirmation as a statement said in the present tense describing yourself in the ideal outcome of your goal. It helps to write down your affirmation and read it during the day a few times. An example of an affirmation would read along these lines: I am grateful, relieved, and

proud that I am or have (Describe your goal in one sentence)

3- Now say that goal in the present and in the positive.
Example:
My goal is to weigh 72 kilos and to become a financially abundant successful entrepreneur.
Transform it to:
I am so grateful that I weigh 72 kilos and am now financially successful in my successful profitable money-making business.

4- Sculpt your answers. They are inside of you already, but by chiseling away at the outside, the truth and clarity of your wishes, aims and goals will become exposed with clarity.

5- Why are these goals important to you? Write down all the 'Why's. Those answers will motivate you on your destination when the going gets tough.

6- Which challenges do you anticipate could be difficult to overcome?
Make sure you list them. This is not focusing on the negative it is simply a practical way to prepare contingency plans that if needed will save time and panic energy.

THE POWER AND ENERGY OF THOUGHT

Thoughts, whether conscious or subconscious create emotions, and emotion is energy. The marriage of action energy with thought energy quantum leaps your inner vibrations. This conception process is law.

Before your body became matter, it was pure energy. If you vacuum out all the emptiness in your body, which by the way is pure energy you will be lucky if you are left with a pinprick of matter!

17 seconds of a single focused and held thought starts the energy combustion. This is not an analogy.

We are only energy. First, we are energy which intensifies into matter. Focused thought for 17 seconds will act like the carburetor in a car.

As soon as that combustion is activated, it becomes electromagnetic and will join other similar thoughts that are out in the universal matrix of energy, resulting in a higher vibration.

This is where science and research show that thoughts vibrating for 68 seconds produce a manifestation. That manifestation can be situational or physical.

Take a moment to go on YouTube and look at some of the videos of Uri Geller who regularly produced physical manifestations by bending metal spoons, knives and forks solely by using the focus of his mind.

He was so powerful that when he appeared on French television in the 70ies the show presenters warned the T.V. viewers to either shut down their television sets or be prepared for clocks to change and beware of your nice heirloom family silver bending out of shape! It happened more than once.

The power of visualizing is such that 17 seconds of uninterrupted laser focused visualization is equal to 2000 physical man-hours or put differently 1 year of 40-hour weeks cycling.

It gets stronger. Now boost that to 34 seconds of focused laser intensity visualization and the equivalent is 20,000 hours of physical action.

And 60 seconds amounts to 2 million hours of focused action.

That is what is called, to work 'SMART AND NOT HARD'.

Trust in your higher power, we all have inner power nuclear strength. When that power is unleashed, it automatically brings into physical or situational reality a 'Manifestation'.

Manifestations are not religious or magical. They are the result of our energies Higher or Divine Power.

The purpose of our life is to manifest by choice, and the proof of a successful life is to manifest what we want and not be the victim of other people's beliefs.

The masses have accepted unwittingly and at times unknowingly because it is much easier to accept another's belief rather than take responsibility for one's own belief. After all, if it goes wrong the quick cure is to shift the blame away from yourself on to someone or something else. Sadly, this is what happens to most people.

But not to the winners of the game of life. Think about it.

Your attention is the most powerful creative tool of all. Take control of your own life and future. You can, EVERYONE can.

Choose thoughts that mirror the reality of what you want, feel it happening now, and you have already started the planting process of growing what you want by aligning yourself energetically with the same frequency of your desired outcome.

With practice, you will become a good luck magnet. Marcus Aurelius said. *"Good luck is when preparation meets opportunity"*

Intuition becomes a byproduct of Visualization. Intuition can only exist on your inner or outer knowledge of a situation or object. At that point you can recognize that something you know is reappearing again but not in a familiar or inspiring way.

A thought radiates energy and the intensity of that energy emitted on a repetitive basis will affect the surroundings, whether physically or situationally. Buddhist masters have been proclaiming this for centuries.

Walt Disney said, "If you can see it, you can do it" So get started on creating your mental images, as they are fundamental to the process of reaching your goal.

A piece of art is born in the mind and the eyes of the artist. Only much later does it become physical and viewable by yourself.

The fabulous power within is covered by old, repeated experiences which have forged negative patterns in your belief system. Stand under the shower and wash your negativity away allowing your inner diamond sparkle and golden glimmer to shine freely and brightly as you love more, smile easier and live inspiringly.

A fabulous life starts with a choice, show up for yourself and enjoy choosing what you want as your ideal reality.

Now is the time to fine-tune the clarity of the vision you hold and see, smell, hear and feel yourself living your goal.

The clearer your imaginative arrival the stronger the magnetism is activated. We are electromagnetic living creatures. We attract the identical of the energy frequency we radiate.

VISION BOARDS

Use this guideline to categorize these sectors. As you fill your vision board with images and photos that represent what you want you are confirming to your subconscious mind that you have them already. This is one of the first steps of creating the life of your dreams and taking responsibility for your choices.
- See your physical body as you want it to be., Health, beauty. Energy. Vibrant.
- In your wildest dreams, how would you like people to describe you? Imagine them talking about your talents, personality, your qualities and how they feel around you.
- Cut out photos of your ideal office or place of work, your home, the type of technology that you use and have become comfortable with.
- Describe your circle of friends, family, work colleagues. Who would be your favorite mentor?
- What is your financial situation in your ideal world? Write out the amount of capital or income you want to have to live the lifestyle of your dreams. How do you manage your money? Do you have a secretary who does your admin or are you super clever and manage your own money because you have learnt and understand investment strategies? How much is your life insurance worth? How well are you generally insured? Car/ Home/ Travel/ Goods/ and so on.

Do you get the idea? You want to make your ideal financial situation very clear and enjoy a positive frame of mind when you think about your financial situation.
- Are you connected to nature and spirituality? If so, describe how do you see yourself spending 1 hour a day on yourself.
- Are you comfortable with your spirituality? How do you live it and what do you enjoy thanks to being spiritual?

For me the word 'Spirituality' means the utmost power which is invisible to the naked eye yet is energetic and super-intelligent. Spiritual substance guides us and accompanies us while we voyage through eternity in an unmeasurable and unrelated moment in time in the physical body of humanness.

While we test drive our current 'human' model whilst laying the groundwork for the next model which we will come back to test drive when the moment is right for our soul's ongoing creating possibilities. Spirituality and its experiences derive from our applied knowledge of activating on demand our thoughts, emotions, and physicality.

In an ideal situation the time should, may or will come when all humans will be able to activate their mind body spirit thought connections interdimensional as easily as we take a jet today to go from one side of the globe to the other in a 12-hour time span!

That was not even thinkable 100 years ago by the masses, though it appears that very ancient civilizations did use their powers much more than our cultures do today.

Mankind has 'unlearned' but now mankind is re-discovering its inner strengths, powers and what many people construe as 'magic'

This is a little check list to help you become aware of what and how you are internally seeing, feeling, hearing, or even tasting.

1- Is your image in color or black and white?
2- Are you seeing slides or a movie?
3- If it is a movie, is it in normal speed or slow motion?
4- Are you in the image or seeing it from the outside?
5- Is the picture clear or fuzzy?
6- Is anything standing out in the picture?
7- Is there a color that resonates with you?
8- Are you looking at it from the side the top or the bottom?
9- What is resonating with you emotionally as you see the picture?
10- Are you hearing any voices and if so, are they low or loud?
11- Do certain words stand out more than others?
12- Are you speaking or are others speaking?
13- What is being said and how is it affecting you?
14- What tone of voice or sound are you hearing?
15- As you are steeped in your imagination are you aware of your breath?
16- Do you taste your own saliva differently?
17- Where in your body are you aware of the emotions that you are feeling whilst in the process of your visualization?

At the end of your increased self-awareness, checklist can you determine if what you felt is what you wanted to feel or not.

If you do not feel what you want to feel, simply re-draw in your mind exactly the outcome you want to have and create in your imagination all the ingredients you need to achieve that feeling of success.

IMAGINATION & INTUITION

IMAGINATION'S POTENTIALS!

Grow in your mind then grow in the belief of yourself. Dare to dream, dare to lose sight of what you know and see now. Go out and up until everything you imagine is new. Champions and superheroes were also Mr and Mrs Everyone like you and me... until they saw themselves as Mr and Mrs Someone.

The visions you choose to create now in your imagination will without a doubt become your reality. The clue is to create your reality by design and trust in your mind to alter your future.

Imagine yourself at your best consistently 2 minutes every day for the next 90 days... And that will be you sooner or later!

Lucid dreaming is another term for imagining. Lucid dream with your eyes shut or open as you are living the life you yearn for. Zero inhibitions, zero fears. Go deep in the core of your essence emoting your true power because you know you can do it.

Everyone has imagination, but few control it. Most people just let their mind roam aimlessly and therefor they lose their self-power. Imagination is identical to a waterfall. It is beautiful to watch for a few moments but then the water disappears into nothingness. So, build a dam at the bottom of the waterfall, the water is still beautiful as it falls but it now transmutes into energy.

Focused use of imagination under laboratory conditions at the Beth Israel Deaconess Medical Centre which is a part of the Harvard Medical Centre has demonstrated that the sustained practice of imagination forms new

structures in the brain and body by way of synapsis and neuronal connections. This has a widespread use as it proves how the placebo effect produces cures in many instances of physical diseases and resulting symptoms.
Some people discover what is... Others create what is yet to come.
Imagination is the seed of what is to come! Use the sheer power of your imagination.
Thoughts are the source of imagination. But thoughts just like every other structured entity has laws. It is vital to grasp the importance of your thoughts. Thoughts shape destiny!
Everyone's realities are the fruit of their thoughts. If you don't like certain aspects of your reality, choose the corresponding aligned thought to produce the circumstances of your wish.

Your life is not the flower of chance... but the result of your inner thoughts, and beliefs which orchestrate you 'being'. Our circumstances come, go, or evolve as all sentient beings are the creative powers of their destinies. The surest way to get specifically what you want in life is to fine tune your conscious and focused thinking, by doing so with awareness and integrating your emotions while being mindful of your intuitive messages.
The more you fine tune your awareness the more you will have clarity of mind and perception of why you are experiencing whatever it is in the 'now'. Interpret what you are experiencing, by taking 'alone and quiet time'.
In the theatre of your mind... where you are safe... start by going beyond where you know you can go or where you feel comfortable. Oscar Wilde said, *"We are all in the gutter, but some of us look at the stars"!*

As you look higher, further, and deeper you will start to feel the adrenalin. Now you are pumping mental energy. It is more important to daydream and expand your imagination then it is to stack your brain with endless facts. **One creates and the other stores.**

IMAGINATION IS A 'WILL BE' WHILE KNOWLEDGE IS A 'HAS BEEN'

Developing your imagination is learning and creating your new ways of "HOW" to think instead of the brainwashing habits most people live by which is "WHAT "to think.

When you develop critical thinking, your imagination expands as your start to see a situation from a different point of view, since you are asking yourself 'What if' questions. Your imagination will deliver your answers.

Sadly, as children we have been conditioned to ignore the imagination.

'Only a figment of your imagination' has a negative undertone, instead take that 'Figment of your imagination' and develop it, run with your questions and ask more questions based on your answers. That is the taking the action to developing your imagination.

Expanded imagination will find its roots in your emotions.

When you start from a place of positivity your outcome will be better even though great poetry, operas, ballets, and art that have been created because the artist was in the deepest moods of depression or sadness. Extreme emotions produce change.

Emotions are like the financial markets, if you are aware of what the underlying trend is, you can make money either by going short or long.

So, when you are in happy mode make some positive visualisations and if you are sad use the visuals to pull yourself out of that state.

Make money, make a name or make a change. But to make anything you must first exercise your imagination continuously and daily. Use it or lose it, and I suggest you use it. Because the loss you will incur will be a treasure that floats by and was well within your reach.

Awaken your imagination by thinking creatively at least 5 minutes 3 times a day, imagining creates energy and defers hope.

TRANSITION STEPS

Transit from creating images to feeling the emotion,
Hold that emotion for 17 seconds daily for 2 weeks, increase it to 34 seconds for the next 2 weeks, and then ramp it up to 68 seconds for a month. By then your body will have processed vibrational frequency attached to that emotion and your subconscious will be emitting it to the universe numerous times as it is now becoming an integrated part of your subconscious beliefs.

It is a powerful manifesting tool.

Those seconds represent energy which can be measured based on the energy produced when pedalling a cycle. As thoughts activate combustion each time that your laser is focus on your thoughts, they activate energy and intensify like a ray of sun coming through a glass windowpane. The heat increases in quantum surges.

- 17 seconds of focused thought equals 2000 hours of pedalling a bike.
- 34 seconds of focused thought equals 20,000 hours of pedalling that bike.
- 68 seconds of that same focused thought equals 2 million hours of pedalling that bike.

And to help you visualise how that translates into watts, imagine 10 children pedalling as fast as they can on an exercise bike can get a TV to work!

To amplify the vibrational strength message of those positive emotions into the cell's membranes simply squeeze your thumb and index finger for a moment while you are enjoying the imaginary emotions. Now you have anchored the corresponding emotions and vibrations of what you want to experience into the sub consciousness of your cells.

Think of your imagination as the physical movement side of your body. You needed a long time and daily explorations to figure out how to initially move your body so you could walk, feel, see, and touch what you wanted to.

As a little baby you learned instinctively how to turn over, and next your body followed your curiosity and you started to crawl. When admiring people oohed and ahead as they excitedly helped you to stand on your two little legs encouraging you to go forwards as they stood at your level with their arms outstretched their smiles of encouragement and sounds of loving admiration fuelled every baby step your little legs made.

Time and daily experiences evolved into learning to run, ride a bike, climb over fences, rocks and trees, jump, glide, modulate your walk, move your body to music, and as you were encouraged into sports you associated your mental speed to your body's movements.

The encouragement of loving adults while you went through those physical processes was very important in your development. But when it came to catching you daydreaming you were told off, and sadly that is the period when a child must be encouraged the most.

Don't fear, it is never too late, we are always able to re-pattern our brains neuro paths. Discover more as you read up on neuroplasticity.

You are the captain of your destiny and as an adult as well as hopefully a self-improvement junkie, it is your responsibility to develop your ability to wonder, be curious and learn to ask yourself and other questions. It won't happen in a week. It might take as long to imagine then it did for you to walk. But every day will be progress and every lucid daydream will be another seed planted into your future reality.

The basic component for imagination is an image, it bases itself on what is stored in its memory banks and from there will start the long road from reproducing in your mind's eye what it sees to producing what it does not physically see… YET! You are planting your seed into the soil of the universal energy matrix.

Imagination is completely subjective. It is your private property. In your imagination there is no right or wrong. Trust it and trust yourself. Just like every seed is different. There is no right or wrong seed, but they will each come out the earth as the correct and exact manifestation of the seed that it was when it was planted into the soil.

This chapter is not a treatise on imagination, but when you accept the power of your imagination you will want to use and develop it as your own creation workshop. We all bloom differently.

Association of ideas is a good spark for imagining. Take the example that you want to plant your garden but have no idea what it should look like. Logically you could read up as much as you can on gardening because intellectual wealth provides a more abundant crop.

Take photos of plants and flowers and lay out photos of bricks and stones, donkeys and insects, unrelated furniture such as bedroom furniture...This is to help stir your imagination into other areas where normally you might not think of those when creating a landscape for a garden). Now relax and play around with the photos for a few days and use the photos as pieces of a puzzle. Very often the results will produce in your mind the type of unexpected garden you will like.

Insert sounds and smells. They don't have to be logical, the more illogical and ill matched the ingredients are, the stronger the imagination is jolted. Freedom is an ideal breeding ground for unexpected creations. Wait for fireworks! Start your tantalizing imaginary voyage now.

Imagining is thinking. It takes time to develop. Genius is the result of patience. Use your mind well, with focus and clarity. Develop it, treat it well, and give your mind worthwhile and educational information. Don't just watch any program that appears on TV. Choose the books and magazines or articles which will give you a larger vocabulary on subjects which stimulate you. If you don't take the time to look after your own interests then you are the ideal prey for the mass media, and you will become a zombie with no ideas or opinions of your own. How sad. Govern yourself with your mind as it is the mind of the universe.

TIP: To produce results from your imagination identify the areas and sectors in which you have a void. A creative act is born from a 'need'. Necessity is the mother of all inventions!

Imagination connects to inspiration which in turn feeds itself in the unconscious activity of the mind.

TIP: If you feel you can't create the image or can't see your wish in your mind with clarity, it could be because your higher intelligence knows it is not the right moment for you to 'see' it yet. Simply write down on a separate piece of paper whatever words you can apply to your fuzzy goal currently. A psychic phenomenon will occur, and you will get your vision or answer unexpectedly. When that happens know that it is not a coincidence but the result of your preparation.

VARIOIUS EXERCISES TO STRENGHTEN YOUR IMAGINATION

Choose your favourite mood.
- Do you like to be in a state of anticipation and hope, or of security and safety?
- Do you prefer to get high on happiness or are you more comfortable with melancholia?

There is no good or bad. Just acknowledge what works for you. This is also known as your 'comfort zone'

Connect your imagination to the awareness of what you are feeling in your body.

These questions will help you anchor the feelings that you enjoy and soon those will be the only feelings you will experience.

You are training your subconscious mind's radar to only seek out situations that will bring you the opportunities to live those feelings which you think of.

The yellow car syndrome. Yellow is an unusual colour for a car, but when a person decides to buy a yellow car, suddenly it seems that only yellow cars of all makes, and sizes are cruising on the road! Your subconscious has instinctively blocked out what you are not focusing on.

There are certain high energy frequencies in key states which facilitate manifestation. To help yourself anchor those ideal states into your DNA identify a situation which produces the feelings in your body that you enjoy. Now go through these steps:

On a scale of 0 to 10 with 10 being the highest, what level of intensity are you feeling as you think of that lovely situation? When you have <u>identified</u> your level of intensity; form a circle with your thumb and third finger and squeeze tightly. You are re-enforcing that vibration to your subconscious.

The timing of this process is important because you want to do it daily for at least a month until 'your' feel good factor is well recorded into your DNA.

Describe the uniqueness of the situation that you are creating which is producing the feeling you enjoy. Once you identify that uniqueness transfer it into another situation and gradually create all situations to incorporate that feeling. You are identifying the stimulus needed to give you the feeling you enjoy.

Finally, now that you identified all the necessary ingredients needed to produce the stimulus which will create a situation either in your mind at first but then definitely in reality later, you want to be sure to continually reproduce that image two or three times daily for a month.

You can change the scenes in your mind, as your imagination will create more and more imaginary situations with weaker or stronger stimulating sensations.
TIP: Build from the images which produce the strongest positive sensory sensations.
Connect your imagination to the awareness of what you are feeling in your body.
The sooner you anchor the feelings that you enjoy the faster they will become most feelings you will experience. You are training the radar of your subconscious minds to only seek out situations that will bring you the opportunity to live those feelings.

EXERCISE WITH A PENNY! Pennies from heaven!
Hold a penny in your hand 3 times a day… and allow yourself to imagine the excitement you are feeling when you find that penny.
Don't focus on where you are going to look for the penny, simply entertain the feeling of how lucky you feel when you find that penny.
See how many pennies start to appear in your life.
Each penny is the symbol of your ability to manifest anything else you want in your life.
But start with a penny from heaven!

MENTAL MOVIE Detail is important when creating your mental movie; create everything that you want. If you are harbouring negative memories or images from the past, this is the moment that your mind will instruct your body not to react emotionally to those images anymore. Instead create in total security what you want. You are the actor; the screen writer and the director so write your script and allow the Higher Power and the universe to get on with producing the movie.

It is important here that if your dream depends on someone else joining you; for example, a romantic partner, a work colleague, or boss that you do not put a face on that actor. Leave the face blank. That is because you can't make someone else do something unless it is right for both of you. The right person is out there and by creating your movie with clarity, the universal language of vibrations will deliver to you the right person who will be sharing the scene you wish to share.

At some time in the future the scene or situation you created will occur. And you could experience 'déjà vu'.

If you are preparing for an interview, prepare it in the theatre of your mind.

It is easiest to build your mental movie from a familiar base.

- ✓ Start by dressing yourself in clothes that you have and feel comfortable in.
- ✓ Include in your mental movie the exact salary, bonuses and perks you want.
- ✓ Then introduce yourself to your interviewer and script a few sentences of introduction which will give a good first impression.
- ✓ Say those sentences out loud to yourself as you look into the mirror every day wearing the clothes that you will wear to the interview
- ✓ Fast forward the interview to the end, where you thank the interviewer for having offered you the position at the salary and with the perks you wanted.

VARIETY is the key to success when building a library where your imagination can go and retrieve. Set your intention at times to build up your memory bank. The simplest way to develop one's imagination is to base a concept on something already known and to let it flow and evolve from there. Look at as many different pictures and videos of landscapes, plant life, animals, urban and country architecture when you have a moment with the intention to use it when needed to expand your imaginary platforms.

As you are looking at those images, imagine how all your other senses would be affected if you were in those scenes.

- ✓ How would that feel on your skin?
- ✓ How would it taste and what would the texture feel like in your mouth?
- ✓ Hear the sounds in the background.
- ✓ Close your eyes and transport yourself in the scenes you contemplate.
- ✓ Focus on the details!

When you find yourself receiving impressions or emoting; train yourself to look at the detail as that is where the symbolic significance lies.

Note: It is the process of a lifetime!

THE DEVIL IS IN THE DETAIL

- ✓ Start with stills and move to videos.
- ✓ Open a photo or a document and time yourself for one minute as you study while noting as many details as you can.
- ✓ Now write a bullet point list of all the details you remember.

✓ Go back to the photo or document and see what you missed.
✓ After doing it daily for a month, do the same but on a 1-minute clip of a video. Choose any video clip on YouTube. They are easy to play back. It is best to simply choose the first minute of any video and change the video every day.

Within 2 months you will notice how much sharper your self-awareness has become. You are now starting to govern your own life with your own mind.

STRETCH YOUR IMAGINATION BEYOND THE REALMS OF YOUR REALITY & CONDITIONING

Research various social habits according to the past centuries and different cultures. Put yourself in a social situation and imagine what it would be like.

This works well when you choose a situation that is 180 degrees opposed from your current life.

In your imagination change gender, age, and transport yourself instantaneously to another continent. If you are a leader today imagine you were a slave or servant before. If you are an old man today, imagine yourself being Catherine de Medici; a 14-year-old virgin bride! And if you really want to have fun; see yourself as an extra-terrestrial and tell us what life is like on your planet.

For it to work you must play the game and really believe you are in that situation. This is a productive version of the parlour game called "Charades"

TIP: *Tell your make-believe story to an audience and convince them of what you are seeing.*

Inspiration & Intuition are active acts of unconscious imagining. It is your inner breath. Your truth from within. The inner messages you are perceiving are your values. What is necessary for you to be abundant?
Obey your intuition and reap the fruits of your courage. It takes self-confidence. Trust the concept that spirituality speaks your hidden truth.

INTUITION

The "Raison d'être" of intuition is to freely connect with the matrix of the universe. Unexpectedly, when seeking to understand life in general, intuition gives answers to questions you did not even know you were looking for and shines a light on our expanding potential. When you are in the flow with your intuition you will see with hindsight that you 'KNEW' something before you formed a conscious 'THOUGHT.
I would like to suggest that the only way *it* 'knows' is because *it* recognises something, perhaps a scent, a sound or a frequency. That 'je ne sais quoi' as they say in French is a vibration which in my opinion can only be stored in the electromagnetic field of our bodies while at the same moment it is instantaneously tapping into the universal unconsciousness. This has to do with non-locality.
Exchange messages back and forth as clearly as if you were talking to your mentor on the phone. The greatest energy of the universe is nature, but sadly today technology has launched a movement of isolation. Virtual sex and virtual communication are but some of the ways designed to cut us off from each other. None the less as you pay attention to your feelings and inner vibrations you

will always be connected to the universal energy, home of your intuition.

Don't second guess your feelings. Give them a free rein and instead allow your intuition to become your leader.

Intuition is a fleeting inner music whereby you can learn how to recognise your own melodies.

- Pain of any sort is a warning that you are doing something wrong, listen to that message of consciousness and keep on correcting yourself until your inner energy quietens.
- Peace is the green light that you are on the right path.

Mentally wander around on the different mind-reprograming platforms on which you develop your ability to focus and enlarge your thinking and imagination beyond your current knowledge of reality; this is where and when you start to expand your intuition.

We live in a 3-dimensional universe, but there is a universe of 4 dimensions and the 4th dimension is time.

Even though we don't see time, it is one of the measures we live by on this planet.

The trick is to recognise the perceptions that come to us from the 4th dimension and reconnect immediately to your reality.

The proof of the pudding is peace. Peace happens when you are living in the absolute present moment.

Emotions come from memories or projections. Either we are living in the past or in the future. If you are not enjoying 'how' you are feeling switch your attention to the absolute present moment, focus on your breath, focus on the feeling of your clothes on your body, focus on anything in the now for a few minutes and allow the effects of the unwanted chemicals to transmute into light and energy and burn themselves out.

Of course, it is in your imagination but so is your past and your future! Only the present is real NOW. That is a small action of consciously creating your peak state of being.

There is a tidal wave movement currently to become isolated. Data shoots up and down the information highway, virtual sex, wars; car races, horse races and online betting are bringing the thrills to most of the global population whilst making sure we don't have to interact with one another in flesh and bones. Yet it is vital that humans connect to each other physically, mentally, and emotionally in 'real' reality and not always in 'virtual' reality.

Intuition feeds off the energetic interaction which emits and receives vibrational messages between the super conscious and the subconscious. That is where truthful information is exchanged.

Listening and acting on intuition is for the brave since initially you are walking out into the unknown. Trust that your intuition is speaking your truth and that better ways will be revealed.

Until the digital revolution became our norm, the only way of accessing and processing information came by the energy channels of our instinct. I am afraid that due to this overload and overreliance on technology many people are losing their basic and most trusted informant 'THE INSTINCT'.

Anyone who follows their "North" otherwise known as 'intuition' has what it takes for leadership at any level. The more intuitively you live the happier you are. Natural untapped creativity floats automatically to the surface setting the right goals while you move towards them pushed by invisible intuitive nudges which feed your innate self-confidence as you realise how right you are each time to follow your gut feeling.

POSITIVE THINKING

Whether you win or lose, the choice is up to you. When you 'decide' to take the action to make it happen your attitude will determine your attitude and control your path and journey ahead. Real **AI** Is also the fact that **At**titude **I**mpacts life and experiences.

You can't change the past, but when you decide to improve your attitude, your future will automatically be brighter. Meaningfulness of life is about 20 % what happens to us and 80% how we react to the situations.

Use William Shakespeare's words "To be or not to be" The choice of how you will be lies 100% in your court.

Make the conscious choice to seed your positive attitude in your mind and then enjoy the experience in its palpable reality.

Your mind is transforming your thoughts into plants like the seeds in the garden. But it is up to you to plant the seeds. If you don't pay attention to the specific seeds and choose exactly which seeds you want to see blossom, the bad weeds will soon sprout above ground.

Avoid pity-parties unless you are doing EFT. Then of course it is vital to fall temporarily into that mode but only for the duration of your tapping sessions.

Be strong and cope well, and the world will stand with you. Fortitude and good luck are the proof and results of a good mind-set.

Do what you must do to the best of your capability. Use a role model for inspiration, and not as a comparison, otherwise you might become emotionally defeated.

Inject massive amounts of effort and energy to fulfil your potential.

Become ferocious about making your life meaningful. It is about how you feel about yourself in the now, and not what your past provided. Your future lies in the choices you make in the present and the efforts you apply to reach your goal. The past does not constitute the future, so stop fearing the future. Instead design it to your own tastes!

Create your self-image from all the components that are your values and your wishes. Choose who you want to become.

If you snooze instead of choose you will lose!

When mistakes occur just say 'thanks for the lesson', re tweak and calibrate your path to continue forward. We are like airplanes, 90% of the time a plane is off course but with a few tweaks on the automatic pilot system the pilot lands the airplane on the airport it was set to land on.

Source Energy, Abraham Hicks

You are more productive by doing fifteen minutes of visualization than from sixteen hours of hard labor.

CHAPTER TWENTY-TWO

LOVE LIFE TO LIVE LIFE

Twenty years from now you will be more disappointed by the things you didn't do than by the things you did.
Mark Twain

LOVE IS A 4 LETTER VERB. It comes in many shapes and forms.
Self-love is the first step to self-empowerment. Love is an art, steeped in spirituality and proven scientifically.
It is an art because each person feels and expresses it differently and it is scientific because the energy frequencies measured on endless and countless scientific research studies namely at the Heart Maths Institute but also at numerous research facilities worldwide show the measurable difference in each subject's physical and mental health as the love frequencies increase.
Love is not only a noun it is also a verb, meaning love is 'Action'. Where does Love live? In your body. You are pure vibrant love when you feel expansive.
The moment you enjoy self-loving you are creating and positively expanding your life's reality. But the moment you start to denigrate yourself, you are in auto-destruct mode via negative thinking and the attached downwards spirals of the matching emotion and vibes.
Of course, we must be realistic and examine our errors, but we are not our errors. We are our unfulfilled potential. Strive to be better than yourself, your inner Genie is waiting to be activated. Enjoy the challenge, become fearless and limitless. Release your passions and give them the space to develop. If you strangle your passions

everything you do becomes hard and tiring. When you let your passions rip, they will carry you forward on the magic carpet of your inner-renewable energy.

TIP: *Do what YOU love.*
When you love yourself, you are being thankful for the lesson of learning from what you analysed, perceived, and processed incorrectly but most importantly; unproductively. It hurts on the moment to acknowledge failure but as you decide to look at that failure you are instantaneously in real time turning the odds around in your favour by learning from the lesson and proceeding again but with more knowledge and experience, knowing you are getting closer to your goal. You can choose to change your thoughts or moods as you catch them next time and reverse them too positive. That is living the verb of love, by taking positive action on yourself

Don't bother looking around for love, it will come easily to you the moment it recognises itself in you. We attract what we emit in vibrational frequencies. And those frequencies come from loving and accepting the greatness in you. Be natural, don't pretend to be what you are not. You are unique, enjoy your uniqueness. Give of your love lavishly to yourself and others. The more love you give to yourself, the more love you get from others.

Loving and loved people feel positive by conscious choice.

The acid test to self-love is:
- If I really loved myself, would I do it?
- How do I speak to others? Do I speak in the same manner that I like to be spoken to?
- What food to do I eat, what do I drink. What exercises am I doing?
- Become the person you want to love.

- Be in love with yourself Being is another version of saying: "I AM."
- The 'I' stands for Intention
- The 'A' stands for Action
- The 'M' stands for Manifestation.

That is your Genie's formula.

HAPPINESS AND SUCCESS

**Success is getting what you want
Happiness is wanting what you get**

NEW START:
The first step to happiness is to love yourself. Do everything to make yourself feel as secure and as happy as you do to make a child feel like that. Start loving yourself at age dot!!! Give yourself all the love you would give a new-born Baby. No matter what is wrong with that baby your heart pours out love to it. Remember, Love is a verb, which means do what love does, it looks after you, it makes sure you are eating well, thinking clean empowering thoughts, exercising not only for your brain but also for your body.

Have you seen the video on YouTube of two premature twins? One is healthy and the other twin is fading away fast. The maternity nurse decides to pick up the healthy twin and places it on the bed next to its weak dying twin. You see the arm of the little baby instinctively stretch out to go over the weak twin's shoulders, and within seconds the machines showing the vital signs of the weak twin pick up and within days if not hours the sick twin is saved. It was the instinctual love energy from its strong and healthy twin that injected life back into the weak little body of the other twin.

If you want to see the video email me on nicole@nicolepetschekuk.com and I will send you the link. And for those of you who are reading this book on a digital platform here is the link. http://youtu.be/jVBWdC1zeFM

Imagine your heart with an open valve on the top. Take a pitcher and pour the liquid golden love into your heart.

This is fun. even though it is working on yourself it is fun work. Nothing serious. Only light-hearted. Close your eyes, look deep into your pink heart and whisper into your heart's ears, "Life Hugs Me"

Be gentle and patient with YOURSELF. There is one thing that heals every problem, and that is: to love yourself. When people start to love themselves more each day, it's amazing how their lives get better. They feel better. They get the jobs they want. They have the money they need. Their relationships either improve, or the negative one's dissolve and new ones begin. Blocks crumble and doors open.

Loving yourself is a wonderful adventure; it's like learning to fly. Imagine if we all had the power to fly at will? How exciting it would be! Let's begin to love ourselves now.

Life has no meaning other than an opportunity to create a meaning.

SOLUTIONS TO HELP YOU LEARN HOW TO LOVE YOURSELF:

1. **Stop All Criticism.** Criticism never changes a thing. Refuse to criticize yourself. Accept yourself exactly as you are. Everybody changes.
   When you criticize yourself, your changes and transformations are negative.
   When you approve of yourself, your changes and transformations become positive.
2. **Forgive Yourself.** Let the past go. (Use Ho'oponopono Chapter 17) You did the best you could at the time with the understanding, awareness, and knowledge that you had. Now you are growing and changing, and you will live life differently. Keep what is good and change the road map to get you the results you want in the future. All you must do is change your path and the content in this book as well as the wide choice of proven and tested exercises and techniques will guarantee you results.
3. **Don't Scare Yourself.** Stop terrorizing yourself with your thoughts. It's a dreadful way to live. Find a mental image that gives you pleasure, and immediately switch your scary thought to a pleasure thought.
4. **Be Gentle, Kind and Patient**. Be gentle with yourself. Be kind to yourself. Be patient with yourself as you learn the new ways of thinking. Treat yourself as you would behave and treat someone you really love.
5. **Be Kind to Your Mind.** Self-hatred is only hating your own thoughts. Don't hate yourself for having the thoughts. Instead, gently change your thoughts.
   Did you know that the heart is the 1st organ that develops when you are happily creating yourself in your mother's womb? That makes your heart the oldest and most

developed part of yourself. Your heart is storing memories and all your deeply rooted experiences. You can pull them out whenever you are ready to focus on yourself. KNOW YOURSELF!
Electrophysiology testing proves that the heart receives information first before passing it up to the head-brain. Random generating research proves that the heart picks up on significant emotional events relevant to everyone before the event occurs. That is also known as Intuition.

The give and take are far more active from the heart's side then the brain's side. Thereby proving the importance our emotions play in the creation of the reality of our lives at all levels. After those emotions travel up to the brain then they become conscious. Most people though are not tuned into their own emotions and thoughts; algorithms of the emotions flow into our body organs, limbs and nervous system and become an integral and forgotten part of our ruling subconscious. Becoming part of your belief system and from then on forwards in your life those beliefs will be pedalling round and round on your inner hamster wheel.

We KNOW with the head, but we LEARN from the heart. And as the colloquial saying goes 'Speak from the heart" The reason being that the next organ to form after the heart is the tongue.
Use your heart as your GPS it will guide you to every possible outcome you desire: Wealth, success, and happiness- your intuition will take you anywhere you want to go.
Speak from your heart, only say what you want, if you don't want it, DON'T SAY IT!

As a child, you were completely connected to your heart. Get back on that old children's tricycle again and your intentions will surface in your reality. Re-connect with your heart to get a better understanding of yourself and your place in the world. We all have a seat reserved for us. Take your seat and not someone else's. You will be happier and more successful because your feelings and thoughts are pure, therefore aligned to your truth that will benefit yourself.
Life loves you… but to enjoy its love, you must love yourself first. Then you will enjoy the love of and from life.
These are some good, positive, and productive ways and reasons to become the victim of yourself.

Praise Yourself. Criticism breaks down the inner spirit. Praise builds it up. Praise yourself as much as you can. Tell yourself how well you are doing with every little thing that you approve of. Of course, the more aware and conscious you are of yourself the more honestly felt compliments you will be able and excited to boost yourself up with.

Support Yourself. Find ways to support yourself. Reach out to friends and allow them to help you. It is being strong to ask for help when you need it. Several clever minds and like-minded people are more productive than one person alone. Remember, no one can do it on their own. Andrew Carnegie hired Napoleon Hill to research and write: 'Think and Grow Rich', here is the Master Mind definition: 'Coordination of knowledge and effort, in a spirit of harmony, between two or more people, for the attainment of a definite purpose'

Be Loving to Your Negatives. Acknowledge that you created them to fulfil a need which most likely was a lesson to live through. Now you are finding new, positive ways to fulfil those needs. So lovingly release the old negative patterns, see the patterns in your mind and watch them dissolve into a sparkling light like the sparkling trail of a magic wand as the glimmering diamond lit stars of the wand disappear into the ether of universal energy. They have served their purpose; you have had the opportunity to learn from that lesson and do things better in the future.

Take Excellent Care of Your Body. Give the same and more love to yourself that you dish out on other people. Learn about nutrition. What kind of fuel does your body need to have optimum energy and vitality? Learn about exercise. What kind of exercise do you enjoy? Cherish and revere the temple you live in. Self-Care is not selfish. When you have helped yourself, you are in strong position to help others.

Do Mirror Work. Look into your eyes often. Express this growing sense of love you have for yourself. Forgive yourself while looking into the mirror. Talk to your parents while looking into the mirror. Forgive them and thank them as well. At least once a day, say to yourself while you look at yourself in the mirror, "I love you; I really love you!" Life mirrors back all your unconscious thoughts, thank your mirror for sharing your secrets with yourself.

Love Yourself Do It Now. Don't wait until you get well, or lose the weight, or get the new job, or find the new relationship. Begin now—and do the best you can. One of Mae Wests powerful sayings was: 'I don't like myself, I am CRAZY about myself'.

Have Fun. What comes first to mind when you think about fun? Remember the things that gave you joy as a child. Incorporate them into your life now. Find a way to have fun with everything you do. Let yourself express the joy of living. Smile. Laugh. Rejoice, and the Universe rejoices with you! Having fun quantum generates energy, excitement, and enthusiasm. Laugh, smile, giggle, dance and see the wow factor in as much as you can.

Make PEACE your 1st CHOICE. Sereneness breeds the developing ability to be self-aware. Have you noticed how each time you are entertaining panic, stress, or negative thinking you flip into victim mode and forget that you have the CHOICE to opt for peaceful thoughts in that moment?

Choose to say the TRUTH. Even if it is uncomfortable on the spur of the moment. Accept what it is and tell yourself if you like it then you are being rewarded and if you don't like what you are experiencing, you are better off to learn the lesson now, go through it, see where the error was made and figure out how to do it better or right next time. One small step at a time. You will learn more about this and you understand the depth, power, and benefits of Ho'oponopono in chapter 18.

Spring cleaning. Make a commitment to identify, let go and heal all the traumas from your past. Make a list of anything you can remember. The mere fact that you remember something means it must be released. Don't judge if it is too small or insignificant. When you clean your house if you see even a small dirty spot on your white sink, you will wipe it away. You won't say to yourself" This is too small a dirt spot to bother about, why tire myself'. Let go of anger you are holding towards anyone including yourself, and then move into forgiveness.

a. Identify the uncomfortable and ugly moments. They are wasting your energy.
b. Let go of the past. tap on each situation.
c. Let go of the anger and use Ho'oponopono and say to yourself 'I love you – I am sorry for... - please forgive me- Thank you."

Now that you have cleaner foundations, and your energy is vibrating with clarity and peaceful frequencies start using your unique manifesting energy by envisioning your dreams. For a dream to manifest into the reality of your life you will use tools that will help you to activate 'EMOTION" because emotions are the quantum turbo power that transports, and transforms 'wishes' into 'matter'.

Become the creator of your true self and your dreams. Clarify the vision of your dream goal. Make it as specific as possible. Use creative visualisation, journaling, and vision boards. You will find more detailed ideas and instructions in chapter 17.

I do repeat myself throughout the chapters, but that is because I know when you see a message from various angles it will anchor more securely and permanently into your understanding. Humans are messy, there is so much going on in and around us. And if you have the slightest bad habit in your subconscious, it will activate unwanted manifestations.

That is why I urge you to try all the different tools and find out for yourself which techniques feel best for you. Use that or those tools now. It is more than likely that as time goes by you will evolve and shift and the tools you like now, will not feel as comfortable or fulfilling to you in the future. Then it will be time to become familiar with other tools. 'THINK ACHIEVEMENT & WATCH IT HAPPEN 'is not about doing some exercises over the weekend and expecting to see measurable and durable results on Monday despite that there might be the 'One-minute wonder' occurrence.

Believe that you are Aladdin and that your Genie is hiding inside your subconscious and only waiting for you to clean up your messy emotions and gain more clarity so that your Genie will come out through the dust and help you to adopt enabling mind changes for life.
I speak about Aladdin and yes; it is a fairy tale, however; fairy tales were written to capture the most important creative talent we are all born with; our imagination. Fairy tales are written for children, we were all children once, it is up to us to recapture our imagination and use fun and fairy tales to lighten the process. We are all Aladdin, and we all have a Genie. Please for your sake, let him out of your lamp and follow your Genie's guidance to live your dreams.

CHAPTER TWENTY-THREE

JUST IN TIME TO BECOME YOU 2.0

The one thing that no one can buy, borrow, steal, or deal in is time. Time is a very useful motivator and tool for those who want to grow, accomplish, contribute and in other words achieve.
Take care of your days, and let the calendar take care of the years, just like you take care of the Pennies and let the Pounds take care of themselves.
Which group of people will you choose to belong to?

- The majority 90% group who are interested in learning and experiencing but do not commit and carry through on their action orientated coaching and self-development and improvement?
- Or are you choosing to be part of the 10% minority group who do whatever they have to do to create their desired future?

The choice is yours; I hope you decide to join the exclusive, successful, happy, healthy, minority.
You made it this far towards the end of 'THINK ACHIEVEMENT & WATCH IT HAPPEN' so I dare to presume that you will make the 2nd choice.
Through personal experience, I promise you that even though much of the content seems either too easy to do, or nor serious enough I urge you to trust that once you implement regularly and practice the advice and the tools described in this book, your results will be surprisingly better than what you even dared to expect in the beginning.

Follow your inner voice and not the voice of other people who will always have an activity for you to do for them while they proceed towards their own goals. As Steve Jobs said "Have the courage to follow you own heart and intuition. They truly know what you want to become. Everything else is secondary." Put your energy into action by doing what it takes to reach your target.

Following is a check list that you can use to give yourself some guidance as all the bullet points will contribute to your self-development and improvement. The benefit of a calendar is to help you measure your progress.

If you can find a year planner with daily squares and hang it up where you can see it every morning it is a great reminder; that you come first. Make sure to also enter your commitments and rituals into your working agenda. Do not compromise yourself for the sake of outside work.

At the start and end of every month give yourself an honest self-assessment on a scale of 1 to 10. The fact of measuring is very helpful and empowering. Become clear on knowing what drives you as you find out what actions you want to or feel need to be taken to accomplish your goals and grow as a person.

It helps to plan the time to integrate these bullet points into your life. You are the vehicle that is going to drive yourself to your success. Spend your time credits on yourself. Prepare your monthly calendar in advance, to make sure you mark out the 'MY TIME' first.

- Clean-up my inboxes/ mail trays / and pending files.
- Weekly make time (20 minutes min) to self-introspect in my life and find out what is not working.
- Daily make time (20 minutes min) to meditate or connect to my intuition and see what comes up for me as a solution to change what is not working for me. There are

numerous ways to meditate- Just find one that works for you.
- Which relationships do I want to improve? What actions could I take?
- What literature, conferences, courses can I take either online or in person? You will want to invest not only time but also money in your continuous learning.
- At the end of the week or the month. Ask yourself 'What lessons have I learned from doing my focused actions? Everyone makes mistakes. Mistakes are failures unless you don't learn from them. Allow failures to become lessons.
- By now you have read I believe 'THINK ACHIEVEMENT' and have come across several success tools that resonate within yourself. Choose 2 or 3 of them and make sure you block out the time in your monthly calendar to DO the work. And not just KNOW about it. The difference between knowledge and action is RESULTS.
- My new SUCCESS HABIT. The only way to create a habit is to use self-discipline by repeatedly carrying out a certain action. After a while your body and mind will automatically demand that action to be undertaken by yourself for you to FEEL good.
- Use the 'Information Ladder' throughout ALL your goals.

a- Gather as much **Data,** which are only cold facts. However, those facts are needed to get the ball rolling. You can always add, delete, or change as you progress. But make sure you have a solid platform of information about your goal.

b- Next is **'Information'** which boils down to the question of '**WHAT**' is relative to your goal.

Information is different from 'Data' in so much that it comes from the Latin verb of FORMARE, it means to 'Form' and that forming starts in the mind. Data is the necessary ingredient for information.

Write down your '**KNOWLEDGE**' on '**HOW**' you would choose to act on reaching your goal. Even though it is very important as I state in the book to start first with 'WHY' as the 'HOW' will appear. Become involved in your own road map.

c- 'b' right above is a big step in avoiding procrastination and I will explain why. Many people wake up with a great idea, and they automatically see the end result of their idea. That is brilliant and very helpful. But I have seen many people stay on the 'High' of their end result, yet they never get to the starting gate. And they don't get started. If you are a procrastinator (read the chapters 5 & 6). It is very helpful to take a step backwards, spend about 40 minutes a day every day for 10 days in a row, simply writing down your roll-out plan step by step. As you go from day to day your 'innermagination' starts to feel comfortable. It takes a while, and it most likely will not be the right route to take. What it accomplishes is to give you a sense of familiarity and confidence that when you start, you will learn and discover what to do next in a better way as you go along.

If you hear your inner chat saying, "You should be further along by now" Ignore it, do not succumb to despair or pessimism, trust your intuition, and become comfortable with the fact you know you are getting your act together and that you are only in competition with yourself. From this place of peace, you will start to get pulled instead of pushing yourself.

d- **WISDOM** is the result of your know-how, experience, and your opinion of the best options available.

- Dedicate a certain amount of time per month to grow, learn and practice a new skill. Keep on doing it until you carry out that task in an excellent manner and you have now mastered a new success habit.
- What is your affirmation for the month? Tie it in to your overall goal.
- Mark up in your daily calendar 15 minutes of uninterrupted time to close your eyes while you visualise your goal as having already happened.

Data = WHAT
Knowledge = HOW
The more repetitive daily focused time you spend on yourself using these techniques and tips, the better you are training yourself for automatic goal achievement.
There is something satisfying about making changes and improvements in ourselves knowing that we are doing it for the right reason, which is to become unstuck even though our subconscious fears uncertainty.
Your brain will never be satisfied enough because your subconscious is used to you feeling stuck rather than wanting to change all at once.

You might think you are changing when you constantly research, study and go to seminars but you are just indulging yourself in procrastination. Of course, it is good to learn and study, but it must always be accompanied by action.

That is why that wonderful book was written, called "Face the fear and do it anyway'. The brain is always faced with fear and uncertainty when looking into the unknown. Many people become overwhelmed and start to self – stress as they have a deep need for clarity when they want to change their behaviours. Ignore it; trust me that the tweaks come as you change.
The more you change the less fear you have and the more empowered you become.
It helps to write down a chosen action and enter the action in the daily, weekly, or monthly calendar. Recording an action in the calendar is equivalent to putting your foot in the stirrup, vault on to the saddle and start riding yourself to success while changing and transforming. It takes focus and time.
Don't fall into the stalling trap, that you must do it all at once or that you must know everything before you start. Your subconscious is communicating to you in the hope that you get scared and loop backwards into staying as you are. Remain the master of your mind.
Remember that your subconscious system is very clever and knows which negative words trigger get you to avoid change. When you become aware of that, you will become empowered. Just like you would not allow a little child to wind you round their finger unless you consciously decide to play into the child's game.
Take a step back, plan your daily 'SELF - TIME 'and enter it into your daily agenda making it a priority and

not allowing ANYTHING else to change your 'MY TIME'.

The best is to spend 15 minutes early morning and 15 minutes at night looking at your vision board and list of self-empowering statements re defining your desired outcomes. Sometimes your mind will focus and at other moments your thoughts will be drifting but with your vision board in front of your eyes you are programming your subconscious into the success formulas you are aiming for.

CHAPTER TWENTY-FOUR

CREATE YOUR FUTURE

When I let go of who I am, I become what I might be.
Lao Tzu

You have read and hopefully absorbed a lot. In this chapter you will bundle the information together and put it into practice creating the future you want for yourself.
Those who want to change the world usually do.
The old Chinese energy art and science of Feng Shui advises that to make room for a new and better life, you want to get rid of the old. Here are a few guidelines that will declutter you and your environment to welcome in a new future.
Start by cleaning up the filing cabinets of your mind.
Are your bank accounts balanced?
Do you have a draw full of IOU's which you owe? If you do, make sure to pay them off as soon as you financially can.
What about a lot of promises and commitments which you have not kept? If that is the case, address each one and each person or company and renegotiate. Then start holding your promises this time round and enjoy your own celebration as you can tick off one kept promise after another.
Is your folder and your desktop on your computer a mess with word documents and folders all over the place?
Yes? then take off a few hours at a time, sit down with some nice inspirational background music and put all your files into a logical order. You will be amazed at the increase in efficiency in your work.

Do you have family members and friends you have not spent time with since ages?
If so, make time to enjoy quality time together. Friendship and bounding are not something to be done when you have finished the other chores on your TO DO list. Do it today, just like the old song of Frank Sinatra who sings, 'Let's forget about Domani..." and do it 'today'.
Each decision you make sculpts your future.

All the drawings, exercises and questions in this book are designed to help you obliterate brain fog to see clearly and realistically where you are in the present moment so that you can decide what your destination will be. It is highly probable that you will want to create lasting changes in many sectors of your life. Self-motivate yourself to create the 'Get up and Go' spirit that will fuel and sustain your motivation to allow you to revolutionise your relationships, finances, health, and career.
Use your current momentum. Don't succumb to what could be a valid reason to delay your goal reaching journey by saying you will start when: You are thinner/ fatter/ healthier / richer/ retired/ the children have left the house/ moved to a new country / job/ relationship and the music goes on! Those are the reasons why most people never achieve much if anything in their life. Generate your own momentum and roll with the ball. Notice how your results will propel you automatically to your next result and so on.
Always keep your eye on your goal until you have taken a measurable step in that direction. Stack all the advantages in your playing field. When and wherever possible immerse yourself into the ideal environment of your goal. If you want to be a downhill skier, live in the mountains. If you want to be the best dressed person in your

community don't hang out with those who always look like if they just rolled out of bed and didn't even bother to comb their hair or brush their teeth. Choose an environment that will understand you and support you as you advance towards your goals. If you want to learn German don't go and live in China!

Success is there for everyone, and success comes when you are 'RWA 'Ready. Willing. Able. to receive it. The stars, the universe, our Higher Power, and ourselves are all on the same team to creating our individual future.
Be honest with yourself. Look inwards with transparent sincerity. You need an Auto-Map of yourself. Just like the GPS of your car. To get you to a destination the GPS needs to know where you are currently positioned. If you don't know where your car is now, your GPS is worthless.

On the following Wheel of Life select each section one at time and grade yourself from the lowest score of zero to the highest score of 10.
The 10 score signifies that you are completely happy and satisfied with that sector of your life in the present moment, while on the other hand zero signifies the worst score. Don't compare yourself to other people you know. This is only about yourself. This wheel of life is helpful to evaluate your potential. You decide for yourself what you want in each sector and remember to remain faithful to your own wishes and goals. This is not the time to be listening to well-meaning advice from friends, families, and coaches. To manage your life in its journey of achieving your dreams and goals a tried and trusted measuring tool is essential, because you cannot manage anything

without measuring it. The Wheel of Life is a very practical tool to easily measure your own progress.

As you can easily see from this sketch, if it was the tyre of a bike or a car it would not roll very far before it crashed to the ground.

The tyre and its spokes need to be well aligned and even. Your finished honest sketch will show you very easily which sectors of your life you want to boost so that all the slices are well aligned.

Take your time and fill in this 'Wheel of Life'. Feel free change the titles of the sectors but keep the different sectors since a well-balanced and fulfilled life is comprised of many parts.

On the following pages you will find columns and lines. Fill them out, take your time, think about what you really wish for and aim to achieve. Naturally, you can change the names of the sectors but make sure they match the name of the pie slices on your 'Wheel of Life'.

For each pie slice, write out in the following columns or make your own columns and tape them to a big board so that you can read them easily every day.

Do not underestimate the value of not only taking the time to write down your choice of 10 actions you will undertake, but also the fact that your eyes will look at them every day on your board or in your book, the actions gradually become so familiar that you are absorbing new habits by osmosis. You are now on a chosen platform designed to launch you towards success.

PHYSICAL HEALTH SEX & EMOTION

Write out 10 things that you choose to do to reach your goal:

	NOW	SIX MONTHS TIME	
RELATION-SHIPS: • Career • Family • Friends			• 1 • 2 • 3 • 4 • 5 • 6 • 7 • 8 • 9 • 10
FINANCIAL ABUNDANCE: • Savings • Investments • Disposable Income			• 1 • 2 • 3 • 4 • 5 • 6 • 7 • 8 • 9 • 10

	NOW	SIX MONTHS TIME	
HEALTH: • Physical • Weight • Mobility • Mental Health • Emotional Health			• 1 • 2 • 3 • 4 • 5 • 6 • 7 • 8 • 9 • 10
TIME MANAGEMENT: **Do you have enough time for:** • Friends and family • Your hobby • Expanding your culture • Your own physical well being • Special interests			• 1 • 2 • 3 • 4 • 5 • 6 • 7 • 8 • 9 • 10

- On top of each column write down the number where you believe your life is now and another number for where you are aiming at.
- Here is a checklist to help you identify steps and aides that you can rely on to increase your chances of reaching your target number 10 and having a well filled out "Wheel of Life."

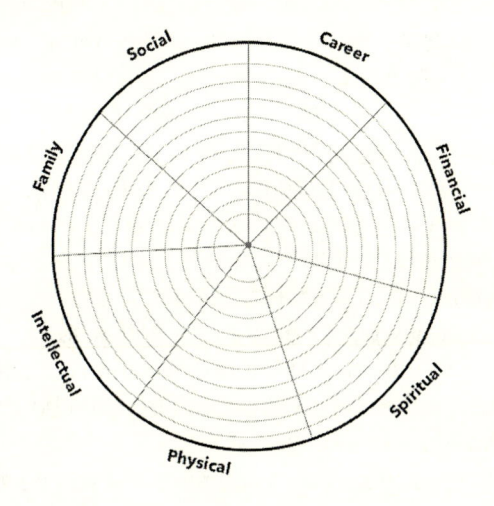

Wheel of Life diagram with sections labeled: Social, Career, Financial, Spiritual, Physical, Intellectual, Family

Think of it as a pilot's check list before he starts the plane. Even though the pilot knows the plane inside out, he is responsible for all the people on board. You are responsible for your life.

Take your time doing this very important step.

I would suggest doing only 1 slice of the pie or column per day. It looks very easy at first glance but if you do it well and in depth it will require clarity and focus. It is tiring to travel inwards and that is your most important journey.

As you go through each column one at a time, this is a very thorough check list. Take your time, don't rush through it, and as you proceed feel free to come back make amendments as you see fit and gain clarity.

a- Create in your imagination a convincing and clear picture of what you want to achieve. Your imagination has no limits. If you have many overlapping ideas, write them down in your workbook. When we see things written on paper, they are easier to focus on, and sometimes we realise they are not as important as we thought previously, or the opposite might be true, and you might realise they are much more important than you had 'thought'
b- What are some of your strong motivating reasons to act?
c- Just like in the G.R.O.W. model, identify where you are today in relation to your ideal target.
d- Find a mentor whom you admire and who is willing to advise and guide you? What qualifications does that person possess to be able to substantiate your choice in them as a worthwhile mentor?
e- Would it help if you took a course, or do you need official qualifications to reach your goal? If so, list the courses, degrees or training schemes that would further your chances of success.
f- What daily action will you take to increase your chances of success in this area?
g- What are your inner conflicts or limiting beliefs?
h- Identify a club, a group of people or an individual who will be helpful in bringing you to the next level.
i- Write out a short description of your new ideal self.
j- Enjoy celebrating all your achievements, no matter how small they are.
k- Give more than you expect to get out of life and life will always be abundant.

Following are some platform questions. Answer them in writing with your own words. We are the result of our questions more than of our knowledge.

1- Since you want to raise your life and lifestyle to the next level or even higher, describe what are 2 or 3 aspects of your personality or behaviour that you feel you must change as soon as possible?
2- Which aspects of your life do you believe are necessary and helpful to adapt, delete or change to reach your next level? Your emotions? Your time management? Your abilities and competence in your work?
3- Which of the above aspects of your life that you described are the most important?
4- If you don't focus on your transformation and don't achieve your goals how much will that cost you?
5- What will you miss and who will you disappoint if you don't achieve the life goals you have set yourself out to achieve?
6- Describe how your life will be better when you change that aspect of your personality or behaviour.
7- What will your energy levels be like when you make those changes?
8- How will you be expressing your happiness when you reach your goal?
9- Write down and describe how your success and well-being will be perceived by other people.
10- What do you think blocked you in the past from reaching your goals?
11- Are you honestly determined to make the necessary changes now to achieve your goal?
12- WHY?

Start decluttering all aspects of your life today. You can only pour new and delicious wine into an empty glass.

As our thoughts determine our feelings, behaviours and ultimately results. It stands to reason that you will have to change your thoughts to change your results.

And that is easier said than done.

About 80% of our daily subconscious thoughts are the same as the day before, they can only be changed by going into the operating system of our life which is our subconscious mind. The mind is not situated only in the brain but more so in your entire body and in the field of the universe. Your body is the operating system of the subconscious mind. When thoughts appear, they translate into feelings in the body. That is the moment to nip them in the bud if you are conscious and self-disciplined enough to change them. The most efficient way to deeply change your thoughts is by conscious awareness otherwise known as being mindful.

13- For 20 minutes daily day, close your eyes and turn off all exterior sensory systems. No incense and music simply overcome your urge to move around. Give yourself an order to sit still like you would tell a dog to sit still and not move. 20 minutes seems like 3 hours, but it is only 20 minutes.

Set your alarm and do not move until it goes off. It might take weeks or months depending on the person, but this is the best way to eventually penetrate your subconscious operating system and allow it to be reprogramed by your commands.

Listen to the clock's tick tock. It is time now to ensure you are doing what you love.

The acid test to that statement is that you enjoy the action so much you don't even notice time racing by, and you are happy to do it even if you are not getting paid for it.

Another tell-tale sign that will tell you that you are living your life's purpose is that you are good at whatever it is that you enjoy. You have a natural talent or feel for it, this will automatically lead to you achieving what is meaningful to you.

Create your future to the best of your ability, let go and realize that some people, events, situations and things are part of your history, but not necessarily part of your destiny. Trust in your goals, trust in yourself.

CHAPTER TWENTY-FIVE

EXERCISES & TECHNIQUES

Excellence is a habit. Aristotle

Transformation only happens by DOING.
Learning is important, but the knowledge does not last for ever ... unless you implement your learned intellectual knowledge into action the accumulated knowledge just gets stored as cold facts and data.
However, transformation lasts for ever because you have taken the action to make it happen daily
This chapter is full of different types of exercises to suit a wide variety of individual transformational needs. Some are designed to allow you to unlearn bad habits and others are designed to reprogram yourself into good habits. None of them result in instant gratification and the processes require a steadfast commitment.

STAY POSITIVE

Keep your thoughts positive because your thoughts become your words.
Keep your words positive because your words become your actions.
Keep your actions positive because your actions become your habits.
Keep your habits positive because your habits become your lifestyle.
Keep your lifestyle positive because your lifestyle becomes your destiny.

This chapter is dedicated to the 'Action' person. Reading is one thing but applying what you read is where the benefits anchor in the memories and vibrations into your nervous system and deliver 'ACHIEVEMENT'.

First simply read through the whole chapter just like you would study a menu. Then choose 3 exercises which appeal to you. If after a while you feel that perhaps this exercise does not suit your style, then go back to the menu and choose another one. Aim for having a weekly option of 3 exercises that you become familiar with so that every day you spend the required amount of time on your self-improvement.

If you have trusted me this far while you read the book, then you will feel comfortable with the easy application of these actions.

The exercises are simple but require focus and self – commitment which comes with practice and not just with knowledge.

1- **GIVE YOUR BODY TIME OFF FROM YOUR 'STRESS ROUTINE'**

Make yourself comfortable, and warm and be sure no one or nothing disturbs you. Set your phone alarm to ring in 15 minutes. It is best to sit down with a straight back and both feet flat on the floor. You might fall asleep if you lie down.
- Close your eyes and mentally scan your body from top to bottom and up again. Short & fast, don't stop at any point, literally scan your body like if you were running through a bar code scanner.
- Take 7 deep breaths inhaling through the nose, keep your shoulders down and bring the air into your belly and expand your belly with the air.

- Exhale through your mouth and tighten your tummy muscles to push all the air back out through your mouth.
- Then take each of your limbs starting with your right arm, then your left, then your left leg then your right leg. Stick the arm out, tense it for the count of 10 seconds then let your arm drop to your side.
- Next lift your leg and heel about 6 inches from the ground, tense it for the count of 10 seconds and let your leg and heel drop to the ground

Make sure you tense as tight as you can and suddenly release.

While you sit down imagine feeling a gentle warm cleansing disinfectant water bubbling around gently in your whole body cleansing you from the inside out. Imagine feeling those deliciously warm tingling bubbles gently caressing and cleansing your insides.

2- BREATH

Inhale through the nose to the count of 2
Hold your breath for the count of 3
Exhale through your nose to the count of 4
Do this 7 times.

3- THE TRIPLE PERSONALITY SET OF QUESTIONS:

Get to know yourself from all angles. Loving yourself is being curious about yourself, discover yourself with the same wonder as you discover the aspects of the person you are starting a new romantic relationship with. When you are in love, you love your new partners quirks and faults as much as you love them for their qualities.

You will need 3 chairs. Put them in a small circle facing each other.

STEP A:

*Sit on the **YOURSELF** chair*
Personality 1: Answer all the questions as 'Yourself'
1- How are you behaving towards a personality group such as: (Love-Relationship-Success-Power- Good Health- Financial Abundance?) Those are various personality groups. From now on they are abbreviated as PG
2- How do you feel about (PG?) take each PG one at a time, Love, Relationships, etc.
3- What are your beliefs about that specific (PG?) Choose one personality group each time you do this exercise.
4- Why is (PG?) important to you?

STEP B:

Sit on the chair of your **Personality GROUP**
(Love – Relationship-Success- Power- etc.)
- Use your body language and sit in the chair physically as your P.G.
- Emit a sound bite as to how your PG sounds when talking. Maybe it is a scream or groan of pleasure or a resounding 'Yes' or a simpering 'Maybe'. But make sure you communicate to the other two chairs who you are via your soundbite.
- What is your posture like? Are you sitting upright or slouched in the chair? Are your legs crossed or swung over the side of the chair? Are your legs still or twitching with nerves? Be aware of how you would imagine an actor portraying your PG in a movie scene.
- Describe your dress code.

1. When (You, PG) spoke about yourself (YOUR NAME) earlier on what feelings were coming up for you?
2. How do you (PG) feel about (YOUR NAME'S) behaviour towards yourself?
3. What behaviour are you (PG) manifesting towards (YOURSELF?)
4. What are (YOUR PG's) values?
5. What are your (PG's) beliefs about your current values?
6. Do you (PG) feel rejected by (YOUR NAME)?
7. In what ways are you (PG) making a commitment to change your behaviour towards (YOUR NAME)?
8. What actions do you expect (YOUR NAME) to make or take in (PG's) life?
9. What can you learn from having heard (YOUR NAME) talk about your (PG)?
10. How has your (PG's) perception changed about (YOUR NAME)?
11. Are you (PG) treating (YOUR NAME) differently then you are treating others?

STEP C:

Sit on the 'ELDER AND WISE ONE'S' chair.
You are the ELDER & WISE ONE in the village now. Stand up and move over to the chair you designated for the elderly wise person to sit on.

1. What does (YOUR NAME & PG) sound like? Give a soundbite.
2. What do you think of the elder persons posture and behaviour?
3. How are (YOUR NAME and your PG) behaving?
4. Since you are sitting in the Elder Wise Persons chair now, and looking at the chair where YOU and your PG

are sitting, describe in your own words how are they feeling towards each other?
5. In your opinion of the Elder Wise Person what does YOU and your PG believe about each other?
6. What do you as the Elder Wise Person believe or feel are their individual values?
7. In your opinion as the Elder Wise Person what do they have to learn and understand?
8. Do you get the impression that their perception is shifting?
9. What else do you think, or feel would help them to improve the quality of their reality and lives?

STEP D:

Sit on the **YOURSELF** chair again.
Now, after having heard the 2 other people's opinions, namely the Elder Wise Person and the designated PG answer these questions as YOURSELF.
It is now time to move back to the chair which is designated as YOURSELF and revert into your own personality and answer these questions without analysing your answers. Simply say out loud what comes to your mind.
You can of course easily record your own session. In this case I always feel it is easier and more truthful to simply speak out your answers spontaneously rather than writing them down because when we write sometimes, we have too much time think about what we are writing, and we change the honesty of what came first to our lips. There are no right or wrong answers. You are yourself and that is what and whom you want to meet and get to know and understand. It is the start of a long relationship between; Me, Myself and I.

1. How did you feel hearing your (PG) saying all those things about yourself?
2. How are you going to modify your behaviour towards your chosen (PG) now?
3. What do you believe about your chosen (PG) and welcoming your (PG) into your life for ever?
4. What is important to you about your chosen (PG) evolving and moving forwards?
5. What can you learn from your chosen (PG)?
6. How has your understanding of your chosen (PG) changed?

STEP E:

Sit on the '**PG PERSONALITY GROUP**' chair.
Which Archetype describes you best?

5) **The Monkey that does not want to see:** If you don't have the courage to deal with what scares you, that unfaced fear will rear its ugly face and come back to bite you in your bottom. But when you open your eyes and look at what you fear head on, you will be able to cross that bridge of where you are to where or what you want to be in a much more confident manner when and if that situation does happen again.

6) **The Monkey, which is timid, shy, and self-effacing:** will sadly discover that other people will be quick to steal your glory! So, stand up and speak up for who you are and what you believe in. Give yourself a voice and discover the enjoyment of getting used to sharing your opinion and vision.

7) **The Monkey with his pedal to the metal!** Do you tend to get things done with and over as fast as possible? Beware, it is one thing to get things done, but it is wiser and more efficient to do them a bit slower but well. Haste

makes Waste. For an airplane to lift up into the sky it starts its taxiing journey at 20 % of its cruising speed. If it went from zero to 800 kms /hour, it would never be able to lift off the ground.

8) **The Monkey with the fur coat**: He is always freezing. Anything unfamiliar that comes your way, scares you so much that you freeze in your steps.... fur coat or not!

9) **The Monkey on the starting line**:
One monkey will go forward and continue to go forward even when he realises, he or others have made a false start or have gone off in the wrong direction. Instead of cutting its loss's he finds it easier to continue and see how things turn out.

The other monkey will stay where he is when the bell goes off, because he will not be convinced that its method is the best way. So, it will keep on delaying the departure until it has all its ducks neatly lined up in a row.

Both above monkeys need to tweak their default modes.

STEP F:

Wrap up questions to be asked by the facilitator or coach if you have one otherwise you can ask yourself the questions.

10- What was it like when you (YOUR NAME) were being your own (PG)?

11- How did you (Your Name) feel when you were in the chair of the Elder Wise One?

12- In what areas have you (YOUR NAME) changed your perception towards your (PG)?

13- What vital points did you learn concerning your (PG)?

14- What path is right for you (YOUR NAME)?

15- Why do you (YOUR NAME) feel that is the right path to take?

16- What are you (YOUR NAME) basing your decision on?
17- Describe how your (YOUR NAME) relationship towards your (PG) has shifted?
18- What will you (YOUR NAME) do differently now to allow your (PG)to integrate your life and keep it there?
19- Make your wheel of life and connect the dots.
A wheel of life helps to see the segments which need tweaking to be on par with the other segments.

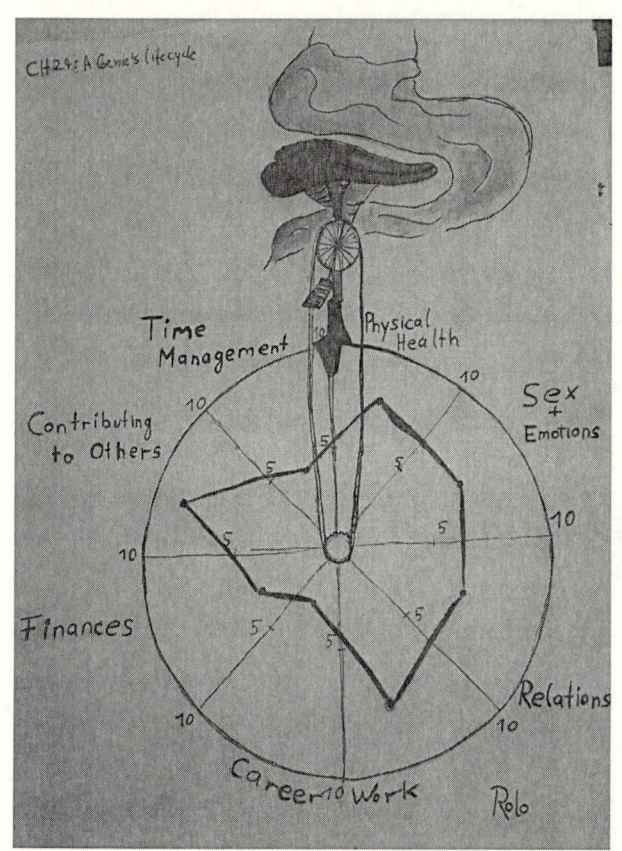

That way you have balance in your life.
See if your cycle wheel will turn like a wheel

Now connect the dots and numbers with a red pen like in the sketch above. The smoother the lines are between each segment the easier the wheel of your life will roll forwards in life.

Feel free to replace the titles with a key word of your own choice.

To get started sit down with someone you trust and start brainstorming about 10 or 12 different sectors or areas of your life which are meaningful to you.

If you could not care less about sports but on the other hand know that you need to do physical exercise regularly you can write 'My workouts' for example.

Now draw a line from one area to the next being sure to write the measures on each line, starting at zero in the centre up to 10 on the outer circumference. The aim is to have all the areas in your life balanced. If you see that one or more are below par with the rest, then work a bit more on that or those areas of your life until your self-grading system brings them all in alignment. It is always easier to go forward with car tyres that are all balanced!

1- Nature
2- Physical
3- Financial
4- Career
5- Network
6- Relationships
7- Body
8- Sex Life
9- Self
10- Culture
11- Friends
12- Spiritual
13- My time

14- Rest & Relaxation
15- Charity work
16- And the list goes on ……..

DEVELOP YOUR PHYSICAL BRAIN

To boost brain capacity and intelligence choose at least one of the following exercises and do them DAILY for a minimum of 3 months.
- Spend 5 minutes everyday handwriting with your opposite hand. I always like to spend that time writing on my gratitude. Because I am writing slowly as it is my non-dominant hand, the focus I am giving to my writing slows down my brain and allows me to not only think about what I am grateful for, but it also gives me the time to 'FEEL' the gratitude which is good for the neuroplasticity of our brains!
- Do at least 20 minutes of physical exercise every day. It helps your existing neurons to thrive and develop instead of shrivelling up. It also helps your hippocampus to increase in size, the bigger the hippocampus the easier it is for you to learn and to remember. As they say. 'Use It or lose it'
- Chose something new to learn every day so that your brain stretches its capacity and automatically forms new cells and connections. This only counts if you must understand and figure out something new. For example, a new piece of technology or reading up on a subject which you hardly have any knowledge about.
- Do cross word puzzles or Sudoku as a bit of a brainy daily workout.
- Eat a lot of fish, excellent omega, and a few walnuts every day, which are very rich brain food.

INTUITION (Refers to Chapter 14)

Some auto training exercises to open your intuitive channels:
If you find that you don't make on the spot decisions, you most likely don't hear or trust your intuition.
- Practice by writing down questions that can only be answered by a simple 'yes' or 'no'. Immediately after the question draw a little box after the yes, and another little box after the no.
- Read your question again a few times out loud and then go about your day without thinking about the question or the answer.
- The next morning return to the piece of paper, pick up a pen or pencil in your hand, shut your eyes for a second or two and as soon as you open your eyes tick either the yes or no box. Don't second guess yourself, just make a tick. Trust yourself, it can be compared to kinesiology when muscle testing always delivers the right answer.

It is useful to help you gain insight and clarity. An example could be that you must employ a new manager, but you are lacking clarity on what their responsibilities should be. So, write down a list of all the actions and responsibilities you are lacking clarity on as to whether they should ultimately be doing that in their new job, and see how many you tick off as yes and as no.
That will help you formulate your job offer with more clarity.

TIP: Get used to doing these intuitive exercises in a calm, noise free environment. Intuition needs peaceful surroundings to blossom.

Hone your inner intuitive voice daily to improve your decisions and behaviours. Watch how your reality improves.

Thanks to the tremendous advances in technology science is now able to identify 'intuition' and follow its path. There is no doubt left that intuition is far more beneficial to us then conscious thought caused decisions.
Sonia Choquette is in my opinion the continuously blossoming flower about intuition.

UNCOVERING LIMITING BELIEFS

1. Find a picture of yourself as a small child, preferably a picture before you were 7 years old. At least twice a day look at the picture and smile at it and pour love on to the child in the image. You only must do this for about 30 seconds, more if you prefer but 30 seconds is enough to get things flowing. It's a very simple exercise that evokes old memories. Notice how you feel when suddenly a long-forgotten event or situation appears in your awareness. Look at that memory on the screen of your mind being aware what you are feeling today from your adult perspective. There is no right or wrong, it's only an exercise in noticing how you can dial up and recall experiences.
At the time whatever behaviour or belief, you developed after that situation might have helped you then. But examine that belief today and be honest as you ask yourself" "Does that belief hinder or help me today"?
2. To further uncover old limiting beliefs and trapped energy I would like you to do some free writing.

Start of by breathing the rounds with a finger on the 3rd eye and breathing up and down through alternative nostrils about 9 times for each side, follow this with some heart meditation, as a guide meditate until you are aware of your heartbeat with your fingertips then continue for about 5 mins. Once the prep is done start to write, and for the first few weeks I would like you to focus and write about your life from birth to 7 years old, let whatever comes out come out even if it seems insignificant information just write and have fun with it.

CLOSING LINES

Thoughts and imagination create reality. 'THINK ACHEIVEMENT & WATCH IT HAPPEN' explains some of the approaches of your partnership to the universe and how to create your reality so that it meets your wish list.
You really are Aladdin, the sooner you start polishing your soul, beliefs and emotions, your Genie which is your supra-consciousness or your connection to Divinity will come out of your soul's lamp and deliver you to your goals.

HOW TO GET INTO YOUR HEART

We have all heard that everything starts from the heart, but for many of us, those are only nice words. Learn how to create your own happiness, it takes practice and patience in the beginning because you want to change your brainwave patterns by being mindful and allowing your intuition to blossom.

Turn this into your daily ritual and you will become centred, grounded, and connected with your Higher Power.

<u>Step by step:</u>
a- Light a candle
b- Focus for a minute on your breath. Feel the cool air inhaled in your nostrils and feel the exhale through your mouth.
c- Breathe in as you count to 7, then block your breath for a count of 7 then exhale to the count of 7 and keep your air blocked for another count of 7.
d- For the next minute or two focus on the wavering flame. Notice how it gets higher or shorter, wider, or slimmer, notice the colour variations of the flame.
e- This helps you stop your mind chatter and enjoy the moment.

Be aware of the 'moment,' otherwise you miss out on enjoying your life. If you are living in the past or living in the future your brain is busy remembering or creating, but when you live in the moment your brain is resting and relaxing.

Feel the love in every one of your moments. It is thrilling and feels as good as when you are falling in love. You can't and don't want to stop that warm rush in your body. In mindfulness all senses are heightened, you are LIVING, yet at the same time the mind is calm focused and peaceful. Stay with those feelings for a few minutes.
f- Now you are ready to think of 5 things that you are grateful for, when you think of them allow your heart to FEEL the gratitude. If you find that difficult simply think how you would feel without the object that you 'know' you

are grateful for. You will get a jolt. Do not stay with that 'down – feeling' though.

Release it immediately and get back to enjoying the feelings of gratitude. Try to stay immersed in that feeling for 17 seconds if you can, as the days and the weeks pass by stay even longer with that feeling.

When you go through 5 things that you are 'FEELING' feel the gratitude that you are feeling now. Then give yourself the time to feel the warmth of gratitude daily, your brainwaves start to form 'happy' frequencies.

Depending on whether you are already a happy person or not, it will take you between 3 months and a year to make 'happiness and peace' your default personality.

Done daily you are setting your body up to enjoying excellent health and vitality regardless of your age or circumstances. Everything starts with your ability to focus on gratitude in the moment. You hold that power inside of you, it just might take some inner searching and exposure to your strength and vulnerability.

Self-transformation, and improvement happens when you become self – aware. It is not a destination it is a voyage. Create the life of your wishes. Going into your heart is the biggest and most exciting journey you can take. It is much more exhilarating then running after any goal. Those goals will become your reality when you live from your heart.

The journey and arrival take place for everyone but each person at their own pace. Happiness, mindfulness, peace, self – confidence, happens at your own pace. It is not a race.

DON'T OOGLE GOOGLE

From time to time, you will have questions which will show up as stumbling blocks to reaching your target.
Rather than surfing Google train your brain to become your neurological coach.
Following is a fun exercise that helps develop your intuition. The best answers come from within and not from Google.
Close your eyes and invite your role models for an evening in a lovely large room, the windows are open and the luscious fragrances of the garden float into the room making you heady with the scents.
Here is an interesting guest list, in case you are short of a few.
Elon Musk, who went from 0 to 60 in a few years all on his own.
Jackie Ma from Alibaba who started out with nothing.
The Dalai Lama, Oprah. Nelson Mandela, Martin Seligman the founder of Positive Psychology, and feel free to keep on adding other amazing guests.
Feel their joy at seeing you as you welcome them to your soiree. They know that they have been invited because you value everyone very highly. And they are delighted to be able to help you. All you must do is ask them for advice on how to solve whatever issue you might have at present.
But suddenly you feel overwhelmed in front of all these great human beings, and you don't want to waste their time or appear a fool ... and so you freeze.
The pacifists in the room tell you to breathe deeply, exhale and relax. Someone else seeing you realises you

have become tongue tied which explains why you can't even formulate your question let alone ask it.

One of your guest gurus tells you to yawn, another tells you to visualise all your thoughts going into individual envelopes and throwing them in to the river.

Now that you are relaxing, write down the first 5 questions that come to your mind

Read them and tick off the most important ones in order of priority.

Ask yourself the questions out loud and notice if that is the correct question you are looking for an answer for. We are the result of our questions more than of the information we receive.

If the question does not reflect your search clearly then reword the question.

Once that is done, in your mind's eyes and ears, see your guest and hear his answer. Whatever you hear in your imagination, jot it down.

If you don't hear anything, then be patient, the answer from within will come to you.

You are your own best advice.

In Jill Bolt's personal journey 'My Stroke of Insight 'she formulates this question: "Is God a mathematician"? When Jill Bolt PHD, gave a Ted Talk she explained how she saw digital squiggles and numbers during her stroke and realised her brain was decoding.

Our DNA is our programming software emitting accordingly the information and instructions on how our bodies will perform. It is the biological command headquarters located EVERYWHERE in the body cosily embedded in each one of our cells

It is our genetic blueprint. And just like architectural blue prints they are changeable. You don't throw out a computer because it is not working You just change the program, And the same is true of our bodies. We can affect our DNA. It will determine how well we age and evolve according to our beliefs. Remember that you have the choice and the ability to change your belief.

The mind and the body react to human language (think of NLP) for those who have studied something about Neuro Linguistic Programming.

Sir Francis Crick the first man ever to have identified the DNA in 1953 is known to have commented that "The DNA is far too complex to have started on earth and therefore must come from another dimension).

Scientists have identified to date 5% of the genes and have simply named the other 95 % junk DNA. But 1% of the human's DNA is not found in any other living animal or plant. I presume that must be the divinely intelligent 1%.

Personally, I am far from being an expert on the body's DNA system. But through my work which is specialising in helping my clients to **sculpt** their targets and goals or live their dreams, I know from experience that one of the reasons of everyone's hurdles without exception are negative beliefs which are running the show while the subconscious mind takes over the show.

So, when I coach clients, I help them stay far away from revisiting those negative beliefs and instead guiding, coaching, and mirroring them to live in their minds and their imagination the goals they are reaching for as if they were already in the throes of them.

Water, like crystals is a powerful **enabler of energy transfer**. Our bodies are 70% water. So, drink a lot of

water before during and after your exercises. It facilitates the cells to transfer the messages swifter to the DNA.
The ideal tempo for drinking water is 1 glass every hour. That keeps your brain humid all the time. If your brain does not get water, the neurons die of thirst! And if you drink 4 glasses because you are thirsty and have not had any water for a few hours, rest assured that a higher-than-normal number of neurons have already died. So, drink a glass of water every hour.

DAILY SEGMENT INTENTIONS

Segment intending separates my day into segments. Breakfast... work... sports, etc.
Would it not be nice if when I work on my project, I become super inspired?
Wouldn't it be nice if when (my assumption happens) everything will drop into place!

STATE OF EXPECTANCY

Waiting for money. You are frustrated but when your friend calls you back and gives you the tracking number saying the check is in the mail... you feel different. That is a state of expectancy. In other words, you visualise the money already in your account. You are totally relaxed; it is a sense of certitude. Like a pregnancy. You are taking care of yourself and preparing for the baby to arrive. Know it is happening but wait a bit.

PROCESS YOUR PAST
IN 4 EASY AND LOGICAL STEPS

1. Identify your block and link it to the past (Refer back to Chapter 5)
2. Write a 'feeling' letter to whom or whatever you believe is the culprit of your block.
3. Write a response letter from whom or whatever received your letter and write down what you imagine would be in their reply letter to you.
4. Write a connection letter, acting like a mediator outlining both sides of the story and agreeing to identify a middle ground with which both sides will feel vindicated, and are happy to bury the past and to go forward on a new solution orientated footing.
5. It is best to write these 3 letters in the flow. Just write what comes up and don't pay attention if it makes sense or not.

REMOVE THE POISON FROM YOUR DEFAULT HABIT OF COMPLAINING.

A complaint is a valid statement. And not complaining does not mean to ignore what must be changed in your opinion. You must face the music and dance. But there is a lighter step that you can learn when you dance to the 'Complaint Music'

1- First, be very clear in your own mind exactly what your complaint entails and word it down to one or two sentences. It is useful to talk straight and clear about the problem, but do not make it worse than what it is and

especially engage in gossip or any other non-constructive and non-related chit about the problem.
2- Secondly, prepare your counterpart for the upcoming complaint by presenting it in a clear, concise, and respectful manner.
3- Use a peaceful & moderated tone of voice.
4- Use an opening sentence along these lines: "I wish to engage your help in finding a solution to this issue/ thing that I have."

By saying it that way, you have flipped that person or people from 'victims of your complaint' to your new team- member'. The arsenic of the complaint has been removed, and everyone is now solution orientated.

5- From now on in, instead of re-iterating the object of your complaint, replace it with the word 'That Thing'.

Things are neutral, the word 'Thing' does not have a strong vibrational energy.

6- SAMPLE: "Hi John, if you have a moment, I would like to ask you a favour. Would you be so kind and brainstorm or help me find a solution to the falling sales that your division is showing in the weekly figures".

Practice the above approach for 3 months, you will develop your own style of communicating your disappointment in such a manner that you will engage rather than irritate the person or people with whom you have a bone to pick.

Get ready to be amazed at your vastly improved results.

POSITIVE AFFIRMATIONS.

Endless books, webinars, conferences, and workshops have been and are given on the benefits of positive affirmations. Let's point out that documented neuro -sciences experiments show that when words are repeated, they hardwire and create a belief. Therefor the power of saying affirmations out loud and regularly wire into the subconscious belief system and end up becoming reality. Since you will be hopefully saying an affirmation, you are automatically boosting your immune system simultaneously. The healthier you are the smoother your energy flows and the easier it becomes for your subconscious mind to believe what you are saying.
Have you noticed that you when you were or are in love, people tell you that you look great and glowing? Have you noticed that when you vibrate with the frequency of love you are and feel healthy? No aches and pains!

Don't take this personally as I obviously don't know you, but it is quite probable that you are in the habit of talking about what is not working in your life and therefor your life is reflecting the truth of what you are saying.
So, reverse that bad habit of talking about what is not working and change your mood by saying out loud to yourself as if it already was happening what you want to achieve. That is an enhancing positive affirmation.
Use your ''self-awareness' to reverse your negative statements to saying and believing that the positivity of what you are saying is true and therefor is becoming true.
Focus with ultra-awareness of the shift in your mood the moment you say your positive affirmation. Keep tabs on

your self-induced mood swings as you say your positive affirmations out loud.

Craft and create your positive affirmations to enhance your feel-good factor. You might have to voice them or write them out and then read them back a few times until you are happy with how you feel when you say your new positive affirmation. You can be flexible here and change the wording or the angle on your positive affirmation after a few days or weeks, as you notice that you react better to a different way of saying the same thing. Words have power.

Here are a few generic positive affirmations that apply to everyone in every sector of life.
Feel free to tweak them to meet your own goals.
- I am enjoying my newfound self-confidence and trust in my abilities.
- I am attracting joyful and positive situations into my life.
- I am amazed at my superpowers of positivity
- I enjoy the zen aspect of my life and notice the solutions which appear effortlessly to me.
- I am always changing for the better.

G.R.O.W.

G.R.O.W Model is an excellent tool for achievement in excellence. It facilitates and accelerates the quality of solution identification and achievement. It is quite involved and therefor it is laid out step by step in chapter 7 GOAL SETTING.

5 BEFORE 5

At the end of your workday, before you go home or leave the office, not too late because by then you are too tired. Write down 5 things you want to get done the next day. Those become the 5 first actions you do the next morning. You will be waking up with a mission! You will be accomplishing more than most people do in a month.
It is a just a habit to get used to doing. It is like walking your dog.!

REWIND THE DAY

Before you lay down or close your eyes at night, take 5 minutes to play your day backwards from whatever time it is now for you, and play your day backwards. See and relive all the events. Each time you come to a moment in the day which you did not like, or it did not go as you wanted it to go, simply do a 4 step Ho'oponopono on it to erase the memory of what you did not like. As you make a mental note of the time of day when it happened. Next step is to replace in your mind that moment with a scene of what you would have preferred.
Now continue your day backwards until the moment you woke up.
When you are back at the start of your day, run your memory back to now again, and when you get to the time at which that incident happened, replace it with what you wanted to happen instead and then go forward until you are back at your bedtime.

Do these 5 times in a row, and the repetitive play back deletes the unwanted events from the subconscious memory and re-installs instead your chosen version of the events as you want them to happen.

SPIRITUAL GOOGLISED WATER

Pour yourself a good big glass of water before you go to bed. Put both hands on the glass and give a command to your subconscious.
Give me the answer tomorrow morning after I drink the 2nd half of this glass of water to: And now ask your question.
When you wake up in the morning, drink the other half of glass, and notice how fast you will receive the answer to the question you asked before you went to bed.
I learned this exercise in a workshop from Oliver Madelrieux who is an amazing French pharmacist and thoroughly understands how the neurochemistry of the brain works.
It is the same concept as the stock taking model called; LIFO= Last in First out.
Olivier Madelrieux spends months at a time in Hawaii and is full of spiritual tricks that work.
You have just read a big menu of different approaches to self-improvement. Obviously, you are not going to do them all, but I urge you to test a few of the exercises that you feel attracted to and a little bit stretched and challenged when you carry them out.
Please keep this book handy where you can easily reach for it every day and just open at one page, you will be keeping your mind alert on your own self-improvement.

All the exercises work, I have been using them in my workshops for years, as well as with my private clients. But there are horses for courses. Trust your intuition which ones will help you the most.

Take the time, to implement some of these exercises repetitively at least for 3 to 4 months your results will automatically improve.

Life is dynamic, not just knowledge.

Since we are soon saying goodbye to each other, let me share with you how I wake up and how I go to bed.

When I wake up, I spend a few minutes laying down and visualising my day ahead, as I want it to be. If any worries pop up in my mind about the day not happening as I want, I push those thoughts out of the spotlight saying to myself that I am in 'My Time' and I can think what I want to think about my day ahead.

Then I do a few things very slowly but consciously. I enjoy brushing my teeth, feeling the nice minty feel in my mouth before sitting down for 5 minutes and while I drink a hot squeezed lemon juice during which I continue to map out my day ahead in my imagination as I want it to be. I am creating my day.

Whatever happens, happens. But I know that with time I strengthen my neural pathways to deliver what I want to happen.

At night , after I sit down on my bed, before I swing my legs up and into my bed , I sit on the side of my bed, with a big glass of water, which I enjoy feeling the water slide down my throat, and I say out loud to myself, " Since anything I want is possible, dear Higher Power thank you for delivering the following to me tomorrow......."

I then lay down and say a few rounds of "I love you, I am sorry, please forgive me, Thank you."

(Ho'oponopono)
I ask you dear Higher Power to transmute the negative memoires I hold in myself, which are the causes and reasons of all my blocks and upsets, as well as in the life of those close and far to me, and to transmute all my problems into positive future memories of happiness, good health, success, and financial abundance.'
Thank you, I bless you, I love you. Good night.

And now I lay my little head down and drift into sleep.

10-9-8-7-6-5-4-3-2-1 -BLAST OFF!
Start here… this is your beginning!
Bon Voyage.

ABOUT THE AUTHOR

From Swiss educated debutante to Knightsbridge special events planner, and from competitive downhill racer, international polo player, and corporate and personal empowerment mindset coach Nicole Petschek has already lived many lives in this lifetime.

A serious polo accident introduced her to the world of mind mastery, and she has never looked back.
Fully awakened to the unlimited potential of the mind-body-spirit connection; Nicole applied her passionate & inquisitive nature to investigating & obtaining measurable results by applying proven methods that successfully re-train the brain and the subconscious.
Based in Munich, Nicole coaches globally personally, and on Zoom both in French and English.

www.nicolepetschek.com

Table of Contents

CHAPTER ONE 13
LINKING YOUR MIND TO YOUR GOALS

CHAPTER TWO 21
MIND'S MAGICAL MIRACLES

CHAPTER THREE 33
CONSCIOUS & SUBCONSCIOUS

CHAPTER FOUR 71
IF I COULD DO IT... SO, CAN YOU

CHAPTER FIVE 89
WHO AM I?

CHAPTER SIX 131
KNOW WHAT YOU WANT

CHAPTER SEVEN 145
GOAL SETTING

CHAPTER EIGHT 177
BURY PROCRASTINATION

CHAPTER NINE 195
HONORING YOUR DREAMS

CHAPTER TEN 201
DREAM OUT OF THE BOX

CHAPTER ELEVEN 213
YOU ARE ONLY ENERGY

CHAPTER TWELVE 233

ROCKET BOOSTING CONFIDENCE

CHAPTER THIRTEEN 241

RELATIONSHIPS

CHAPTER FOURTEEN 255

CELEBRATE SUCCESS

CHAPTER FIFTEEN 263

WHERE IS THE MONEY HONEY?

CHAPTER SIXTEEN 279

CHANGING YOUR POINT OF VIEW & FOLLOWING YOUR INTUITION

CHAPTER SEVENTEEN 295

ENERGY MEDICINE

CHAPTER EIGHTEEN 325

DELETION TOOLS

CHAPTER NINETEEN 369

NO BLAME ATTRACTS FAME

CHAPTER TWENTY 381

CUT A YEAR IN 12 SLICES

CHAPTER TWENTY-ONE 399

VISUALIZATION & INTUITION

CHAPTER TWENTY-TWO 437

SOLUTIONS TO HELP YOU LEARN HOW TO LOVE YOURSELF

CHAPTER TWENTY-THREE 449

JUST IN TIME TO BECOME YOU 2.0

CHAPTER TWENTY-FOUR 457

CREATE YOUR FUTURE
CHAPTER TWENTY-FIVE 463
EXERCISES & TECHNIQUES

europe books